Praise for John Pelan's *Darkside* anthologies

The Darker Side: Generations of Horror
Winner of the Bram Stoker Award
for Best Anthology
Nominated for an International Horror
Guild Award for Best Anthology
A *Locus* New & Notable Book

"A refreshing change . . . Pelan owns an increasingly sure grasp of the dynamics of putting together a worthy original anthology."
—*Locus*

"If the reader is one who gravitates to the type of horror that creates a lingering, perhaps even haunting feeling . . . this is a collection worth reading . . . most horror fans will find something to enjoy."
—*KLIATT*

"*The Darker Side* offers several somethings for somebody. And several bodies for everything. This is Grand Guignol entertainment at its finest. Buy it, enjoy it, and store it in a well-lit room."
—Rambles.net

Darkside: Horror for
the Next Mill

"A solid roster of l 0
pages of original hor
Omni

"The contributor list rea no's Who of Contemporary Horror Writers."
—*Lip Dink*

A WALK ON THE DARKSIDE

VISIONS OF HORROR

Edited by John Pelan

A ROC BOOK

ROC
Published by New American Library, a division of
Penguin Group (USA) Inc., 375 Hudson Street,
New York, New York 10014, U.S.A.
Penguin Books Ltd, 80 Strand,
London WC2R 0RL, England
Penguin Books Australia Ltd, 250 Camberwell Road,
Camberwell, Victoria 3124, Australia
Penguin Books Canada Ltd, 10 Alcorn Avenue,
Toronto, Ontario, Canada M4V 3B2
Penguin Books (NZ), cnr Airborne and Rosedale Roads,
Albany, Auckland 1310, New Zealand

Penguin Books Ltd, Registered Offices:
80 Strand, London WC2R 0RL, England

First published by Roc, an imprint of New American Library,
a division of Penguin Group (USA) Inc.

First Printing, September 2004
10 9 8 7 6 5 4 3 2 1

Cover art by John Picacio

RoC REGISTERED TRADEMARK—MARCA REGISTRADA

Printed in the United States of America

CONTENTS

CROSSROADS

Don Tumasonis

Near midnight, obsessed with breaking up asphalt in the middle of the lonely road out in the sandy pines, I did not notice the sheriff's deputy, even though I was half expecting a visit, after what I had done the last time.

"Wooo!"—a pause, and then—"Eeee" was the first thing I heard. "Looky here! Who's come back for a visit!"

"Officer, I can explain . . ."

"Don't bother, little buddy—just drop that pick nice 'n easy and put your hands up behind your head, real slow. You're under arrest, for destruction of public and private property, for obstructing traffic, creating a public nuisance, trespassing, for making me work too hard, and—well, a whole lot of other things too."

I did as I was told, easing the pick down, while turning slowly. I could see that Fatty, as I had come to think of him, or Farnum, as I later found his name to have been, had his hand on the butt of his service revolver. For some reason, he used no flashlight. What with the moonlight and my fairly good night vision, I was also able to see that the flap of the holster was still buttoned shut.

Cornpone was obviously viewing this as a big joke, some goll-danged carpetbagger crackpot, a nut, who got his rocks off cutting holes in state property, specifically roads, for reasons unknown to any others than said crackpot, now finally caught red-handed. He really didn't seem to think I was dangerous—that much was clear. Only an object to harass, humiliate, jail, fine, and send on his Yankee way, sadder, bruised, possibly sodomized, certainly lighter in the pocket, but wiser. Fatty was wary, but not too much so, probably lulled by what he took to be the humorous aspect of it all.

It wasn't a joke for me though—it was a matter of life or death.

Which made it easy for me, when slowly straightening up after having laid the pickax down, to unobtrusively glide my hand along my torso as if in the motion of putting my hands up, pulling out in one smooth grab the .38 I had tucked into my waistband, safety off.

Fatty was looking down the wrong end of the barrel before he even knew it.

"Now hold on there mister, I wasn't meaning no harm. I'm just doing my job like . . ."

"Shut up."

"Now lookit. You just can't . . ."

"I said shut up." I had the revolver at arm's length, high up, pointed straight at his face. He shut up. I told him to turn around, saying that if he followed my orders, he wouldn't get hurt. He nodded. I could see the sweat start to stream down his jowls.

I removed his piece from the holster, and threw it deep into the bushes nearby. With my gun touching the back of his head, I made him march into the swamp. When we were far enough in, up to our ankles, we stopped, and I told him to drop his pants, told him I wanted to tie him to a tree with his belt.

While he was lowering his breeches, with the mouth of the weapon hard up against the base of his skull, I could feel his trembling, conducted from the bone past the thin skin and hair to the pistol like a voice through the membrane on a phone.

And then I shot him.

Maybe I'd better start again. What I'm trying to do is tell the story like it happened.

Things have gone so far along, events have taken over, that I thought I'd better write this down, just in case. About how I wound up here, a murderer, on the run from the police and worse. Leave a record to show I'm not crazy, out for thrills, or covering up a crime. I killed because I had to, or thought I had to.

After all, it was only a few short months ago that I was a nice guy, an upright cit, grad student, minding my own business.

My world was still whole, though on the verge of crumbling—an accident I saw coming at me like a locomotive aimed at a car stalled on the tracks, me in it, and the doors welded shut.

A whole world, did I say? It was dented.

Dented because I had finished my graduate work in a non-defense-related field, comparative religions, specialty: eschatological movements. Wrong choice.

Dented because I had no children from my marriage just recently gone up in smoke after six turbulent years, the divorce finalized about the same time I finished school, leaving me with my young self exposed to the draft.

I mean, with all my scheming and strategy, I was sure that I was safe. It took a while for me to realize that I was one of those unfortunate few caught up by the system that shouldn't have taken me. But it did, in the form of the well-known printed letter with the infamous opening: "Greetings: your friends and neighbors . . ."

I had no friends and neighbors so low and despicable

who could do this to me; a machine had cooked it up, upon discovering that I was suddenly open to the breeze: draft fodder, ready for the maw of the monster, the more attractive for my being a prime specimen, an excellent example to show any other smarty thinking of cheating the system "Slip up once, buster, and you're going to the 'Nam!" Me, an old man of twenty-six. I should have been safe.

I had about five weeks—five weeks left to my independent life, which I suddenly saw to be only the illusion of freedom.

Oh, and dented, too, because the rock band I played in, the one I'd helped set up years back, finally on the verge of big time, catching wind of my deferment running out, cut its potential losses, its gangrenous limb, and dropped me. Fine friends. Just when things were getting good.

With my world collapsing around me, I was at first too disheartened to fight back: I felt that I had shot my bolt, and there was nothing left to do. If I split for Canada or even Sweden, which I see now, too late, to have been the wise choices, I would be free, perhaps even beginning to enjoy things. I really have no history of ethical principles that would net me noncombatant status, and I was not ready to go to jail. As it was, with few options left, I began to see myself as guilty, one who let others take the heat and bleed for me. I was horrified at what was happening, but all further will to struggle against fate was gone. I felt limp, and in some strange way, almost looked forward to my induction as ironic justice.

I had my long hair clipped—I didn't want the army doing that—and sat around a few days, listless, doing nothing, just letting things flow over me without thinking too much about anything, haunting the record shops by day, the local hangouts at night, killing my fears and anxiety with raw scotch and beer.

A few days into this developing cycle of despair, I was in the Columbia shop, up Main Street, in Rochester, where I had studied. Mental anchor lines cut or slipping, I looked for other things than those I did from habit. I was probably ripe for what happened—always attracted to the obscure, the offbeat. With the failure of those stratagems guiding my safe little world, I decided to sample something other than the usual diet of rock in which I normally indulged at the rate of a new bought record each day.

There was a small section of racks with "Blues" on the bin separator label. I had earlier bought one or two fairly tame records by Josh White and Jimmy Reed, and those were the extent of my knowledge of the blues. Innocuous as they were, I had liked them. Perhaps more blues would perk me up. I lighted on a disk I hadn't seen before, a pressing of some Library of Congress tapes—Son House and one or two other Mississippi singers, made back in the forties. I was skeptical, anything that old, monophonic . . . But still, I was adrift, and open to impulse. Maybe something unfamiliar, something that could lift me up. Get out of the rut.

When I took the LP home, and played it second side first, I was disappointed beyond words. The recording quality was horrible. The acoustic sound was raw, the idiom just plain primitive, and worse, incomprehensible and bland. I was already conjuring mental plans for returning the record for full value. Tim, at the store, who I knew well enough to chat with, would probably let me exchange it for something else.

I then threw on the A side. Even if only one song was good—but this looked hopeless. The first band repeated, in my view, the crudeness of the other side. I was already resigned to going back to the store.

Then *that* song came on. We all know Keats, "peak in

Darien," the rest. Well, it happened then. My spine went cold, the hair on the back of my neck stood on end, goose bumps stood up all over me, etc.—all the usual clichés, which happened, this time, to be true. "Sun Going Down." And further on, "Country Farm Blues." Something strange, wonderful was happening. Something whose existence I never would have suspected, left on my own for ten lifetimes. What *was* the artist doing?

I had neglected the liner notes, putting the record straight on the player when I came home. I looked at the comments more closely, and then I had it: both tracks were done with a bottleneck on the little finger, gliding it along the strings. It was that I had heard: That glissade of eerie notes, running a graveyard arpeggio down my spine, was a slide run along bare and wrapped steel, like a Hawaiian guitar.

I played those two cuts over and over. I had discovered my own new continent. The draft, Vietnam, the breakups with my wife and the band—all forgotten. I devoured the notes while listening, and there I came across a fact I filed away as a useless, but interesting curiosity: Son House had been "rediscovered" in Rochester a couple of years before.

Over the next ten days, I took a crash course in the blues; specifically, I tried to find all I could on the bottleneck style. There wasn't much recorded available locally. In my search, I stumbled across a folk song magazine that had a lot about blues, and there were some references there, but nothing really helpful on performance technique. I worked on my guitar for days, using a metal comb, a jackknife, a piece of thin tubing, but was unable to duplicate, or even come close to the notes I had heard on the record. Of course, I realize now, I wasn't much of a guitar player. Then.

What happened next was so coincidental that, looking back on these last months, I wonder if it was any coincidence at all. I had stopped going to my usual hangouts, not much more than a couple of weeks before the U.S. government was about to seal my fate. With the thought of soaking up as much new experience as possible (the prospect of an *end* to all experience was staring right at me), I started trying out new bars. I also wanted to avoid running into my ex-wife, who was still frequenting our old haunts.

In a folk club called Jimmy's on St. Paul Boulevard, run by a pair of genial ex-cons with a taste for long-haired college girls, I saw by chance a handbill stapled on the wall for an evening of blues with none other than Son House. The venue was a place across and further up the river, left bank of the Genesee, nearby the lake.

I was astounded. I had never imagined the old bluesman was still playing. The date given was two nights ahead. I made sure that I was there.

Not too many people had shown up; a handful, about twenty or so, mostly guys, although there was a couple or two. The place was a tiny coffeehouse, with a small low stage in front of the plate glass street window. It was blowing outside, a cutting wind carrying polar cold down past the Laurentian Shield, crossing Ontario, bearing its chill. I placed myself closer to the stage than anyone else, having made sure to come early for the best seat, and waited eagerly, full of anticipation for the performance to begin.

We must have sat an hour or more after the start was scheduled; a couple of people got tired of waiting, and left. Finally, on the verge of leaving myself, two men entered the room. Son looked frail, and even a bit scared, walking to the stage. He stumbled on the low step, but his young white partner, Spranger, a local folky who was hired to give moral support to a man perhaps too shy to play alone, caught him just in time and helped him up. I felt sorry for the poor old man, and then I saw him take a swig from something in a brown paper bag.

His numerous pulls at the bottle of whiskey turned the joint performance into near disaster. Spranger played alone, and then with Son House. Their duets never really caught fire, styles and temperament never matching. A few sparks were given off, but nothing more, and the evening was heading toward catastrophe after a relatively short time: a near-tragic display of an old man past his prime, wrecked by alcohol and self-pity.

Perhaps out of embarrassment, many of the few spectators left early; the spectacle of the master nearly falling out of his chair, maudlin and at times weeping, hardly managing his guitar, was almost unbearable.

The evening being over, so to speak, before it began, I was loath to leave before getting a few photographs with my camera, and perhaps a word or two with the great man. Others, not many, lingered on. Son stumbled down from the dais, to a chair by a café table, the entire time profusely apologizing.

With the pressure off, he became more relaxed, and the hangers-on drew him into conversation, much of it revolving on his guitar technique. Warming up, he showed us his open tunings, a revelation to me, and then, with only a handful of people remaining, and a few more pulls at the bottle, he erupted unexpectedly into a performance that froze the blood in the veins of everybody in that room.

The slither of the slide on steel, his raw voice, his eyes gone completely wild, would have had me running for the door, if I hadn't been so transfixed, with everyone else.

I don't know how long the session lasted; time was

stopped, it did not matter in that space the bluesman had carved out. It was beyond time. Its power was immense.

Then, just as abruptly as it started, it was over. There was a frail old man sitting three feet in front of me, with eyes, although perhaps a bit jaundiced, no longer shooting flames, the guitar and that *voice* now silent.

It was just as if you had been sitting quietly in some restaurant with your girlfriend, and with no warning, she suddenly did a spectacular shamanistic turn, with voices from all corners, luminous blue lights floating in the air, flying drums and the rest, and then afterward, dropped it, returned to eating peacefully, engaged again in pleasant conversation. Where was I? she might say, picking up on the last coherent word.

One collective breath was let out, I think, by everybody watching. People got up, moved around, away. They were shaken, like myself, by what they had just seen and heard. Some got coffee, others were chatting in one or two small groups. I think they were just trying to restore themselves to normalcy, asking: What was that? Did I really see it? Did it really happen?

Then, unexpectedly, I had Son to myself, and I put the question to him that had popped into my mind fully formed, in the short while after he had ended his astounding performance.

He was pulling at the bottle again; when my words had sunk in, he looked at me, and suddenly caught my wrist, frail old man or not, in a grip of iron. I heard him out for the next five to ten minutes, during which we were fortunately left alone. After, when he dropped his grip, I was utterly dumbfounded.

What had happened was my asking a question that Son had doubtless heard enough times over in the year or two since his “rediscovery.” When I put it to him, he probably had his answer down pat.

What I asked him, was about the Robert Johnson rumor. Even in the short space of time encompassing my snap course in the blues—as in Mississippi bottleneck style—I had come across the legend. It is impossible to avoid. Briefly put, Son and his sideman playing back in the early 1930s were pestered, the way he told it, by a “youngster with a dissatisfied mind, ’bout eighteen.” Not bad on the mouth organ, allowed to sit in on account of that, a sort of mascot, but not to be allowed to touch the grail of the guitar. “Couldn’t play. Scare off the customers.” Little Robert Johnson, a cast in one eye, got tired of the off-putting big boys, upped and disappeared. Ramblified, maybe. No one saw him for a year or two. Comes back—what?!?

This young man, couldn’t tune a guitar, let alone play one, now has the upper hand. Instead of sulling up, like before, he astounds his former mentors, playing with unheard-of virtuosity, independent bass lines, searing melodies, zinging the slide, something absolutely new and even frightening. He dies a few years later, stabbed, or poisoned, or shot. No one knows what happened. He has changed the face of music, although it’s taken some time to percolate down, to really influence things. Like now.

There were rumors, lots of them. How did—let’s face it—an utter incompetent, a guitar nincompoop . . .

Most of the explanations are dark, very much like the rumors flying around Paganini in his time. No one knew quite what to believe, because Robert Johnson is the only one who knows. And he ain’t talking, now, or ever.

So what I did, is I asked Mr. House what *he* thought had happened.

And perhaps caught off guard, tired, a bit confused, he

whispered to me what I think no one else had ever heard until then. Now I understand why he turned to lay preaching. And hits the bottle so hard.

There was a name mentioned. I turned things over in my mind the next few days. Forget about post-divorce depression. As many women as I wanted. Absolute fame and respect. And if none of it was true, a guaranteed deferment, forever, as long as I timed things right. No more sweating, lying awake at night, and wondering if my fate was facedown in the Asian mud, a bullet through my forehead, Mekong water washing my blood away.

Oh, I made it down to New Orleans, all right. The *name,* amazingly, was still around. Everyone knew who she was, I could see it in the faces, the fear, when I said who I was looking for. Money got me contacts, and eventually, with time running out, an appointment.

I *found out*—I won't say any more—and took thereafter the Greyhound to a backwater county, rented a car, and drove to a sleepy delta town. I had the things I needed with me, and made a few local inquiries, hoping that my profile was low. It wasn't and twice, poking around during the next moonlit nights, I was almost caught. I wish now I had been.

There was the slightest bit of confusion about the final set of directions I had received—maybe it was on purpose, the juju woman's way to really give me time to think over what I was aiming to do. Or maybe it was just her failing memory.

Regardless, the small ambiguity sent me wandering to two obscure crossroads out in the middle of the country, on two successive nights. The wrong crossroads, but that was okay, since I still had a few more nights before I had to report to the recruiting station in Buffalo. But I had to watch my step; local law was, if not exactly onto me, at least viewing me with real suspicion. Who wouldn't in a town of 852 registered souls, where the hog-calling contest was the year's big event, and you're a Yankee stranger checking into the hardly ever used hotel with no particular stated purpose in mind, just "scouting out fishing locations," and the like.

Uh-huh.

It was on the third day in town that the deputy, Farnum, pulled me aside. After a half-hour check of my driver's license by radio to the state police, and probably the FBI, I was let go, in a none-too-friendly fashion. I went back to where I was staying, and waited for the night.

At third try, I finally found the right place. It was farther north than what they say, those people who claim to know a lot, but don't. How I knew I had the right place, I won't tell; let's just say that a certain object was buried there, whose finding, and character, made it absolutely certain that I was at the bona fide spot that had been described for me in that café a week before.

It was out in the middle of nowhere, on private land; for a car to pass by, and interrupt my work, would be unbelievably bad luck. My luck this time, held.

Once I had dug the hole at the unpaved crossing to the proper depth, there was nothing more to do than sit and wait until midnight neared. I had given myself plenty of time, so I just leaned back and had a cigarette, listening to the night noises, but mostly reviewing the details of the ritual as it had been given to me.

About a quarter to, I began to take things out of the sack I had with, and arranged them in the specified order around the pit I had dug out. Everything properly in place, I unfolded the scrap of paper on which the formula had been written. With a pocket light, I gave the words one last glance, to be sure I had them right. Walking counterclockwise slowly, with a bottle of cheap red wine in one hand, I recited the phrases I had memorized. At each point of the compass, I stopped, took a swig, then spat it into the hole. At each of the three full circuits, I stooped for one of the objects I had earlier placed at the periphery of the pit, and dropped it in.

Once I had completed the ceremony in the correct order and detail, I picked up the gunnysack, which was lying off to one side, and took out the two last objects: a large black rooster, with its feet bound, and beak wired shut, and a small paper cutter—the type that looks like a breadboard, with a swing blade attached to one edge by a pivot bolt.

I looked at my watch, and saw it was two minutes before midnight. I took an old-fashioned razor from my pocket, opened it, and carefully cut the twine that bound the rooster's claws. Its spurs were clipped, so there was no danger involved. I set it down standing, smoothing its comb with my hand, at the edge of the pit, precisely in line with the north arm of the crossroad. I said a soothing word or two to calm it down. But it was quiet, probably dazed still from the drugged corn I had fed it earlier.

With one eye on the ticks of my chronometer, set precisely to the National Standards Laboratory radio signal just that same afternoon, I waited the few seconds remaining.

At midnight precisely, with a sharp swoop of the blade, I sliced the rooster's head from its body, throwing the severed part into the bushes far away.

What followed was hard to accept, but I saw it with my own eyes—the rooster, instead of falling over, did the normal: it ran around in time-honored circular fashion—like a chicken with its head cut off.

Nothing special about that. Anyone who's lived in the country has seen the routine; what's just an expression for city folk, but a gory and grotesque reality, literal as the words that express it.

What was wrong here, however, was the manner in which this particular chicken had decided to follow habit. It ran at a slow trot clockwise around the hole, all the time spouting its small geyser of blood into the dark opening. Coincidence? Reflex? Just happened to run around at the required distance to prevent it from tumbling in, yet aiming the spurts of blood precisely into the black vacancy the whole while?

Weird and upsetting as all this was, it could have been a quirk of nature. I could handle that.

What got to me, though, was the fact that at each cardinal point of the compass, at each spot where a road met the dug-out hole, it stopped for a moment, its neck—or where its head would have been—bent toward the black depths as if listening.

It was at that point I knew this was real—I had up to then held a certain amount of belief in reserve, telling myself that I was carrying out a quaint, if rather drastic folkloric ritual, in the interests of amateur scholarship. But now I felt the bottom drop out of my stomach, knowing what was ahead of me, and knowing that the chain of events I had now started, had to be followed through to its conclusion. That, or worse, much worse than I could possibly imagine would follow. I had a previous participant's word of assurance, if only secondhand, on that. Think about that, whoever is reading this.

With its third orbit completed, the rooster halted, right on the dime, on the northern point where I had set it down. The blood stopped jetting—I had difficulty grasping that a rooster, no matter how large, could have held quite so much blood.

It held itself steady for a moment, then arched its body and the ragged remains of its neck in the familiar style, as if to crow. Only an obscene gurgle of blood emanated. And it fell neatly into the pit.

Every hair on the nape of my neck and back was standing. I could feel gooseflesh invade every inch of skin, as uncontrollable shivering overtook me. There was no explaining *that* away. It had gone exactly as described to me in detail. I knew I was in deep, really deep.

In spite of shaking, I did what was proscribed, but required. The paper cutter was my idea; the ritual was unspecific here, and I could have used a knife, but I just saw it as the quickest way of getting things done.

I set the cutter down on the south side of the excavation's bloody rim, as was the command, seating it firmly in the sandy gravel. Satisfied that it would not slip, I lifted the blade to its full vertical extent, and placed my hand flat, palm down, at a slight angle on the board, its four fingers extended straight out, over the edge of the cutter and above the hole.

I admit there was a moment of hesitation, but not after what happened next. While I looked at my fingers for the last time, I took just a momentary pause, perhaps to think over if I really wanted to do this.

It was then I heard the sounds—they were faint at first, and seemed to be coming from all directions. When they got nearer, I realized they were concentrated, some large multitude or mob walking on each of the roads to the crossing. Toward me.

The sound was like large and massive horses' hooves, muffled in cloth, in burlap, shaking the ground. They were getting closer, very close, and then stopped. I shook, without looking up—I did not want to see. I had a feeling that whatever was out there was watching me, ready to pounce if I did not continue with the irreversible train of events I had set in motion, and soon. A wind picked up then, from all directions, and began to blow, steadily, growing stronger and stronger. Noises started coming out of the hole.

At which point, I lifted the handle of the cutting blade high with my right hand, still looking at my fingers.

Then I chopped them.

I had, not unexpectedly, fainted, and afterward I thought myself lucky not to have bled to death. On the other hand there wasn't all that much blood around; maybe most of it had gone into the hole, along with the fingers. When I came to, I wasn't so concerned with details, eager as I was to finish the job and get myself out of there. If I had had more time, and wasn't shaking while patching myself up, thinking about what I had done, I might have had a look after the missing blood. As it was, I was fully occupied with applying the "poultice" the practitioner had given me. Once it was on, I filled the hole, tamping it down and covering it with dust, so no one could see that anything had gone on there.

I got a large pair of gloves, and stuffed the fingers of the left one with some wadded paper, and went around wearing it to avoid questions. My thumb and a strap across the back held it in place. It may sound like a recipe guaranteed to produce blood poisoning, but by now, after all I had experienced, I had *faith* in the rest of what had been told me, so I didn't go to a doctor, although I was tempted for a while.

There was no swelling of my arm, no colorful green, yellow, or black shoots of dying flesh decorating the limb; other than a slight fever and dizziness, and—of course—the loss of use of my hand, I really didn't feel that bad at all.

I went back to Rochester, by Greyhound again, and sat out the next few days reading back issues of *Sing Out,* technique books on playing blues guitar, and listening to old and new records of blues singers, whatever I could get my hand on. While soaking up the riffs, I could feel there was something going on inside the glove, under the dirty bandage, but adjured not to look, I left it alone, until the date I had been given.

Time finally came, and while I was removing the glove and stinking bandage, I'm not quite sure what I expected. Once everything was off, I went to wash my hand, which was half encrusted by dried blood. That done, I gave it a close look.

The cuts had been clean, and the wounds were totally healed. What was even more remarkable were the stubs I had remaining; these resembled the tips of actual fingers, and not some amateur butcher job. They were round, smooth, with the familiar whorled patterns, and even had the beginnings of nails. In fact, my hand looked like it had suffered from some birth defect that had left the fingers with part of one joint, and not a ragged remnant of the unskilled amputation of which it was the result. I could feel, I thought, bone and muscle and perhaps something else, pushing, striving against the constraining envelope of flesh.

I made my scheduled trip to Buffalo, right on time for my slated induction. The army docs took one look at my truncated hand, and wondered how I had ever been called up at all. 4-F. I tried to show manly disappointment at my rejection. I think I succeeded, almost convincing myself.

The fingers grew at the rate of about a third of an inch every two weeks. After seven weeks, I could see the first joint forming on each of the reborn digits. About the same time, I noticed the dots. There were two of these on the pad of each finger. At first, they were barely visible, but with each day, they became clearer, until they showed as sharply as if tattooed. They were lined up parallel with the fingers, and were very small black spots, perfectly round. The inner ones, nearest the palm, had each an additional thin curved line to the left of the bottom dot, touching it, like outline suns peeking out from black eclipsed moons.

I could hardly wait.

It was hard sitting around, waiting for the fingers to recover to their full extent, and the temptation was great to pick up a guitar, particularly on my regaining flexibility and motion. Nonetheless, I heeded the warning I had been given. It was absolutely imperative that I did not touch a stringed instrument until a certain sign I had been told to watch for appeared.

That would have been almost impossible in Rochester—boredom alone would have had me lifting a guitar at home or at a friend's. What I needed was more distraction than the upstate town could provide, to get my mind off my left hand. I still had some money left, so I decided to head to Manhattan, and check into the scene. In four to six weeks, from the look of it, my hand would be ready, and I would conquer the world with my guitar. In the meantime, I could get myself a small room, and see what was going on in a very rapidly developing musical scene.

I settled in on the lower East Side in a cheap and ratty one-room, all I could afford, and began walking the Village nightly during the next few weeks. Amazing riffs and runs were beginning to form themselves in my head. It was something for which I had no gift before, lack of invention complementing my hopeless playing. I was sure now I would be able to translate my new visions to notes; I was totally convinced. I began laughing to myself inwardly, I nightly heard what had become, to my ears, the hopelessly inept guitar work of others I once thought inspired. I could barely contain my eagerness to blow them out of the water, in just a few weeks more.

It was just about then that it happened, that I by pure chance, wandered into the place that changed everything.

The Café Whá is in the heart of the commercialized west end of the Village, where the tourists tend to go to gawk at the threatening new tribes that seem poised to take over the country, LBJ or not. Visitors avoid the scruffy East Village, more poorly lit, with a sharper edge of danger and potential mugging, unless there is a concert at one of several rundown halls or old movie houses, when pleasure balances the risk.

I had passed by the Whá numerous times on my visits downtown: just another downstairs dive with no chairs or tables, and pretty nondescript at that, hard put competing with the numerous poster and head shops, book stores selling the revolution, and clothing emporiums with unisex changing rooms. These, and the button shops with "Frodo Lives" badges in Elvish (counterbalanced by those exhorting "Nuke Hanoi"), the snack bars with deliciously greasy pizza by the slice and the record stores and live music, the crowds spilling off the sidewalks onto the streets like some lively oriental souk, all with a brilliant carnivallike edge, light up the night. Dope sellers approach you every five feet with half-furtive offers of quality weed, consisting mostly of grass clippings from Washington Square. These are easily recognized at a distance, and easy to be quit of by simply offering *them* a nickel bag, preempting any offer to you. But it's the strange new people themselves, with their hair, their wild uniform, that are the real attraction.

Given so much ferment, new shops with interesting wares are going up by the score, almost weekly, there's always something new. But if you cruised the area as often as I did, you would have eventually seen the more obvious, and would be examining the less-noticeable details tucked away in the crannies. So one night, waiting for my fingers to completely grow back, I walked through the doorway, down the concrete steps through the combined haze of ten kinds of incense and more than a hint of pot, to the cellar where things were going on.

Whoever was playing was taking a break, so I bought a beer at an inflated price, and looked around. The whole club was spattered with gobs and dots and patches of fluorescent paint—the floors, the walls, and ceiling. Black light turned it into the kind of place where everything glows: the paint, your teeth, anything white you're wearing.

Watching the crowd, admiring the women, I didn't notice the band was back until they started to play. I didn't pay much attention to the music at all—the first five seconds, that is, when someone strummed a loud, weird, introductory chord that rattled me awake, as if I had been sleepwalking until then.

I turned toward the band, but didn't see the lead guitarist: There was the standard mix—a bass, the drummer, a rhythm guitar—minus the main man. Puzzled, I swung my gaze around, past the couples and solo acts who were already filling the dance space, when I spotted him.

He was the negro in the bathtub, literally so. That is, the guitarist, off by himself, was standing in a white porcelain tub placed near one wall. Gape-mouthed like a weekend tourist, I started to draw closer, past the twisting dancers, when he played the next notes.

I froze. It was like nothing I had ever heard before. It was like hearing Robert Johnson, or Son, for the first time, but different; a lightning flash ran up my spine, whacking my brain stem while simultaneously sending warmer and warmer pulses through my body in waves. My left hand tingled a lot more than the right, but I paid little attention to that, dazed as I was by the incredible revelation that was now unfolding, as it were, before my very ears. I felt that God, or somebody else, was in back of that guitar.

I must have shuffled forward unaware, stunned and pulled by the music, until I found myself in front of the man, close enough to touch him, since the bathtub he was standing in was mounted on the floor, there was no stage or proscenium. He was right down there amongst us, with us mortals.

He had a shock of hair like an aborigine, and a headband around it. The mustache was not quite Zapata, but getting there. He had great teeth, too, and a ready smile, and there was something exotic about his cheekbones and his eyes.

The music was rough, but all there, I mean, it was no music that everybody else played; this was space music, never seen or heard on the planet Earth before, having the nature of *just landed.* Hello Earthlings. But it was him, nobody else, unlike anything else, a new continent coming into view.

This guy was doing things impossible, that I never dreamed of, at least until I saw his hand move up and across the neck of the instrument. Then, without thinking, I began, just a little at first, then more, in a way I can't explain, to con what he was doing. It was like when you have those stubborn last pieces of a jigsaw puzzle that have been off to the side all the time, and you finally, only a few more spaces to fill, at last comprehend where they should go. And my comprehension was just as amazing to me as the raw and powerful music itself.

Between those riffs that he made look effortless, he peered up with those lazy eyes, giving the false impression that he was coming up for air, folks, just having a look around, when in reality he was in full control. I think what he was really doing, was looking to see if this amazing music, never conceived before in the history of the planet, was connecting with anyone.

He looked around me, and past me, and then, as if he just happened to notice, looked me in the eye. And burst out with a radiant smile, and while his picking hand squeezed the strings that seemed to play themselves, he lifted the other hand from the frets and gave me a short, sideways wave, right out of Spanky in *Our Gang*. His grin said, *Look, no hands*.

But then, I almost collapsed—naturally, since following the movement of his hand, I saw on his fingertips patterns of dots identical to those on my own half-grown fingers.

He must have seen the shock on my face, since, without missing a beat, without dropping a note, he cocked his head to the side slightly, and winked a quizzical eye, as if to ask *What's happening, man?*

I felt almost too weak to stand, so I backed away, jostled by the writhing dancers, and leaned against a nearby wall, knocking back the rest of my beer. Only partly recovered, I kept on watching his fingers move, thinking to myself all the while: *Yes. Precisely! It all makes sense, it's just the way you would do it!*

He would now and then look over my way, keeping an eye on me, I think, which was smart enough, given all the stone-doped crazies passing through on any given evening, ready to react in any of a million unpredictable ways. Every now and then, he would make eye contact, like he was asking *You alright man? Everything okay?*

It was then, I think, he realized, slowly at first, then with his grasp of my insight increasing, that I saw and *knew* what he was doing. I could see it in his eyes. And that astounded him, although he played on as if nothing had happened. A pro.

When the song was over, he motioned me over with

his head. I saw his wary look as I approached, but he was unquestionably curious. It was then, without thinking, perhaps out of nervousness, that I took my shortened hand out of my pocket, marks visible.

That stopped him cold. His jaw dropped, and his eyes nearly bulged, and it was only then that I realized he had seen *my* hand. And now he stood there, silent, just shaking his head in consternation, from side to side.

We were close enough to talk, and he asked me, over the din of the crowd, "Where'd you get *that,* man? You know twenty-seven? Three time five? Black and red? You gotta be careful! Come here, I'm gonna tell you something. . . ."

Dazed, I walked to him. He leaned over, so no one could hear him but myself.

And he told me.

So that was it. Somewhere along the way someone had left out some awfully crucial details, crucial for my own health, safety, and well-being. And that was only in *this* life. . . .

I felt cheated, and enraged. I spent a lot of time kicking at and breaking furniture in my room, before my anger let out, and I sat down, feeling like a deflated balloon. I realized I was acting the fool, and that trashing the apartment was hardly going to solve my problems, if there was any solution.

The guitarist, if I had him right—and for once, somebody had told me something concrete, in a noncryptic fashion—had implied that whatever it was, it would happen to me sometime during my twenty-seventh year. Just like Robert Johnson. It was too late for the Whá guitarist; he had already made his choice and reckons on four more years or so. During which time he is determined to make his mark, which I am sure will be a big one, before he has to go.

I was skating on the edge, on a lot thinner ice than I had ever imagined. My fingers were growing day by day, and would be ready soon. I had been told not to touch a guitar, or any stringed instrument until they were "normal" again. My chance acquaintance from the Whá explained why. If there was any hope of reversing what had been done, I had to keep away from music stores, bars where bands played, schools, anywhere there was a possibility I could touch or accidentally come in contact with a fretted board. And in the meantime, I had to find out *if* the process could be reversed. He owned that he had never heard of that happening before.

But my fingers had already taken a life of their own, and the noise I heard around me, ordinary traffic, the sounds of pedestrians walking the pavements, the whisperings of the very air itself, were translating themselves into music in my mind and then, without conscious volition, to little jerks and movements of the new digits. I found myself drawn without thinking toward places where guitars are found: a park bench, music schools, museum displays. I think the fingers, the hand, were taking over, and trying to make me transpose those yet imaginary notes inside me into sound, tremendous music that would awe and astonish all who heard. It was almost out of control. To top it all off, my twenty-seventh birthday was nine days away.

So it was important that whatever could be done, had to be done quick. I went south as fast as I could drive, going day and night, down to Louisiana, using a rental car. I wasted several days calling around, trying to find my original contact, the woman in New Orleans. She seemed to have vanished into the depths of the earth. I was near panic, when another name was given to me.

* * *

That's why I went to the crossroads again. I didn't trust the instructions I had been given; I didn't at all care for the smirk on the face of the yellow-eyed crone who had given them to me in a backstreet fortune-teller's shop, charging me two hundred for something not guaranteed to work. Not that the money made much difference if procedures failed.

She wouldn't even let me see her face-to-face; I had to walk backward into her room, to tell her my problem, and left walking forward. I talked looking at her in a mirror. Her voice oozed skepticism: I shouldn't go to the crossroads *now*—I should wait until the end of August, or the beginning of February. I told her I didn't have the time.

She just shook her head. Her directions were hedged about so heavily with the conditional: *If* you do that . . . *if* it come to you . . . *if* you hear that noise.

Yet I had no other choice, with time ticking away. Which, with my steadily increasing panic, goes a long way toward explaining why I became careless, advertising my existence in a town where I was unwanted, persona non grata from before, where my presence was bound to awaken suspicion, and set the dogs of law upon my trail.

No matter. Now it's done and over with.

I lost another day after first going out to the crossroads, only to discover that it had been paved over since my previous visit. My twenty-seventh was by now only one day away. I bought myself a pickax and a crowbar to break up the blacktop; I already had a shovel. I was dropping hints, if I had thought about it at all, left and right, forward and back, up and down, for every grandmother, half-wit, and daughter-in-law to see for miles around. Not to mention Fatty, the deputy, who probably saw the potential arrest as the icing on his cake.

* * *

Once I had disposed of the body, I went back, ready to get things moving, since with the road surface cracked open by my earlier efforts of the evening, all I had to do was widen it out, and dig. I had given myself plenty of margin, just in case something—like Fatty's visit—should momentarily disturb proceedings. After all, I was not in any position to make mistakes. I had long ago put aside any dreams of guitar fame and glory, and was ready to go to Vietnam in a wheelchair, if they wanted me to. Only one thing was important now, and that was reversing the Covenant, if at all possible. I was giving it my best shot.

Set to dig, I thought all of a sudden about the deputy's car. He had walked up on me, meaning he must have parked it out of sight so he could approach me unseen in the dark. If it was near the main road, I'd better move it, in case anyone saw and got suspicious. There was still time enough to do that.

I didn't have to walk far: it was hidden by the trees, just around the bend. He must have cut the engine by the main road, and glided silently down the incline to where he had left it. I wanted it out of sight, maybe put it in the swamp for good measure. It was unlocked, but there were no keys. It would have taken too much time to go back where I had left Fatty and dig around for them; somewhat illogically, I began to root about inside the patrol car, looking for an extra set.

There was an object resting on the front seat, covered by a tarp, probably a shotgun, I thought. I took off the covering in the darkness, to move the thing aside, while I was already moving my other hand, the right one, toward the glove compartment.

Something like a violent shock struck the other hand, and I looked to see what I had in it. Even in the starlight, it was easy to tell.

An electric guitar.

* * *

Of course, I didn't give up. Even though I knew whatever I did from now on was futile. I found that out pretty quick when I opened the hole deeper. Nothing was in there, although I was certain of the precise spot. I could forget any ceremony with the previously buried objects; they were missing, and a ritual only using what I had brought this time would make things worse, if that were possible. I admit, I trembled mightily, once it all sank in.

Since then, I've thought of the irony involved. Deputy F, if he'd only come a few minutes later, after I found out I was done for, finished—why, he'd still be walking around today, bragging about how he had caught a big offender. Biggest criminal in years. I wouldn't have resisted. But done is done.

That's the whole story of why I'm in this cabin in the woods off the Interstate, hiding out. They'll find me soon enough, of course—it's just a matter of time. The police in fifteen states are looking for me, and I can imagine my picture regularly on the TV. Sooner or later—probably sooner—I'll be found. Not that it matters, really, considering what I'll be facing further down the line. My debts to human law and custom will look like nothing, compared to *that*.

So there's only one thing left to do, in whatever time I have remaining. That's why I took the deputy's guitar (Farnum was quite a good fingerpicker, I understand from the newscasts on the car radio) and bought the tape player and mike on my way here. I don't need an amplifier for what I have to do. Whoever gets me first, the law, or the *others*, I'm going to leave *something* behind.

My fingers are tingling already.

Mike:

How are things out at Waolatchee Sheriff's Office?

I reckon you've heard plenty of rumors about what happened up our way, so I thought I'd better send you some info outside the proper channels, sub rosa, so to speak, since the DA, Herrick, has put a tight lid on all evidence.

I managed to make a few copies before he grabbed everything. As you will see from the enclosure, the perp sounds like a winner, a real nutcase. He is, or was, by his own admission, a cop killer, so at least we know who did it for sure.

When we took the call, we went in armed for big game, with seven cars—3 from Jefferson County, and 5 from here. We weren't sure on the ID, but after Farnum's killing, we weren't taking any chances, especially since a fair number of tips gave us a pretty good idea of what we had. Car rental agency, lumberyard, music store, that sort of thing.

There was no car there—we found that and a rental trailer, still attached, further up a farm road. The cabin was shuttered and the door closed. Milliken and Perez, two of our biggest boys, sorta snuck up on the porch, and rammed it with all their weight—we weren't gonna give the bastard a chance, if we could help it.

Problem was, he had barred all ingress. The doors and shuttered windows were backed solid from top to bottom with two-by-fours, screwed into place, we found out later! Perez got a dislocated shoulder and Milliken fell flat on his butt. The door didn't budge.

Well, we'd blown our chances of surprising him, so we headed for cover, told him over the bullhorn to come on out. Nothing. There was a phone line in, and we tried calling him. No answer. A real stubborn customer.

We waited a while, got up reinforcements, and

waited some more, hoping to starve him out, but nothing doing. So finally we got some fellers—volunteers all—with bulletproofs on, who went to work on the door with crowbars and a sledgehammer, while half the police in the state, it looked like, covered them. Man, if I told you we weren't sweating when all this was going on, I'd be a liar.

They finally got a hole through the woodwork, and pitched some CS through the opening. No sound came out, while they worked to knock down the door. We had masks on, but nobody was going in until the gas had cleared. We figured the guy might've had a mask of his own, since he hadn't come out, and might be waiting for us. We wanted to see what we had when we went in.

Now, are you sitting down? You'd better, to get ready for this: When our men entered, there was nobody there. I mean, it was just a one-room, with a bed, a washstand, a chamber pot, and not much else. Someone had locked themselves in there, nailed the place shut from the inside, and then left—don't ask me how. There wasn't any sign of walls or floorboards removed or replaced; or at least that's what forensics say. From the way things were nailed together, it should have been impossible for anyone to get out without removing the two-by-fours: the walls were solid log cabin, the floor a concrete slab, and the roof was untouched. The one light was on.

What we did find were the following:

> The manuscript, composed of the top leaves of a yellow legal pad, otherwise blank, transcription herewith enclosed.
> A small satchel, or man's travel bag.
> Several sets of men's underwear and socks.
> On the floor, a set of men's clothing; in the pockets, ID, including driver's license (NY state),

social security card, university ID, a wedding photo, and a key chain with car and house keys, and a wallet with $510 and some change.
A couple of ball point pens.
A comb.
A bar of soap.
A man's safety razor.
A few tins of canned food, some empty.
A stainless steel fork.
A medium screwdriver.
A wood saw.
Assorted long screws, several boxes.
A hand drill, with three bits.
A pair of shoes and socks, thrown on the floor with the outer clothing.
A man's onyx ring, gold, 18k, standard jeweller's issue.
A man's wristwatch, Bulova waterproof.
On the bed (unmade), a box of .38 ammo, opened, 13 rounds light.
On the floor, a .38 Smith & Wesson revolver. It had been fired; all the chambers were empty, with 6 expended shells on the floor, together with 6 live rounds, same place. It looked like someone was trying to reload, and got nervous. There were cavities from 6 rounds that had partly penetrated a wall from the interior side, tightly clustered around one spot. Rounds matched the gun, according to lab. They're being checked against fragments found in Farnum's skull.
Two quart bottles of JD (green label), one empty, the other half so. No glass.
A 3-inch length of polished light steel tubing, crushed.
An Ampex tape deck, with 4 reels of 3M recording tape, and a recording microphone. The

state acoustics lab at the university is looking at these now, at the DA's request. From what I hear, these have got some very faint scratchy guitar music, awful stuff, wild junk like nothing never heard played by man before. Modern "music"! The tape, I'm told, breaks off in the middle of playing. No voice.

An electric guitar, Farnum's or the body thereof, connected with a jack to a tape deck socket. The neck was missing, apparently ripped(!) from the body of the instrument. We searched the woods, and haven't found it. The strings were snapped, with only twisted wire remaining on the body of the guitar. It looks like someone left in a hurry.

Oh, and last of all, a scrap of paper, torn off from some other pad we haven't found yet, in the same handwriting as the original of the copy I sent. Text reads:

You can run, you can run, you can run but you can't hide. You can run, you can run, you can run but you can't hide. It was down by the crossroad, that where I began to slide.

Any ideas?

JIKININKI

Joseph A. Ezzo

Resumeshiokure . . . meshiokure . . . meshiokure . . .

The noise, an outlandish hybrid of the twittering of birds and the trilling of crickets, but with human speech nearly thrown in, had been incessant since Les Finley had returned to his home in Tucson. He could never recall hearing it before, and wondered if some new species of birds or insects had invaded the neighborhood since his departure. Aside from the noise, which loomed only as a kind of trivial annoyance far in the background, he had far more prominent concerns. Les stood in the front yard of his next-door neighbor and best friend, trying to gauge the response of his neighbors to his new situation.

"I don't get it, Jerry. We're living in the twenty-first century, for crying out loud. Why would people be bothered by the fact that I have an Asian wife now?"

Jerry, who had lived next door to Les for over a decade, and who, along with his wife Althea, had been a pillar of strength for Les in his darkest hour, merely shrugged. "Well, you know this is a conservative town, Les," he said evasively. "And a fussy neighborhood. No one's moved in or out of it in more than five years."

"What does that mean? Look, you know me better than anyone, Jerry. You know what I went through not long before I left for Japan. That divorce, the emotional pain I endured. You saw how it tore me apart, how it soured me on just about everything in the world. I taught in Japan for three years. A long time to be away. Is it so shocking that I should come back here to Tucson with a wife from Japan?"

"And then there is . . . well, she's a little . . . it's just kind of unexpected, you know? No one knew, that sort of thing."

Les snorted. "What is it you're really trying to say, old buddy? I know you better than that, and you're beating around the bush, is all. Out with it, how about it?"

"Well, I don't know exactly . . . Les, you're my good friend, you know that, I wouldn't want anything bad ever to happen to you. You know—"

"Get to the point, Jerry."

"Fine. She's . . . well, Les, for one thing, that blond hair I think is throwing people."

Les's eyes widened. "You want to tell me everyone's decided to ostracize me in my own neighborhood because I have a Japanese wife with blond hair? Don't these people know anything? Almost every young woman in Japan colors her hair these days. So do a lot of young men. A lot of women—and men, too—think that the naturally black hair looks heavy on a woman. Women like to soften that by lightening their hair. Blond is not unusual. It's not a sign of a woman being sleazy or loose or anything of the sort. Japanese go in for trends big-time, and coloring hair is very popular right now."

Jerry was holding his hands out in front of him. "Okay, okay. I hear you, Les, and there's no need for the rest of the block to, as well. Okay, fine. But then, too, you keep saying 'young.' She looks to be about fifteen—"

"Oh, stop it! She's twenty-six. She has a master's degree in . . . oh, kiss off, Jerry, I don't need to explain myself to you." Les walked away, then turned and spat. "Friend," he fumed as he headed toward his front door.

"Les, take it easy. People are a little uptight, is all. Maybe it doesn't really have much to do with her. But you know, I mean, just what is this deal with your wife's granny, huh? Lurking about in the shadows every night? Making all that noise. That's giving us all the creeps, man."

Les stopped just before his front door. He turned and glared at Jerry, face reddening. "What are you talking about? That's nonsense. What kind of crap are you pulling, Jerry? There's no one here but Maiko and me." He shook his head as he pulled open the door. "I never thought you'd stoop to listening to such drivel, Jerry. I thought you were above all that. I guess things really have changed since I got back." His voice carried into the house, and Maiko came to greet him.

"Who you were talking to?" she asked, looking around to see if he was alone.

"No one . . . nothing. Forget it." He shrugged, took his wife in his arms. "You doing okay? You happy about coming here with me?"

Maiko blushed. "Of course! What do you think? I'm so happy with you, Res!"

He held her close. "Thanks, sweetie. That's just what I needed to hear." Then he held up a hand. "But . . . try to say my name again. L-l-l-les."

"R-r-r-l-l-l-les."

"Excellent. Keep working on it."

Maiko sighed. "I try. But you know it's hard for me. We don't have this sound in Japanese."

Shortly before midnight, after Maiko had fallen asleep, Les crept out of the bedroom and to the front of the house, restless and still annoyed by Jerry's comments. Standing in the living room, he surveyed the three windows there. One of them was set in the front wall of the house, the other two on the side. Then he strolled past the front door to the dining room, which likewise had a window on each the front and side walls, and from there entered the kitchen. The kitchen-dining area protruded from the main portion of the house, so that the kitchen window over the sink provided a view of the backyard. He began his investigation with this latter window, then worked his way to the dining room and living room. Six windows in all, and none of them offered a view of anything but various patches of his property, just as it had been since he first bought the house. No grandmother lurking about, anything like that.

Les sulked over the next few days, wondering why Jerry had gone to such outrageous lengths to defend the pedantic attitudes of the neighborhood, so much so that he had trouble sleeping, and found himself coming out of a fitful slumber at three thirty a.m. To his surprise, Maiko was not in bed with him. He pushed off the sheet and sat up, but just then he heard her footsteps on the tile floor of the hallway. Without acknowledging him, she slipped back under the sheet and fell asleep at once.

"Maiko?" Les whispered, touching her gently on the shoulder. "Is everything okay?" She felt unusually cold, or so he thought. He listened to her breathing for several seconds, then lay down again. Over the next four nights, the pattern repeated itself. Les never stayed awake long enough to see Maiko leave the bed, but when he managed to roust himself, usually between three and three thirty, she was gone. He never had the chance to get out of bed to find where she was, because each time she returned to the bedroom just after he awakened. Not once did she acknowledge him, but climbed into the bed and fell immediately asleep, her body cool and slightly moist.

The pattern, like Jerry's excuses, weighed on Les, and

he turned increasingly surly and evasive at the technical college where he taught. He felt sure that the general lack of sleep contributed to his state of mind, and therefore stopped off at the local Walgreen's one afternoon on his way home and picked up the strongest sleep medication in the store. Maiko and he spent that evening watching *American Beauty* on a cable movie channel, and later, as Maiko was showering, Les got himself a glass of water and addressed the bottle of sleeping pills. The telephone rang.

"Yes?"

"Am I speaking to Lester Finley?"

"Who's asking?"

"We'd like to enroll you in our new credit program that allows you to consolidate—"

"Not interested. Please take my name off your calling list." Les felt his patience quickly slipping away.

"But please, sir, if I could just have two minutes of your time, I think you'll find—"

"I think you can go pack sand, you prick!" Les slammed down the telephone.

"Who that was?"

Les looked up suddenly, saw Maiko in a white robe, a towel girdling her head. "Why you yell rike that, Res?"

Les sighed wearily. "It was . . . nothing . . . just someone with nothing better to do than bother me. Just . . . listen, Maiko, I need to settle down a bit. How about some tea before we go to bed?"

Maiko smiled. "Mmmm. Okay. I can make." She started to head toward the kitchen when Les got an idea. He held out a hand.

"No, sweetie, I'll do it. Here, just relax in the living room. I'll take care of it."

Maiko kissed his cheek. "Okay, but first I go to dry my hair." She turned and walked toward the rear of the house. Les gathered up the sleeping pills, went to the kitchen. He hastily prepared two cups of Japanese green tea, then dissolved four sleeping pills in one of them.

When three a.m. arrived, Maiko was sleeping like the dead. Les crept from the bed and made the rounds at the windows in the front of the house. The last window he looked out of faced Jerry's house, and there he saw someone standing.

It was a woman, as Jerry had suggested. She seemed to be waiting, cast so deeply by the night that she appeared as a faint silhouette. *Who are you?* Les asked silently. *What are you doing in my yard? And what do you want with my wife?*

Resumeshiokure . . . meshiokure . . . meshiokure . . .

The annoying twittering-trilling grew in volume, and, as it did, Les perceived the woman turning her head to either side. She repeated the gesture several times, with increasing rapidity. Was this woman, then, the source of the bizarre noise? Then it seemed that the woman stopped moving her head, became very still, and Les sensed she was staring straight ahead, at the living room window, and that somehow she could see him perfectly, despite his concealment behind the curtains. He shuddered involuntarily and stepped back from the window, breathing hard. He glanced in the direction of the bedroom, then slit the curtain open again. The woman was gone.

The following day Maiko was still asleep when Les left for work. Restless, he canceled two afternoon classes and returned home at noon. She was up, dressed in a red kimono (one he had not seen before) and sitting at the dining room table, sipping tea and picking at a croissant. She appeared to be very upset.

"What's up?" Les asked casually.

Maiko did not answer, merely lowered her head. "Maiko, what is it?" he asked with concern.

She shook her head. "I feel . . . bery bad, today, Res. I hurt . . . eberywhere."

He sat down next to her, took one of her hands. "What's wrong? Do you need to see a doctor?"

Maiko shrugged, looked away. "I wish to be in Japan," she whispered. Perhaps she had intended for Les not to hear this, but the words reached his ears very clearly.

Les collected himself. "Tell you what. How about if I make us some lunch? Then maybe we can do something fun in the afternoon, maybe some shopping. How does that sound?"

Maiko did not look up. In fact, it seemed to Les that she had not even heard him.

Les got up and went into the kitchen. *Whoever that woman is,* he said to himself, *she's doing something very bad to Maiko, and means to hurt her. I have no idea why, but I can't let it go on.*

After lunch, which Maiko did not touch, he drove to the Walgreen's, to buy not more sleeping pills, but Vivarin. As he pulled his car back onto the street where he lived, he found himself behind Jerry. The two departed from their vehicles at the same time and exchanged greetings.

"Sorry if I sounded a little harsh to you the other day," Les remarked, clutching the small Walgreen's bag. "Things have been a little strange of late. But I think they're starting to get under control."

Jerry grinned. "Good to hear. I hope you weren't offended by anything I said, it's just that—"

Les waved him off. "Say no more, Jerry. It's just a question of adjustment. You know, learning and adjusting. Have a good one."

At eleven that evening, Les popped two Vivarin and chased them with a strong cup of coffee. Maiko was already in bed, having retired there very quietly some time ago. He joined her there, found her sleeping. He lay in the darkness, glancing every few minutes at the illuminated digital clock on the nightstand. The stimulants in his system rendered him impatient and irritable, and by midnight he was out of bed and pacing anxiously about the house. Every few minutes he stuck his head in the bedroom doorway. He even ventured out onto the back porch for a short time, via the side door, where the heat of the August evening quickly chased him back inside. He punched through the cable channels with the sound muted, drank a glass of orange juice, paced about some more. A dozen or more times he went to the side window and opened the curtain slightly, but saw no one outside.

He lost track of the hour, found that he had to relieve himself. He was in the kitchen at the time, and chose to use the bathroom in that part of the house instead of the one in their bedroom. He felt unusually faint while sitting there, nearly falling off the seat a couple of times, and finally understood that his body's need for sleep was far stronger than the Vivarin and the coffee. As he exited the bathroom and came round into the dining room, he heard muffled steps on the other side of the house. He reached the living room to see Maiko's back disappear in the hallway. When he got to the bedroom, she had slipped back under the sheets and was sleeping soundly. Sighing with grave displeasure, he lay down next to her, but failed to sleep. By the time he had to get up for work, he surmised he had slept less than an hour, and was in no shape to teach.

The following night, he was too cranky and exhausted to devise a coherent plan. He awoke sometime after four a.m., not surprised to find Maiko absent. When he decided to get out of bed and go after her, he found he had no strength whatsoever, merely lay squirming like a jellyfish. Then he heard one of the outside doors open and close, and then Maiko's now-familiar footfalls in the hallway.

"Did you have a nice visit with your grandmother, or whoever that is you go to see every night?" Les asked, but his fatigue was so great that the best he could do was whisper, and he was unable to hear half the words he tried to articulate. By the time he had finished asking, Maiko was in the bed and asleep.

Over the next two days, Les tried a slightly different approach. As he failed to figure out why he could not broach the topic with Maiko, he instead threw himself into his teaching, hoping that would ease the growing obsession he was developing. Much to his dismay, he realized that his anxiety was only mounting, and he had to do something. Fortunately, he arrived at this conclusion on Friday, with no more work in sight until Monday. He went to bed with Maiko, then slipped out into the living room once she had fallen asleep. Once again he juiced himself with coffee and Vivarin, set himself resolutely to getting to the bottom of this bizarre mystery once and for all. He sat in the living room and flipped through cable channels, and every ten minutes he rose and walked through the entire house, closely monitoring the outside doors. Occasionally he glanced out the side window, but did not see anyone. As three a.m. neared, he felt certain tonight he would make a breakthrough; he did not feel drowsy or sleepy, only determined. He also moved as quietly as possible so as not to miss any sounds of the night. The twittering-trilling was there, but sounded very distant, in that foggy realm where a person is not sure if he is actually hearing something or simply fooling himself into believing that he is.

The minutes ticked away. Shortly before four a.m. he thought he heard stirring in the back of the house. Then he heard the toilet in the bathroom flush. He braced himself, listened intently. Now the twittering-trilling noise rattled clearly through the air. It gathered strength at the same time Les heard footsteps in the hallway. The side door opened; Les leapt to his feet, then held himself. All this waiting, this preparation, and he suddenly found that, at the moment of truth, he was unsure what to do. He made no effort to follow Maiko, but sidled to the window and looked out. The woman was there, waiting. Les stared, as if unable to move, and a few seconds later the woman was joined by a second figure. Les realized then that Maiko and the woman appeared to be the same height and shape. They stood close to each other, but if they spoke, Les could not tell, as the only sound filling his ears was the infernal noise that (he now understood) had been brought here by that strange woman.

Resumeshiokure . . . meshiokure . . . meshiokure . . .

He peered fixedly at them. The woman extended an arm in a whiplash motion. Maiko shied away, both hands out in front of her. Les winced, trying to will himself to act. He tried to call out to Maiko to get away from the woman, but his throat felt painfully constricted. The two women moved about one another in a circle, stopped, moved again. They repeated this several times, all the while the woman extending a menacing arm, Maiko protecting herself with both of hers. After that they stopped moving, and stood very close; so close, in fact, that Les could make out only one form, as if they had somehow melded. Then the figures separated and Maiko took a couple of slow steps backward, then turned and ran. The woman remained with her arm extended as Maiko disappeared from Les's view around the back of the house. Les heard the side door open, then her footfalls in the hallway.

So, at last I've witnessed it. There was something foul and sinister here, just as Jerry had intimated, and he would not rest until this business was settled. Why had Maiko not said anything about this? Why had she not enlisted his help, but was electing to suffer through this on her own? Why did she appear to be willing to endure this every night? Perhaps her thinking did not really matter; he was now aware. He turned his attention back to the window; the woman remained where she was, and now, free of the paralysis that had gripped him moments earlier, Les moved. He ran to the kitchen and produced a large flashlight from under the sink. Then he bolted outside, around the side of the house, flashlight ablaze. "Get out of here, damn you!" he shouted madly, directing the flashlight toward the woman. "Get out and leave us—"

The beam of the flashlight fell across the figure before him. Les gasped loudly. The "woman," if that indeed was what she was, was horribly disfigured, her face nearly featureless save for the deep pockmarks of rot that streaked it. She also possessed what appeared to be a mouth; it hung gaping open and was studded with festering stumps of blackened teeth. Her hair—or at least whatever it was growing out of the top of her head—was white and spidery, and matted against the sides of her face. She raised two bleached hands, consisting of little more than bone and nails, in front of her. Les cried out and threw the flashlight at her, then raced for the front door. He looked back once, to see the flashlight explode into a cascade of sparks, although clearly it had not struck the creature.

Resumeshiokure . . . meshiokure . . . meshiokure . . .

The noise was the loudest he could remember now, seemed to be reverberating against the walls of the house. Shaking uncontrollably, Les managed to go to the side window and glance outside. A wall of flame stood behind Jerry's house and his own; the repulsive thing that had been trying to hurt Maiko was caught in the middle of it, and was dissolving rapidly. The noise continued to grow as she disappeared in the fire. Les then saw a brilliant flash of lightning in the night sky, followed by the rumble of thunder. Another bright peal ripped across the sky, and the thunder was so loud it nearly shook the floor where he was standing.

An earsplitting shriek filled the house. Les whirled around, heart pounding. Frenzied footsteps sounded in the hallway, and Maiko burst into the living room, running out of control and screaming. If she saw Les, she did not acknowledge him, but rounded the corner of the living room and headed into the dining room. Les rushed to follow her, caught up to her in the kitchen. Her screams were now accompanied by heavy sobs.

"Maiko, for God's sake! What's wrong with you?"

"What have you done?" she roared, eyes wild. "Why, Res? Why? Oh, why?"

"What do you mean? What did I . . . there was . . . something out there. I know about it now. I found out about it. It was trying to hurt you. I don't know why . . . I don't understand at all, only that it's gone now, and it can't hurt—"

"What are you talking about, Res?" Maiko bawled, smiting her forehead in despair. "That wasn't some creature sent to harm me! She was my *hannya,* the spirit that guards me. She came to me from Emma-o, to protect me from the *jikininki.* She's been with us since we stepped onto the jet in Narita." Maiko wrung her hands, began to hyperventilate. Then she screamed loudly again. Les took a step toward her but her voice stopped him. "Those of us who continue to respect the old traditions are all given such protection if we choose to go from Japan. The *jikininki* follow us eberywhere. It is how they are, they are dead and not dead, so filled with greed and hate.

Neber are we safe. And now—" Maiko burst into tears, began shaking uncontrollably.

"Maiko, my love, what on earth are you saying? This is absolutely crazy! Do you see that? What kind of—"

"You don't understand!" she screamed at the top of her lungs. She began dancing madly around the kitchen, as if eluding something. "She was one of the Hags! She was my *hannya*! She was—"

"She was some monstrous, decaying thing!" Les shouted back. "Trying to get at you, and I was only—"

"She was . . . no, no, no she wasn't!" Maiko fell to her knees, crying so ferociously that Les felt shivers ripple through his entire body. Maiko was on all fours now, pounding the floor of the kitchen feebly with a fist. "She was an emissary from Emma-o, the king of the afterrife. She keeps the *jikininki* from me!" Then she looked up at Les, a severe madness in her eyes. "She keeps them from . . . she was protecting . . . *us*!" She wailed loudly, pounding the floor now with both fists. "You killed her, you *killed* . . . do you know what it means for me . . . for you . . . don't you hear their cries, what they're saying . . ."

Les placed both hands at his ears. "This is the craziest thing I've ever heard!" he cried out. "Maiko, get a grip. You're not some superstitious farm girl from the back country. You're a city-bred woman with a master's degree, you've traveled to a dozen different countries in your life, speak three languages fluently, and I'm supposed to believe you buy into this drivel you've been laying on me? Is that insane, or what?"

She looked up at him, the intensity in her eyes replaced now by a hopeless fear. She opened her mouth, but the only sound Les heard was an earsplitting crash against the front door. Les's heart jumped into his throat. A second crash shook the entire house, and was echoed by Maiko's screams. Les held out his hands to try to calm her, but she was not looking at him. Her mouth now hung open, her tongue rolled grotesquely against her lower lip, and he could no longer see the pupils of her eyes.

A third violent discharge erupted against the front door. Les felt his legs begin to buckle as he reached down to Maiko. "They're dead!" Maiko shouted suddenly; Les could see only the whites of her eyes, yet she knew exactly where he was, for she grabbed the front of his shirt as soon as he was close enough. She pulled him toward her with uncanny strength, and he was helpless to move against her. "But they don't rest! They feed! They feed! Without stop! They feed! They need corpses!" She was screaming at a level that turned Les's blood to ice, and in a voice he had never before heard.

"And they need a hu—" Les saw her lips continue to move, but her voice was drowned by a fourth crash, a splintering explosion that sent fragments of wood from the front door blasting through the living room and dining room. Several pieces caromed off the dining room wall and fell near Les's feet.

The sound of heavy feet, accompanied by a nasty, high-pitched buzzing, filled the front of the house. Suddenly Maiko lurched to her feet, both hands on Les's shirt, and shoved him back into the wall with such force that he struck the side of his face and stood momentarily dazed. The recoil of her effort, however, caused her feet to slip out from under her, as if a carpet were pulled away while she walked, and she fell backward, the base of her skull striking the range. She hung as if suspended in midair for a second or two, then crumpled to the floor, a massive puddle of blood pooling quickly around her head.

Les barely had a chance to take a terrified step toward her when the kitchen erupted with rushing bodies. They swarmed viciously until they covered every square inch of the floor, and then they piled themselves on top of each other until there was virtually no empty space in the room. Thrusting themselves against Les, their buzzing ringing his ears into a punishing stupor, they set themselves upon the lifeless form of Maiko. When standing on the floor, they barely reached Les's waist. They were possessed of short, stubby limbs, bloated torsos that ran with open sores and were clotted with decay, fed upon by armies of worms, grubs, and other monstrosities so repulsive that Les was certain they had no name. As they moved, they left tracks of putrid slime in their wake. Their heads were large and bulbous, consisting of little more than an enormous, gaping mouth studded with thousands of protruding, needlelike teeth that likewise teemed with the unspeakable fiends of the grave.

Resumeshiokure . . . meshiokure . . . meshiokure . . . meshiokure . . . meshiokure . . .

Through the haze of terror, Les realized that what he was hearing was in fact speech. Now that initial sound became intelligible to him. *Resu . . .* it sounded vaguely like Maiko's speech. There is an *r* sound in Japanese, and sometimes it is used in foreign words, for sounds not present. Like *l*.

They were calling him by name.

Meshiokure . . . he knew enough Japanese to begin to pull these sounds apart into words. *Meshio o kure . . . meshio o kure . . .* spoken not as a polite request but a rude command. . . . He gripped both sides of his face with his hands and bolted out the front door, screaming at the top of his lungs. Rain fell in sheets around him.

The outside light shone next to Jerry's front door. Les saw the door flash open. "Les, Les, what is it?" he heard Jerry call out through the storm.

"Help me, Jerry! Help—" Before Les could finish his sentence, Jerry was charging toward him in the downpour, hands in front of him. In the middle of his driveway, Jerry suddenly froze, lit up by a bolt of lightning that struck him with smoking fury. Jerry collapsed in a burning heap, the stench of his smoldering flesh filling the air. Les fell to his knees and vomited as the *jikininki* moved in, devouring the misshapen heap that had been Les's closest friend. They fed in a frenzy, their vicious teeth clapping together in chorus, silencing the rain and replacing it with a hideous, earsplitting drone.

As soon as Les had managed to empty the contents of his stomach on the grass next to Jerry's driveway, the front door of Jerry's house banged open and shut. He looked up fearfully.

"Les? Is that you?" Althea stepped from the house, her plump form moving cautiously in the rain. "Les? What's going on? Where's—"

Les waved his hands savagely. "Althea, don't! Go back in the house! Don't come any—"

But then it seemed to Les that Althea saw, and at least knew, if she did not understand. She cried out ferociously and ran toward the smoking remains in the driveway. "Althea, no!" Les screamed violently. "Don't come near! Don't!" The louder he yelled, the faster and more determined she approached. Then her foot skidded along a film of rainwater and was swept upward. Her body jerked forward in a half somersault, and she landed, arms flailing, directly on the top of her head. Les heard the vertebrae in her neck snap, saw her body unfold onto the driveway, head twisted at a hideous angle. Her hands and feet twitched for several seconds, then became still. The wails of the *jikininki* immediately followed, and they pounced.

Resumeshiokure . . . meshiokure . . .

Outside lights were being illuminated at the neighboring houses. Les heard several doors open. He thought, above the cacophony of the *jikininki,* he heard someone call out, "What the hell's going on out here?" He pushed himself to his feet, began running around in crazed circles.

"Go back into your houses, everyone! Don't come near me! Save yourselves, don't come near me! Don't come—" Then he collapsed in the grass as they approached. In his mind's eye he replayed Maiko's dying moments, the movement of her lips as her words were drowned by the bellows of the *jikininki*. Not a polite request, but a rude command. A command spoken by superiors to one not worthy of their time. Now he saw her mouth very clearly, and the final words that formed there. He had heard the first four words of her last sentence: "And they need a . . ." Now he saw the last two: "human slave."

Resu, meshio o kure. Meshio o kure.

Feed us, Les. Feed us.

Lightning crackled and exploded overhead, and he heard someone scream.

THE VANISHING POINT

Mark Samuels

John Keyes sat and stared at the empty little bottle.

He'd taken the last three of the pills two days ago. And now he was experiencing the first stages of withdrawal. An invisible barrier between him and the world had been breached. The cotton-wool numbness he'd become accustomed to gave way to anxiety. There was a cold sheen of sweat on his brow. When he wiped it off it returned within minutes. In his left ear he could detect what sounded like the fluttering of tiny wings: but it was obviously an auditory hallucination.

Keyes lit his twenty-seventh cigarette of the day. He tipped the ash into a coffee cup filled with butts.

The realization was upon him that the moment to act had come. Not to act was unthinkable. Everyday sights and sounds that seemed normal to others were for him like scenes from a nightmare.

Four days ago he had checked into this crummy hotel with no clear plan of action. His only motive had been to get away from all those who knew him back in the city. Keyes had walked out of his office at five thirty p.m. as usual, got into his car, and simply driven hundreds of miles along the motorway until he discovered the hotel by accident. It was the sort of place used mostly by drivers for overnight stopovers to break up a long journey and avoid falling asleep at the wheel. The building had three floors, and eighty rooms. Everything about it was functional, from the neglected concrete-and-glass exterior to the cheap prices it charged.

And now it was time to go. Even here Keyes was aware of the gulf between him and the rest of the human race. His social skills had degenerated to the point where conversation and making eye contact with another human being overwhelmed him with panic. Without the pills to assist him, such essential interactions were nigh impossible.

During his stay, Keyes had come to know every detail of his shabby hotel room. He left its confines only to pick up food from the nearby petrol station's convenience store. They sold tins of baked beans and pork sausages and he would take two cans back with him and eat the contents with a plastic fork while sitting on the edge of the bed. The mattress sagged in the center from the weight of a legion of sleepers. When he lay there, in the hollow, he would gaze up to the cracked and peeling white paint on the ceiling, and imagine he was looking at the landscape of the Arctic Ocean from a great height.

His other diversion was to sit in the easy chair, looking through television guides. He was too fazed to read any of the articles but would stare at the photographs of celebrities, most of whom he did not recognize.

The images were glorified counterfeits: The celebrities' imperfections had been airbrushed out or digitally removed. Keyes found the search for these enhancements engrossing and would make his own amendments with a pen. He began by adding wrinkles and lines but warmed to his task, as he got further into each publication. Eventually he was defacing the photographs to the extent that the TV stars' faces were slashed and torn.

He knew that what he was doing was a futile attempt

to fight against what he termed the tyranny of "sham-existence." Psychotropic drugs had dulled its effects to the extent that he was almost able to ignore the surrender of the human race to this phenomenon of sham. But the medication produced only neutrality; one more means of ensuring his tacit compliance if not his participation. Early on, when he first recognized the all-pervasive nature of the sham-existence, he had talked to others about it. However, they did not seem to realize that all apparent solutions were equally part of the problem. Science, psychology, religion, and philosophy were likewise only manifestations. There seemed only one viable way to circumvent the circus that is sham-existence: annihilation.

And this was the only avenue that was left open to Keyes, since he could no longer tolerate existence in an imitation universe.

His plan of action, such as it was, consisted of setting out on foot north of the hotel until he reached a suitable point of departure. He imagined walking blindly into traffic or hurling himself from a motorway flyover. These were two possibilities that appealed. Either way, it was still to be decided. Keyes did not wish to plan his demise carefully. If he did so, he would doubtless have considered each method's drawbacks and been ensnared again by sham.

There was one object in the room that he had tried to ignore: a practically obsolete television set. Keyes had even thrown a sheet over it in protest. This device was the ultimate embodiment of all the junk he was leaving behind.

Keyes had stopped watching television once his last set had broken down several years earlier. He'd meant to replace it, but as time passed he discovered that it was no longer something he required. When he saw a television now, usually in a bar or some such public area, he was more aware of its hypnotic aspect and the amount of time it could steal from a person's mental life. Keyes believed that it was a drug (albeit of an electronic rather than pharmaceutical nature) more addictive than heroin. He had often warned television viewers about the way that time passed without one realizing it, whilst the machine's cathode rays bored into the fragile tissue of the human brain, rotting it away. There are studies conclusively demonstrating that television is the most effective form of mass subjugation ever devised. Where television is readily available to all members of a society, voyeurism rapidly becomes the dominant creed.

So why was he standing there, thinking about seeing if the television set worked? Could it be that he had had so little contact with the wider world these past few days that he wanted to be reassured that it went on just as idiotically as before? He took off the sheet that covered it, and turned the dial marked ON/OFF.

There was a sudden burst of crackling from the set and its screen was filled with black-and-white static.

That was it. There was nothing else to be seen.

Keyes leaned forward to examine the front of the TV more carefully. He could not spot any channel buttons, but there was a large UHF dial, which he began to rotate first clockwise and then counterclockwise.

And a single channel finally appeared on the screen through the static.

Keyes sat cross-legged on the floor watching the broadcast unfold and was oblivious to everything else. He smoked incessantly; the blue whorls and ripples of tobacco vapor drifting across the screen's light.

It was an emergency network and not regular programming at all. No other channels could be received by the set, despite Keyes's tuning all the way through the VHF frequencies. For the first few minutes, there was only a test pattern. A right to left scrolling announcement at the bottom of the picture declared: *A state of emergency has been declared. Wait for the next broadcast.*

Finally the test card was replaced by a series of images.

The transmission was of extremely low quality, like a relic of the 1950s: blurred, half in focus, and distorted. Keyes would have believed that it had come from the dark side of the moon.

The voice-over had been slowed down to around half normal speed while, in contrast, the pictures flashed across the screen with bewildering rapidity. They consisted of a series of abstract moving images, one after the other, appearing to have no sequential connection. Their inexplicably eerie nature lent them the aspect of being scenes from a nightmare.

Keyes saw grinning plastic mannequins seated in a cinema watching a film of themselves as if the screen were a gigantic mirror; he saw a cityscape of skeletal tower blocks through which poured the light of the rising moon; he saw earthworms climbing skeletal TV antennae on rooftops; he saw flies crawling out from mobile phones; he saw lichen-covered eyes reflected in a city office window; and he saw a motionless escalator choked with bleeding computer components whose circuit boards, wires and machinery were spilt like exposed human entrails.

The voiceover was as follows:

> The latest report we have is that . . . consciousness is returning and the return is proving successful . . . we have the numbers to succeed . . .
>
> At night the world is ours . . . after sunset we have control . . . our dream-scientists will soon solve the problem of immobility in daylight . . .

Central Control confirms that the infestation of human aliens in this borderland should be cleared by 104/Alpha Time . . .

Unless this borderland is quickly occupied it will be lost to us . . . Embarkation to another dimensional sector is not possible . . .

Remember that disorientation quickly passes and that you will rapidly become accustomed to functioning here . . .

. . . life in the inorganic and industrial . . . as it was in the beginning . . .

The human aliens must be displaced.

These beings are a threat to our plans.

The dream-scientists assigned to your region are experimenting on direct alterations of quantum and atomic structures in order to facilitate our more rapid migration . . .

These instructions come direct from Central Control . . . Our continued existence is at stake . . . Compliance with them is mandatory . . .

This is not a simulation . . . The interruption in paradisal consciousness is real . . .

I repeat: This is a state of emergency . . . Dream this world into death . . . Let chaos fall like rain

Finally, the images and voice ceased. The familiar words reappeared at the bottom of the screen: *A state of emergency has been declared. Wait for the next broadcast.*

Keyes's cigarette trembled. His hands were shaking uncontrollably. He managed to put it to his lips and suck some blessed smoke into his lungs.

Was this transmission being broadcast across the country? If so, why wasn't the hotel filled with panicking hordes? Why didn't he hear police sirens wailing? What he'd seen had been nothing less than an announcement that the human race was under attack. Even if the transmission was on an unusual frequency, it had to have been picked up by the authorities. Why weren't they doing something? Had no one else seen it? Or were those entities *already* in control of the entire area and all operations within it?

As if in response to this last thought, the television screen flickered; the picture of the test card disappeared, and was replaced by the sight and sound of static.

Was it a *two-way* transmission? Were Keyes's *own* thoughts, not to say all of those who had witnessed the broadcast, being monitored?

What he thought he'd seen must be a hallucination. It had to be. Or was it the last attempt of sham-existence to re-establish control over his thoughts? Was sham-existence finally deploying the most powerful weapon in its armory against him? Surely it was one or the other. In any case it could not be allowed to affect his course of action.

Keyes looked at his watch: seven thirty p.m. It was as good a time as any to leave. He put on his raincoat, closed the door to his room behind him, and made his way along the corridor to the hotel stairway.

He exited through one of the crummy hotel's side doors and traversed the half-deserted car park. With a vague sense of recognition Keyes saw his own vehicle occupying one of the spaces and knew that he would never drive it again.

Ahead of him lay a scrubland of small hills. Rain began to fall from a slate gray sky and the dull nothingness of twilight made the landscape shadowy and unreal. When he looked back to the hotel a few of the rooms had their lights turned on. The illumination was sickly, and seen through drawn green curtains. It looked like patches of phosphorescent mold. Such was the effect of the darkening sky that the hotel resembled the lot of a film set: all facade and no substance.

Keyes thought of this clichéd metaphor and smiled in a laconic fashion. He could elaborate on this metaphor, he thought, and say that he felt very much like an actor taking his leave of a performance in the middle of a scene. An extra whom the cinema audience had scarcely noticed and whose unscheduled departure would not impact upon the action.

As Keyes trudged across the dreary scrublands, up and down its seemingly endless series of troughs and hillocks, he experienced a profound sense of liberation. It was good to leave everything behind and lose oneself in this wasteland. But no sooner had he begun to savor the feeling when he realized that sham was again trying to thwart him from carrying out his escape. Why not go back, he thought, now that he felt so much better? Things were surely not so bad that he had to end it all? More drugs could be obtained. Existence could be made bearable, couldn't it? Keyes drove the palm of his hand into the side of his head, jarring his skull. Stupid, stupid! The charade was just trying to trap him.

Keyes now began to half stumble forward; he concentrated on trying to exterminate all the rational thoughts in his mind that might lead him to make that same mistake again. He had to remember that those were not *his own thoughts* but an imitation, a mental nexus imposed upon his brain by the outside world.

He lost track of time.

After climbing over a rise, Keyes at last saw the lanes of a motorway. He wondered why he'd not heard the noise of traffic in advance; but this question was swiftly answered. It was deserted. No cars sped along in either direction.

He clambered down the bank but lost his footing. His

ankle had got caught in a half-concealed tendril, and he twisted it as he fell. When he tried to get up and put weight on it the pain was so intense he collapsed by the roadside.

Perhaps the motorway was disused. Only around a quarter of the overhead lights actually seemed to work, and even some of those flickered as if the power supply were intermittent or else they had fallen into a state of disrepair. The tarmac was riddled with cracks and even several potholes.

As he lay there in the darkness, with his body slumped on the surface of the roadside, Keyes saw a lone vehicle approaching. Its headlights cut through the gloom, the two circles of illumination growing larger and brighter.

Keyes lifted a hand to shield his eyes, and the car pulled up to a halt a few yards in front of where he lay. The driver got out and walked toward him with an oddly stiff-backed gait, his form silhouetted in the glare of the headlights. The man's joints creaked as he bent down to examine Keyes.

Very shortly afterward Keyes blacked out, for the next thing he knew he was seated beside the stranger in his car and they were traveling along the deserted motorway. His head felt clearer after a time, and though he was grateful to the man for the attempted rescue, this sense of gratitude was mingled with dull resentment. Sham-existence still had him.

The stranger didn't seem to be aware of the fact that he had regained consciousness and Keyes let his eyelids flutter open in order to take in his surroundings. The car was in a shocking state of neglect. Thick dust covered the dashboard and the windscreen was caked with insect remains. Around Keyes's feet were balls of crumpled newspaper and other debris.

Keyes let his head loll to the side in order to glance,

with half-closed eyes, at the driver. He wore a boiler suit and leather driving gloves. A muffler was wrapped high across his face and this, together with the baseball cap he wore, made his features indiscernible.

The car was cruising at sixty miles an hour, and the stranger had no difficulty avoiding the worst parts of the poorly maintained road. The movements he made were sure and swift as he skirted around objects ahead. Keyes made a groaning sound in order to alert him to the fact he'd awoken, but it elicited no response.

"Thank you," Keyes said eventually in a dazed mutter, "for picking me up back there."

Nothing could have prepared him for the shock he now experienced. It was not the actual words he heard that were chilling but the ridiculous voice that uttered them.

"You seemed," the stranger said, "to require my assistance."

He screeched just like a ventriloquist's dummy. For a moment Keyes was dumbfounded and wanted to believe that the stranger affected the voice in some bizarre attempt to be funny.

If he noticed Keyes's discomfort, he made no sign of acknowledgment, but followed up his statement by saying in the same horrible vocal parody: "Feeling better now, eh? Feeling better?"

Keyes nodded and mumbled his thanks. The pain in his ankle seemed to shoot halfway up his leg, but he didn't want to discuss it. He turned to look out the window, feigning indifference, when he was trying to concentrate on seizing the first opportunity to get away from this demented character. They passed the wreck of an abandoned vehicle just off the deserted motorway. Keyes just had time to glimpse a shattered windscreen before they hurtled by.

"Smoke?" the driver said, his cracked voice breaking the silence between them.

"Thanks," Keyes replied.

The stranger fumbled around in the glove compartment and drew out a packet of twenty Marlboros. His movements were jerky and forced.

"Here, light mine for me will you?" he said, discordantly.

After lighting his own cigarette with a match, Keyes lit the other.

"Enjoy," he said, passing the second to the driver.

Keyes drew the acrid vapor into his lungs and settled back. God, he needed that nicotine hit! The stranger brought his own cigarette up to his mouth and appeared only to be mimicking the action of smoking. He didn't inhale or exhale but let the fumes waft around uselessly. It was as if he were mocking Keyes's actions.

Paranoia, thought Keyes: nothing else. This must be another wave of withdrawal effects. He ran his fingers across his forehead and found it damp with sweat. Mere paranoia or not, he had to get out of the car and away from this person. It was imperative he did so. Damn his twisted ankle! The whole lower part of his leg felt swollen and useless.

He decided to ask the driver what his destination was and tell him it was out of his way, but that he'd be grateful to be dropped off at the next junction. He could try to hitch another ride.

"Where are you headed?" Keyes inquired in a reasonably level voice.

"Why . . . nowhere, of course, the same place as you," he replied with a little giggle.

"Stop the car here and let me out."

"But we're not there yet. Aren't you enjoying the ride?"

Keyes pulled at the door handle. It wouldn't budge.

The driver chuckled again.

"No other traffic on this stretch of the motorway," he said. "You might as well sit tight."

Well, that's true enough, Keyes thought. He'd seen no other moving vehicle despite the miles they'd traversed, and anyway it was not possible for him to walk. His cigarette had burnt down to the filter and he dropped it to the floor, crushing it into the debris with his one good foot.

"Why," the stranger asked in his ventriloquist's-dummy voice, "why were you lying by the roadside back there?"

There was nothing to lose by telling him, Keyes thought. Perhaps he'd even stop the car and let me get on with it. The thought might actually appeal to his warped sense of humor.

"My ankle . . . it . . . no . . . the truth is I wanted to escape from this sham; to do myself in by walking into the traffic."

"Oh, how quaint!" he replied, chuckling once again. "Don't you know that nothing is dead? What makes you so special? Are you not made of matter? Why should consciousness be confined to the living?"

The idiot began rambling in a singsong fashion and Keyes turned away, peering into the darkness beyond the window. He tried to blot out the sound of the other's voice and concentrate on what he saw instead. But his arm was clasped in a viselike grip, as if the fingers beneath the gloves were made not of flesh but of wood or plastic.

". . . All sorts of things might wake up after sleeping for a very, very long time: The trees might sing songs, plastic and metal might shudder into motion, and the stars might chatter out their secrets across the void . . ."

Keyes saw more wrecks on the motorway, their engine parts scattered over the tarmac, and in the flickering overhead light it seemed almost as if they twitched with dim life.

". . . Don't you know that lifelessness is just a disguise . . . that sentience is everywhere . . . that you humans have been trespassing while we were somnolent. . . ."

Was it another hallucination or did the car wrecks ahead seem to be crawling along like damaged cockroaches? And what was the noise Keyes detected, a noise like the buzzing of a million bloated flies, seeming to emanate from the scrubland vegetation?

The stranger let go of Keyes's arm and instead grabbed him by the throat. The car bounced across the road and juddered to a stop halfway up the embankment, beneath a flickering motorway lamp.

In the struggle that ensued Keyes dislodged the driver's baseball cap and muffler. His head was made of plastic, like an oversized doll. Glass eyes, filled with television static, stared sightlessly back.

". . . trade your sham for mine . . . there is no reality . . ."

His voice crackled as he closed his grip on Keyes's windpipe.

". . . wait for the next broadcast . . ."

ANTHEM OF THE ESTRANGED

Lee Thomas

The name of the show was derived from the practice of lifting a stone to see what filthy species had taken up residence in the dirt below. Though the apt title was not lost on any of the production staff of *Picking Up the Rock*, it seemed to completely elude the endless parade of poseurs, losers, and has-beens that populated its installments; one of which, Michael Donnelley was about to meet.

Normally, Mike scheduled interviews at the studio or in one of half a dozen mediocre restaurants in the valley. But tonight, at the request of Tommy Gunn, he had parked in the armpit of Los Angeles, where pathetic victims of the Hollywood dream could still feed their fantasies on the scraps of Tinseltown, like pilot fish at the ass end of a shark.

The cold wind lifted trash from the yards, passing litter from one dying field to the next. He scanned the buildings for house numbers and reminded himself to deny any future interviews that might require his setting foot on such tainted ground.

He groaned at his surroundings; this was not the life he had planned.

Picking Up the Rock was a digital graveyard for one-hit wonders with predominantly unsavory eulogies written to their memory. Overdoses, sex scandals, and bitter rivalries got the bulk of the air time because those were the creatures the audience expected to see writhing beneath the stones of fleeting celebrity. The show would be pointless if it spotlighted a well-adjusted, successful post-celebrity. Nobody wanted to hear that Tommy Gunn of late-eighties glam-metal sensation Lipstik had parlayed his band's top ten single, "Power Tool," into a successful dry cleaning chain and continued to live in the lap of luxury.

Where was the fun in that?

Fortunately for everyone—audience, producers, researchers, and Mike himself—Tommy Gunn had succumbed to addiction and alcoholism. His descent into dependence had culminated in a ten-car pileup on the 405, ending the lives of his spokesmodel wife, Kandee Kane, and their year-old son, Ethan. By the time Tommy had come out of rehab and performed his community service, Seattle had given birth to the grunge movement, and Tommy had found himself without a record label.

These days, Tommy Gunn produced porn videos for Wet Angel Productions (scoring all of the epics himself, of course), and occasionally making guest appearances on screen in the hopes that his fame among sleaze would sell a few extra cassettes. His six-bedroom manse in the Hollywood Hills had long ago returned to the care of the bank that had financed it, and Tommy now resided in a beat-up shack in Silverlake; the very shack Mike noted upon taking the corner as the ugliest house on the block.

But despite the fact that the Gunn house was hideous, from its leprous brown paint to its jaundiced trim, the home had drawn a few curious passersby.

Half a dozen shadows moved silently across the lawn like monks on a sacred pilgrimage, their heads uniformly bowed. Though Mike could not make out their faces in the gloom (because Gunn's house was not only the ugliest on the block, it was the only one without a porch light burning), they all seemed to be wearing similar costumes: part rag, part robe.

Mike stopped on the sidewalk and watched this bizarre aggregation slowly herding across the overgrown lawn, cautiously avoiding the refuse and rusting garden tools at their feet as they made their way to the front of the house. Mike briefly wondered if he had made a mistake with the date or time of his appointment. Perhaps he was supposed to meet Gunn tomorrow night, and tonight was coven night at the Gunn household.

But the robed visitors did not seem to have been invited. Their destination was not the front door. Instead, they took up places on either side of the cracked cement porch and placed their hands on the flaking paint and rotten wood of the house's facade, where they remained like six delinquents told to assume the position by an arresting officer.

The display of worship put a tingle in Mike's belly. Disturbed by the sight, he considered turning around and returning to his Celica to put some distance between himself and this Silverlake freak show.

Just as he decided that retreat might be a good idea, the six shabby monks turned from the house and gathered at the center of the lawn in a single tattered huddle. One of the monks lifted his head as if to sniff the air, and his face fell under the bath of the streetlamp.

The skin had been pierced dozens of times with small silver hoops, carving scalelike shadows on his face. The monk's eyes lacked irises. Dime-sized pupils, all blackness and depth, bored through orbs the color of watermelon juice. A taller pilgrim, a woman, noticed her companion's distraction and also looked up at Mike. A triangular hole gouged the space that had once held her nose, and beneath the nasal chasm an ear to ear grin split the woman's face in half. "He sees us," she sang lightly.

"Impossible," the male told her before dropping his head.

The troupe turned away from Mike and began to sing a low harmonized chant as they worked their way toward the sidewalk and ambled down the street like a single poorly formed beast. Despite its shabby appearance, this beast had a beautiful voice and a lilting melody on which to exercise it. The tune—seemingly without words, but rather a series of well-crafted vowels—remained in the night air even after its singers had taken the next corner and disappeared.

Their song still playing in his head, he stepped onto the lawn and realized he was being played for a goof. Gunn had set up this show as some sort of publicity stunt.

Now, Mike would probably be met at the door by some buxom dominatrix who would lead him to her "Lord and Master." He prepared himself for whatever else Tommy Gunn decided to shoot in his direction after he rang the doorbell, but was surprised when the door opened to reveal a rather small man, ten years his senior with a receding hairline and a pronounced potbelly, who wore jeans and a black T-shirt that had faded to slate gray. A pair of crimson lip prints painted the front of the shirt, and the word "Lipstik" was scrawled below. Thick pouches had formed under Gunn's bloodshot eyes and his once attractive face was now puffy and wore at least two days' growth of beard.

"Hey," Gunn said in a rasping voice. "You're Mike, right?"

"Yes," he said. "Mike Donnelley, and you're Tommy Gunn." The haggard man nodded his head. "That was quite a show you had going on out here," Mike said to let

Gunn know that his production had been noticed, but that he wasn't getting away with anything.

Gunn looked into the street over Mike's shoulder and scanned the neighborhood. His brow was furrowed, and he looked back at Mike as if the journalist had claimed to be Marie Antoinette. "What show?" Gunn asked.

"Okay." Mike smiled and stepped over the threshold, passing the confused musician and taking in the furnishings of the man's home.

The rooms were pretty much what he had expected to find. Old furniture, once very expensive and stylish, sat crammed into a space one-tenth the size of the room the pieces had been designed for.

"Normally when we do one of these pre-interviews we go over our research to verify information," Mike said as he walked through Gunn's living room and poked his head into the small, dark dining hall. Again, furniture too big for its environment had been situated, leaving little room to pass on either side of the crystal-topped dining table and the chrome and glass cabinet against the wall. "Then," he continued, "we just want to hear it from your lips. Tell us your story."

"Right," Gunn said. "And then you show a lot of pictures of twisted metal and me with a bottle in my hands."

"Good," he said. "Then we're on the same page."

Gunn's cheeks flushed crimson before he shoved his hands in the pockets of his jeans and made a vague shrugging motion. "So why should I tell you anything?" he asked. "You don't give a shit about anything but the accident."

"That's not true," Mike countered. "Your foray into filmmaking is also of great interest to us."

The corners of Gunn's mouth dragged into an angry frown. "We create our own salvation, buddy," he growled. "Once those vultures at Arista and Kandee's parents were done with me, what choice did I have? I was broke, and nobody was buying the music anymore."

"And yet so few of your peers went on to create classics like *Angela's Asses, Mary Potter's Secret Chamber,* and my personal favorite, *Crouching Pussy, Hidden Snake.*"

Mike had been with *Picking Up the Rock* for just over two years and found himself appalled, not only at the sheer volume of fallen pop stars, but the uniformity of their indignation. He couldn't remember a single one of these men or women that would admit to being a mediocre musician with a single marketable song, nor could he remember one that seemed even remotely grateful for their fifteen minutes of fame. So he wasn't surprised by Tommy Gunn's assertion that the world had forced him into a life of low-budget porn.

"We create our own salvation," Gunn said again.

"Yeah, yeah," Mike said. "What is that? Some of Lipstik's timeless lyrics?"

"It's from the Bible," Gunn told him. The small man with the receding hairline opened a low cabinet and withdrew a bottle of scotch. He poured a few slugs into a tumbler and turned to Mike. "You want a drink?"

Mike dropped onto the sofa and shook his head. "I thought you were clean these days."

"Doesn't matter anymore," Gunn said, lifting the glass to his nose. He inhaled the fumes of the whiskey and closed his eyes.

"So is this part of the show?" Mike asked, remembering the odd monks performing their ritual only a few minutes before against the side of Gunn's house. "The bad boy is back, complete with drugs, booze, and Satan worshippers?"

Gunn again furrowed his brow and shook his head. "I'm moving on," Gunn said dreamily. He toasted the air with the tumbler and poured the whiskey into his mouth. "Shrugging off the coil and taking my act on the road."

Mike didn't have a clue what the burnout was talking about, so he took a guess. "You're going back on tour?"

"No," Gunn said. "That was a small dream, and I woke up in a bed of shit. What I'm talking about is the dream of dreams, the lord of all dreams."

Mike laughed at the performance of euphoria. "So you're completely fucked up right now?"

"Not yet," Gunn said with a smirk. "You know, this interview's kept me going for the last few weeks. Knowing people were going to see some of the videos and hear the music again really got me pumped. But then I saw the show. You make us look like clowns."

"We prefer the term 'freaks,'" Mike said. "Now, can we get down to business here?"

Gunn bowed lightly. "What do you want to know? My blood alcohol level when I drove into the back of that truck? Or are you more interested in the coke? Maybe you'd like me to tell you what it felt like to have my wife's head fall into my lap while the rest of her was pinned to the car seat by a sheet of corrugated aluminum? Or better yet, finding my son's body shredded on the side of the road? That's a good story, because I wasn't sure he was dead at first. I thought he was trying to crawl, but foolish me, that was just postmortem muscle spasms."

"Let's start with the blood alcohol level," Mike said. "Then we'll segue into the death throes."

Gunn lit a cigarette and, squinting through the smoke, pointed a finger at Mike. "You know what hurts the most, buddy?"

"Probably a piece of corrugated aluminum at about eighty miles an hour," Mike said, "Now, if you don't mind . . ."

Gunn slammed his palm on the makeshift bar; the concussion rumbled through the room. Gunn's face stormed with agitation. "Who the fuck do you think you are?" he roared. "You come into my home and act like you're doing me a favor by dragging me back over that road. I came out of rehab six months after losing my family and realized there was nobody waiting for me anymore: no audience waiting for a new album; no wife waiting at home; no child waiting for his daddy; no friends waiting for the next party. I woke up one morning with nothing, and I didn't even have the chemicals to make the pain stop." Gunn finished his drink and poured another, his hand still pointed at Mike to keep him silent as he pursued his intoxication. "You gotta have somebody waiting, man," Gunn told him earnestly. "That's the only thing in this fucking world that matters, knowing that somebody's waiting out there for you."

"Touching," Mike said blandly.

"Can you say *pathetic*?" Mike asked of the table of men. "I mean, the guy is polluted on alcohol and cocaine, drives his family into the back of a repair truck and he's looking for sympathy. Then the asshole ups and disappears before we can get him on camera. The crew showed up last week, and the *looze* was gone. So now we have to use stills whenever we quote the dickhead or we have to run one of those cheesy-ass videos on mute so people can hear Phil doing the narration."

"He's lost a lot," Jim said. "My guess is, he's done some suffering over it."

Mike sneered at his boyfriend, who could have found Hitler's good points, and took another sip from his Manhattan. "Fine," he said. "He's suffered, but who the hell hasn't? Jesus Christ, he's not a martyr; he's a spoiled little brat. No, he's worse than a spoiled little brat; he's a fame-seeking has-been with more skull than hair and a food baby the size of a bowling ball. Even worse, he can't stop whining because nobody cares about his crappy songs anymore."

"I always thought he was kind of cute," Charlie Nixon said.

"Of course you did," Mike said. Charlie thought anything male was kind of cute, but only because Charlie was a completely uninteresting-looking man who had the chinless charms of a mounted bass.

"Well," Ray Thornton said, "it seems Michael is entering one of his moods. We'd better be going."

"So soon?" Mike asked. Ray and Charlie had been sucking down his alcohol for the last six hours, and Captain Brilliant needed an excuse to leave? "We'll be serving breakfast in about an hour."

"Charming . . . as always," Thornton said as he rose to leave.

Ray Thornton was Jim's ex-lover, and Mike had no qualms about offending the man or driving him away. He felt it was completely unnatural that the two had maintained a friendship after their breakup. This new age of tolerance was annoying; he preferred the good old days when exes were treated with loathing and spite.

He remained at the table as Jim escorted their guests to the door. He imagined that the appearance-conscious Jim would be apologizing for Mike's outbursts and toasted this image with his cocktail before draining the glass.

Jim was a sap—a very cute, very sweet sap.

The sweet sap returned to the dining room and began clearing the table.

"Leave those for morning," Mike said. "We don't have to be up early."

Jim put down the plates he had stacked and leaned on the back of a chair. Mike thought he looked remarkably cute when he got that serious look on his face, basically because Mike could never quite take Jim seriously.

"I'm staying at Ray's tonight," Jim said quietly as if announcing that the results of his latest test had been positive. "I just don't want to be here right now."

"Because I can't find the bright side of a chemically dependent burnout?"

"Because you can't find the bright side of anything," Jim said sadly. "You're so damned angry all the time. And I don't appreciate the way you've been treating our friends."

"You mean your ex-boyfriend?"

"I mean everyone, Mike. Ever since your father died, you've gotten nasty."

"That's not true. I was always nasty. You just used to have a sense of humor."

"That's because I thought you were joking around. But you're not. You're serious about the lousy things you say to people. You're serious about the lousy things you say to me, and I don't deserve that."

Mike couldn't help but notice that his boyfriend was genuinely upset, and he thought that perhaps he should take the man seriously just this once. But instinct overpowered intelligence and he said, "Ray must have broken world records giving you that spine implant at the door."

Jim gave one last, sympathetic gaze before saying, "Good night, Michael," and leaving the room. A moment later, Jim left the house.

Mike sat in a chair beside a sweating blob of dough named Ed whose fat fingers raced over the editing board as images flickered on six video screens before them. Behind them, a perpetually nervous young woman gnawed her thumbnail.

The editing room was barely the size of a walk-in

closet but had so many dials, lighted buttons, and monitors, they might have been orchestrating a moon mission rather than performing surgery on digital signals. The reek of videotape and dust filled the room. Mike's throat tightened against the plastic pungency, and he wriggled to get comfortable in his chair, growing more irritated by the moment with the editor and his mousy assistant. But then Mike's mood had been anything but "up" over the last few days.

Jim's desertion had stung, and nights of minimal rest had eroded what little patience Mike retained. His sleep had been disturbed by dreams of cloaked monks, chanting their contagious melody into the darkness; their song of oddly arranged vowels played lullaby as he slipped into drunken unconsciousness and acted as alarm throughout the night, pulling him from scenes of rock stars, car accidents, and mutinous loved ones.

Even when he was awake, that song rolled through Mike's head. But instead of reveling in the pleasing tune, his nerves grew raw at its repetitive invocation.

"They're going to make us recut this," Ed Hoeffer said, drawing Mike's attention back into the editing chamber. "We're supposed to go to air Monday, and they are going to cut the shit out of it."

"Leave it in, Poppinfresh," Mike told him.

After six nights of sleeping alone, and not sleeping well, Mike's attitude had gone from bad to *blender*. Instead of stirring up shit, he now had himself set to frappé, and anybody that got caught in his carafe was going to find himself liquefied. As a result, Mike wasn't going to take any shit from a lard-assed knob jockey. Besides, he wanted to make sure Tommy Gunn had a scenic trip down memory lane.

"It's powerful," he said.

"It's sick," Ed countered.

"Now I want a slow fade from the 'Power Tool' video," Mike said. "Get the shot of him dancing across the stage with the bottle of Jack Daniel's in his hands and dissolve it into . . ." Mike checked his book to find the tape and time designation he had noted that morning. "Tape three, four-oh-five."

"No way," Ed said, throwing up his hands. The big man pushed himself away from the editing board, sending his anxious assistant, Tammy, against a rack of videotapes. "Sorry, Tam," Ed said.

"It's 'kay," the intern lisped.

Michael took over the recently vacated chair and called up the archived news tape with its sweeping shot of the interior of Tommy Gunn's crumpled Jaguar. Mike would keep the sound track of "Power Tool" playing over the scene, boosting the volume for the lyric line "if ya make me choose, you're gonna lose," as the glare of a floodlight captured the bloodied leather of the car seats and came to a jerking pause when it encountered the nest of hair surrounding Kandee Kane's severed head.

Unfortunately the head, left on the seat by Tommy after his escape from the wreckage, had been placed face-down, so all the camera caught was a teased platinum cloud, resting like a toy dog amid the shards of glass and human fluid. "Fucking perfect," Mike announced as he sprung from the chair. "That's a wrap. Tack that between what we've already got, and don't touch a frame or it's your ass."

Ed, the moist hulk of geek, looked at Mike as if he had just defecated on the chair between them. Mike smiled his broadest grin and waved his fingers as if to a child before leaving the stifling air of the editing room.

He felt considerably better, almost giddy, after creating the video ode to Gunn's downfall, and once he was away from the stink of tape and back in his office he decided to call his boyfriend, if only to have someone to share his amusement with. Jim had left a message on voice mail (the third in two days), insisting that he needed to speak with Mike.

Swelled with beneficence, he dialed Jim at work, ready to talk and (if Jim was a good boy), ready to let him come home.

But Jim wasn't coming home.

"What are you talking about?" Mike asked angrily. "What has Ray been saying about me?"

Jim, ever the weak-willed diplomat, replied, "Ray doesn't have to say anything about you, Mike. I just can't take it anymore. Your anger is contagious, and I don't like feeling that way about people. Maybe you should see someone."

"I should see someone? The world is full of assholes, and I'm the one that needs therapy?"

"I'm sorry."

"Yes you are," he replied and slammed down the phone.

Mike left his office and stepped into the bright afternoon. He lowered the top of his Celica convertible and drove through the low buildings lining Sunset Boulevard, past the palm trees, standing sentinel over Brentwood and out toward the ocean. When he reached US 1, he turned right, and instead of heading into Santa Monica as he had planned, he drove north hoping to find a place to park the car and get his thoughts in order.

He pulled into the parking lot of a seafood joint in Malibu where Jim had taken him to celebrate some event or other about six months ago. He turned off the stereo and stared at the ocean. The waves crested low, rippling with white foam. The sky was bleached a pale blue, and silver tips capped the restless waters in the distance.

His life had been a clean slate when he'd come to Los Angeles. Few friends and an intolerable family had given him little to regret when quitting Portland to pursue a new life in Tinseltown. In those ten years, he had put together a relatively decent living, a few more friends and a relationship with Jim: all of which now seemed as insubstantial as the foam disintegrating on the shore.

Jim was as good as gone. Mike's "friends" were comprised of drinking buddies who collectively had the depth of a bottle cap, and he felt certain that his career was about to take a drastic turn for the nonexistent in light of his creative contribution to the Lipstik segment of *Picking Up the Rock.* Ten years ago, a clean slate had seemed challenging, even exciting, but at this point in his life, Mike wondered if the independence he'd been so proud of had been little more than well-designed self destruction.

And for the span of a heartbeat, he understood why someone like Tommy Gunn might want to *shrug off the coil* and take his act on the road.

A lilt of song broke over him like warm waves, instantly extinguishing the flame of self-doubt. Mike pulled his eyes from the water's shimmering caps and scanned the parking lot for the source of the flowing chant. He looked back at the ocean to see if the song rolled from the surf as it certainly held the cadence of tide, but he could find no source for the tune.

Mike checked the rearview mirror and saw a short derelict standing behind his car. His heart leapt, and he spun in the seat; he opened his mouth to tell the bum to move on but something about the stocky form was familiar. Besides wearing the tattered robes of the monks he had seen on Tommy Gunn's lawn, the bum also wore Tommy Gunn's face.

The head and eyebrows had been shaved, leaving a

smooth egg with the features of Lipstik's lead singer, looking remarkably serene and sympathetic. Mike was shocked to see that the whites of Gunn's eyes had been stained pink.

With barely a hint of effort, Tommy Gunn rose into the air and came down silently into a squatting position on the trunk of Mike's Celica.

"Get offa the car," Mike roared. "You freak."

When his command was not honored, Mike uncoiled and cranked on the ignition. A low thread of red liquid passed before his eyes, swirling in the air like a tendril of smoke. Its progress enthralled Mike to paralysis as it wove around the steering wheel. The fluid encircled the handle of the car key to kill the engine and then rolled over the dashboard where it splattered against the windshield and continued to squirm.

A word, *Wait,* appeared on the glass.

Mike shot a look over his shoulder. Gunn's watermelon-juice eyes stared back; the musician's index finger pointed at him not in accusation but in communication. The end of the finger had been sliced open and a thin rope of blood pulsed from the digit, but instead of succumbing to gravity, it danced in the air and made words on Mike's windshield. With a flick of his head, Gunn sent Mike's attention back to the glass.

Life and death are but two options, the crimson letters read. The note smeared and then a new message appeared in its place. *There is another way.*

"Who said anything about life or death?" Mike asked.

The question is coming.

"I don't think so," Mike said. "I'm not opening my wrists over a prick like Jim."

The teeth of loneliness gnaw slowly.

"You're going to have to do better than that," Mike said, but when he turned to face off on Gunn, the man was gone. He quickly searched the parking lot, anxious to maintain a fix on the monk's position.

A robed figure scurried up the side of the restaurant like a spider, but this wasn't Gunn. Even from the distance, Mike could tell that this was one of the other monks. His eyes drew a line from the restaurant, over US 1, and up the road to the north.

The monks were everywhere. They stood on rooftops, their silhouettes cast against the washed-out sky and the silver-tipped waves. They sat on the gravel shoulder of the highway like large deer brought down by racing fenders. A group of ten stood twenty feet from the side of his car, but none of these was Gunn.

Gunn lowered out of the air and returned to his crouching position having traded the trunk of the car for its hood. The thin trail of visceral ink spun around his form like a ribbon; red splashed on the windshield, and Mike jerked back against the seat.

A token, the words read.

"Why don't you just tell me what you want?"

What do you want?

"My sanity returned in good working order," he replied.

No, the red letters challenged. *To belong.*

"Belong to what?"

Anything.

Mike laughed, and the volume of the outburst startled him. "I'm not you, Gunn. I didn't fuck up my life playing rock star. You pissed everything away and then wondered where it all went. Well, face it buddy, nobody wants you around."

A father's words, the red letters charged.

"Fuck you," Mike roared.

Why else here?

And then Mike remembered the evening that Jim had

brought him to this place. Mike had received a call from his brother earlier that afternoon to relay the news that their father had died. The ever-sympathetic Jim had been more upset by the news than Mike, who had seen the drunk's passing as the removal of a well-pierced target and certainly nothing irreplaceable.

They were not close, not even speaking when the old man had died. The distance and dismissal had been the result of his father's final words to Mike before he'd moved to California.

Face it, kid, no one wants you around here.

His father's exact words were scrawled on the windshield before him in swirls of Gunn's blood. Mike began trembling in the car seat.

Tears slid down Tommy Gunn's face as his finger conducted circles of fluid in the air. The other monks on the rooftops remained motionless, carved from the bleached sky as wind tore at their robes. The message on the windshield blurred, and then Gunn was writing again.

A token.

"A token of what?" Mike asked. "For what?"

A token of you, the message read. *To become what you are.*

"Exactly what do you think I am?" he asked, his voice weak and shaking.

One of us.

"Who are you?"

The estranged. The disaffected remains.

"If I give you a token, what then?"

We become one.

"And what did you give, Tommy?" Mike asked, some part of his mind accepting this dementia as the only reality left for him. "What was your token?"

In reply, Tommy Gunn touched the collar of his robe and gently pulled the folds back to reveal the hairless body beneath. The flesh was smooth and pink like that of a monstrous child, only this child had been damaged. A deep wound the size of a fist had been carved in Tommy Gunn's throat; a similar injury appeared between his legs. Both wounds were raw as if fresh, still glistening like meat on a butcher's board.

The eunuch closed his robes. The tears he'd shed for Mike had dried in glistening trails on his cheeks, and his features radiated warmth and caring.

Somebody's waiting, the crimson line read.

Somebody's waiting.

Mike woke the next morning to the blaring trill of his telephone, which cut painfully through his hangover. "Yeah?" he asked.

"Why aren't you at work?" Jim asked.

Because they fired me, Mike thought.

As he had suspected, Ed Hoeffer had gone to the show's senior producers with a copy of the Lipstik segment, and they had agreed with Ed's assessment that the cut was not only exploitative, but also perverse. Mike's vision would no longer be required by *Picking Up the Rock.*

"Why'd you call here if you thought I'd be at work?" Mike asked, and then quickly regretted the sarcasm. "I'm sorry. I'm not feeling well this morning."

The rush of concern in Jim's voice when he asked, "Are you okay?" brought Mike close to tears.

"Fine," he lied. "Just a touch of the flu or something."

"Do you need anything? I was going to come by this morning and pick up a few things anyway. I can swing by the store on my way in."

"That's okay," Mike said and then quickly added, "Thank you. I just need to get some rest."

"Why don't I wait until tomorrow, then. I don't want to disturb you."

"No. I'd like us to talk, if that's okay."

After leaving the parking lot in Malibu the previous afternoon, before finding out he'd been fired and completely immersing himself in a clear swamp of vodka at Mickey's, Mike had put a lot of thought into the encounter he'd had with Tommy Gunn. The words, "Somebody's waiting," had run through his head so many times that he had put them to the monks' chant.

Once those words had vanished from his windshield, Tommy Gunn and his fellow monks had similarly vanished. They had not become dust or smoke, but had simply stepped from their places on the rooftops, risen from their seats on the roadside and faded into insubstantial blurs. Then, their forms were caught in the wind, a spiraling gale that carried each of the monks from their perches and blended their material together with a vicious swipe until a single mottled cloud blew away on the rapid current of air.

Mike had been left alone then with the words of his father and the words of Tommy Gunn, each answering the other in a repetitive loop:

Face it kid, no one wants you . . . to belong . . . face it kid . . . somebody's waiting . . . face it . . . we become one . . .

"Mike?" Jim asked. "Are you still there?"

"Yeah," he mumbled. "I'm sorry, what did you say?"

"I said, I'm worried about you."

"You don't have to be," Mike told him. "I'm going to be okay now."

Mike left the bed and put on a pot of coffee before stepping under the hot spray of a shower. He shaved and brushed his hair before throwing on a pair of jeans and an old white T-shirt. He sat in the living room with his coffee and stared out the window at the neat row of houses across the street.

On that night in Silverlake in Tommy Gunn's home, the musician had told Mike that the only thing that mattered was to have somebody waiting. Gunn had sought his salvation and made his sacrifice in order to be accepted—in order to belong. No longer a welcome citizen of this world, Gunn had chosen to enter another.

Mike pushed his tongue over his teeth, straining the muscle under it until he had as much of the spongy meat exposed as anatomy would allow. He clamped down carefully with his teeth.

Surely it was his tongue they would want for their token. Like Tommy Gunn's voice and manhood, it was Michael's tongue that had created his estrangement from the world and therefore it was this that he must sacrifice. He strained a little harder to get more of the pink flesh over his teeth and then bit down again as a dull ache rose in his jaw.

He didn't know why he felt compelled to practice this exercise; it was foolish.

He had no intention of joining Gunn or his disaffected remains. Unlike the lost musician, Mike felt he could make a place in this world; he need only sacrifice the use of his tongue rather than its substance.

We become one, appeared on his window in a sudden splash of red.

Mike turned to find Gunn and two other monks in the entryway. The three stood shoulder to shoulder, the rags of one's robe melding into the shreds of the other. The man with the multiple piercings like a chain-mail mask nodded his head, and the loops of steel penetrating his skin rippled over his features in agreement. The woman with no nose and the ear to ear grin breathed deeply as if aroused. Tommy gazed at him with warm appreciation.

"The tongue," the grinning woman whispered. She crossed the room and held out her hand to Mike, helping him to his feet. A pool of blue-gray fluid swirled deep within the cavity where her nose had been. This same roiling tide covered the back of her throat and tongue when she opened her mouth to say, "Take my breath and make your offering." She dipped the expanse of her mouth toward Mike.

He pulled away. "I'm not going with you. I belong here."

"No," she told him. "You belong with us." Fire flashed behind the pale pink lenses of her eyes, and the rolling steel gray tide in her mouth foamed violently. "You belong *to* us."

Mike jerked his hand out of the woman's grasp. He backed away with quick, stumbling steps and collided with a solid wall enveloped in the folds of shredded robes. Gunn held his left shoulder and the pierced man gripped his right. Through the window, Mike saw the other monks, dozens of them, gathering to witness his conversion. They climbed to neighboring rooftops or walked somberly over his yard, their heads lowered in reverence. Each retained some vestiges of humanity but their appearances had been perverted, mangled by whatever token they had deemed substantial enough to gain entrance to the order.

The woman unhinged her jaw, and it fell open to reveal a pulsing tongue, bright red and marbled like freshly slaughtered beef against the swirling blue-gray pool beyond. Her teeth, no different than Mike's own, were nonetheless frightening in their number as her spacious smile allowed him a view of their entirety. Mike drew a panicked breath and held it as her lips found his skin.

Her mouth locked over his face and her tongue pressed at his lips.

The penetration of the woman's tongue, parting his lips and prying open his clenched teeth, fueled his struggle, but the crushing weight of the robed bodies at his back kept him immobile as the woman's teeth clicked lightly against his.

Mike's chest thundered with fear and the need for oxygen, but he refused to take air from the disgusting chasm of teeth and tongue. Even as her jaws clamped together, severing a more substantial piece of tongue than Mike himself could have offered, he maintained his asphyxia. He needed to scream for the agony in his mouth, but he had forgotten how to breathe.

The woman pulled away, spitting Mike's tongue into her palm and wiping the blood from her lips with a long stroke of her forearm. The mound of spongy pink meat pulsed in her hand and then exploded into a thousand tiny specks, which rose into the air like vapor and evaporated.

"He didn't take the breath," she sang in a minor key.

"Then he's lost," the pierced man dismissed, lowering his head as if to pray.

The world spun to a blur, and Mike was aware that the demanding hands and bodies had released him. He tried to close his eyes, but his swimming mind refused the command. Warm blood filled his mouth and ran down the back of his throat to pool in his belly. The pounding in his heart grew to an unbearable thunder, and finally he gasped sweet air.

The last sound he heard before dropping to the floor was the low chant, so musical and pleasing, coming from every corner of the world to lull him into darkness.

"Somebody's waiting," Tommy Gunn told him.

A warm hand touched his face, and Mike's eyes shot

open as he struggled to remove himself from Gunn's touch.

But the hand didn't belong to Tommy Gunn or any of his order.

"Hey kid," Jim said.

Mike tried to return the greeting but agony flared in his mouth, bringing tears to his eyes and chilled sweat to his neck. The television, mounted high up on the wall of the hospital room, flickered over Jim's shoulder; it was also muted.

"You had a seizure," Jim told him warmly, returning his palm to Mike's cheek. "They're going to be running tests on you for the next couple of days, but they said you'd be okay."

Mike grasped the hand on his face tightly, squeezing it close to his cheek. Jim looked down on him with an expression of kindness that was absolute and loving.

He needed to speak to this man, but did not possess the means. Mike wanted to apologize, to find some way to mend the bridges before they fell away completely. If he could do that, if he could make one solid connection to this world, then no other world would ever matter again.

He made a motion in the air as if requesting a check from a restaurant waiter; he needed a pen and paper; he wanted to write Jim a note.

His fingertip tingled lightly before a geyser of blood shot into the space over the bed. The red tendril rolled nonsensically from the tip of his digit, creating a pattern of swirls and lines over the bed like graffiti. When Mike pulled his hand away, the crimson thread whipped back against the wall to splash the clean white surface.

"Jesus," Jim hissed. His eyes had grown wide as he stumbled away from the bed.

Mike made a gesture to placate his retreating savior, and the ribbon of blood snaked across the room, mocking gravity and nature. He screamed for Jim to stay, ignoring the pain in his mouth, but Jim had already opened the door to escape the snake of fluid writhing in the air between them.

The door slammed.

Then he was alone in the silence. He tried to recall the monks' chant in the hopes they might come for him, but he already knew he had been denied entrance to their order, just as he had been banished from Jim's.

The exile of two worlds gave up the song and lost himself in the weave of blood. He followed each curve and line before wiggling his finger to change the design, in which he lost himself again. He penned messages to the gods in the sterile air. Eventually, he authored Gunn's slogan—*We become one*—and then decided he didn't like the sound of it. The Exile made an adjustment in the lettering and cast it against the wall for permanence. The trail of blood ran dry, and he stared at this final message until sleep pulled him away, knowing the message would be there for him when he woke—would always be there for him.

One.

SOMETHING IN THE AIR

Michael Laimo

It all happened just three days ago, at a time when life was running its normal and rather mundane course through Darien Falls.

The day was January 18th. During the night, a northern front blasted through our little slice of upstate New York, dragging the temperatures down into the single digits. When morning rolled around, the sun exerted itself in the cloudless sky but couldn't permeate the layer of frost on the front lawn. Breakneck gales were still beating their way across the hills into the village, and beyond the field out back, Capson Lake shimmered beneath the spineless sun like a long flat mirror.

I'd just finished my breakfast, an egg sandwich that hardly sated my appetite. The growl in my stomach made me reach into the cupboard for some cereal, but Sharon sighed and gave me a bit of a cross look. I'd promised to pick up some things at Wegman's, the essentials like milk, bread, cheese, etc., and was now being silently reminded of it. She'd run out of space for her notes on the magnetic refrigerator pad and had expressed displeasure with the slight inconvenience. I told her to simply hang another one. She ignored me and told me to go out and get the things she needed so she could start the list anew.

It was a played-out routine between us, one not worth arguing over so long as I stayed married to the same woman.

"Weather's gettin' bad," she said, despite the glaring sun.

"Sky's clear. Ain't no sign of a storm."

"Wind's still blowing, though."

Indeed it was. It'd kept me up half the night, the endless sound of it howling about the eaves and whipping twigs and debris against the shingles. Toss single digit temperatures into the mix, and yeah, you had yourself some pretty nasty weather, cloudless skies or not. So I bundled myself up in the Gore-Tex jacket Sharon gave me for Christmas, then poked my head into the den. Kevin had a blanket wrapped around his shoulders and was doing his best burrito imitation on the couch. Sharon leaned over to attend to the fire, amply providing me with a pleasant view of her rear. There I stood, admiring the scene until the wind rattled the windows and made me realize, with dismay, that I'd soon be leaving the warm comforts of home for a Sunday afternoon encounter with the elements.

Little did I know.

"Anything else you need before I leave?"

"You got the list, right?"

"Yep."

"That's all we need."

Another stronger gale shook the windows. Kevin loosened the blanket around his head. "Dad, TV's been out all morning."

"Well, I suppose that's to be expected, with the wind blowing like it is. Plus there's ice all over the wires."

"Let's just hope the power stays on." Sharon tossed another log onto the fire. Sparks showered the hearth in a comforting display of warmth. Kevin pulled the blanket back over his head and made himself one with the sofa cushions. He'd probably be in the same position when I got back. I figured in a few more years he'd be the one running errands for the Queen of the Household and I'd be wrapped in a blanket staring at my wife's ass. Until that day . . .

So I said my farewells, and left through the front door. Immediately a sharp gust hit me in the face. The sting of it was shockingly harsh against my skin, as though I'd taken a slap across the cheek. I wrestled the jacket's hood up over my head and walked briskly to the car, looking up to see the naked branches of the elms out front groaning restlessly beneath the wind's flexing muscles.

With the wind and the cold weather and the bitterness of it all, you'd figure there might've been a helluva storm on its way. But the sky had never looked clearer, or bluer. In comparison to the clouds of yesterday, it exhibited a radiant hue like a tropical ocean contrasting the stagnant murk of Capson Lake. It was deeply brilliant, utterly fascinating, not a wisp of a cloud to be seen. *It looks painted,* I thought. *It looks unreal.*

More wind came, but unlike the sharp punching gusts rattling the windows and slapping my face, this wind shifted, unsteadily at first, then purposefully and in portions, against my face, my legs, my body, like frisking hands. I shuddered in its embrace, and despite the bitter cold, felt an immediate sweat breaking out against my back. I squeezed the keys in my gloved hand, then opened the door to the Dodge pickup and got in, slamming it shut and thereby closing out the invasive draft, which pounded the vehicle and nearly cradle-rocked the entire chassis.

Amidst the protective confines of the cab, I heard the wind seeming to vocalize its unruly intentions, or perhaps, I imagined, its frustrations for not being able to get to me. It whooped against the windshield, screamed about the sides, and whistled loudly at the rear before departing with a roar. It sounded almost musical in nature. Throw in the creaking tree boughs for percussion, and you had yourself one mighty chorus of nature's elements.

I pulled the truck around and headed up the driveway, which ran three hundred feet to Pikes Road. The layer of icy frost on the grass reflected the sun's rays in a glimmerful sheen, and I imagined that from above it must've looked like a great suntan reflector. As I steered along the crunching gravel, clawlike tree shadows swayed violently in the choppy path of the driveway. The fierce wind kept whistling and whipping at the pickup, causing the steering wheel to joggle in my grip.

I passed the cluster of elms lining the front lawn, and was just thinking how pitifully weak they looked in their leafless state when a sudden flash of light from above lit up the windshield, demanding me to shut my eyes. A loud crack filled the air and I yelled "Holy shit!" and then it was raining dead twigs all around. A few splinters showered down in the rear of the cab, but I heard the real bulk of the damage hit the ground just feet behind the tailgate.

"Shit!" I yelled again, then stopped the truck and twisted around to peer through the rear windshield. What I saw explained the loud crack I'd heard, but . . . well, let's just say I was having a good deal of trouble believing what'd just happened, and did not dare get out of the truck just yet.

I'd assumed that a branch had snapped away from one of the trees, and that much in part was true. But you had to multiply that branch by about twelve or fifteen, and that's what I now had in my front yard. There were tree branches lying all over, splintered boughs severed from their trunks, rising and poking every which way. The messy scene and sudden odor of burning wood reminded me of the time I'd visited the logging plant up in Newcastle where the lumberjacks chainsawed the logs before trucking them up to the paper mill. What you had left was a knotted abundance of fireplace wood that you could cart away for free in your pickup. Seemed as though I had enough firewood now to last me through the winter, compliments of Mother Nature. And to think: I didn't even have to lug it home. Woo-hoo.

Sharon emerged from the house, her face pinched with worry. "What the hell happened?"

I lowered the window. Bits of wood flew into my face. "The wind, I guess." I grinned uncomfortably, feeling as though I'd just told a lie; it didn't seem possible that a single forceful gale could do such damage. Then I remembered the flash of light I saw just before the branches came down. Lightning, perhaps. But that really didn't seem at all possible; there were no clouds in the sky. So then how could this have happened?

"Well, you'd better hurry up home." Sharon looked more than concerned, and I knew she'd end up hiding out in the dark basement—a thunderstorm ritual of hers—if things got any worse out here. "I don't like the looks of this."

"Just stay in the house," I said, and at that moment the screen door whipped from her hand and slammed against the house.

"Ahh! Jesus!" She pulled the door back and quickly closed herself inside. Hello basement.

I shut the window, then took a deep breath and rolled the Dodge to the end of the driveway, where I made a left turn out onto Pikes Road. The wind had left its mess out here too. Branches and twigs littered the entire road. An azalea bush, uprooted from Lou Henry's yard across the street, lay against his mailbox post like a large roadkill.

Slowly I moved the pickup forward. Not fifty feet

down the road I heard another sharp crackling noise. I cringed and hit the brakes, half expecting a tree limb to fall onto the truck. When I looked out the driver's-side window, I thought I saw a hissing reptile—it looked that way to me until I realized a power line had snapped. It dangled from the top of the street pole all the way to the asphalt, where it writhed angrily like the snake I imagined it to be. There were black scorch-marks in the road like some July 4th amateur's aftermath. Above, the wire leading from the pole to my roof was still intact; if it had snapped over the dry trees, there definitely would have been an inferno to contend with.

I inched the car up the road, away from the wire, then tried to cell-phone home to see if the power was out, but no connection could be made—only static met my ear. Maybe there's a storm coming after all, I thought, and immediately knew better than to turn back. If the power failed, then I'd need some candles and kerosene in addition to the food on Sharon's list. And with the wire down, it'd take a good while to get the juice flowing again.

The road leading into town was also badly littered with debris, making the going slow and difficult, and every now and then I had to navigate around some larger branches. Halfway into town an old oak had uprooted from its place at the forefront of someone's yard and lay across the road like a dead dinosaur. I had to four-wheel the Dodge over the grass in the yard across the street to make my way around it.

Although the wind appeared to have calmed down for the moment, the damage left in its wake was wholly troubling. In addition to the twigs and tree limbs, mailboxes, newspapers, wood shingles, weather vanes, and other outdoor items swept the area. There were downed wires on almost every street corner, and on Willets Place an entire telephone pole had fallen on someone's house.

Flames and black smoke rose ominously into the sky (the clear blue sky), intimidating the lone fire truck at the scene. At this point, realizing the severity of the damage, I turned on the radio for a report, but caught only static across the board. First the cable. Then the cell phone. Now, the radio. *This is worse than I imagined.*

Finally, I turned onto Main Street and slowly made my way into a mostly deserted town. A sharp blast of wind shook the car as if in protest of my arrival, but I ignored it and moved on, pulling the truck into the Wegman's shopping center. The large parking lot was only spotted with cars, perhaps a dozen in all. Two light poles had come down, arched over like broken flower stems. One had fallen atop someone's Ford SUV, crushing the roof into a jagged U shape. A state police cruiser sat near the scene with its door open and its lights blazing, a heavyset uniformed cop leaning against someone's car about twenty feet away. I parked a good distance from the cruiser then got out. The wind, suddenly strong again, nearly took the door from my hand, and I had to muscle it to get it closed.

I strolled over to the cop, purposely scraping my feet against the blacktop to alert him of my approach. He must've heard me coming but never looked up. His freckled face remained downcast, shoulders hunched, eyes squeezed shut. When I got to within five feet of him, I could see icy tears pouring from his eyes. All I could think was, Jesus, something very bad is happening, something very bad is happening, over and over again.

"Are you okay?" I asked the cop. Dumb question, but what else could I have said?

He shifted toward me, and that's when I saw the gun. He had it in his right hand, pointed toward the ground. He opened his tear-filled eyes and looked toward the sky. His shoulders started shaking and sobs blurted from his lips.

"Jesus, what's wrong? What's . . ." I had a difficult time finding the right words. My heart started doing backflips, and I looked around a quick moment to see if anyone else might be nearby—someone with their wits about them. I saw a woman running into Wegman's, but that was it. Running into Wegman's. As if trying to get away from something. . . .

"It's over," the cop blurted. "The prophet was right. They've come."

In the distance, I heard a scream. A human scream. It warbled down into a sick gristly wail, then died. It seemed to have come from inside the supermarket.

"What's over?" I asked weakly, keeping one eye on his gun and another over my shoulder toward the supermarket. I wanted to grab his collar and scream "So what the fuck is going on? And what are you going to do about it?" In thought, I answered my own question: *Apparently nothing*. Here there were screams. And downed poles. And crushed cars. And all the cop could do was babble and cry.

"Yep, yep . . . they've come. There's nothing anyone can do about it."

"Who's come?" My heart was pounding, not particularly at what he was saying, but because of the simple fact that a cop was standing before me, highly unstable, and with his gun drawn.

And then something totally unforeseen happened. The wind picked up. Again it prodded my body and face; oddly, it seemed to have come from numerous directions, along with that eerie feeling as if hands were forcefully fondling me. The cop yelled, "Not me, you bastards!" He raised the gun, arm trembling wildly; it looked as though someone had grabbed his forearm and was trying to shake the gun loose from his grip. There came a brilliant flash of light from above (like the one I saw just before the trees snapped in my yard), followed by a sirenlike missling noise in the distance that abruptly came to an end with a tremendous explosion. It rocked the earth beneath my feet. I spun around in a panic, trying to keep my balance. Far off in the distance, perhaps three miles to the east, I saw a tremendous plume of black smoke rising into the air.

"What the fuck?" I yelled. "Are we under attack? What the fuck?"

"The planes," the cop said, eerily calm. "They're falling from the sky. Every goddamned one of them. And there's nothing we can do about it."

Planes? Falling from the sky?

I wouldn't have believed him hadn't I seen the smoke in the distance, or the thin trail of white vapor leading down into it. I heard some car alarms blaring in the distance, then a shriek of brakes, then a crash. People started yelling and I saw a man in the intersection of Main and High gesturing uncontrollably, as though on fire. The rise and fall of the town's fire siren began its boundless toll. Never in my life had I felt such an overwhelming pouring of disquiet. It was as though the entire town was all at once falling apart at the seams. Maybe even the whole world.

The planes are falling out of the sky. I saw it, but I didn't believe it.

"The wind!" the cop yelled.

Head spinning, I turned back to face him. He was heaving, as if about to throw up. The gun wriggled wildly in his hand, then fell to the asphalt with a dull clunk.

He repeated, "The wind . . ." and then he started choking and jerking around and moving like the man I saw in the intersection, who, by the way, was still there shaking and trembling uncontrollably, feet glued to the ground. The cop was screaming now as if in excruciating pain, but it did him no good. I thought he might be having some kind of seizure until I realized that his uniform was rippling too, as if caught in a strong wind, and then he was virtually lifted off the ground and carried away from me. I could see him trying to fight whatever had him in its grasp—his hands moved ponderously as if under water, his booted toes dragged along the asphalt—but it seemed only to exhaust him. His body spasmed and twitched, and at one point he went head-over-heels in a complete somersault, looking remarkably like an astronaut in a no-gravity environment. A tiny cyclone of dust twirled around him, encapsulating him as it carried him away.

"The wind," I said to myself. *It's taking him away.*

It carried him to the intersection where six other people were now gathered. Everyone there was behaving in a similar fashion: twitching as if being prodded with electricity, yet obviously unable to move from their current positions. I recalled the sensation of the wind coming at me from multiple directions, how it purposefully seized me and clutched me, as if trying to manipulate me. I imagined that if it had come at me stronger, with more direct intent, then I might not have been able to move, like the others in the street who were trapped in its bouncy, muscling command.

I reached down for the gun, but a gust of wind took it away from me, sending it across the parking lot into a growth of weeds alongside the building perhaps a hundred yards away. This little trick brought about feelings of hysteria in me. It made me want to go home. It made me want to see if my family was all right.

Suddenly, I heard a squelch. It came from the police car.

The door had been left open and the police multiband radio was on. Pacing crazily, I tried my cell phone first, but the network was still down. In the far distance, I heard another huge explosion. The ground reverberated beneath my feet. *Another plane,* I told myself. *Jesus Christ.*

I looked at my car, then at the police car, then at the people in the street, then back to the police car. If there were any answers to be had, they would be found on the other end of that police radio. So I ran to the police car and shut myself in, running my hand against the steering column and feeling out the keys, which were still in the ignition. I figured I might be better off taking the police cruiser home, given the sudden circumstances.

I looked back out at the people gathered in the intersection, perhaps two dozen strong now. They jostled together frantically, like lottery balls in a clear tank, unable to break their bounds. Their clothes rippled madly under the force of the wind, and the hair on their heads flew up in the tunnel of air spinning just above them. Away from the crowd, two middle-aged men drifted in from around the corner of Elm. They floated about four feet off the ground, as if tethered on strings, one partially clad in pajamas, the other completely naked. Once the crowd seemed to be in their sights, the wind picked up speed and sailed them down Main Street—they looked as though they'd been shot from cannons. Their bodies convulsed, mouths wide open, cheeks rippling from the aerodynamic force. The ferocious wind then hurled them like sacks of laundry right into the stormy mix of people. The collision was fierce and loud. Screams erupted, carried out by the twisting storm, and a mad wash of blood spun away from the fray in a thick splatter across the intersection.

The radio squelched again and then a male voice crackled on, startling me. I moved to grab the microphone from the mounting bracket, but fumbled it and was unable to retrieve it: I couldn't tear my sights away from the insanity outside. I was paralyzed with fear, and numb with the fact that as long as I remained in the car, I appeared to be safe. But then what? Would the wind let me drive back home?

A hiss of static shot out from the radio. I fingered the receiver and the voice came back, loud and clear from the tinny speaker. I focused my sights on the dangling microphone, away from the madness a hundred yards away:

> ... so I'm at the Woodlawn Police Department, and there's no one here at all, the place is empty. Down the road there's a large crowd of people. There's maybe a hundred or more of them, men, women, and children, all amassed together in what I can only describe at the moment as an unbreakable cluster. I know that doesn't seem to make any sense, but they're under some sort of . . . of physical influence. It's the wind that's doing it, but I have no explanation for it, and I don't think anyone does, really. I mean, it's just gone fucking batty . . . it's like it's alive, man. It's picking people up and moving them around into these groups, and then it surrounds them with these little tornadoes. They're all over, these storm-held masses. I just came in from Lakeview twenty-five miles away and passed four of these crowds on the way. In Ashborough the crowd was so big, I had to stop the car and get out so I could get around them. It was so fucking strange . . . I mean, I just walked right by them . . . well, I kept a safe a distance, stayed at least fifty feet away, but I really couldn't get any closer because the wind wouldn't let me. Man, it was so fucking surreal, I could see all their faces . . . the ones on the outside, they were looking at me. Their faces were all bloodied and battered, torn up from the wind and debris. I could see them trying to

reach out to me, as if I might be able to help them or something. Yeah, right. I'd tried once, took a step closer to the whirling dervish, but the wind kicked me back—it felt as if I'd taken a sharp punch to the ribs or something. It's really fucked up, I mean, the wind, it just pushed me away, as if I might've been some kind of threat. Makes me wonder . . . why doesn't it want me? I mean, I ain't complaining, but for some reason, it just doesn't pen me up like the others. It goes as far as to feel me up, but then it just blows me away as if I taste bad or something. Heh, blows me away . . . get it? Aw Jesus, I'm losing my fucking mind. Yeah, I mean, as far as I can tell, I'm the only one left. And then the planes . . . Jesus Christ, man, they're falling out of the sky like hailstones. It was early this morning, maybe about two a.m., when all this started. I'd heard on the radio that there were reports of bright flashes in the sky and extreme turbulence, and that all the planes still in the air couldn't land because the weather patterns suddenly went haywire and the wind started knocking the planes around like punching bags. Of course, the planes eventually began running out of fuel, so they had no choice but to try to land, and they broke up as they made their descents. Last I heard, before the radios went out, was that there'd been about eight hundred fifty planes in the air when this all began. I heard one go down about two hours ago, near Lynnfield, and I figure they're still dropping like flies . . . Jesus, man, I mean, what the fuck? Am I the only one left? Is there anyone out there that can hear me right now?

I wiped a tear from my eye, then picked up the microphone and placed it against my lips. "I'm here."

* * *

Ten minutes later, I clipped the microphone back into the bracket and looked toward the intersection. There were at least a hundred people out there now, jammed together in an unwanted pushing-shoving match, with many more being added by the minute. Most of the new arrivals found themselves caught in strong gales that blew them violently and unsympathetically into the fracas; a few others made more conspicuous entrances, with lesser winds dragging them along the road as if fettered by leashes; by the time their bloody carcasses were propelled into the collective, they'd become mostly unrecognizable as humans. And the noises that came from the crowd, well, they could easily drive a man insane—a man lucky enough not to be inside. Every captured person did their damnedest to scream and shout and yell (I imagined the pain-induced vocalizations as being mostly involuntary), and the collective volume of such came together to sound like a sea of lost souls bathing in the lavas of hell. Well—that's how I imagined it.

I'd earned myself a heckuva headache, probably from all the wind beating against my ears. It was at this moment I realized that the fire siren had stopped tolling, probably had some time ago, and the only sounds that could now be heard were the high moans of the wind and the shared anguish of those caught in its tight embrace. *This is hell,* I thought, and suddenly wondered what the cop had meant when he said, *The prophet was right. They've come.*

The man I spoke to who'd holed himself up at the Woodlawn Police Department was named Kelly. He was a biker who, like me, had remained untouched by the winds, and we both decided that there had to be more of us out there, and that we should make an effort to join forces and hunt for the truth of the matter. He told me that he would remain at the Woodlawn police station until I arrived. At that point we'd take some time to formulate a plan, and hopefully make contact with others like ourselves. I told him that I was going to head home first to check on my family, and then I'd make the thirty-mile drive to Woodlawn. He suggested that I find a motorcycle somewhere, but I told him that my wife and ten-year-old son couldn't ride. He didn't answer me. He just told me he'd play with the radio until I arrived. He must've assumed that I'd be arriving alone.

I rolled the car across the lot, staring out at the crowd which had swelled beyond the edges of the intersection, now down Main Street. There had to have been about five hundred people in there now, some of them familiar faces: Jud Barlowe from the hardware store; my next-door neighbor Phillip Deighton; Phillis Darmody, Kevin's third-grade teacher. The wind still whipped about them fiercely, and a thickening layer of debris circled the crowd like a planetary ring. The car rocked and jostled, but had not been directly influenced by the wind; it seemed only to be affected as an outside encroacher to the prime directive, whatever the fuck it was. Then I remembered what Kelly had said, that every time he came too close to the crowd, he'd been "blown away." Perhaps this was what was happening to me also. As if, like he said, I tasted bad.

I decided to move on, to allow the crazy scene to progress toward its inexplicable resolution. And did it ever, with me as its witness. I didn't know what to think, how to feel—well, I *could* feel my mouth hanging wide open and my eyes bulging and my breath staggering in my lungs, but other than that I could do nothing but white-knuckle the steering wheel and watch the extraordinary scene unfold before me.

Before I made it across the parking lot, a familiar flash of light emanated from above. It flickered a few times, like an expiring lightbulb, then shifted from a flash to a glare and illuminated the entire area in a constant glow. It blinded me, as if a searchlight's beam had been pointed at my face. I squinted and cupped my hands around my eyes. The environment grew brighter, and when I looked up I saw a tiny sun riding down from the blue sky, a fiery ball of light the size of a small house. It hovered in the air perhaps two hundred feet above the whirling tornado, as silent as its appearance was sudden. It remained there unmoving, as still as a boulder and seemingly transfixed on the activity below it. Soon a high droning sound emitted from it, something oddly mechanical-sounding despite its nonmechanical appearance. With this, the tornado and the debris and even the people began to swill up into it. At first only a few dark bodies shot up into the light; crazily, I thought they looked like lemon pits being sucked up through a straw. But soon more people started making their way up the funnel. The whirl of dust and debris went from dirty gray to blood-red as it fully ascended into the ball of light. In a time less than five minutes, the light had drawn everything up into its wake—the tornado, the people, every shred of debris—leaving the street free of any evidence. With its mission accomplished, the ball of light geysered upward into the sky and quickly disappeared, taking most of Darien Falls with it.

And then, almost immediately, the wind died down, leaving me alone in a ghost town.

Despite the lack of mankind, it had been an even slower go returning home than it had been coming into town. My watch had stopped at 9:14, but I estimated perhaps three hours having passed since I left home for Wegman's. I still had Sharon's grocery list in my pocket, and prayed it wouldn't end up as my very last hold on her existence. A few clouds had returned to the sky, only some thin wisps, but a welcome sight nonetheless.

During the drive home, while I maneuvered around dead animals and fallen branches and some crashed cars, I ran the dial on the police scanner from left to right. This time I heard Kelly again, searching for others, and a preacher man who cried of the scourges of hell and the immoralities of mankind through a dry cracking voice. I listened to his diatribe for a few minutes, and was about to change the frequency when he pulled a passage out of the book of Nostradamus that sent a chill through me and made the hair on my arms stand on end:

At the nineteenth sunrise, one will see great fires in the skies,
Wind and light will extend towards earth: circles of life will form
Within the circles, death, and one will hear cries,
Through wind, and fire, death awaiting them.

I thought it too coincidental to be true, unless the preacher with the hoarse voice took liberties upon himself to exaggerate the prophecy, if one existed at all. Then I thought of what the cop had said: *The prophet was right. They've come,* and I turned the scanner off, deciding for the moment that I'd sampled enough apocalyptic talk for the time being. I made it to Pikes Road and turned left toward my home, praying like hell that God had spared Sharon and Kevin despite my shortcomings and sins in life. The downed tree was still downed, and I followed the tracks I'd made earlier across my neighbor's front lawn. I passed the broken electrical wire that no longer snapped and popped, and finally turned into my driveway, the sound of the gravel under the Dodge's tires a familiar welcome to my slammed mind.

The wind had made a mess of my house. Shingles peppered the lawn; the gutters dangled from the eaves like those few tree branches still clinging to life; all of the windows had shattered. I ran in through the front door, calling, "Sharon! Kevin! Where are you?" But there were no answers.

In the den, Kevin's blanket lay halfway out the window, skewered on a thick shard of glass still in the window frame. The shard, and the blanket, had blood all over it. I walked over to the window, peered outside. A trail of blood led ten feet away, then abruptly ended, *as if he'd been picked up and carried away.*

I shoved my fist in my mouth and bit back my tears, shaking my head in denial. What made me think that my family would be spared from the loathsome wind and its harmful intent? I looked up at the sky, wondering where Kevin was now. Whether he was alive or dead.

More clouds had filtered their way in. Birds chirped happily from the injured trees. It seemed somewhat evident that the essential duties of the wind had been completed, and taking into consideration the most optimistic viewpoint, life would have to continue on with those few remaining people to build upon its offerings. It seemed an unfathomable task, especially with those memories of Kevin lazing on the couch and Sharon tending to the fire.

I thought of the last time I saw Sharon, the screen door whipping from her grasp, how frightened she was of the advancing winds and the storm she thought would come.

The storm . . .

The basement!

I walked to the basement door, knowing that she would've hid herself downstairs in an effort to soothe her storm-driven anxieties. I opened the door. The darkness beyond the threshold of the door was forbidding . . . yet acted a possible means of salvation for my wife. *Dear God, please . . .*

"Sharon?" I called.

And she appeared like an angel from the heavens, her feet pounding the staircase, falling out of the darkness, hands grabbing me, holding me, tears streaming from her eyes, cries spilling from her mouth in a pure outpouring of comfort and relief. I hugged her back, tighter than ever, making sure she'd stay with me forever.

"You survived," I said through my tears, wondering how many more people were still buttoned up in their homes, drumming up the nerve to emerge into the aftermath of the storm.

"The wind . . . it blew in all the windows . . . it took Kevin. I ran to the window, but the wind, it tried to take me too. I had no choice . . . had to lock myself downstairs. Jesus Christ, I saw Kevin flying away into the sky." She cried hysterically, then blurted, "Was it a tornado, was it? *Was it?*"

I didn't know what to say, so I just nodded my head. "A very bad one."

"I was in the basement," she cried. "I didn't know what to do!"

I hugged her tighter and rubbed her head. Nothing I could say would ever alleviate the grief running through her body. "We need to leave here, for now. There's someone in Woodlawn waiting for us."

She didn't ask any questions, and I didn't mention anything about what'd happened while I was away. I looked into her eyes, and she at once knew that I'd experienced something extraordinary this morning, something inexplicable, and with this, gave me the benefit of her trust.

I grabbed her by the hand and led her outside, and for one brief harrowing moment wondered again how many people were holed up in their homes, hiding in their basements and their closets, peeking out only to see if it might be safe enough to grab some food and water.

When we reached the Dodge, I knew at once that there weren't going to be any survivors hiding in their basements, or their closets, because in a matter of seconds the wind made its undeniable purpose known, and made me realize that it was preselecting its victims and would get to them no matter what, no matter when, and I knew this because when I looked to the sky I saw the clouds suddenly evaporate, and then I saw a great flash of light illuminate the environment, and then the wind swooped in and snatched up Sharon like an eagle dive-bombing a mouse in a field, tearing her away from my grasp and carrying her over the roof of my house into the distance, toward Capson Lake and perhaps all the way to Deerfield where there would most likely be another mass herding of humans awaiting her arrival.

I stood there dumbfounded, considering the truth of what'd just happened, a ten-second incident that defied imagination and rewrote the book on fear. In this time, the clouds returned and the wind died down and I was left alone wondering, *Why not me? Why not me?*

Now, I sit three days later at a Motel Six in Latham, writing all this down on a composition ledger I lifted from behind the front desk. There's twenty-three of us now, we each have our own rooms, lucky, I suppose, to have found enough with the windows still intact—I'd decided that these rooms didn't have any people in them at the time the wind blew through. We passed by a few plane crash sites, but didn't dare approach the still-smoldering ruins. There's ruination everywhere, but still, no bodies. The only people we've found were alive, and they're with us now. We're all armed—protection from the dogs roaming about. Kelly and I are leading the coalition of survivors, and know there are plenty more out there. We just have to find them.

And when we do, they will ask us the same question: *What caused this?*

And we will tell them: *It was something in the air.*

GOD'S FIST

Paul Finch

Skelton didn't know which one of the photographs he found the most disturbing.

The first depicted the aftermath of a brutal lynching in Serb-occupied Kosovo; a man, who had been murdered by being hacked and disemboweled, had been hoisted into the air on a metal pole . . . several children, presumably *that* same man's children, were screaming and crying and trying to console each other around his dangling feet. The second featured a murder actually in progress; it had been taken during the atrocities in Rwanda, and showed a black child—perhaps no more than two or three years old—naked and curled in the dust, but shrieking with pain and terror, as two black men clad in baggy jungle fatigues and big, heavy boots stamped it to death. The third picture was an odd one, but was explained by the rough caption someone had handwritten on the back of it: *Congenitally deformed prostitutes, Rio.* It displayed a hellish backstreet-slum, where two women waited idly amid the trash. One wore a very short dress and high heels, the other a halter top and tight shorts. There, the charm—if "charm" is the correct word—ended: The woman in shorts had both her legs in calipers—the right one ended in a hefty club foot, the left tapered down into a stump just about the place where the ankle should have been; the woman in the dress and heels had a nice figure and shapely legs, but bizarrely, her face had sunk inward—scrunched, like a deflated football. Presumably, they'd both got well used to their disabilities . . . by their shoulder bags and saucy postures, they were touting for business.

Skelton crouched looking at the pictures for several minutes, his heart thumping. He'd seen a lot of nasty in his time—especially during his ten years as a beat cop in one of the city's most run-down districts—but never anything quite like this. A moment passed, then he laid the pictures to one side and continued to empty the filing cabinets, shoving files and folders into the various cardboard boxes. When he'd been told the narrow, dusty room was a library, the least he'd been expecting was reams of heavy books—probably videotapes and microfilm cans as well. Of course, newspaper libraries were slightly different. He should have realized that when he'd first found out where it was they'd be working today. Not that this operation was a newspaper as such—*The Catholic Echo* was a hefty broadsheet that came out weekly, but it catered exclusively to the Catholic communities of Britain and Ireland, detailing the latest developments in church affairs, plus world-news items of interest to the religious-minded. The majority of the photographs in the drawers reflected this, showing groups of monks and nuns smiling, priests posing beside their altars, celebrities launching charity events, or landscape views of St. Peter's Square, Knock, and the Holy Grotto at Lourdes.

Skelton looked again at the three horrific photographs. Even a church newspaper had to cover the real world, of course—the downside of life. There'd also been shots of dismal ghettos, discarded syringes in gutters, nervous

British troops on the bombed-out Bogside streets—but these three particular images had an unsettling quality all of their own. He gazed at the prostitute with the head like a kicked-in football; at the mangled remains of the Bosnian father, the weeping, wailing children gathered beneath him. Again, Skelton placed the photos to one side. He wasn't sure why he didn't throw them into the boxes with all the rest—at least, he wasn't sure yet.

"Ray!" said Jervis, sticking his tousled head through the door. Jervis was Skelton's foreman. "How you doing, pal?"

"Almost there." Skelton closed a couple of the fuller boxes, then stood.

Jervis nodded. "Good . . . 'cause we want to start shifting the computer gear next."

The tousled head disappeared. Skelton glanced around the narrow room. The shelves were now bare, the bulk of the drawers hanging open and empty. The company librarian had already removed the various A, B, C, D, and so-on stickers from the fronts of them, as well as the posters on the walls and the sheaves of old back-copies from the rack underneath her desk. Her own personals had also been taken, which meant there was virtually nothing else in there. Apart from the three black-and-white photographs. Skelton glanced at them again, considered tossing them into the last box . . . then slid them under his overalls.

Outside, the newsroom was alive with people bustling back and forth: removals men mainly, but also secretaries and admin girls, plus a couple of the journalists who the company management felt would be more of a use than a hindrance during the move to new premises. One of these was *The Catholic Echo*'s editor, Len Hoggins. His name suggested a plump, perhaps piglike man, with a mop of greasy gray hair and an irascible, middle-aged temperament. In fact, that couldn't have been further from the truth. Hoggins was only in his midthirties, slim, a smooth dresser, and rather good-looking in a blond "film star" sort of way. He was patient with his staff, polite to visitors, and of a generally amenable nature.

He was also a complete bastard—at least, that was the way Skelton felt about him. And Skelton ought to have known, he having been a classmate of Hoggins's all the way through infant, junior, and finally middle school. Of course, time had rolled on since then, and Skelton and Hoggins's paths had long since diverged, though, for all that they still recognized each other.

"Ray!" said Hoggins, stopping Skelton as he carried two of the boxes through the *Echo*'s old reception area. The journalist was apparently delighted to see his one-time acquaintance.

"Len," said Skelton, also stopping.

There was a momentary silence. Skelton was well aware that his overalls pants and T-shirt were coated in dust, and that he was sweaty and rather bedraggled. Hoggins, on the other hand, seemed unaffected by the toil and panic around him. His blond hair was combed neatly back in a crisp wave, not a strand out of place, while his white shirt and florid silk tie looked as if they'd just arrived from the dry-cleaners.

"So, long time no see," said the newspaper boss after a moment. "How are you?"

"I'm okay," Skelton replied.

For the first time, Hoggins seemed to notice his former pal's workclothes. "You're not with the police anymore, then?"

Skelton shook his head. "Nah. Got tired of it."

That wasn't entirely the truth, but Skelton certainly wasn't going to tell Len Hoggins that it had been more a case of the police getting tired of *him*.

"How's Mary?" the journalist asked.

Skelton shrugged. "Okay. I see her from time to time."

The message of that wasn't lost on Hoggins. "Oh dear," he replied sympathetically. "Trixie?"

"She's fine. I get access once a week."

"Sorry to hear that, Ray."

Hoggins's commiseration seemed genuine enough, but Skelton knew that it wasn't. Len Hoggins was just about the most ingenuous person he'd ever met.

"It's all right," the ex-cop said. "Life's a lot quieter."

"Suppose so. Anyway . . . where you living these days?"

"Got a flat down Bagley End."

Hoggins nodded, his expression neutral—clearly unsure whether further pity *(because Bagley End was seven blocks of semiderelict council tenements, and basically a junkie sewer)* would be welcomed, or whether it would be deemed an insult because it openly implied that Skelton now really had sunk to the bottom of the pile.

"So, this is . . . this is what you do, then," the journalist finally remarked.

"Yeah. It's laboring, mostly."

"It's certainly keeping you in shape."

Skelton nodded. His dusty T-shirt did little to conceal his broad chest, bull neck, and massive arms and shoulders. "I always liked to work out."

"Yeah . . . I remember."

At that moment, Jervis approached, tapping his watch. "Ray . . . time, eh!"

"I'd better get on," Skelton said.

Hoggins slapped him on the shoulder. "Yeah, well . . . it's good to see you again, Ray. Presumably we'll keep running into each other while the move's on?"

"Very possibly," Skelton replied, moving away. "See you."

* * *

That evening, when he got back to his flat, Skelton stripped down to his jockey shorts, and went into the bathroom. He was thirty-five years old, and stood six feet, three inches tall. He was very strongly built—according to the scales, he weighed fifteen stone, seven pounds, and thanks to the dedicated fitness program he followed, none of that was flab. He looked at himself in the mirror: His hair was still jet-black, almost oily, but at the moment unruly and badly in need of a trim; thick black sideburns ran down either cheek; the face in between them, once reasonably handsome, was now pitted and stony.

Skelton contemplated this for a moment, then went back into his pokey little lounge. Its furnishings were sparse—an armchair, a single wardrobe, and a chest of drawers with a portable TV on top. Beside the small electric fire, there was a variety of weights and dumbbells. Skelton got to work on them straight away, breaking off only for a second to flick on the early-evening news, which wasn't particularly uplifting: the latest batch of Middle East peace talks were floundering—the body count in the streets grew alarmingly as the region's so-called statesmen haplessly bickered; an Iowa gun-buff had committed fourteen murders as he strode through a shopping mall, shooting people at random—later investigation revealed that he'd held his cache of weapons legally, even though he had numerous gun-related offenses to his name; a British MP had been exposed for loitering in public toilets and behaving indecently with young men—the leader of his party had later gone on air to describe the incident as "a great personal tragedy"—for the MP—not, it seemed, for his wife and kids. Skelton watched and listened in silence as he exercised, his torso now gleaming with sweat, his deltoids and pectorals—already hugely developed—now bulging all the more as blood suffused them, his biceps hardening, standing out like wood, the veins in them as thick as cable.

Later on, after he'd showered and changed, then eaten his usual evening meal of poached eggs, fruit, and rye bread without butter, Skelton called Mary. A man answered the phone whom Skelton didn't recognize—he was young, with a loutish Manchester brogue.

"Yeah?" he said.

"Is Mary there?" Skelton asked.

"Who wants to know?"

"Her ex-husband. Who are you?"

"A friend."

"I see." Skelton paused for a moment. "So . . . is she there?"

"Er . . . I'll just see."

"You don't need to sound so worried," Skelton advised him. "I'm not planning on coming round."

"I'm not worried. Why should I be worried?"

"Just get Mary, I haven't got all night."

When Mary finally came on, she didn't sound particularly enamored.

"What is it?" she asked.

"I see you've got company."

"What's that to you?"

Skelton mused. "Nothing. I just hope Trixie's being treated with the respect she deserves."

"We're not bonking next to her playpen, if that's what you mean."

"Glad to hear it . . . though it's a pity you're *bonking* at all. That dickhead sounds fifteen years younger than you."

"Ray . . . have you just rung up for a fight, or what?"

"No," he said after a second. "No . . . I just wanted to let you know I'll be okay for Sunday."

She gave a bitter chuckle. "You're always okay for Sunday. Why are you bothering ringing me to tell me that?"

"Perhaps I just wanted to hear your voice."

"Well, I don't want to hear yours. So if that's it, I'll go."

"That's it," he said.

The next thing he knew, empty airwaves were buzzing in his ear. She hadn't bothered to say good-bye.

Later on that evening, Skelton walked across town to the ten-screen multiplex, where the latest Hollywood blockbuster was showing. From the very outset, it was a blood-streaked ballet dance. Men were mowed down like watermelons, shot spectacularly to pieces, dying in elaborate patterns of slo-mo carnage. At every instant of course, the hero scowled and frowned through his commando face-paint, and shook off his bumps and bruises, and pumped his trigger finger, and threw in the odd quip, and stamped on heads and punched guys out and slashed and hacked and kicked them to oblivion, and left trails of exploding cars and buildings in his wake. The whole thing was a dazzling display of pyrotechnics, the endlessly expanding fireballs glaring red and orange on the mesmerized audience, the quadrophonic sound system thundering above, beside, below, the gunfire rattling from cinema wall to cinema wall, the very seats vibrating . . .

It might have been impressive, Skelton thought later on as he left the theater, if he hadn't seen it all so often before. The truth was, he felt numb to that kind of thing now. He supposed it would be the same on the world's most death-defying roller coaster. If you tested it twenty times a day, the adrenaline would soon stop pumping. Of course, if you tested it twenty times a day, you would probably increase your chances of at some point being involved in a terrible accident, as well. That was worth thinking about.

By the time he got back to his neighborhood, the girls had started to appear—haggard scarecrow shapes on the dingy street-corners. The dealers were now abroad—dark outlines in graffiti-covered doorways. It was only ten o'clock, but drunks were also in evidence, slumped against the grilled shop-fronts or lying senseless on the litter-strewn sidewalks. There were raucous sounds from the pubs. From one of them—The Mechanics, a scummy little drinking-hole squashed under a railway bridge—a stool came hurtling through the window, curses and screams accompanying it.

Skelton ignored it all. He strolled casually past, and let himself into his flat without a backward glance. No one in this district really knew him, but his look alone was enough to dissuade the opportunist muggers and addicts, while the crumbling block in which he lived hadn't seen a decent burglary in several years because, let's face it, what was in there to pinch? Of course, there were certain other creatures, in more distant parts of the city, who might well give Ray Skelton hassle, and worse; as a copper, he'd never knocked on the custody office door if he could smash his latest prisoner's face into it instead, while all his arrests—even those for minor offenses—had been made with the maximum use of thumb-in-the-eye and knee-in-the-groin, because he'd always believed in leaving the toe-rags no illusion about what breaking the law on his manor meant. Yes, there were many individuals who'd be interested to know where he now lived, though the British police didn't willingly issue such information, not even when it concerned an officer they'd eventually, angrily, dismissed from service.

Once indoors, Skelton made himself a mug of tea, set

his alarm clock for six, and then, as was his habit, turned in early. For once, though, he didn't settle down in bed with a Jack Higgins or Robert Ludlum; he settled down with three glossy black-and-white photographs. He looked at them again, hard, letting his mind wander. There were so many injustices in the world, that just putting a tiny proportion of them right seemed beyond the combined powers of all the human agencies set up to serve the cause of good. There were so many instances within his own personal experience. More than once, he'd dragged the bloated, rot-riddled corpses of OD victims out from foul, flooded storm drains, knowing full well that nobody would ever be blamed let alone prosecuted. One freezing winter, he'd broken into an old lady's home, to find the occupant on the kitchen floor, encased in ice; it was anyone's guess how long she'd been there—only her failure to return library books had finally aroused interest. Then there'd been the turf war, where several teen hoodlums had hauled a rival gangbanger up to the top floor of an eight-story block, thrown him off, and when they'd come out at the bottom and found him still alive, had dragged him back up and done it again. That last incident had occurred in this very neighborhood, Bagley End. Not surprisingly, no one had ever been arrested for it, because nobody round Bagley End ever saw or heard anything.

Skelton went to sleep still staring at the photographs.

The transfer of *The Catholic Echo* from the outskirts of town to a new, more central location was completed within five days. Over the years, it had outgrown its former premises—a purpose-built but relatively small editorial and print center on a suburban industrial-estate—and was now relocating to the third and fourth floors of a palatial Victorian building on the city center's main trunk road, quite close to the railway station and, more importantly, the borough's impressive cathedral. There was much lugging of furniture and machinery from the backs of wagons, then up and down stairs, and into and out of lifts. It was a chaotic and physically draining business, but by the end of the week the bulk of the heavy work had been done, and come Friday afternoon, the journalists and tele-sales girls were back at their desks, and Jervis and his removals-crew were relaxing in the nearest pub.

"I was wondering if I could book some time off?" Skelton asked through the wreaths of cigarette smoke.

He'd just provided Jervis with a pint, so he didn't expect a reply in the negative; he wasn't disappointed.

"Should think so," Jervis said. "Next contract doesn't start till a week Monday. When were you thinking of?"

"Next week."

Jervis shrugged, then took a swig of beer. "Sounds good. You'd only be sitting round the warehouse, otherwise."

The weekend passed for Skelton in its usual desultory fashion. He window-shopped most of Saturday, then in the evening went for drink in a couple of city-center bars, but meeting no one he knew, went to the cinema again to take in another movie. This one wasn't an actionfest, but neither was it especially memorable. Halfway through, Skelton found that his attention had wandered and that he'd lost track of the plot. He wasn't especially concerned; he had other, more important things on his mind.

On Sunday morning, he caught a bus to Hawkley Wood, and knocked on the door of Mary's semidetached two-up-two-down, keen to see his daughter. It was a bright autumn day, and the bubbly four-year-old was coated and bonneted in preparation for his visit. Curly blond ringlets hung down either side of her pretty face;

she had woolly tights on and smart, knitted mittens. She looked about as cute as a little girl could, which was more than could be said for her mother. Mary appeared behind her, looking haggard and hungover. She was still caked in makeup from the night before, and her once lustrous golden hair was a lank, unwashed mass. A half-smoked fag drooped from her mouth, and her dressing gown only partially covered her once voluptuous but now hefty nakedness. Skelton got the impression she was in a hurry to get back upstairs, where somebody—he suspected—was waiting for her.

"We'll be back at five," he said, as Trixie took his hand.

"No later," Mary replied. "It's getting dark early now."

Skelton felt like asking why darkness should pose a problem when Trixie was with her father, but he let it go. He didn't see any point in upsetting the child with yet another row blown up over absolutely nothing.

The first place they went to that morning was St. George's parish church. Skelton had been raised a Catholic, and though he wasn't practicing, he felt that the things it stood for were inherently decent and should therefore be passed on to children if at all possible; they could make their own minds up about it when they were older. Mary didn't care either way—she was nominally Church of England, though the truth was she had no religion at all. She'd hardly ever visited a church, but she didn't mind Skelton taking Trixie to one because she didn't expect anything of consequence to come of it; it certainly hadn't done where *he* was concerned.

As usual, they stood at the back during the Mass, Trixie more fascinated by the various statues and stained-glass windows than the actual service—especially the towering figurine in the porch. It was an armored knight, St. George himself, a red cross on his flowing white tabard, his long steel spear thrust cleanly through a hideous black dragon that writhed beneath his foot. Her father was less easily distracted, though he too tended to struggle to stay interested, depending on how monotonous the priest's delivery might be. On this occasion, there was a distinct droning quality to the overlong sermon, and despite his best efforts, Skelton's attention began to drift. He found himself glancing through the titles of the various church newspapers in the rack next to the font. *The Tablet* was present, *The Universe, The Pictorial* . . . and *The Catholic Echo*. Despite all the mayhem of moving-week, Len Hoggins and his team had still managed to get a paper out. That was professional of them, Skelton thought . . . grudgingly.

He picked up the *Echo* and began to flick through it. Hoggins had always been sufficiently motivated to get things done if it suited his purpose, Skelton recalled, but how he'd ever got to become editor of a religious publication was a total mystery. They'd known each other well at school, but Skelton remembered Hoggins as a political firebrand—a left-wing one, it went without saying—even as early on as his third year at Secondary Modern. Later in life, Skelton heard that Hoggins had got arrested as a hunt saboteur, and several months after that, had been hauled in again for throwing stones at police lines during an anarchist rally. Surely all these things were on the militant atheist's agenda? Or had Hoggins mellowed as he'd grown older? Had he genuinely, perhaps, found God?

Skelton had scanned through the *Echo* numerous times in the past—this wasn't the first occasion he'd been bored at the back of a church—but now he actually read a few articles, just to put himself in the picture. The first one he came across dealt with the inner-city disturbances following the recent death in police custody of a suspected heroin-trafficker. Skelton had heard about the incident—it had been all over the popular press—but as far as he was aware, the prisoner had choked on his own vomit while asleep in a cell. There were no suspicious circumstances, though this was not the line *The Catholic Echo* was taking. In their version, police spokesmen were largely ignored, while the deceased's solicitor, plus his grieving mother and father, were quoted at length, their angry tirades dotted with explosive words and phrases like "killed," "cover-up," and "those responsible." Further down, the column moved away from specifics into the more general area of public disorder and the sociological reasons for it. Again, it was a fairly simplistic attitude.

"In many urban ghettos there is now a siege-mentality, thanks to heavy-handed policing," read one inflammatory extract. In case that left the reader under any illusions:

> Stopping and searching, aggressive questioning, the detaining of youths for no reason other than it is late at night and the youths concerned have a criminal record, is a clear infringement of human rights and a misuse of police powers.

Just to finish off:

> If this sort of behavior continues from the police, then one can't help admitting that inner city communities will feel justified in venting their frustration on the streets.

"They will if this fucking rag has anything to do with it," Skelton said under his breath.

He remembered his own experience of an urban riot. It

was quite a few years ago. He'd been only a young constable at the time, but he and various others who'd been on the TSG training course had been bussed as reinforcements down to Wolverhampton, where it was really kicking off because a drugs raid had emptied a few squats.

Skelton didn't think he'd ever forget the sights that met his eyes that night: Entire rows of shops, and the flats above them, were blazing out of control; rubbish of every description littered the streets—trashed cars, overturned dustbins. The mob itself had been well-organized, its frontline soldiers carefully masked with scarves or ski masks, and heavily armed with bricks, pipes, bottles, Molotov cocktails, and even jars of acid pillaged from the local, now wrecked and burned, comprehensive school. They'd barricaded off certain accessways, and from the gantries above were bombarding anyone who tried to get through; they'd laid rivers of petrol down, threatening to ignite them if the police tried to advance up the central street; they'd formed grenades out of twisted nails, to throw at the dogs and horses; they'd scattered tacks and broken glass to destabilize any attempt to rush them in armored vehicles. And behind it all, in that vast swathe of run-down city which they'd declared their own, crimes of every description were in progress: robberies and beatings, aggravated burglaries, rapes, woundings, arson and vandalism on an unprecedented scale, and of course, wholesale drugs-dealing. For all of the rest of society's navel-gazing, for all the academic reports and public inquiries, and the deluge of guilt-driven sociological discourse, *that* had been the real reason behind the riot—crime, defiance, and rampant do-as-you-will!

Of course, Len Hoggins and his cronies wouldn't know anything about that. On the other hand, perhaps they might . . . and just didn't care. That wouldn't be very public-spirited of them, Skelton thought as he folded the paper and shoved it back into the rack—just as it wasn't very public-spirited to use religion as a wooden horse for politics. Skelton noticed a foul taste in his mouth as he gazed at the *Echo*'s now crumpled front sheet. He wanted to hawk up a wad of phlegm and spit it at the thing. But, of course, he couldn't. He was in a church. You didn't do things like that in churches. Just before he went out, though, when the Mass was over, he glanced again at the cyclopean figure of St. George. The saint's armored foot clamped the dragon's neck with crushing force; the lance transfixed its flesh with merciless precision; from beneath his raised visor, the holy warrior stared down at the impaled beast with a look of vengeful glee. Doing the Lord's work wasn't necessarily all grin and bear it and turn the other cheek.

After Mass, Skelton took Trixie for a McDonald's, then spent the afternoon with her in the nearby park, where she played on the swings and fed the ducks. Long before five o'clock, she was bored and wanted to go home. He'd been separated from his wife and daughter for two years now, and the child was starting to grow away from him. It hadn't helped that he didn't have the money or imagination to treat her the way other divorced parents treated their estranged kids, and this day in particular, cold and damp from midafternoon onward, made things especially hard. For once, though, Skelton wasn't too concerned. He walked his little girl home early, and said good-bye to her with a simple wave from the gate at the end of the path.

His ex-wife looked at him puzzled, wondering why the usual cuddles and kisses were absent, but Skelton said nothing to her. Preoccupied, hands deep in his jacket pockets, he wandered away.

* * *

John Pizer represented the new breed of midrange gangster—the sort who lived at home with his wife and kids, and even had a legitimate job, but about whom the trappings of extra income were always visible: he drove a BMW, his coats were sheepskin, his jewelry exclusively gold and of the chunky variety. To all intents and purposes, his daily life was perfectly normal: he gave his children lifts to and from school, walked his dog daily, sent flowers on anniversaries, and cards and presents at Christmas. But if you looked a little closer, all the signs were there: the words "LOVE" and "HATE" were tattooed on his big, notched fists—they'd faded a little over the years, but they were still visible; his broad bullet-head was always shaven to the bone, his only facial hair a trim tuft of beard and a small, neat mustache; his frame was squat and square, hinting at excessive brawn behind the civilized facade; and if you perhaps got your order in before him at the bar, a glint—just a glint—of ice-cold menace might appear in those steely eyes as he fixed them on the back of your head—in which case, you'd be well advised not to turn round.

As a former cop, Skelton knew John Pizer of old—at least he knew *of* him. He knew, for instance, that Pizer—who'd begun his illustrious career offering protection to hotdog and hamburger vendors outside football stadiums, but who then served time for GBH and later progressed as muscle for larger, wealthier outfits—now dabbled in smack, Ecstasy, and illegal steroids, but mainly ran sections of the red-light district, providing outlets where the hardest of hard-core porn was available and controlling the dozens of good-time girls who waited in the salons and parlors, or if they were drabber, skinnier, more visibly damaged by the life, in the roach-ridden alleyways and backstreets where only the most desperate punters would seek them out. He knew that Pizer had now attained that relatively secure underworld status, where he continued to reap the rewards but rarely got his own hands dirty, instead having numerous fall guys, or in his case *girls*, to take the rap.

"Hey, John!"

Pizer halted. It was just after eight, and he was taking his normal morning walk with his young pit bull, Ivan. He was dressed in a snazzy designer running-suit and flash trainers, but as always, was distinctive for his gold-encased hands and his pink, shaven dome. Even so, he hadn't expected to meet anyone he knew. He was just cutting through a narrow ginnel to the park, when he heard the voice. He turned . . . a tall, heavily built man, wearing jeans and a denim jacket, with a shock of black hair and dense black sideburns, was approaching.

"Who are you?" Pizer asked.

Beside him, Ivan started to growl.

Skelton smiled. "Got a message for you."

"Yeah?"

"From God."

Pizer looked puzzled. "Uh?"

Skelton jerked his right arm forward, the monkey wrench shooting out from his denim sleeve, landing neatly in his right palm. "But this white-trash ornament gets it first."

And without another word, he raised the heavy tool, and smashed it down on the pit bull's head. There was sickening wet crack, and immediately the dog collapsed in a yowling heap, going rapidly into violent convulsions. Pizer stared at the dying animal with disbelief . . . then turned on Skelton in a screaming rage.

"YOU FUCKING BASTARD!"

Eyes starting from his head, he thrust a hand under his tracksuit top, and yanked out the Browning 9-mil he always carried for protection—but Skelton was prepared, lashing down again with the wrench, sweeping the gun across the alley. Pizer gasped as his fingers on that hand broke, but he hadn't earned his early criminal corn with a meek and retiring nature, and before his assailant could strike another blow, the gangster lowered his head buffalo-style, and charged. He caught Skelton in the belly and drove him into a tottering retreat. The ex-cop felt his balance give, and the next thing he knew, he was toppling over. The alley wall came hard against his back. It knocked the wind from him—and the monkey wrench from his grasp.

Pizer was now butting and clawing, hacking in punches. *"YOU'RE DEAD . . . FUCKING DEAD!"*

Skelton knew he'd lost the initiative. Even with his superior strength and size, the gangster was a ton weight and pinned him down efficiently. Only by forcing his forearm into Pizer's throat and pushing as hard as he could with it, could Skelton finally lever the hoodlum up into a position where he could slam home a punch. His aim was true, and even at short range, his knuckles connected firmly to Pizer's mouth, drawing out globs of blood and broken teeth. Stunned by the pain, the gangster loosed his grip, and the ex-cop was able to thrust him away with his knees.

For a split-second, they separated—panting like racehorses, rising painfully to their feet. Then Pizer launched himself forward, head lowered again, barreling into Skelton's midriff. This time the ex-cop was ready, and with both fists clenched together in a bone mallet, bludgeoned Pizer on the back of the neck. The hoodlum kept his feet but wheeled drunkenly away. Skelton followed and kicked him in the belly, then in the face—his steel-toe-capped boots making maximum impact. Now it was Pizer who staggered into the wall, virtually cross-eyed. His guard had dropped, and Skelton caught him with a massive right hook, then with a left. There was a snap of jawbone, and blood spurted over the brickwork.

"How do you like it?" Skelton gasped, as the gangster fell senseless at his feet. "Not much fun when *you're* getting the pimpstick, is it!"

The steel-capped boots flashed in repeatedly, dealing crunching blows to body, limbs, and head—especially head. Again and again, Pizer's skull rebounded from the wall. When Skelton had finished kicking, he started stomping—one foot at a time, then both feet together, all of his considerable weight behind them.

Of course, it couldn't go on indefinitely. Once a minute or so had passed, reality came swimming back. All at once, the ex-cop felt the chill of the autumn morning, heard the bustling traffic in the next street . . . he looked wildly round for witnesses. There was no sign of anybody at either end of the alleyway; the windows above, belonging mainly to offices, were still blank and in darkness. Mopping the sweat from his brow, Skelton scooped up the monkey wrench and revolver, and stuffed them out of sight under his jacket. He was about to set off walking when he spied the dog. It was still alive . . . barely, tongue lolling out, body lying flat . . . almost deflated, its chest rising and falling in panicky rhythm. Skelton gazed down at it, for a moment—feeling his first pang of regret. From mercy rather than cruelty, he lifted the wrench and hit the animal a second time. This one did the job.

Skelton felt his bruises only later on, when several hours had passed and the adrenaline had finished coursing through his body. Not that he could afford to sit around and recover.

The first thing he did when he got back to his flat was strip naked, then put on a pair of work gloves and wrap every item of clothing he'd worn in plastic bin-liners, including his old boots. After this, he took a long, very hot bath, washing his hair and scrubbing his fingernails. Once he'd dressed again—this time in smart casuals—he put his gloves back on, picked up the bundles of clothes and the wrench, and set off on foot. He walked for several miles, wending his way through the ginnels and backstreets, every so often tossing a package into a skip or dumpster. The wrench, he deposited in the canal. Only when he'd done this did he return home and assess the situation. As far as he knew, there wasn't a print left which even the best SOCO team would be able to read. The DNA, of course, was another matter—Skelton knew his DNA would be all over the crime scene: blood, saliva, fragments of skin, hair, earwax. Theoretically though, it didn't matter. There were no samples of his DNA in the databank, as he'd left the police long before it had been required of every officer to provide one. At the end of the day, *none* of it mattered—so long as his precautions earned him sufficient time to do the things he had to do.

It was early evening when he finally got round to plastering his cuts and rubbing antiseptic ointment into his grazes. Then and only then did he settle down in front of the TV and relax—and slowly tear to strips the photograph of the congenitally deformed prostitutes.

Phil McGregor was Lib-Dem councillor for the city's large Wilberton ward, and though he had ambitions to go much higher, for the moment he was content. Regularly quoted in the local press, and easily recognizable in the district for his green three-piece suits and round-lensed John Lennon specs, he was a popular and respected man who was fully prepared, for a short time at least, to enjoy his little corner of empire.

But despite his being outspoken on social issues and a

keen defender of the environment, there were several less savory aspects to Phil McGregor's character: for example, he was living with a woman whose marriage had fallen apart because of the affair the councillor had conducted with her, while in his mid and late teens he'd been busted twice for possessing cannabis and three times for having LSD, instances his political opponents would never let him forget, though in the manner of so many astute and unscrupulous campaigners, he'd managed to turn these minus-points to his advantage. The fact that he had "a partner" rather than a wife was something he made an issue of—it fitted in neatly with the hip, libertarian trends of Blair's Britain; while his colorful past eminently suited the self-image he garnered of intellectual rebelliousness—in the mid-eighties he'd been prominent in the local students' union, vociferously opposing everything from American cruise missiles to imports of South African fruit, and more recently, had tried to take the government of Great Britain to court over its bombing raids on Iraq, a ploy which had failed miserably but which had raised his public profile no end. Of course, by then he'd done away with his long hair and straggling beard, his stinky old Afghan coat and flared jeans, to cultivate the slicker shirt-and-tie image he'd eventually use as his springboard into local government.

In fact, Phil McGregor seemed to have done impressively well out of his days as an activist. With zero qualifications—either work-based or educational (*he failed all his exams*), a criminal record, a habit of shouting people down in arguments, and to top it all, bad breath, you'd have expected to find him, by his fortieth birthday, a miserable recluse, out of work and permanently stuck in low-rent accommodation, rather than a prospective MP whose opinion was always sought and whose presence was required at all the most fashionable parties.

At least . . . this was Ray Skelton's view, as he waited in the dark beyond the lecture-hall door. It was nearly nine o'clock and the debate was drawing to a close. McGregor was in there somewhere, on a panel with several other VIPs, discussing the whys and wherefores of a possible Lib-Lab pact. When it was all over, the students would stream out and invade the local pubs. They'd try to take some of the celebs with them, and would probably succeed with McGregor as no doubt it would be suggested they'd treat him to "a couple of drinks." Occasionally with Phil McGregor, his true persona shone through—he earned a lot more money than all of those students put together, but he was never backward in coming forward if a bun-fight was on offer.

As expected, the entire crowd came out together, so Skelton had to withdraw into the shadows and bide his time. He followed them across campus at a distance, until they reached The Earl Buchanan pub, where they went inside. Again Skelton hung back, securing himself a spot under the elm trees in the park across the road. It was two hours later when McGregor finally reemerged. He'd clearly been drinking, though he wasn't quite drunk, sauntering along, hands in pockets, rather than going for his car. By sheer fortune, the councillor chose to take a short cut across the park. It was in its deepest, most unlit section where he met Skelton. No sooner had he spotted the hulking shape beside the path, than what felt like a cannonball exploded in his face, and the world became a dizzy, downward spiral of noise, pain, and confusion. . . .

When McGregor finally came round, his numb, sticky cheek rested on cold stone. He groaned, shifted position . . . his left temple began to throb, loose teeth waggled beneath his probing tongue. Wearily, still half dazed, he levered himself up into a sitting position. The concrete floor was black with oil and soot, and rolled away into shadow on all sides. By the still, dank air, the councillor had the impression he was indoors somewhere—though in a cavernous place, a warehouse or vehicle depot, though by the looks and feel of it, a derelict one. Slowly, his eyes attuned to the dimness. He thought he could make out vague shapes close by—scraps of rubbish littered across the floor, waste paper, dead leaves.

Far above, there was a broken skylight, naked stars visible beyond it. Only the faintest illumination spilled down from this, but a moment later even that was blotted out as a tall, broad figure came and stood in front of it. McGregor swallowed hard . . . a bolt of ice went through him. He'd recently put his name to a newspaper campaign to rid the city's nightclubs of their aggressive, bullying doormen, and now assumed this incident was a response to that, which was unnerving to say the least. Though he thought he knew how these things worked, he couldn't be exactly sure. They'd already clobbered him, so most likely he'd now get the warning, though he couldn't rule out another kicking—just for good measure. Mind you, the more cuts and bruises he walked away with, possibly the better: *Crusading councillor defies gangsters . . . ; 'They didn't scare me,' says McGregor . . . ; Mob strike out, but MP-in-waiting shrugs it off . . .*

"How're things in South Africa, Phil?" Skelton asked in a quiet voice.

"Eh?" McGregor was baffled; no threats, no intimidation? "What . . . what do you mean, South Africa?"

"How are things in South Africa? Simple enough question."

"Okay . . . I guess."

Skelton was amused by that. "Okay? You call a murder epidemic okay? You call law and disorder on a terrifying scale okay?"

"All right . . . it's not okay," McGregor said. "Jesus . . . what is this?"

"FUCKING RIGHT IT'S NOT OKAY!" Skelton shouted, the words thundering in the vast, empty building. A moment passed, the echoes ringing and ringing as they died away. He lowered his voice again. "So much for your antiapartheid dream, eh?"

"W— what?" McGregor's voice was tremulous.

"It was you, wasn't it," Skelton said, "who organized the big student party in the town center on the day Nelson Mandela got released?"

"Well yeah, but . . . I mean, things are better over there now than they were."

"And how the fucking hell would you know?" Skelton wondered. "You ever been to Africa?"

McGregor tried to swallow again, but his mouth had gone dry. "N— no."

"Didn't think so," Skelton sneered. "But you've still got a lot of opinions on it . . . at least, you always used to have."

"Look, just tell me . . . what's this about?"

"Led any more demos recently, Phil? Any more sit-ins?"

"W— why would I?"

"Oh, sorry." Skelton gave an ironic chuckle. "There are no calls to ban fruit exports from *black* African tyrannies, are there! No demands to cease trade with genocidal nutcases who happen to be the same color as the poor sods they torture and starve and terrorize. . . ."

"Look, I don't know what you're on about—"

"Liar! You do! You *fucking* do!" Skelton paused for a moment . . . the councillor, now clearly visible in the dim starlight, was already a crumpled, cowering wreck; it was almost pathetic. "Any idea what would happen if you tried to organize a demo somewhere like Nigeria, Phil? Zimbabwe? Mozambique?"

"No . . ."

"No?"

"I don't know that much about it," the councillor protested.

"That never stopped you in the past," Skelton retorted.

"Look, I've always opposed abuses of human rights—"

"No you haven't! Only where it was fashionable, only where it made you look good in front of your friends—and by doing that, you've helped protect some of the worst criminals modern politics has ever produced."

McGregor shook his head, bewildered. "It's not true—"

"Put this on," said Skelton, pushing something forward.

Whatever the object was, it first bounced like a football—though it was much larger—then it rolled lazily across the narrow space between them.

"What is it?" said McGregor, puzzled even as he caught hold of the thing.

It was heavy, coarse—made from thick, damp rubber. There was an odd chemical smell about it.

"Put it on!" Skelton ordered.

Then it struck McGregor what he was holding—a car tire.

"Oh God!" he screamed. *"No . . . please!"*

Skelton produced the Browning. Starlight glinted on its shiny chrome finish. He pointed it at McGregor's legs. "Put it on or I'll kneecap you . . . then put it on you myself!"

Shivering violently, staring at the gun in mute terror, the councillor hurriedly lifted the tire and looped it over his head. Instantly, cold fluid slopped over him. The smell—now he recognized it.

"Christ in a cartoon!" he gibbered. *"This thing's full of petrol. . . ."*

"'Course it is," Skelton replied. "You think I'm playing at this?"

As if in answer to his own question, he struck a match. The flickering finger of flame reflected in McGregor's now goggling eyes.

"Wait!" the councillor said, his voice a strangled whimper. "Just wait a minute! What . . . what do you think you're gaining by this?"

"Gaining?"

McGregor began to cry, tears streaming down his cheeks. "What kind of justice do you think you're striking a blow for?"

Skelton smiled in the half dark, a jack-o'-lantern vision to his victim. "You're perceptive, I'll give you that."

"Go on then . . . tell me!"

"Your kind of justice, Phil," Skelton replied. "*Your* kind."

And then, with a shrug and a sniff, he threw the match. . . .

Later that week, after Skelton had torn up the picture of the black child being trampled to death in Rwanda, he went over to St. George's to be confessed.

The church was empty and in gray half darkness when he entered. Opaque shadows hung like curtains between the pillars. There was a dank chill in the air. Rain fell in drenching sheets against the outer walls and stained-glass windows, hissing aloud in the high airy vaults of the old and venerable building. Only the altar was illuminated, four meager candles throwing twinkling light on the white cloths and silver chalice.

Skelton strode forward, genuflected once, then entered the confessional booth and knelt. For several moments, he heard nothing. It was even darker in there than outside in the church, but the air was rich with the scent of wax and wood-polish. He sensed rather than saw the elegant oaken panels around him, could imagine the ivory crucifix hanging just to his right.

"Are you ready, my child?" asked a deep and stately but vaguely muffled voice.

Directly in front of Skelton, a sheet of semitransparent gauze was tacked over a square aperture. Beyond it, the dark outline of a head was visible. Pale light set it in broad silhouette.

"Father," said the ex-cop, "I just wondered . . . I just wondered if it's possible to be God's strong right hand?"

There was a brief, puzzled silence, then: "God's strong right hand?"

"His fist . . . so to speak."

The priest paused again. "I'm afraid I don't understand."

"Here on earth," Skelton tried to explain. "Father . . . we all have a mission in life. I firmly believe that. But is it possible that some of us might only come to discover that mission much later on?"

"My son . . . this is a confessional. I'll be happy to debate these issues with you at some other time, but for the moment—"

"This is a confession!" Skelton blurted. "Of a sort. I thought that you, a priest, would understand what I'm saying."

"I am trying, my son . . ."

"You see, Father, there is certain breed of creatures among us, who are guilty by default!"

The priest's voice remained calm and resonant, though by his tone he was now humoring the supplicant, gently playing along as if he'd sensed trauma and was trying to salve it. "Guilty of what exactly?"

"Crimes," Skelton said. "Against the rest of society. But the sort of crimes that go undetected."

"If they truly *are* crimes, they won't go undetected by God."

"That's precisely my point." Skelton struggled to control his excitement. "The Lord works in mysterious ways, does he not, Father?"

"My son . . . I fear I'm missing something here."

"Then answer me this . . . is it possible that those of us who deserve it, will be punished here on earth?"

"That's not my understanding of doctrine," the priest replied slowly. "If you mean does God intervene in our daily affairs in order to teach us lessons . . . then, no."

"No?" Skelton whispered. This couldn't be correct. He *knew* it couldn't.

"We will only be judged in the afterlife," the priest added. "That is God's teaching. Until then, we have free will."

The ex-cop gritted his teeth, had to bite back rising anger. "How can you say that, Father? For *my* sins, I lost everything . . . my job, my home, my family. How can you say such a thing?"

The priest paused to consider. "I think I'm beginning to understand you now . . . you're trying to make sense of the difficulties life has thrown at you?"

"Not quite . . . it's more that I'm trying to make sense of the problem-free lives enjoyed by others."

"Well . . . we don't know that's the case for certain, do we." The priest's tone was now reproving. "Everyone suffers hardship, my son."

"Some more than others," Skelton replied.

"As I say . . . we don't *know* that, do we."

Skelton knelt there for a moment, helpless. This was not what he'd wanted to hear, though perhaps in his heart of hearts he'd expected it. He hung his head.

"Of course," the cleric reflected, "we're all entitled to our opinion."

Skelton glanced up again. Oddly, subtly almost, the priest's voice had altered. As before, it was deep, educated—yet now there was a new note in it; a taunt, a crafty insinuation. Beyond the sheet of gauze, the dark outline of the head hadn't moved, but the supplicant could imagine its eyes fixed upon him. Skelton felt a brief chill of unease. Fleetingly, he wondered when *official* confession times were and if he'd perhaps wandered in during an hour when the booths were supposed to be unmanned. Aside from this tiny room, the rest of the church was steeped in deadening silence. If this wasn't an official confession time, then who exactly was he speaking to?

"Our opinion?" Skelton whispered, wondering why his hair was suddenly prickling.

"As I say . . . free will," the stentorian voice replied. "We can think and believe what we like . . . none of us knows anything for sure."

"But the rules of faith—"

"Can be interpreted differently from one person to another." The voice paused for a moment, to let its words sink in. "We each of us must find our own way."

"We each of us have our mission," Skelton said again, though now it was a statement rather than a question, and aware of this, the voice made no answer. Abruptly, there was silence. Not even a breath stirred from the shape beyond the portal. It simply waited.

Eventually, Skelton joined his hands. "Forgive me, Father, for I have sinned . . ."

" 'O generation of vipers, who hath warned you of the wrath to come!' "

Hoggins glanced up from his desk, surprised by the

voice. The last person he expected to see was his onetime schoolmate, Ray Skelton, the visitor's chiseled face waxy pale between his big black sideburns, his huge frame clad shoulder to foot in shiny-black motorbike leathers.

The editor sat back in his chair, not sure whether to smile or frown. As far as he was aware, no one had made an appointment to come in and see him today, least of all this curious character. "I'm sorry . . . what?" he finally said.

Skelton closed the door behind him, shutting out the trilling phones and chattering voices of the newsroom. The small office was suddenly snug and quiet. It still smelled of fresh paint and new carpets.

"Matthew three . . . verse seven," Skelton explained. "I thought you, the editor of a Catholic newspaper, would have recognized that."

Hoggins gave a puzzled, vaguely amused shrug. "I can't repeat the gospels parrot-fashion."

"Neither can I," the ex-cop replied, hands behind his back. . . . Hoggins noticed, with a jolt, that Skelton was leaning against the door, making sure it couldn't be opened from the other side. "I only remember that little gem from when I was twelve, from when that psychotic old hag of an RE teacher quoted it repeatedly at me as she hauled me by the hair to the headmaster's office."

Hoggins tried to mask his growing concern. He'd never seen a face as white as Skelton's now was—at least, not on a living man. The deathly pallor brought out the intruder's eyes like dark jewels.

"Miss . . . er, Miss Burns, wasn't it?"

Skelton nodded. "That's right. Bad-tempered bitch with a hearing aid . . . and the thing never bloody worked. Always had to scream everything, so she could hear herself."

"I remember that." Hoggins struggled to keep the

tremor from his voice. As cautiously as he was able, he slid a hand across his desk to the intercom button. "What was it you'd drawn on the blackboard while she was out?"

"I hadn't drawn anything," Skelton said. "Somebody else had. It was a cunt . . . an open cunt."

"Oh, yeah." Hoggins winced as he remembered.

"Sorry, is that sort of language inappropriate in here?"

"Well . . . it's a bit strong."

Skelton considered. "We're both red-blooded fellas, though. We can take it."

"Yeah."

"That's what you told me that day . . . remember?"

Blankly, Hoggins shook his head.

" 'Cheer up . . . you can take it!' " Skelton said. "That was after I'd got six on the arse. I mean, it wasn't as if I wasn't used to it . . . what with my old man off his head on ale all the time and walloping me like there was no tomorrow. But it still seemed unfair. 'You can take it', eh?"

Hoggins tried to make light of it. "Kids are so sympathetic."

Skelton agreed. "Still, I learned something that day . . . *GET AWAY FROM THAT FUCKING BUTTON, LEN!*"

Terrified, Hoggins snatched his hand back. He then blanched at the sight of the heavy revolver the intruder had suddenly pulled on him. The journalist wanted to duck, to dodge, to run for his life—but he didn't dare; in fact he went rigid.

"Jesus, Ray . . . what the . . . what the fuck's going on?"

With slow deliberation, Skelton trained the weapon on Hoggins's forehead. "I learned," he said, "I learned that it isn't so much the justice of the act . . . as the example. Miss Burns didn't drag me out of class that day because I'd been bad. It was because *someone* had been bad . . .

and because though she didn't know who, she didn't like me, so *I'd* do. The message would be lost on no one, you see—not even the person who'd really done it—I mean, he wouldn't own up, but he certainly wouldn't do it again. *Eh, Len!*"

Hoggins had raised his hands, but he could only shake his head, perplexed. His entire world seemed to have shrunk to that little black hole in the revolver's muzzle. "You're . . . you're telling me all this is about *that!* Jesus Christ, Ray . . ."

"You're very quick to take the Lord's name in vain, Len. That's twice now."

"Look . . . we were kids!"

"But you weren't a kid during the Kosovo crisis, were you?"

"What?" Hoggins couldn't be sure what he'd just heard. The eyes of the man accosting him now gleamed with fanaticism.

Skelton felt under his jacket and drew out the one remaining photo of the three he'd stolen. He tossed it onto the editor's desk. Hoggins glanced down at it with fascination. It portrayed a gruesome scene from the most recent Balkan war—a mutilated man hung in tatters above the heads of sobbing children.

"While I was working here, I found this," Skelton explained.

Hoggins was none the wiser. He shook his head desperately. "I remember it. So? Look . . . a freelance tried to sell it to us. It should've been returned to him."

Skelton couldn't resist smiling at that. "I just knew you didn't use it in the paper."

"'Course we didn't!" Hoggins blurted. "We'd have been hauled over the coals for publishing a picture like that."

"And of course, it would've increased public sympathy with the bombing campaign."

Again, the journalist shook his head. "What?"

"Len . . . I don't recall exactly, but I have no doubt at all that you and your newspaper took an antiwar stance during that crisis."

"You're not making sense," Hoggins blathered. "We're a religious newspaper. We're not likely to promote war, are we!"

"Do you promote torture and mass murder?"

"Of course not."

Skelton jabbed a finger down at the photograph. "Then why withhold this? Why . . . when it made it crystal clear what those Serb police units were up to, and why military force was needed to stop them! Why bombs *had* to be dropped! Why, for once, 'making love not war' was a load of irrelevant bollocks!"

"You're going to kill me for this?" Hoggins stammered. "Politics?"

Skelton shook his head. "No, Len . . . I'm going to kill you for the same reason I killed John Pizer and Phil McGregor."

The journalist tried to reply but couldn't; even in the dire peril of his situation, those two names sank slowly in.

"For the same reason Miss Burns had me caned that day when I was twelve," Skelton added. "To make a good and lasting example."

"*You* killed Councillor McGregor?" Hoggins whispered, the horror of that incident flooding back to him. His face twisted with revulsion.

"Interesting," said Skelton. "When it really comes to the crunch, you're less concerned about the criminal."

"You . . . you *necklaced* a man?"

"Doesn't seem so righteous when it's one of your own, does it."

"One . . . of my own?" Hoggins stuttered. "He was . . . never one of my own."

Skelton considered that for a moment, then shrugged. "Possibly true. He was just a poser. You're an actual *doer* . . . which makes it even more appropriate in your case."

The journalist now stared at the intruder with something like pity. "You've really lost it, pal. You've really—"

"Enough talking!" Skelton barked. "Get over here!"

Hoggins remained firmly in his seat. "Why?"

"We're going into the newsroom."

"Why?" the journalist asked again, but now Skelton crossed the room and dragged him roughly to his feet, jamming the gun into his ribs.

"Like I say—to set an example."

"Look," Hoggins jabbered as he was propelled out through the door and into the main office, "this is all wrong . . . who the hell made you judge, jury, and executioner?"

As the two struggling figures appeared, a stunned silence spread slowly through the ranks of reporters, subs, and tele-sales girls. People rose unsteadily to their feet, phones were dropped, fingers tapping out tattoos on keyboards continued to tap, but lost all rhythm and pattern. From the nearest desk, where the secretaries worked, there was a stifled scream. . . .

Skelton held his ground until sure he had the full attention of the startled office, all the while holding Hoggins in front of him like a shield. With careful accuracy, he then fitted the muzzle of the revolver into the nape of the newspaper boss's neck. Hoggins tried to flinch away, but his captor held him in a firm grip.

"This is one way the Serbs liked to do it, I understand," Skelton whispered. "It's an old KGB method."

"You fucking madman!" Hoggins whimpered.

"Just concentrate on saying your prayers, Len, 'cause you *need* to!"

And at that precise moment, Len Hoggins found his courage. The desperation of fight or flight finally took him over, and with as much force as he could muster, he lunged his elbow back, catching Skelton hard in the midriff. The ex-cop's flat, firm belly didn't yield, but air hissed through his clenched teeth, and for a second he was off balance, and then all hell let loose . . .

People ran and shouted; a sturdy young man standing close by, ventured bravely forward; a secretary grabbed up a phone and began to shriek into it . . . and Skelton pumped the trigger as hard as he could, two or three times.

And it made no difference.

The gun didn't fire.

Skelton had handled firearms many times during his police service, but he had never been permitted to carry one on duty, and had never really been trained to use one. He'd thought the safety was off, but the truth was that he hadn't known for certain. As panic now erupted all around him, the deadly weapon was suddenly little more than a lump of steel in his hand. Though even lumps of steel have their uses.

"The Devil protects his own, eh!" Skelton snarled, yanking Hoggins back by the collar, making sure that he didn't escape. "Not on my shift!"

And with savage, over-arm swipes, he began clubbing the journalist on the cranium. Not once, but repeatedly, each blow ripping flesh and hair asunder, showing bloodied yellow bone beneath.

Something then hit Skelton in the face—a thrown

diary—and though he barely felt it, it woke him up to the growing danger of his predicament. Office staff were now bustling on all sides of him, some dashing for the doors, others yammering frantically into phones. With a deafening electronic *whoop whoop whoop* a stray hand hit the fire alarm. And then the sturdy young man lurched forward and tried to grapple with Skelton. The ex-cop turned to face him, stopping only to shove away the sagging, lifeless shape of Len Hoggins. The young man was an editorial assistant of some sort, as his shirt and tie attested—he was burly, perhaps he played rugby or went climbing at the weekends, but he was fresh-faced and young, only twenty at the most, and he'd never encountered anyone whose sole profession was, or at least had become, total violence.

Skelton pounded the youngster, body and head, first with the Browning, then with his free fist. It was a toss-up which of these wrought the most havoc, but the final punch, delivered with neck-breaking force into the underside of the young guy's jaw, lifted him bodily from his feet and launched him over a row of computer terminals like a thing made of rags and cloth. There were more screams and shouts, VDU's hit the carpet in explosions of glass and sparks, a desk fell . . . and now, from some distant part of the city, even over the repeating screech of the fire alarm, Skelton could hear the approaching wail of police sirens.

Knowing the game was up, at least for the moment, he turned and fled, barging out through a fire exit and hurrying down a spiraling flight of concrete steps. Sweat broke on his brow as he ran, and it was chaotic seconds before he even thought to thrust the revolver out of sight beneath his jacket. A moment later, he landed breathless on the ground floor, and quickly pushed his way through the facing door, only to find himself in the gigantic building's ornate lobby—which was now thronging with confused people who had spilled out from the various offices and lifts. Among them, Skelton spotted several breathless members of staff from the *Echo,* all now talking animatedly with a clutch of receptionists and security guards, gesticulating wildly toward the grand staircase. Even as Skelton watched, a police constable came hurrying in through the entrance doors, threading his way into the frightened crowd. The *Echo* staff fought their way toward him. Skelton still considered sidling past, hoping to lose himself in the pandemonium, but now spinning blue lights were visible in the street outside. More police figures could be seen, leaping from cars and vans.

Skelton turned sharply and scrambled back up the fire stair. The building was likely to be a rabbit warren—there should be any number of possible exits; he only had to locate one of them. A moment later, he found himself in a first-floor corridor, with dozens of office doors leading off it, but all now open and silent. The alarm had driven everybody out, which Skelton realized was a fortunate accident. Trying not to run, so as not to attract the attention of anyone who might be left, he moved quickly along the passage, rounded a corner, and set off up another flight of stairs. He was traveling in a vaguely eastern direction, he reasoned—this should take him to the rear of the building, where there ought to be additional fire escapes. As he made his way, he passed one video camera after another. His image would be indelibly printed on the celluloid innards of each and every one, though detection had perhaps been inevitable from the outset. He sought only to escape now in order to replan and reexecute the final phase of his scheme. Hoggins wasn't yet dead; of that, Skelton was certain—and the ex-cop *had* to put that right before he did anything else. He couldn't, in fact he *wouldn't,* leave that sole remaining photograph on his bedside cabinet any longer. He didn't think he could bear to keep looking at it—the hacked, shredded face, the hanging entrails, the splintered lengths of bone . . .

"Excuse me, sir . . . can I have a word?"

Skelton stopped in his tracks and turned. A security guard had stepped out from an office behind him, and though having gone pale because he'd unexpectedly found the man he was looking for, was now warily approaching. Skelton appraised the guard quickly—he was broad of chest and shoulder, but heavily overweight and with a full head of snow-white hair. The bar of colored braids on the chest pocket of his smart blue tunic indicated that he was ex-military, possibly a war veteran. That was a shame.

Skelton mopped the sweat from his flustered brow. "What can I do for you?"

"I . . . er, I . . ."

The security guard came as close as he could, then made a frenzied grab. Skelton was ready, however, slamming two massive punches into the older guy's guts, then locking an arm around his head and throwing him across the passage—or at least *trying* to. Gasping with pain, the ex-soldier clung on to Skelton as hard as he could, wrapping his arms around the intruder's waist.

"Stupid old bastard!" Skelton spat. "Don't make me hurt you!" The security guard grunted something under his breath, his fat old face already blotched purple with burst blood vessels. They wrestled back and forth frantically, but Skelton now felt an overwhelming sense of rage. "Stupid *motherfuck—*" he growled, barreling across the passage and ramming the guy's head into the wall . . . once, twice, three times. Plaster cracked with the force, blood smeared over it. *"YOU WEREN'T ON THE*

FUCKING LIST, IDIOT!" he screamed. *"NOW LOOK AT YOU!"*

It was several impacts more before Skelton calmed down sufficiently to drop the broken body and continue running. Now it was panic-stricken flight again, passage after passage, stairway after stairway. He fancied he could hear shouts inside the building—was that a chopper *whirring* somewhere above? Skelton knew from his own experience that, these days, too many unarmed police officers were getting gunned down in UK cities; armed units were always now ready and available to be scrambled. Let a single firearm appear, and the heavy mob was there in next to no time.

Even as Skelton considered this, he blundered out onto a metal fire escape that dropped thirty feet into the building's main loading bay; already, two police cars were visible there, a bunch of uniformed officers standing uncertainly around them. At the far end of the bay, meanwhile, the security barrier had lifted and a large white van was just in the process of swinging under it, almost certainly an ARV. While Skelton stopped and stared at it, the cops below spotted him, and immediately started to advance up the steps. Hurriedly, he drew the revolver and pointed it at them . . . it halted them in their tracks.

"Back off!" he warned. "Back off . . . I'll blow your fucking brains out."

They watched him warily until he retreated from sight, then a burst of shouting filled the loading bay, boots hammered the steel treads. "It's that nutcase Skelly," Skelton thought he heard someone say, "used to be job. Bladdered every fucker he got his hands on!"

This time, the shit had really hit the fan. As he hared back through the building, a dread sense of defeat was growing on him. Not only had they spotted and trapped him, but they'd *identified* him as well. There'd be nowhere to run after this, or hide—even if he somehow broke out of the cordon they'd no doubt thrown around the entire building. He'd be pictured on TV, in newspapers—he'd be hunted down. Only one option remained, it seemed—*one!*

He halted at an intersection of corridors. Sweat drenched the inside of his leathers, the breath rasped in his chest. Fit as he was, Skelton wasn't used to this type of dashing back and forth, this relentless charging up and down flights of stairs. But if he could somehow find his way back to the *Echo*'s offices, he might be able to finish off what he'd come here to do. He knew that he hadn't killed Hoggins, but he'd certainly knocked him cold—which meant the newspaper man might still be lying there. It was highly unlikely any of the dweebs on his staff would have risked their skins trying to save him.

With new enthusiasm, Skelton took the first flight of stairs down to the fourth floor. As with the others, it was now deserted; coats, bits of paper, the odd pen littered the corridors, indicating the company personnel's indecent speed of departure. The ex-cop made his way through the reception area and into the newsroom. The wreckage of his previous visit was everywhere: strewn paperwork, overturned desks, shattered VDUs . . . and Len Hoggins, still at the far end of the office, where Skelton had left him.

The ex-cop smiled with satisfaction.

The journalist was no longer prone on the floor, but had somehow managed to drag himself up into a chair, where he now slumped helplessly, a beaten king in the ruins of his realm. He looked as if he'd been hauled through a mangler. His normally pristine attire was crumpled and torn and stained all over with blood, his face ashen gray, the hair above it an unkempt mass of gory locks. The only expression the guy wore was one of agonized incomprehension; he didn't seem even vaguely aware of what had happened to him. His wounded head nodded absently, his left hand shivered like a leaf. As Skelton approached, he noticed that Hoggins's shoulders had locked in see-saw posture and that his right arm hung at a crazy angle, twisted in spastic paralysis. Finishing the hypocritical bastard off now might actually be doing him a favor, the ex-cop realized, which wasn't part of the plan at all. Still . . .

As he approached through the devastated office, he turned the gun over and over in his hands, puzzling at its refusal to function. As he'd originally surmised, it was a Browning, a modern and sophisticated model, but infamously simple to use. He examined it more closely; this time, the safety was clearly off, yet despite all the pressure he exerted, the trigger refused to give. It was either jammed or broken, he decided. He turned the gun again, pressed the trigger harder, tried to release the magazine to unload and reload . . .

And was totally unprepared for the thunderous detonation which suddenly shattered one of the windows behind him.

Skelton reacted automatically, hurling himself to the floor and rolling behind the wreckage of a toppled desk. Once there, several moments of breathing hard and breaking out in fresh sweat passed before he dared glance up again. The first thing he saw was the gun—he'd dropped it in his fright, but it lay only five or six feet away. The second thing was Hoggins, still slouched in the chair at the far end of the room—a messed-up, lifeless mannequin, a mockery of the slick young hotshot he'd once been. If all else failed, that alone was a result . . . but all else hadn't failed yet. Skelton glanced back toward the window; only a few shards of glass remained in its frame, but beyond it, on the far side of the street, other buildings loomed, many of their windows now wide open.

Ideal sniper-positions, the ex-cop realized. That had been close.

The time for carelessness was over.

He proceeded on his elbows and knees, snaking his way toward the gun. It was hardly very dignified—but then neither was it very easy; he had gone only two or three feet before exhaustion overcame him. Bewildered, Skelton halted for a rest, hanging his head—and watched in wonderment as a strand of bloody saliva unspooled from his mouth.

Another moment passed before Skelton sensed the icy chill spreading slowly through his insides. He responded quickly to that, trying to leap up, trying to pat himself down for damage, but blinding agony lanced him—clean through, promptly curling him into a knot and throwing him down on the carpet, the force of which blow only added to his torture. Skelton contorted where he lay, cringing at a flaring pain the like of which he had never imagined. It seemed to grow and grow; it was white, searing, it ran through him like a spear but burned in his chest with the corrosive power of acid. With a wheezing gasp, he tried to suck new air into his lungs, but for some reason it wasn't happening. Glutinous gore bubbled in his mouth, gurgled in his throat, perhaps blocked up all his passages, but even if that wasn't the case, his lungs weren't resisting the suffocation, weren't inflating or deflating or even responding in any way at all—they seemed to have shriveled inside him.

Skelton tried to suppress the resulting panic, to batten down the unrelenting pain. There was still time—time to finish his mission, time to defy those bastards out there, who admittedly were better shots than he'd ever considered possible, but who as always were too late and too half-assed in their efforts to enforce the law.

With a blood-thick snigger, he dragged himself out to full-length, then extended his right arm toward the gun. "Jush one," he blathered, "one . . ."

It would take only one shot. Skelton was no expert, but he was only ten or so yards from his target, and if he could just squeeze off one. With a grunting, coughing laugh, his fingers alighted on the barrel of the Browning—which was still warm, which still trickled smoke from its muzzle . . .

It took several seconds more for the meaning of *that* to impress on Skelton.

When it finally did, he might have laughed again, had the shock not added insult to unbearable injury, had it not sent a jolting convulsion through his already shattered form, the new blast of pain bunching him up then grinding him down. The smashing force of the floor against his nose went unnoticed, for suddenly Skelton knew that death was upon him—he was strangling on his own vomit, drowning in his own gore. As he writhed there, things twisted and turned inside him, ragged things, torn and flopping things . . .

And all the while, Hoggins sat there in the chair, nodding and drooling, and staring sightless from under his matted mop of spiky, blood-clotted hair . . .

Skelton no longer saw him. His sight too had given out. Like his vascular system. He couldn't even whimper. The crushing pain had finally become unendurable. Even then it grew worse, worse, steadily worse . . . like the inexorable pressure of some clenching fist.

A gigantic, clenching fist.

"WHATEVER HAPPENED TO?"

d.g.k. goldberg

I am the answer to a trivia question. I was a one hit wonder.

I have a bad case of whatever happened to . . .

I was over before I got started, a *People* magazine retrospective from the starting gate. Someone has to be, why not me?

Okay. Here it is: I had one hit, two chances after that, then a canceled contract and a sleazy manager and all before I was twenty-seven. Skyrocketed to fame and then fizzled without drugs or pimps playing into it—it must have been astrological or something. I was on the cusp of punk with my rotten attitude and traffic-cone tits then all of a sudden it was time for something else: pale waifs in ripped velvet and my tough-girl take-no-prisoners attitude was yesterday's news.

I made buckets of money.

I spent buckets. Not just on massages, managers, and manicures. The tax men, tour hotels, and the touts screaming "Ya gotta spend money to make money" added up quickly. I lived high on the hog, or at least used very expensive makeup, but it isn't like I enjoyed anything. Not for a minute. Not at all. And this isn't an angst-ridden, materialism-sucks confession priming for my appearance on Oprah to hustle my found-the-way-to-live book, so, get over that will you? No. I didn't enjoy anything because I never really *got* anything. I was dragged to expensive restaurants but I could not eat lest I gain weight. I couldn't buy books 'cause I had nowhere to keep them while I toured. God forbid I looked at chocolate and who ever heard of a new song sensation that had the audacity to take a vacation? Saw a lot of great hotels from the service elevator.

Now I live in an apartment constantly invaded by the noise from other people's lives. When I am taking baths in the rust-rimmed tub I hear sounds like footsteps right outside the door. When I claw my way awake and run hot water until it steams to make a cup of instant coffee, the pipes wheeze and whine. I can hear Them Next Door digging in their garden late at night. Them Next Door work odd shifts. I hear Them bumping and thumping, rearranging furniture and planting tomato vines by moonlight. Them Next Door seem to always have the television on—Home Shopping at three a.m.

I don't expect or want you to feel sorry for me. I don't even want you to run out and get me a sandwich even though I am hungrier than an anorexic when the shrink ain't looking. Look, three years ago I got invited to parties where I fought other overly photographed folk for the shrimp on the buffet line. Now I huddle in front of the spitting space heater in the hallway wondering how in the hell people manage to eat protein three times a week. Things have changed.

The walls are so threadbare that I'm never quite alone.

I am yesterday's news. I should do the decent thing and die of a drug overdose.

I read recently that Olga Korbut got arrested for shoplifting. I'm sure someone will give a talk-show insight into her deep psychological problems. I read about Tonya

Harding getting evicted for nonpayment of rent. I am certain that someone will talk in terms of self-destructive acronyms and do a comedy routine. I suspect that Olga was hungry and Tonya needed a place to sleep.

Them Next Door seem to recognize me. I saw Her Next Door a few days ago, she cut her eyes at me and made a sound between a snicker and a snort, wrapped her oversized sweater tighter about her chest and tipped down the walkway to her unit. She has dangerously thin ankles and smells of random death.

I haven't been gone long enough to do a comeback. I mean, Tiffany got a spread in *Playboy* that I imagine brought her a nice chunk of change but she'd been gone long enough to be an *Oh, yeah, I remember.* I don't know if I want to live long enough to get there.

Do you follow the British tabloids? Do you know about Fred and Rosemary West? I thought not. Suffice it to say that they buried a lot of young girls in their garden and that someone is making strange noises next door. Hotel California. Young girls go in but they don't go out.

Some really weird shit lives in my bathroom. Really. Odd bloodstains in the toilet. Weird horrible crunchy bugs skitter across the floor. Something eats my eye shadow. Something.

I'm not scared of supernatural shit. Vampires, witches, werewolves, bring 'em on. Although zombies give me the cringes—the flesh eating thing is shivery and gross—but still, across the board, it isn't the supernatural I fear, instead it is the hideous drab horror of twenty or thirty more years on earth drudging through a job at a shoe store or in a cafeteria after I was a one hit wonder.

It makes me crazy. These young girls. So young that even with a bit of pudge or a wonky nose they are still beautiful because they are young—well, they go into the building next door and they don't leave. They don't leave, I tell you, and I don't know what to do.

No one should ever, not ever, have that one moment when it looks like it works, where it seems like the rest of it is all going to be breakfast in bed atop silver platters with linen tablecloths while deferential minions ask what you would like, no we should not have such moments if after them comes an apartment with too many roaches and the chill winds of winter shivering through the bottom of cracking windows. And, the sense that next door something dreadful goes on.

It would be much much better if I didn't recall Brie when I eat processed cheese.

It would be so nice if there were a man to blame. A boyfriend, a producer, a PR twerp who worked for MTV and decided I wouldn't do . . . not that easy, no it isn't. It would even be easier if I were to blame, if maybe I really had no talent and fucked my way into my one hit. Although how you can fuck enough people to hit number one on the Billboard charts I haven't a clue.

No. It wasn't some evil man or my lack of talent. I pause here. I must. I need you to understand that I was good. Very good. Got it? Fine. We can continue.

Let me tell you about my day, okay? I woke up to the sound of my neighbor's car barfing like news clips of the Middle East and then I rolled over into the coffin of a pizza. Last night I ordered pizza after I got too drunk on Mad Dog to care about how much it cost and I ate half of it in a starved bestial rush then went to bed with the rest. Even before I blinked into complete consciousness I gobbled one piece while watching my belly bulge over the waistband of my faded bikini panties. The weird thing about not getting enough to eat is you can have skinny little arms and legs but get a spider tummy bulge off of two decent meals—bloat like Biafra. Do you remember Biafra? It was several starving countries ago, well I am several one hit wonders ago.

After I inhaled a piece of pizza I struggled erect and shoved the rest of it into the leaky box and then put it in the oven. I ran my fingers through my hair and got clumps of it thick with tomato paste and oregano—organic conditioner? In a high-priced spa somewhere I'm certain that women are plastered with tomato paste. Lord knows ladies do odd things to themselves. Yesterday in the library I read about women getting Brazilians (that's a bare-pussy wax) and then having crystal graffiti pasted on their genitals. They do it in New York and London. Swear to God.

Then, late at night I heard a noise. I banished it. But, if I am honest, which hurts too much, I know that late last night I heard a noise. . . .

I creaked and crawled like a hungover crab to the mildewed shower and blasted my brain with steam. I love hot water. I damn near scald myself whenever I can. It makes my skin itch. I mean, I know very hot water really dries out your skin and all, but damn it feels good.

Not much feels good when you're poor.

Even less when you sense—when you know—that Them Next Door are doing something horrible and you are too bored or too weak or too self-obsessed to stop them.

That's something that has somehow got lost recently—I mean, Dickens knew the real deal, but lately, in this century, the reality is that we all forget how fucking scary poverty is, it is almost like it is too horrible to admit that it happens. And we forget how alone we can be. Not how alone we are, but how alone we can be. Poor is the dead end of alone.

Those girls that visit Them Next Door are poor and young, all bright waxy lipstick and cheap cracking shoes.

A week ago I went to a mall, a long story that, and you don't need to know the why of my going to a mall. But, a week ago I went to a mall. I walked into a department store, the anchor store, one of the big stores that make the mall be there, you know, and it doesn't matter which one, there aren't that many and they are all alike. Anyway I walked into a big three-story chrome and shiny anchor store in a megamall and the first thing that hit me was how clean the air smelled. Really. It even smells different in the Land of Money. It smells different where they sell Clinique, and Estée Lauder, and Lancôme, it smells cleaner than the drugstores that sell Max Factor and Maybelline.

I know, I mean I really know that an acrylic sweater in Nordstrom's is no different from one in Wal-Mart, but God the air smells better.

Waylon Jennings died three days ago. Yeah, right you are saying, wasn't he *old*? But, sixty-four doesn't seem old and you see he was kind of an outlaw and they shouldn't die, they should just disappear. He was part of childhood, I recall Mom waltzing around the cracked linoleum when she'd had one too many cheap beers—she bought beer by the case, incredibly cheap generic shit in white cans with black block print lettering that simply said LIGHT BEER. Anyway Mom would waltz around to "Amanda" and stomp around to "Good Hearted Woman" and now Waylon is dead and I am beginning, I think, to find lines in the corners of my eyes.

More: the one hit wonder that I was. It was Waylon. I did an almost punk—maybe rockabilly—cranked full-throttle cover of "I've always been crazy." Now, Waylon is dead, I have no recording contract, and the cockroaches in my kitchen have a brighter future than I can imagine for myself.

Maybe I should name one of the cockroaches Waylon.

(Maybe I should wonder who is dying next door.) I mean no disrespect. I'm just so lonely. Really lonely. Really. "I'm so lonesome I could cry." And I hate it that this is all taking place in a city. I could handle obscurity if I was in Mooresville, or Peachland, or Darlington, if I could sit on the outside steps at night and smell pine scent while I strained toward the whine of an eighteen-wheeler. But here—a three-floor walk-up with a rust-stained toilet and the mixed smell of jalapenos and cabbage in the paint-peeling halls, it don't feel right.

I was thinking of Waylon but I keep hearing the refrain of one of the Hag's songs: "I'm tired of this dirty old city."

Shit. I am a pretentious little bitch. I wish I could afford to get drunk. All of this shit is a bit over the top for being only twenty-eight. I mean, in the grand scheme of things, is it a huge fucking tragedy if I have to get a job whoring eye shadow at Sephora?

Only, I'm scared. I am scared shitless that when I go to apply for a normal job someone will ask me if I didn't used to be me. And, I don't know how to act anymore. I don't even know what people wear anymore; I am that far out of it. Are pant legs straight or flared or boot cut? I haven't a clue. God help me in terms of skirt lengths. I really don't know.

I'm losing it.

Was George Mendel the dude that turned into a cockroach in Kafka's story or was he the guy that did the things with plants? See? I don't know anything. I may know what goes on next door but I dare not think about that.

Damn cockroaches they are all over the place.

Was it Kate Wilhelm that wrote a story about some sad old bag controlling the cockroaches in her apartment cause she loved them, or was that someone else?

Can you show signs of Alzheimer's before you're thirty?

Am I forgetting shit because everyone has forgotten me?

At least I haven't become a cam girl although I am terrified that's next.

With cockroaches skittering around the sticky linoleum and no fucking way to pay the rent cam girldom fascinates me. I mean, these sad pathetic chicks put up their CD and DVD wish lists and maybe midwestern insurance men really do buy that stuff. *Hi! I'm Taylor and I am fourteen please send Sailor Moon crap.* Does that really work?

Well, why not?

I had a song hit the top of the charts and I can't afford a meal at Mickey D's now.

Maybe I made a mistake with my material. Country? Really?

Nope. It was a fucking great song.

Really.

Damn. Waylon is dead. I only have three cigarettes and six dollars twenty-eight cents.

Cigarettes or food? You know the answer.

Here's a question that I fear: Do old songs remember things better than they are? Or is that just me, always idealizing the past and fearing the future. My future looks kind of sucky right now—the most I can look forward to is a night shift at Kinko's. If I am lucky.

Yeah, luck.

I say that all the time.

I was totally gobsmacked, thrown against the wall, and crushed by fate when Luck showed up in my roach hotel of an apartment. Okay, I'm not dying of a fatal disease, I don't have three handicapped kids and an old man who beats me, so what am I bitching about, right?

I don't know how I fit into the universe and thought I did and it's fucking horrible.

You think I am kidding? Yeah, well, that would work better for both of us, but I am not kidding.

The worst bit isn't the roaches. It isn't the obvious Eastern European smell of my neighbors' cooking, nope it isn't even the fact that I may be the last English speaker in a neighborhood where Spanish or Arabic works better—oh, yeah, I can see you with your useless BA and political correctness now, just cause I said that bit about Spanish or Arabic you feel all warm and fuzzy now, don't you? I mean it is okay that I am in a mess because I am obviously a bigot. Damn. You educated fucks are real pieces of work. I am simply telling it like it is, I am the last English speaker in a block of roach-infested crumbling piss-scented buildings, got it? And just maybe if I had learned something somewhere along the way I could figure out what to do—I mean it's not my fault that my generation rejected Las Vegas, now is it?

I imagine that it is easy to deal with a dybbuk that is outside you—I mean if the demon is *over there* one can cope, can't one? But, if it is in me, what the fuck is the deal? What do I do? I mean really.

And, whatever it is that happens to me, it won't let me sleep. Not really. I try to sleep; I drink myself into numbness each night on wine when I can find the price of a pint. I stumble over my shoes but I cannot sleep. I went to the mental health clinic and whined but the bored and boring social worker told me that no one ever died from lack of sleep. I haven't died. But I'd like to.

Because I cannot sleep . . . because I cannot sleep. I look out the window at two in the morning, at four when the dawn is simply a thin rumor I look out the window after trying to read Martin Amis and researching Rose West on the Internet and telling myself I am imagining things and I think I see my neighbors digging a hole in their backyard.

My apartment, such as it is, is a tiny two-room disaster with rust-stained bath carved out of the guts of a neo-Victorian messy wedding-cake house perched precariously next to a brick bungalow destined to be the starter home for generations of GI Bill couples. From my smudged window I can see the nearly streetlight-lit handkerchief yard and late at night when my own demons are restless I think I see Tom and Jan out back behind their barbeque grill digging into the cold red clay.

I know that my mind's not right.

How could it be? I have clear memories of restaurants where a starter salad cost $12.50 and now I cannot afford Mickey D's so how could I possibly be inclined toward rational thought—but, damn, they are out there night after night digging holes in the backyard. And something else: I'll occasionally see a waif-pretty youngling with pink-punk hair and oversized overalls slip through the hedge and ring their doorbell but I don't often see them come out. The young women I mean, I see Tom and Jan often in their insipidly matched jogging suits walking round the neighborhood with too much gum in their well maintained smiles.

Maybe it's nothing.

And maybe it isn't.

I strain against the mottled window glass lurk-listening for screams but all I hear is the radio from Him Downstairs, my neighbor That Damn Him listens to oldies stations far too often. I hear my own voice warble and blare on the radio from Him Downstairs and I wonder how it is that I am not even thirty and I'm on an oldies station and what is really happening next door? Are they cutting up young girls or am I going mad from protein deprivation—do you know what it is like to have no money?

Last week I saw an almost-slender young woman, pear-shaped, with the small breasts and innocently big ass that some smooth-skinned lassies in their early twenties wear with impunity walk up the walk and ring the doorbell next door. I never saw her come out and I wonder.

I'm insane. I mean I can't possibly see everything that goes on next door, can I?

If they are killing people and I am silent, am I responsible?

Kitty Genovese died before I was born. Long before. 1964 for crying out loud. No one remembers her anymore. No one.

God, my mother used to natter about Kitty Genovese. I am sort of more the Karla Faye Tucker generation. Only Karla Faye was lots older than me too. But, I mean, my mom's generation was into victims and I'm into . . . or my generation is into empowered women. You can't get much more empowered than an ax murderess can you?

I never believed all that Jesus stuff.

I mean, Karla Faye had great hair, really great hair, I envy her that, but even with the great hair I couldn't buy the bit about how the person that killed the person was another Karla Faye and she didn't deserve to die because she was so different. I mean I have to live my entire stupid life having been a one hit wonder—why should a murderer get off easier?

Even roaches remain roaches.

You know there are moments when I am glad I was briefly a rock star, they usually occur late at night when I troll the Internet looking for bio data on people who live on death row—being on death row sucks more than being a failed rock star but I suspect that they are both fueled by the same adrenaline madness that puts "I" at the center of the universe.

I did something really crazy not too long ago. Like that's a surprise. I found a Web site about Issei Sagawa; do you know who he was? He was a Japanese cannibal who ate a Dutch student at the Sorbonne in the early eighties. After spending three years in a benevolent French funny farm he flew back to Japan and wrote four novels, now he does a regular column for some Japanese magazine, and he shows up on talk shows, even did a freaking article for a gourmet magazine.

He was a lot more than a one hit wonder.

Four novels. All of them best sellers. All because he said some girl tasted like tuna sushi.

Anyway, this Web site said that bless his heart, despite his freedom and his cult status and charge cards, he doesn't have many friends. Go figure. And that when he starts making friends with European women they invariably find out that he has a penchant for euro au gratin and they leave the country.

Well, gentle reader, I wrote him.

Shocked?

Well, fuck. He may be a cannibal, but he's more than a one hit wonder. Four best sellers. You gotta respect that.

So I sent him this e-mail telling him what a turn on he was and telling him that I matched his Aryan fantasy fuck, you know, big and pale and blond.

Then I changed my e-mail address because I read the rest of it, the bit where he barbeques his victim's breast and doesn't enjoy it because the breast, once cooked, is too greasy and Lord that offended me, if you are going to kill someone, butcher, and eat her you ought not to denigrate her further by rejecting her titty because it is too greasy.

Besides, what did he expect? After all, a breast is just fatty tissue, isn't it?

They are really more like the Canadians, the Ken and

Barbie murders, Karla and whoever her husband was I forget. You know, Them Next Door. Have you forgotten? What with all this babbling about sushi you might have. Here it is, I e-mailed the Asian cannibal and then wussed out but nevertheless Them Next Door are still doing something.

Tuesday last I saw a spaniel-sweet girl with curly hair tip up to their porch a look of Girl Scout cookies and hope plastered across her pale pudding face. I stood and watched in the window drinking Mad Dog as she tripped the light fantastic up the broken pavement, across the sagging porch and to the abandon hope door. She had sweet calves; biteable calves above neatly rolled white socks.

I drank quite a lot of Mad Dog. It tasted like a cross between grape juice and cheap astringent.

Full of Mad Dog I went quite mad and dressed all in black, not a stretch given my wardrobe, and tipped across the lawn to look into their windows where I predictably saw the young girl wearing only her socks and a cheap vinyl slave collar kneeling before the sweat suited man while his wife held the video camera and the young girl sobbed, snot running down her face and referred to his cock by the mandatory pet name. She did something wrong and he smacked her across the face shattering her cheekbone. The video caught it.

I suppose I could have stopped it.

I could have gone back to my apartment and called the law.

Instead I clutched the windowsill and watched in rubbernecked fascination while he beat her numb and then came all over her no longer such a pretty face. I stood deer in headlights and took sips from my bottle while he rubbed his cock over her bruised lips and pummeled her with his ham-hock fists.

She fell to the floor like a deflated balloon and the air whooshed out her, I thought maybe her soul brushed my cheek fleeing past me to the afterlife.

I slunk back to my apartment, said hello to the roaches and finished the Mad Dog. It wasn't enough, there was not enough to escape the thud of mud, the sound of Them digging and the certain knowledge that we also sin who only stand and wait.

I watched on the news the next day through the haze of a hangover that coated my tongue and throttled my guts the shiny school picture of a girl who would never come home and I wondered what fraction of the murder belonged to me and what belonged to God and how much belonged to you who will not ever own any crumb of guilt but I did not wonder what the newscaster said, there is a question I don't have to ask:

Whatever happened to?

I don't ask.

I know.

INCIDENT REPORT

Michael Shea

After dinner, Detective K went into his den, a cozy but masculine space, he thought, paneled in dark-stained wood. He stood before the broad desk bolted in its nook, the computer equipment deployed to access from the sturdy chair with its smooth swivel, and took pleasure in his workstation. In just a moment, he would settle into his Incident Report, doing what he loved best, pure police work. These last few hours of labor would be an oasis of the Real Thing before a long rotation back into uniform. Officer K was going to serve as Court Security.

A Bailiff's uniform dangled from a hanger on the closet door. K made himself turn and look at it, just for the self-discipline. He'd do six months standing on his head, could carry it off just fine. The other Bailiffs knew he wasn't on a scheduled rotation, but they would be kind enough. Never once, in his seven years since making Detective, had Officer K neglected to maintain a friendly rapport with the Uniforms. You had to be in touch with the ranks, know how to joke with them, never seem like you looked down on them. No matter how high you rose, you needed everyone on your side in police work.

There was a knock, a small, polite knock which registered low down on the door, maybe four feet off the floor.

That would be Tony. And K instantly knew *why* it was Tony. His son had glimpsed the uniform, and was fascinated with cops' uniforms. It was particularly irritating, having to confront his son's enthusiasm, but he reached out and opened the door, giving the boy a mild, patient greeting. "What is it, Anthony?"

The boy squinted a little at the note of reproof in "Anthony" instead of "Tony," but grinned. "Are you going to wear a uniform tomorrow, Dad?" And his pale brown eyes darted past K's shoulder at the Bailiff's husk hanging behind him.

For a responsible father, children were a heavy weight to bear. K could see himself so clearly in this eight-year-old face. How strong, how handsome, how tall a uniform made you feel, back when you were young. It wasn't the boy's fault he hadn't yet learned that the uniform was the badge of the minimum wage—that if your work involved a uniform, you were basically a janitor as far as real skill and power went. You were the EMT grunting the meat into the wagon, not the Doctor. You were the guy in white latex gloves on Intake, making some street-scum strip, and putting his foul briefs in a plastic bag—not the Detective.

"I'm not going to wear it to work, Anthony. I'm going to put it on in the locker room."

Now the boy was shyer, smiling more anxiously. You could see that he sensed there was something wrong about his question, something coy and unmanly. "Can I see you wearing it, Dad?"

"You know, Anthony, that even if I wore the uniform, I wouldn't put on the gun belt till I was at the Hall of Justice." K had, himself young, felt that innocent awe of the bulky, hardware-crusted duty belts, the big black grip of the Smith crouched under its retaining strap like a barely caged bear. . . .

"Why couldn't you?" How could little Tony know how blatant and awkward that kind of firepower felt bulging on your hip? How much realer, more effective, a well-tailored shoulder rig was? So much more mojo it gave you, to be secretly armed.

"A uniform, Anthony, always has a very specific job that goes with it, and you always follow the rules of that job. That way you can be proud of the job that you do."

The kid was so short, too, would surely grow up as short as K himself. He'd long foreseen that if the boy grew up tall, he'd take an indirect pride in his child's bigness, while he would resent having to look up to meet his eyes. But when foreseeing shortness, this too he resented, as an accusation of deficiency. And little Tony unknowingly rubbed it in by insisting on a waxed flattop just like his Dad's.

"What are the jobs for that uniform, Dad?"

K took his time. The boy was really a pretty darn good kid. Was *very* well behaved at the table, and knew how to be quiet when speaking wasn't appropriate. K thought about this afternoon—that trashed-out pair eaten away with booze and drugs, shouting and tearing at each other but chained together. Tony already had more inner worth than a whole block-full of lowlifes like that. His father could see him always carefully weighing the rightness of what he was going to say before he said anything.

But the boy had to learn not to *question* what had already been sufficiently *explained*. K bent to plant his palms on his knees, signalling something Important, eye-level with Tony. The boy straightened.

"You ask me what I am going to do in that uniform, Anthony. I am going to protect the judge and the courtroom from the criminals that are brought into it, and from those criminals' friends in the audience. But you have to understand something about uniforms, Anthony. You might wear several different uniforms. You might be in the Boy Scouts. You might spend a while in the service. And what you'll learn right away, Anthony, is that when you put on a uniform, you don't start asking *questions* about your duties, what you do is *listen* when your duties are *explained* to you. Now we'll talk some more about this soon. You understand? Now Dad has got some work to do."

Once the door was shut again, it took a few moments for his sense of sanctuary to return, for that calm alertness to instinct so important for the best police work. The case he had in hand must be managed perfectly. A Major Felony would be a vein of gold shot through the dark months ahead, hours of investigation, conferences with the DA and, if there was a survivor, courtroom appearances at the prelim and all through the trial. He would, within the khaki husk that hung behind him, remain a Detective.

He slipped into his big, solid chair, within moments was rolling, keying the narrative into form. The keys' clacking dropped like soft rainfall on the silence of perfect concentration as inwardly he returned to it: the cruise down those dogpatch blocks of the West Valley, that grotesque couple trading shouts in the driveway of their pathetic stucco-box tract house, its fenceless and grassless lawn an elephants' burial ground of car chassis and parts . . .

COUNTY SHERIFF'S DEPARTMENT
INCIDENT REPORT/NARRATIVE STATEMENT
Time 7/07/03 @ 1537 *hours*
Incident/crime Domestic violence
Code V Name(s) Untergang, Bridget and Jack
Location of occurrence Plum Valley District, 17 Plum Blossom Place

Case Number K70703B

In accordance with my assignment to County Sheriff's Violent Crimes Investigation Unit, I was monitoring Dispatch while returning from West County (see incident report K70703A) and heard Dispatch broadcast a Violent Domestic Disturbance in progress in the Plum Valley District on 17 Plum Blossom Place. I radioed Dispatch that I was responding, and also radioed the responding Sheriff's Deputies Tully and Hawser to let them know I was nearby and would be on-scene when they arrived. I arrived at Plum Blossom Place at 1544 hours, and viewed both the Untergangs out on the driveway in front of their residence. They were shouting at each other and gesturing violently.

K was really on the alert today, after yesterday's grim little interview, Sheriff Piccolo telling him with a thin, not very friendly smile that he thought a rotation to Court Security, effective the day after tomorrow, would be a good idea. So K got his car on the street at sunup and stayed there, just to be ready to pounce on the first heavy squeal from Dispatch. Nine hours yielded nothing but a backyard theft: a retired old fart's Weber was missing from his deck. K ached to score something real, had risked Piccolo's irritation to reconfirm what was procedural: that during his rotation he could still contribute to cases he had in progress. As the day wore on he had to struggle to fight down the longing for luck that drives luck away. As the sun moved down to the west, he willed himself cool.

And then this squeal. Just what he'd been hoping for, something down in dogpatch. And at his first sight of the place, he began to feel that confidence of luck that brings luck on. It had a guilty verdict written all over it. It stood the edge of a decayed development, the end house on a block dead-ending at acres of neglected fruit trees shaggy with lichen.

He idled, scoping them a moment from the car, and they increased their volume, sensing a police audience. (See? You don't need a monkey suit and a logo on your car, they sense your power.) He watched, and knew these people, knew just what he had here. This was the essence of the Detective's craft—to just breathe in details of their identity from their surroundings. Car parts crowd out the lawn and half cover the driveway, the garage door is permanently wedged open, and the garage's clutter is spilled out onto the other half of the driveway. Instantly K knows that speed and booze are the presiding demons of this place. The Mom, Bridget Untergang, battered, gaunt, and punk-haired at fifty-plus—is and has long been the speed, only secondarily sinking in booze during the crankless stretches. The Son, Jack Untergang, with his thick middle at thirty-five, his soft flushed skin, his potato nose, his squinty red eyes like a crybaby's—uses speed of course, but is and long has been mainly the booze. He's the hanger-on, whining and complaining because she was the Bad Mom. She's the shrieker, the furious self-justifier, and is also guilty and sentimental and a habitual giver-in to the Son's whining. So she supports him, bails him out of drunk tanks, and keeps him his room in this rats' nest.

They're having a classic substance-zombie blowout. How many domestic beefs has he seen move in this pattern? The fight erupts indoors and rages there awhile. Then one of them decides to storm off. The broil moves out into the driveway. Storm-Off hovers by his vehicle and they stage another full round out front. In this case—there's always these insane details—the boozer, as part of getting his battered old convertible road-ready, is putting big sloppy bandages of duct tape across the outside of the passenger door—apparently the guy's door flops open on turns. By the old scabs of tape already in place, the technique's been working OK for a while. Strip! Rip! he slaps on a piece. Then turns on the woman shouting at his back and bellows back, brandishing his roll of duct tape. Watch now. Once he's done with the tape, he'll fling it down as a dramatic gesture.

Sure enough! It bounces from the pavement and lands on a heap of ratty painter's dropcloths and ragged, tangled rope. Detective K begins to feel the magic start to work, that thrill of intuition. Because a true detective is a species, a creature, and that is *his* species, *he* is such a creature. His breed is proven by moments like these, when he vibrates like a tuning fork to a brutal crime in embryo.

> *I identified myself to the Untergangs and told them we had received complaints of a violent altercation from some concerned neighbors. They both began talking loudly to me and shouting at each other at the same time, and I began recording the conversation as it involved mutual accusations and I was having difficulty sorting them out. Bridget Untergang's face showed what appeared to be several scars on the brow and in the areas of both cheeks. I didn't immediately observe any recent scarring, but a long-established pattern of abuse seemed to be suggested. To avoid aggravating their neighbors further, I suggested we talk in the house.*

The inside of the house was a furniture-riot festooned with dirty clothes, cat hair, and jammed ashtrays everywhere. There were miscellaneous tables, all littered with unfinished projects: picture framing, leather tooling, there was even a galvanized tub for candle-dipping all scabbed over with candy-colored wax. Each moment he stood with them in the dust and fetor of their cage, the Untergangs grew more perfectly transparent. Mom's scars—a thick place along her lip there, too—were the history of her boyfriends and exes. By the age of those scars he could calibrate that she hadn't had a man living with her for several years now. He noted there was one table where icons and foldout three-panel religious paintings predominated, a messy little attempt at a shrine, curled black candle wicks in glass sockets, a litter of burnt kitchen matches. Detective K knew she was at speed-freak retirement age, she'd be working at Recovery, doing Twelve-Steps . . . but a photo of three dogs in a glassed frame lay flat on a chair arm. The slanting noon light, gilding every mote of the dusty air, also showed a scumble of white dust on the glass. So, working at Recovery, and still bowing to the glass like she's done since she was a kid. . . . Lot of guilt there, in a speed-mom at this age. . . .

He lets them bleat their grievances, their accusations. Bridget: I've never said a word, not one word, about killing myself! He says that because he'd just as soon see me dead. Because *he* wants to kill me! Wouldn't you! You'd just as soon, wouldn't you!

Translation: Yes, she rants endlessly about killing herself because she feels guilty about fucking up their lives, and what she wants now is for him to tell her that he forgave her and doesn't hate her for turning him into this Zero with a twenty-year-old duct-taped convertible.

Jack: Killin' yourself is all you talk about! I warned you I wouldn't stand for it if you started in again with it! I'm not gonna take the blame! You talk like that and I'm not gonna just stand around and let you go to hell! *Kill* you? I'm tryin to take *care* of you, you stupid bitch!"

Translation: You ignored me all your selfish life, let your boyfriends bully me! But I'm not going to treat *you* like shit, bitch.

> *The subjects were mother and son. Bridget Untergang very vehemently accused her son Jack of wanting to kill her. Jack Untergang insisted that it was his mother who wished to kill herself. This subject HBD by the odor of his breath, but he did not appear to be impaired. Their dispute appeared to be of a chronic, longstanding nature. I informed them that two Deputies were en route, and that I hoped an arrest situation would be avoided. Both the subjects immediately began to calm down. Officers Tully and Hawser arrived.*
>
> *The Deputies had responded to another disturbance at this residence two weeks before, and had found only Bridget Untergang at home. Jack had left sometime before, "peeling rubber" according to a neighbor. The Deputies shared my opinion that this pair were loud, but that they had a pretty stable, long-established pattern, and they were unlikely to come to actual violence.*

Detective K talked to the Deputies out by the curb. He laughed sympathetically—this kind of thing was the dregs of Patrol work. He told them he already had a tape, would take care of the paperwork—said he would go interview the complaining neighbor, which he took to be that gnarled woman glaring from a porch three dumps down. She looked like another speed-crone, maybe a decade or so downhill from Bridget, and self-righteous. "She'll badmouth 'em both all day long if you'll listen," grinned Tully, still young enough to get a laugh from lowlife local color.

K waved them off with an ironic salute. The scuttlebutt of his rotation would have reached them already, and he knew he'd just made a good impression. Had saved them drudgery, and showed himself unaffected by his bureaucratic misfortune.

He went back inside and talked very earnestly with Jack. "I'll be honest with you. I think you're somewhat impaired by alcohol. You're in a treatment program (he saw the guess ring true in the red-rimmed eyes), and I don't want to be hardnose about this, but I think you should go somewhere and sleep it off. I think that would be the simplest way to resolve this whole thing, Jack."

He walked him out to the convertible, made sure he fastened his seat belt. Like an omen, a wink from the future, a half-full pint of bourbon glinted from the seat at Officer K. And next to it, a tire iron. Jack drove off, not peeling rubber but lurchingly, foot uneasy on the gas, and left him musing.

Any cop would say this was one of those calls you made when you tried to cut lowlifes some slack. The odds were good an accomplished drunk like Jack could safely drive to some refuge, and sleep it off.

But by the tingling of his raptor's instinct, this was a major felony on the brink of being born.

He'd already placed his bet. Had not punctured this swelling of their cyclic wrath by taking them into custody. How much more masterful, how much more *beautiful* it would be to intervene precisely when the crime was born, to nip it in the bud. *Beautiful* was not a word he would ever say aloud, nor was *Heroism,* but that would *be* Heroism, to dive in and catch the crime at its incontrovertible point of delivery. And what did he risk? There was no witness to this type of gamble.

He gave his card to Bridget Untergang, expressing the hope that she would relax, maybe take a nap herself, and then walked down to where the neighbor-witch stood glaring from her porch, her skinny shoulders hunched with grievance.

> *When the Deputies had left I suggested to Jack Untergang that he go somewhere and cool off. He agreed and drove off in a late '70s white Chevy convertible with the passenger door duct-taped on the outside. I proceeded down the block to 36 Plum Blossom Lane to interview—*

Another light knock sounded on the door of K's den, this time striking higher on the panels. Karina. She would only venture to knock when he was working if she had a communication from one of his superiors. He went to the door, and stood there a moment, centering himself, before opening it.

"Captain Mullet called. He said you could"—she turned her eye to a message pad in her hand and read with added emphasis—" '*turn in those items when you got out of court.*' "

Officer K nodded equably. "OK. Thank you, Karina."

But she held his eyes, silently insisting that he could tell her more at this juncture. He'd explained his rotation to her, and from that it would be obvious that the items Captain Mullet, who was section chief of his Violent Crimes Investigation Unit, would be referring to were Officer K's Detective badge and shoulder-rigged Glock. Karina was waiting to hear the obvious *said,* though he had already made it perfectly clear to her.

He had nothing but praise and respect for his wife. Look how attractive she kept herself, her eyebrows these flawless little black arches . . . and she put beautiful meals on their table, and her conversation was cheerful. She added a graceful feminine note, made it just what a family dinner should be. But this side of her was where

Anthony's weakness came from. Their situation had been *explained* to her, but she had to keep *questioning* because questioning was her disguised way of *complaining* about it.

"You've gotta excuse me, Karina." He gave her his most patient smile. "I have to finish this report and then run out and do a follow-up interview. Hey, thanks for that ironing job, it looks sharp." Still smiling, daring her to try to probe the subject of his reassignment.

After another hesitation, she smiled, declined. "Let me know if you want anything." He nodded and closed the door.

—Juanita Moran, 63, of that address. She stated that she was very much aware of the Untergangs as neighbors, because she said they lived most of their lives shouting at each other out on the sidewalk in front of their house. Ms. Moran said very emphatically that Bridget Untergang was constantly accusing her son of wanting to kill her.

Juanita Moran's ponytail was dead white. Her lean face seemed strangely seared. As she talked, her eyes gazed down-street at number 17, seemed to look almost fondly at the place where she had seen so much turbulence over the years. He asked her, "Do you think Bridget is really afraid that her son might kill her?"

"Of course she is! She's always *squawkin'* that she is! But then it's all just bullshit too, right? They have their big explosions, their big dramas, and that gets 'em off, they calm back down—Hey! *They* feel better!"

But she also stated that the Untergangs had a longstanding pattern of these altercations. I have made a recording of this interview as well, to be submitted with this report. I returned to Mrs. Untergang's residence and spoke with her inside. She was calm, and agreed with my suggestion that she might take a nap. I gave her my card, and I will call the Untergang residence this evening to be sure that a follow-up visit is not necessary.

Nothing further at this time.

He e-mailed the report to Captain Mullet. As he clicked Send, he felt a weight break free and fall away from him. It seemed he soared for a moment.

It was about two hours after dark. He made a cleaner, clearer copy of the tape, and snapped it into his belt recorder.

Sitting back in his chair, relaxing his body, he reached out mentally. It was a sensation like delicate antennae sprouting from his spine. Reached out for Jack Untergang. Some particle, some few floating molecules of the man—he could almost feel the tickle of them. Jack had lots of nice booze-storing fat. On some backstreet he chugged his last half pint as the sun westered. He snored through the sunset with his jaw sagged open, was still snoring now, but in another hour or less would be waking with a thumping headache, wiping off drool with his sleeve. . . .

K rose slowly, an abstracted expression on his face. He checked his pockets, his shoulder rig, slipped on his dark sports coat. There was something dreamy to his movements but he was not dreaming, he was harkening for that first infinitesimal signal that his suspect had begun to wake, to move toward their point of inevitable intersection. K checked his watch. It was a quarter to nine. He stepped through the side door into his garage, where his black Mustang waited. He mounted up, and ignited the engine.

At 2151 hours, checking the messages on my home office phone, I found I had received a call from Mrs. Untergang. It was somewhat garbled, but she seemed to be expressing some anxiety regarding her son. I called her residence but received no answer. I decided to drive to her house.

Launching into the streets, the rushing air taking hold of him, had a skydiving feel. Free-falling in the wide dark, he steered through an aerial view, envisioned these miles of whispering trees with lit windows beneath them as thick as stars. Somewhere to the southeast, where the city thins out to shabby fragments with rural gaps, offering places to drink and stew in your car, defunct gas stations to tuck yourself behind, dirt spurs that hook into the bushes . . .

There's a twinge of him, a faint signal flare. On a trash-littered spur, scrub oak all around. He's just waking up, raw and grogged out, his roofless car filled like a tub with the night's cold. The man has no memory: each time he wakes up in the mess of his life, it's a revelation. So of course he decides it's time for strength, time to get himself together. He pulls out his vial and scorches his sinuses with vitamin Speed. Again his chronic outrage simmers. Mom, that bitch . . . what she's *done* to his life.

And while K reached out, he drove expertly. He threaded a suburban route, something that he did just for pleasure now and then, because the stream of lit-up houses kindled his imagination. All those boxed lives, glowing with hidden business, some, inevitably, with crimes. Any one of these houses, a Detective could penetrate. Could enter, sift, study, know. K crossed his dominion, the yellow windows spinning past.

Thin and clear as a strand of spider-silk through his nerves, K can feel the convertible move. Jack's driving with verve now, cranked enough to think he's sober. He digs in his pocket and finds he's got a few crumpled ones. Outstanding. Time for some Mad Dog or Night Train.

From the proprietor of Luigi's Liquor. Mr.——, I learned that the subject pulled in a little after 2200 hours. Mr.—— remembered selling him a pint of Night Train.

Now that's more like it. The oak trees whipping past in his headlights, a solid bottle between his legs. The thirty-proof shrink-wraps what's left of Jack's brain while his rage and self-pity burn bright on the wick of the crank. . . .

K has has driven west of the Plum Valley district, and begins to crook briskly through a flanking route of rural roads. He parks in crickety quiet by the rail fence of a defunct orchard. Vaults the fence and sets his feet whispering through ankle-high grass. Moving amidst the shadowy branches, the Detective sees the convertible. Jack is on Garfield, not far from Satsuma. Soon he's going to hook right, less than a quarter hour away.

As K advances the shaggy trees radiate a surprising cold vitality, soliciting him with bristly gestures, startling him—now on this side, now on that—with their closeness. Spooks, naysayers from his own mind's weaker part, warning of complications, tangles, failures. But he treads without hesitation. Such are the boogeymen that cow the second-raters, the hacks that back down from the sorcery that could be theirs. K knows that when you are the true breed, you gamble. You wade out into the wide dark water, you feel the faint bow-waves of the convertible pushing the night air before it . . . and your ship comes in. He smiles in the dark as he moves whispering up to the orchard's farther rim, and the back fence of the Untergang dump.

Dark dignifies the surrounding, turns trash to silhouettes, and makes the one lit window a frontiersman's candle in his cabin on the wilderness fringe.

> *The house was quiet as I approached it. Jack Untergang's convertible was parked in the driveway. A light was on in the living room. I knocked and announced myself but received no response. Because of the distressed tone of the call I had received, I felt it was called for to try the front door. It was unlocked.*

So was the back door. It led him through a utility nook into the kitchen. He stood in the kitchen, testing the house's silence, and found it complete. In the outlying night he felt Jack's fitful but accelerating approach, stretching like a live wire northward out of the Garfield district. He stood there enjoying what he most prized, that last allotment of collected consideration, before he reached out, and irrevocably intersected with a crime at hand.

The kitchen's odors spoke to him as he lingered there. Early in his career, K learned that the smell of a subject's kitchen was one of the first, surprising intimacies his power granted him. They let you in because they fear not to, and you stand in their kitchens and sniff the echos of their meals, the crude smells of the foods that give them comfort. The smell of this kitchen is archaeological. As dense and complex as ruined cities is the architecture of dirty dishes that tower from the sink, from the counters, from the table. In this den of intermittent, desperate feedings, the food-crusts lie in strata, old upon very old. . . . Here feeding has been an irregular frenzy. Here (a room as intimate in its way as a bathroom, a bedroom) the will to live has sometimes flared, always to be decisively defeated. This odor of defeat is the stink of crime—Essence of Felony—the stench of abject surrender to ugliness and disorder. When you let shit crust on you this deep, you are abandoned, Major Crime will find you, and once you are accused, you *will* go down.

> *I stood just inside the front door and called out again. Still receiving no response, I advanced a few steps into the living room. I saw a shape in the doorway to the kitchen. At that moment, Jack Untergang rushed out of the hall to the bedroom. I saw that he had a pistol in his right hand.*

K himself was the shape in that kitchen doorway now. He stepped through it and into a dining area that had been annexed to the living room by the tide of cluttered furniture. Over this jumble, this crazy checkerboard of lit and shadowed trash, hung the echos of years of shouting, and raging, and remorse, and futility. This whole place was a seedbed of violence. The crime he had come to intercept was here already. He felt it like a worm, a big larva in its cell beneath the floorboards. It was just on the point of hatching out, and spreading its wet black wings. He stood watching the front door, all the while feeling its ugliness beneath his feet, struggling to rupture its cocoon.

That tingle of imminence. Jack's growly, duct-taped boat is grumbling onto Cherry right now. K hefts in his mind the whole crime, from commission through arrest, and finds it, yes, tight and true. Go for it. He comes one further step forward and stands poised, watching the front door.

Waits, vibrant as a tuning fork. Any second now, he will begin to hear the throaty motor-noise, like a lion's cough, the approach of murder.

It reaches toward him . . . but makes not a sound . . . and still . . . not a sound. Nothing but silence all around.

Just wait. Just hold still. . . . No.

Sometimes this happens. Sometimes a fated crime ricochets back off into the wild blue yonder of the future, bounces crazily off the runway a few times before it can land. That convertible is coming, but maybe not tonight.

> *The house was dark, and Jack Untergang's convertible was not present. When I knocked and announced myself, I found that the front door was not closed. I received no response, but the excited tone of Mrs. Untergang's phone message seemed to call for some assurance that she was safe. I came two steps into the living room and again announced myself. Though the house was dark, I saw a strange shape in the doorway to the kitchen. I advanced a few steps further into the living room.*

Yet still Detective K stood, letting the silence uncoil around him. It was in this kind of silence, in exactly such mute and lonely hours as this one, that mortal crimes were done. . . .

Well. It still lay in his power to snatch that crime from the dark that hid it, to prove and punish that concealed savagery. K did not deny himself a thrill of pride. To how many men was it given, an accomplishment like that?

He unpocketed, and pulled on, a pair of latex gloves. Stepped back into the kitchen and uncradled the grease-smudged wall phone. Punched in the number of the phone in his den, and while he listened to his message-prompt, unclipped the recorder from his belt, and played into the receiver a brief burst of Bridget Untergang's recorded voice. Hung up the phone, and reholstered his recorder.

Surefootedly he walked a crooked path between jumbled tables, crossing the living room to the bedroom hallway, and a jumbled, doorless closet. He bent to a stack of battered cardboard boxes from which hung sleeves and shirttails like dangling tentacles, and dragged it out of the closet, clearing the closet floor, where there was a hatch to the crawl space below. Lifted this open, plunged down both his hands and firmly gripped, and hoisted from beneath the house—plucked up in a clean jerk Bridget Untergang, bound and mouth-taped, and only vaguely, weakly wriggling in resistance. She is concussed, with asymmetric pupils, but still her eyes, above the bright tape sealing shut her mouth, struggle to focus him.

He drapes her across his shoulder, clamps her one-armed there, and with his free hand shuts the trap, and shoves the boxes back in place. Recrosses the living room with her, ducks into the kitchen and plucks out one kitchen chair, and sets both woman and chair down in its doorless entryway. Here it has been someone's inspiration to install a chinning bar across the upper portion of the frame.

While she twists sluggishly on the floor, he pulls a length of frayed nylon rope from his sports coat. Till this afternoon, it dwelt, like the duct tape, in the Untergangs' trash-choked garage. He pauses a moment, weighing the sequence of his next moves, thinking through the alternatives, his eyes absent while the woman's fractured gaze searches for his face. Nods then to himself and, bending down, fits his hands in two parentheses around the woman's head. Straightens and turns his back to her, and ties one end of the rope into a loop of carefully gauged diameter.

All right. He crowns her with the loop and works it down over her head—snug till it's past the nose, not too loose around the neck. He sees her eyes have found, are disjointedly focused on his face. Remotely amazed, she seems to recognize him for the first time. He gives her that confidential little smile he uses to reassure a subject: Almost done here, Ma'am.

He gathers her gently for lifting—left arm hooking below her hips, firm control of her center of gravity essential to doing this smoothly—then surging upright with her, left arm thrusting her high while his right hand tucks the rope's end over the bar, gets two quick wraps around it, and regrips the free end firmly.

Now he can drop her, and free both hands for the knot. He gives her a sharp downward yank with his left arm as he pulls its support away. OK. Just barely short enough. Her tied feet, heaving like a single limb, a dolphin's tail, buck the air just inches off the floor. He knots the slack end hard around the straining, wavering length that holds her weight, her thrashing will to live, which now, at long last, has fully awakened in her. He steps back for perspective, then ducks around her wild oscillations to topple the chair on the floor behind her, putting it too close for where a true suicide would kick it, jumping off. Steps back from her again, and again judges the whole scenario.

Good. And almost done now . . . she shits herself within the tight jeans. Her eyes are looking for something on the ceiling, something they remember, almost remember, from long, long, long ago.

Nodding again, he plucks one of his cards from his breast pocket. He steps in close once more, reaches round behind her to her bound hands, and slips one end of his card into the spasming clutch of her fingers. Fitfully, she mauls it as she dies. . . .

And, at last, hangs slack.

Done.

His white latex fingers pinched the creases from the

card. He edged politely past her, his hands gently touching her hips to damp down the body's last, slight swing. Faced the phone, let his arms hang, and dropped the card.

Almost complete now, and flawless, he knew this already, but check and check again, never get slap-dash. He retreated farther into the living room, this time for a first-glance perspective on the scene as you came through the front door.

Just right.

Well then. He felt as he always did, completing perfect work like this. You always wanted to delay those crowning touches, never wanted the magic to be finished. But he took out his buck knife, and opened it, and went to her once more.

He sliced her bindings, let one strand drop to the floor, and wadded up the rest. She had good, abraded ligature marks on both wrists and ankles. Reached up to her duct-tape gag and stripped it off. It came off too cleanly. Forensics should detect the adhesive, but you couldn't count on them. He wadded up the tape with the ligatures, then stripped a little shred off the tape's corner and restuck it to her cheek.

He edged past her for the last time, and paused to look back at her before he left. Seen from the back . . . that anonymous touch perfected her: one of the faceless dead that crime had claimed, with that aura of total abandonment they always wore.

He went out by the back door, and dropped the wad of tape and ligatures on the step and watched it bounce into the shallow grass nearby. Climbed back into the orchard and set out to recross it, careful to kick a distinct second path through the whispering grass.

I had called for backup, and as I stood in the front doorway, Officers —— and —— arrived. We ad-

vanced a few steps into the living room as I called Mrs. Untergang's name again. We noticed a shape in the kitchen doorway. Officer —— used his flashlight, and we saw Mrs. Untergang hanging by her neck from a rope tied to a bar across the upper frame of the doorway. . . .

Back in his car again. Taking a deep, cleansing breath and looking at his watch. Found he was precisely poised within the time-stream of this crime. One of those few men who had the insight, and the will. . . .

The clocked recorder of his den phone, the call was ten . . . eleven minutes old. At this very moment he was just driving his Mustang out of his garage. Leisurely, he took his Glock from his shoulder rig and unscrewed the suppressor, which he would have needed for the actual shooting of Jack Untergang, the report of his unsilenced gun not scheduled till ten minutes from now, when he had driven up to the front of the house, and stepped into the living room. Reholstered it, and then took the throw-down from his coat pocket—a little .32 automatic, which Jack would have needed in place of the tire iron he would have walked in with—and replaced it in his glove box.

He fired up the Mustang. Cruising back down the angling rural roads, he radioed Dispatch. He'd received a call from the subject interviewed this afternoon, and was now en route there. The caller, Bridget Untergang, sounded agitated, and it appeared he should have some backup meet him at the residence, where his ETA should be a bit past 2300 hours.

The dark oaks flowed past, the hunchbacked hills of the sullen, untestifying earth. All the murders this earth had witnessed, and disdained to punish! Justice didn't grow on trees. The world's whole weight, dumb and dark, opposed it, truth be told. Justice wasn't just hanging there to be plucked like plums from the crooked, concealing branches. It had to be found, to be dug out. And then it had to be seized, and lifted up. Because it was a torch. Justice was a torch men carried to light the way, some men.

MEMORIES ARE MADE OF THIS

John Pelan

The rain was sheeting down in a nearly impenetrable layer on a November afternoon as I made my way to my favorite pub. The Smoking Leg was as silent as Stonehenge at midnight, all the chairs drawn neatly to the tables with the ashtrays carefully centered. The only sign of activity came from the fireplace where the flames leaped and crackled, the fire being the only disruption of a deathly quiet afternoon. A late-lunching couple sat at one table talking quietly over their glasses of white wine.

My friend Ian nodded to me from behind the bar and poured a cup of the execrable sludge that passes for coffee at the establishment. We exchanged greetings and he gestured to the front page of the morning newspaper, which lay unfolded on the bar, the headlines having nothing really remarkable to say—violence in the Middle East, another dot-com losing millions of investor dollars, that sort of thing . . .

"I didn't bother with the front page this morning," I remarked, "went straight to 'Zippy' and the sports section. . . ."

"Understandable, but you probably didn't see this, then." Ian indicated a short article regarding a psychologist being brought up on charges of ethics violations. The article wasn't really very illuminating, something about the planting of false memories via hypnotic suggestion. Apparently a family was suing for damages and asking for an astronomical amount of money.

"What's this, then? Another of the endless sort of therapies to convince people that there's something in the past they can hang the blame on for things not going to their satisfaction in the present? Nowadays you have mass-murderers claiming they did it because their great-aunt sat them on the toilet backward or they ate too much cotton candy as a youngster or some such. I think it's all pretty much rubbish, but I didn't realize it was illegal. . . ."

"No, it's not illegal; and restoring so-called suppressed memories is very much in vogue. Thing is, I've seen this man's handiwork and quite frankly, a life term or hanging would be more appropriate than the slap on the wrist he's likely to get."

I turned to the article again; the main issue seemed to be that Dr. Vance Harding had caused a man to attack his parents by making him "remember" a childhood of sexual abuse at their hands, incidents that several other family members insisted could not possibly have occurred. The story was fairly compelling in laying out the evidence that Harding's patient was a victim only of false memories and not of any childhood abuse. The insinuation being that the psychologist had planted these ideas in order to prolong the man's therapy and soak his bank account for as much as he could get.

"So you're saying this man's a fraud? That's what the article seems to indicate. . . ."

"No, he's something far worse than merely a fraud. I have reason to believe that he was actually responsible for at least one man's death. The human mind is a pretty amazing thing, there's room for lots of things to be suppressed amid all that gray matter, things that perhaps should remain where they are and not be brought out for any reason. By that same token there's an awful lot of room to *put* things that have no business being there in the first place.

"A man I knew some years ago was seeing Harding as his therapist and the outcome wasn't at all pleasant. I have his journal here if you'd like to read it, it might have something in there you can use for one of those stories you write. On the other hand, at the very least it will give you something to think about. Give it a read and then I'll tell you how it came out and see what you make of it all."

I spent the evening doing a bit of research about this Dr. Harding. A good bit of the material I found indicated that many of his patients "recalled" being forced to take part in rituals involving various sorts of sexual abuse and even human sacrifice at the hands of "Satanists" that were often family members, teachers, neighbors, or others with close connections to the patients. These findings almost invariably resulted in nasty lawsuits and estrangements. Several things struck me as odd; first and foremost was that while I've met a number of Satanists over the years I've never yet encountered one that considered the abuse of children or human sacrifice to be part of their creed. Further, if each of the patients of Dr. Harding had indeed suffered at the hands of a separate cult (which seemed the case as his patients were from many different regions), and were to be believed, then the sheer number of adherents to these practices would be staggering, with covens in every major metropolitan area and black magicians smirking and lurking on every street corner. When you looked at the numbers that would have to be involved for his patients' "memories" to have any credibility it all sounded like something from a bad Dennis Wheatley novel. I came to the conclusion that this Harding chap was a rascal of the worst sort and was assured that this journal Ian had referred to would confirm my expectations.

I got round to the pub late the next afternoon and as promised Ian had a three-ring binder waiting for me. He explained how it came to be in his possession.

"Darrell was a semiregular here before you started hanging out here, I don't think you ever met, though you may have been in a time or two while he was still coming round. Pretty sad guy, boring job that paid well, drank far too much, no girlfriend, no real friends . . . As a bartender you run into people like that all the time, much of the time they just need to talk to someone. Darrell needed something a bit more than that, it was like nothing in his life had ever been better than just sort of a painless mediocrity. Guy like that was a perfect target for a quack like Harding. For a guy like Darrell Dain, paying someone a hundred fifty dollars an hour to tell him that the sad state of his life wasn't his fault must have seemed like a bargain. He kept this journal right up until the end. He left it here one night and I never got the chance to return it. Read it through and then I'll tell you why I think Harding ought to hang rather than lose his license."

The journal was written neatly on cheap lined paper; it covered a period of time over three months. Many of the entries were no more interesting than one would expect of a chap like Dain, who if I'd ever met him would have been almost instantly forgettable. Most days went something along the lines of "went to work, went to the pub, watched TV, etc." However, the relevant entries were extremely interesting. . . .

2/2/93

Dr. Harding suggested I start keeping this journal, and make entries every day, particularly after our sessions. The session today didn't seem to do much, Harding says I'm depressed, hell, I knew that before I went to see him. He also said that there must have been some traumatic events in my childhood. I sure don't remember any such thing. My childhood wasn't very remarkable, we moved a lot because of Dad's job so I didn't have a lot of friends that I stayed in touch with, but I don't remember anything major ever happening except being hit by a car and breaking my legs when I was eleven.

Maybe the next session will be more worthwhile, if it isn't I'll chuck the whole thing, it's pretty expensive.

2/16/93

Dr. Harding hypnotized me today. Afterward he asked me a lot of questions about my older sister, funny, but I hadn't thought about her in ages. The doctor said we're close to getting to the root of my depression. I actually feel pretty good right now, I was going to go out for a few pints, but think I'll just stay in and watch TV instead.

2/23/93

Another session of hypnosis today. Dr. Harding said we're close to learning something and wants to go to two a sessions a week until we "achieve a breakthrough." I told him I thought that was fine. I'm remembering things from childhood that I'd forgotten long ago, I hadn't thought of my older sister Janine in years, she was ten years older and lived with us until I was in junior high. Amazing that I hadn't thought of her until today, I can picture her now as clearly as though she were standing in front of me. She was quite attractive, I suppose, long blond hair that she never, ever cut. I wonder what she looks like today?

More, I wonder how I could have forgotten my own sister! Something awful happened back then, an estrangement or something, I can't recall exactly. I'd put her out of my mind all these years. I think it was a big family scrap of some sort and she left us, never to have contact with us again. Maybe this is what's been eating at me all these years; maybe Dr. Harding can help me remember it all.

2/25/93

Now I remember, and I wish to God I didn't . . . It was as clear as watching a show on TV. I must have been twelve or thirteen. I don't know where my parents were when this all happened, but then they traveled quite a bit. Janine and a man she referred to as "Steven" came into my room and told me I had to go with them. They made me wear a blindfold; I'm not sure where we went, though I think it may have been no further than our basement. There were other people there, when they took the blindfold off I could see that the room was lit only by candles and they had some sort of altar in the center of the room. The rest of it is just bits and pieces; I remember they made me get undressed. I remember they had a lamb and they cut its throat, collecting the blood in the bowl and one man, (Steven I think it was) put something else in the bowl, something he had in a bottle. We all drank, I remember that I didn't want to, but they had the knife and I was scared . . . There was something in the lamb's blood, some drug maybe . . . The rest is just so fragmented and scattered. They made me do *things* then . . . with the other men, with the women, with my own sister. . . . It went on for a long, long time. . . .

How could I have forgotten something this awful? It's clear to me now that I'm missing a year or more of my life! This started when I was twelve, and I remember the preceding year quite clearly. But there's a whole year in my early teens I don't recall at all. I have a vague recollection of having gone to school of course, of the house we lived in, but there's a big blank spot there. When I was fourteen we were in a different city, in Cleveland . . . we'd moved from Dayton, but I recall nothing about the move, nothing about leaving school, nothing. What happened during that time? Dr. Harding has shown me something terrible, and I can only feel that there's something much, much worse that I'm not remembering. . . .

3/2/93

It's coming back thanks to the hypnosis . . . I don't know why my parents were never cognizant of what was going on under their roof, perhaps they were being drugged? Steven and/or Janine are coming for me on an almost nightly basis. . . . Sometimes Janine gets into the bed with me and makes me do things while Steven watches. Other times we go to the place where the rites are held. I don't know what the drugs are that they give me, but I'm not resisting any longer when they take me to their rituals. I can feel the exhilaration of the first time they let me cut the lamb's throat and the warm blood gushes over my hands and bare chest as clearly as though I'm there and feeling the sensation of power that comes with taking a life. I realize that I'm looking forward to them coming for me now.

I remember the feelings and I'm sickened. I was only twelve, I had no idea how evil these people were or how sickly perverse were the acts I was performing at their urging. Every night that we go to the place with the altar now they give me the knife and lead the lamb to me, the other nights my sister and I are in the bed together . . . and God help me, I'm enjoying it. . . .

Harding said remembering my past would set me free. He's wrong, I feel horribly trapped by the shame of what I did. He says none of it was my fault, that I couldn't understand the enormity of what I was being made to do, but that hardly makes me feel any better. I'm so angry I can barely focus on going to work. . . . I hope there's some sort of light at the end of this tunnel. Last night I sat at the pub until closing and they had to call me a cab, I don't even remember coming home. . . .

3/4/93

This was the worst of all, and it's as clear now as though it happened yesterday. Steven and Janine have come for me again and I can tell that something unusual is up. I can sense Janine's excitement, she's practically trembling. Steven tells me this is what I've been prepared for, that tonight there is a special lamb for me. The room is packed with the people. I look at their faces in the candlelight and find that I recognize quite a few from the outside world. Our postman, the lady at the grocery store, one of my teachers . . . These are all fellow worshipers of the Dark One.

I take my place at the altar and wait for them to lead the lamb to me as before. Steven and my sister are chosen for the honor. They bring forth the sacrifice and I recognize her. . . . Her name is Anna, she lives down the street from us. She's eight or nine years old. She's naked and crying as they drag her to the altar and hand me the knife. She's been hurt terribly, I see that a pentagram has been cut into her chest, with droplets of blood still weeping out at the edges of the design. She's been marked for sacrifice; I can see in her eyes that she knows what's coming, and I know what I'm supposed to do. I'm to cut her throat and let them catch the blood in a bowl just like before. . . .

I feel all of their eyes on me; they're chanting *"blood of the lamb, blood of the lamb"* over and over. I'm standing there frozen, not sure what to do; I've killed the lambs before and enjoyed it, but this is different, something in me is shouting *No!* Janine is caressing me and whispering in my ear, *"Do it, please do it, give us the blood of the lamb."* I push her away, I hear Steven hiss *"Do it, you little coward. . . ."* I'm scared of Steven; he's a large powerful man, I've felt his terrible strength before when he *did things* to me. The smoke from the candles is making everything blurry, Anna is sobbing hysterically and trying to cover herself as Janine bends her head back, exposing her throat. Steven has his hand on my shoulder and is urging me to complete the task.

I look at the knife in my hand. The blade is a good ten inches long and razor sharp, the reflection of the flames flicker up and down its length making it appear to coruscate with electricity. I know what I must do. What I *have* to do. I turn as quickly as I can and plunge the knife into Steven's chest. My sister tries to grab me, and almost as though it had a life of its own the knife slashes across her throat. There's screaming and blood, so much blood, and I hear Anna screaming and people running and finally from somewhere the police come.

They sent me somewhere to "rest," and when I got out my parents have moved us to another city to live. Everything's the same on the surface, but strangely unfamiliar. Nothing is ever said of my sister or of my time spent in the asylum. The questions I have are ignored. Did Steven and Janine die? I think they must have, but they're never spoken of again, and I'd forgotten all of this until Dr. Harding made me remember. My own sister seduced me and initiated me into a cult of devil-worshipers that practiced human sacrifice. I've *killed* two people, though maybe it was right and necessary that I did so, but it's awful to have to think about after all these years.

3/9/93

Dr. Harding says I've made a breakthrough and that now we need to work on purging my sense of guilt. I was a child, I was drugged and seduced, not a willing party to their perversions. What I did was closer to heroism than anything else. At least that's what Dr. Harding says. But Harding didn't see what I saw this last weekend. . . . They were back in my bedroom, Janine and Steven were. Whispering to me as like they used to do, promising things. Awful things. They're dead now, of course. They haven't changed since that awful night. They stood there at the foot of my bed urging me to get up and go with them. Steven has a horrid wound in his chest, it looks like the knife went straight through into his heart. Janine is as pretty as ever, but there's a deep gash in her throat where the knife got her. They stood there all night whispering terrible things to me, offering me new thrills if I went with them. Finally morning came and they faded away when the sun rose. The next night they were back.

3/11/93

Harding's no help at all. He says these are figments of my imagination, guilt that needs to be expunged from my memory. He doesn't understand, he wasn't there last night when Janine *crawled into the bed with me* just as she'd done years ago. He wasn't there to see her lover's ghost smirking and encouraging her. He wasn't there to hear their constant entreaties to go with them. Go *where?* I wonder where it is they want to take me and what it is they want me to do for them and I feel physically sick. Apparently they've been dormant all these years until I remembered them and the act of remembrance freed them to haunt me. That's what I am, *haunted.* Haunted and tormented by the people I killed. I want Dr. Harding to make me forget; if I forget, maybe they'll go away again.

3/16/93

They won't go away and Dr. Harding can't help me. He gave me some pills to help me sleep after our session last week but they don't really help. I'm as afraid of sleep as I am of staying awake. If I'm awake I can face them, if I'm asleep and they come there's no telling what might happen. They've come for me every night since last week, and I suspect they'll come every night regardless of whether I sleep or stay awake and wait for them.

I don't know what I can do; Harding says they're just figments of my imagination, manifestations of guilt that I have to work through. . . . That's what Harding says, but Harding hasn't heard them whisper to him, hasn't felt their touch, hasn't lain in bed terrified to move while ghostly hands grope and fondle him. I can't decide what to do, it's getting late. Do I try to sleep or do I wait for them to appear? One thing's for certain, whatever I do, they *will* come. . . .

I closed the book and set it on the night table. Dain's last entry was the one dated March 16, 1993. I didn't know what to make of it; he was obviously a deeply disturbed individual who was in need of far more help than what he'd got from this Harding.

I stowed the journal in my pack and headed to the pub. Ian was busy loading up a batch of CDs on the jukebox when I entered; he gestured for me to help myself to a cup of coffee and finished up with his work. I looked around the room thinking for a moment of all the phantoms the pub contained. The stories that each person that had come in had to tell. . . . How many people carried secrets as terrible as those of Darrell Dain? It was a morbid fancy to be sure, but reading Dain's journal had been strangely disturbing, the idea that anyone might have such a horrible secret suppressed that could suddenly be brought up and given life again.

"You read it all, I take it?"

I nodded and handed the binder to him. "A pretty unhappy chap. What became of him?"

"This is why I think Harding ought to hang. You know that the human mind is a very powerful thing, capable of all sorts of things that we don't fully understand. You and I have both done the firewalking sessions over in Redmond. Quite impossible—human beings can't walk on red-hot coals without having to go to intensive care. At least I thought it was a fraud until I tried it myself, there's no doubt in my mind that the coals were real enough. We both saw them cause a piece of wood to burst into flame before we walked across them. We were hypnotized and walked across them as though strolling through a field of new-mown grass, several other people did the same. Somehow the fakir that organizes the firewalks has learned a way to set free our ability to block out the reality of the heat and the accompanying pain. It's a triumph of the human mind, nothing contranatural about it all. You've also heard of the stigmatics, religious zealots whose faith is so strong that they develop wounds that emulate those of Christ? More indicia of the mind's potential to cause seeming miracles.

"Dain died the night after that last entry was written. He was in here that night until closing and left the journal on the bar where I found it the next morning. I hung on to it expecting he'd be round for it, and he never did show up. Three days later he was found dead in his apartment, he'd been murdered. . . . Cut up terribly, his throat was slashed and there was a pentagram carved into his chest. The killers had taken their time with him yet no one heard anything and there was no sign of forced entry."

"Wait a minute, you're suggesting that the ghosts of his sister and her lover butchered him? You've told me on numerous occasions that you don't believe in ghosts, at least in the classic sense of the word. Are you suggesting that the ghosts of the two people he killed came back from the grave and did him in, that Harding's therapy somehow 'woke up' the ghosts and they came back for revenge? That's a pretty incredible idea, especially coming from a skeptic like yourself!"

Ian shook his head and lit a cigarette, "No, it's not like that at all. . . . After I found out what happened to Darrell, I did a bit of detective work, nothing fancy, but public records like births, deaths, school attendance and the like are pretty easy to come by. You write ghost stories, your natural inclination is to cite the supernatural. What I'm suggesting is actually far worse and can be blamed squarely on Harding's implanting false memories. . . . You see, Darrrel Dain was an only child, he never had a sister."

SHOES

Tim Lebbon and Brett Alexander Savory

Fucking hell.

What's happening to me?

Not just a sheen—sweat *drips* off him, onto the bedclothes coiled around his body, clinging tight. When he flings the sodden sheets away, the cool air breathing in through his little bedroom window is an icy tattoo-gun pricking his skin.

His stomach clenches once. Tight.

He doubles over, bringing his fist down hard beside him. Eyes squeezed shut.

Something inside him is burning. Hot coals in his belly. A fire deep and raging.

He has not felt pain like this in his entire life. He opens his eyes. The dark of the room is rimmed with red flame. Eyes squeezed shut again, tears begin to roll down his cheeks.

I'm dying, he thinks, but on some instinctual level knows that he is not.

Death is kinder than this.

Another flash of pain rips through his abdomen. He rolls off the bed, falls to the hardwood floor, the pain of the impact lost like a gasp in a hurricane. He's all elbows and knees to the bathroom.

Harsh fluorescent light calcifies his burning vision as he opens his eyes again. He cannot see the toilet through his tears. He makes it halfway to where he thinks it might be before another searing burst of pain rips through his belly. His arms quiver, give out under him. Lying on his side, his entire body shaking, teeth chattering, coherent thought melting with every ragged breath, he vomits until there is nothing left inside him but dry heaves. His gut continues to spasm, his jaws locked open, gulping at air.

Eyes open.

Eyes open.

Eyes open.

Close, he thinks. *Please. Close.*

But they won't. His eyes, like his jaw, are locked in this position. Open, waiting for more.

But there *is* no more.

Slowly, like gentle waves of water, the pain is washed away. His breathing returns to normal. The acrid stench of bile stings his nose. His stomach kicks once more, then settles, admitting defeat.

A thousand snuffed candles smoulder inside him.

Eyes close.

Eyes close.

Eyes—

—close—and open, close and open.

He blinks.

Kneels again. Mopping up puke. Head still spinning.

What the fuck was that all about? he thinks. His throat burns. Stomach muscles flinch with every belch he brings up, expecting, bracing for another deluge.

With the bathroom floor still a mess, he stumbles back to bed.

The digital clock on his bedside table glows 4:17 A.M. He has to get up for work in three hours.

"Fuck that," he mumbles, and his gut lightly kicks him again. "And fuck you, too."

Rubbing his stomach, he crawls into bed, the cold breeze still filtering in through the small bedroom window. But this time it's refreshing—no tattoo guns, no ice. No gut-wrenching, white-blind pain doubling him over, squeezing his eyes shut, blistering all thoughts to tattered gibberish.

He drifts into sleep.

Three hours later, the alarm rattles him awake.

What a fucking nightmare! he thinks, but then the stench of puke drifts in from the bathroom, and the smell brings back the memory of pain in his guts. He lies there for a while waiting for it to happen again. He holds his breath, feels his heart worrying away. Cold sweat breaks out all across his body, but it's anticipation of pain, not pain itself.

Need . . . he thinks, but can't decide what. He's hungry and thirsty and his throat is burnt from stomach acid and his guts ache and his elbows and knees are bruised from where he fell to the floor . . . but he needs *something*.

He doesn't want to move, afraid the pain will return, but then the Snooze finishes on his alarm and it shouts again, no subtlety.

He sits up slowly. Head spinning, but that's normal when he wakes. A cigarette will see to that. And caffeine. A smoke and a coffee, that's what he needs. He stands and walks carefully into the bathroom to piss, looking around, expecting to see or smell or feel something but finding it conspicuously absent.

He sidesteps the puddle of puke still on the floor,

stands in front of the toilet. His piss seems to go on forever. He watches the stream hit the water, taking the bad stuff away and leaving him room to pump in more bad stuff. Coffee, yes, lots of coffee, and he decides there and then that he won't go to work today.

That's when it hits him again: a stomach cramp so violent he thinks he's been shot. The pain is too keen for him to shout. It steals his voice and knocks aside his knees, dropping him so that his jaw thumps the toilet pan. Head swimming, he groans and rolls and hugs himself tight, trying to make himself small so the pain can't find him.

When the cramps ease up enough for him to walk, he moves gingerly to the kitchen and roots through cupboards. He lights a cigarette and makes some coffee, swallows a chocolate bar and winces as his stomach rolls around it. Cigarette, more coffee . . .

He sits at the kitchen table, rings in sick. Up all night with stomach cramps, he says.

"You need a rest," his boss tells him. "You've been working too hard."

I sure have, he thinks . . . but is unable to remember exactly what his job is, or where the office is located. He closes his eyes and tries, but there is only a hazy knowledge, like the memory of a bad dream from years before, faded to nothing.

He hangs up, exhales deeply, pumps more coffee into his system. As the last mouthful slides down his throat, the phone rings.

"Hello?"

"Yeah, hi."

He waits a second, expecting the caller to say more, but there is only silence from the other end.

"Who is this?" he asks. His brow furrows. A quick stab to his gut. An echo of last night.

"Never mind who it is, fuckface. Go look in your garage."

Click. Dead air.

His fingers tremble only slightly as he replaces the receiver. He does not understand enough of what is going on to be scared. *Fuckface?* It's too early in the morning to be calling people fuckface.

He pushes back his chair, the words spoken by the man on the phone sinking in.

Garage.

Heart thumping, he gently sets his coffee cup down on the table, crosses the kitchen to the door that leads out to the garage. He turns the brass knob, opens the door, looks around. Seems like a normal garage: car, workbench, power tools, shovels, garbage bins, musty air. Nothing at all out of the ordinary.

He frowns, squints his eyes tight, thinking. Closes the door.

And sitting back at the table, he starts to shake.

Full body tremors. He splashes coffee on his hand, his shirt, the floor. He sets the cup down, hugs himself tight, rocks in the chair.

My name is James Grundson, he thinks. *That's my name. This is my house. That was my car.* He glances toward the kitchen windowsill where a picture of a pretty woman sits—framed by gold, framed by memory. *And that's my wife. My wife. My . . . Where is she? What's happening to me? Why can't I stop—*

James's leg twitches, shoots out, knocks hard into a table leg. It spasms faster than the rest of his quaking body. He moves a hand down from his rib cage, rests it on his thigh, pushes hard, harder, but it won't stop—

—shaking.

Sweat pops out on his forehead, his stomach twists in on itself, wrenching out a gasp. Both hands come back around his middle, squeezing, trying to mash the pain away.

Need something, need something, really need to—fucking shit, what is this?—Christ, it's too much, I can't—

James falls to the kitchen floor. His mind spins, searches for an answer, anything at all to make the pain go away. He knows he *needs* something, but his craving is an elusive thing, a name on the tip of his tongue, and if only the agony would recede for a while and let him forget, maybe, just maybe . . .

He cracks the side of his head against the tiles, shatters one—

need something

—cracks his head against the same broken tile, sending tiny slivers of ceramic into his scalp—

needneedneedneedneedneed

And the phone rings again, rings right inside James's head, shattering thought, erasing more memory, expunging parts of himself he hadn't even known existed.

Until—

The answering machine picks it up.

James's body is a taut wire, humming, stretched, ready to snap.

"I know you're there," says the voice on the machine, the same voice. "Get up. Go look in your garage. Look harder this time. Take responsibility for once in your life, you shitheel."

Another click. The message ends. The machine beeps. James is sure his ears are bleeding, spilling his life onto the cracked tile beneath his head.

Get up, get up.

But his mind can't convince his body that getting up is the best option right now, so he doesn't move, just lies on his side and waits to die. Waits for his head to explode.

Time passes.

No more phone calls. No more electronic beeps to split his cranium in half. No more shaking. And, finally, no more pain.

James Grundson falls asleep.

He dreams of nothing.

James likes dreaming, always has, so when he wakes and there's just a memory of blankness, he tries to go back to sleep. He rolls over on the floor, sees the photo of his wife—

—that is my wife, yes, definitely, it is.

So why the hell don't I recognize her?—

—and closes his eyes, remembering when he was a teenager waking from a dream of fucking his French teacher, just about to empty his load up her arse when he woke, angry at the world for not giving him that, trying to get back to sleep to find any remnants of the dream.

That never worked.

He cannot fall back to sleep, and the recollection of that long-ago, never-finished dream kick-starts something, a pain in his balls, blue-balls. For a while it's almost pleasant, and he's dozing again, but then it feels like someone grabbing his scrotum and crushing it between two bricks.

More pain, so intense he can't make a sound, and he's thrashing on the floor once again. He slices his scalp on smashed tile, and it's almost welcome because it gives him a lesser pain to concentrate on.

Later, awake, sick, the phone rings and he doesn't answer. The machine clicks on again:

"Have you looked yet, fuckhead? You sick bag of *shit.* Go, look what you did."

He can't concentrate on whatever the demented bastard on the phone is talking about. He crawls over to the answering machine, knocks it from the table, smashes it to smithereens across the floor. Its exposed innards mix with a puddle of cold puke.

He needs something to stop the pain, so he goes through the cupboards in the bathroom. Pills, potions, creams, an old dried-up joint behind new packets of soap. Nothing that he sees and thinks, *Yes, that's it, that's it!*

His balls are still aching like hell and he needs to jerk off, relieve the pressure. He makes his way to the bedroom, strips, and starts to work his flaccid cock. But he can't get it hard. His balls sway like two centers of pain, and he can't get it up, can't rise because something is so very wrong, something screaming for his attention, something . . .

"This isn't my house."

Through all the pain last night and this morning he'd assumed familiarity, had no reason to believe otherwise. He was here, asleep, then in such pain that his perception had been turned inward ever since.

"This . . . isn't my house."

The truth of it rings in his ears, quiets the pain a tiny, tiny bit.

He roots through the closet, dresses in some other man's clothes—a nice Italian suit that fits snugly, and fine black shoes that *almost* fit his feet, just a tiny bit too big—goes back downstairs and opens the garage door again. But he doesn't want to go inside.

Finally gathering the courage, he steps through.

It looks just as it should, but there's something in the air, a whiff of knowledge unknown, like a threat whispered in a foreign tongue.

Inside the house the phone screams again.

James steps fully into the garage, closes the door behind him, shutting out the incessant ringing. He only hears it now as a repetitive echo in his mind. Continuous. Never changing and never ending.

He walks slowly around the car, afraid of what he will find.

Near the front bumper, a pair of legs protrude from behind the car.

James claps a hand to his mouth and steps back, away. Gathers himself, then goes back to see the rest of the body, his own body vibrating, threatening to convulse.

He passes around the front of the car and sees the woman, lying facedown in a pool of blood, a spade embedded in the back of her skull.

James's stomach kicks, he loses his balance, has to lean against the side of the car. The pain is less than before, but still threatens to overpower him, send him reeling to the bloody floor of the garage.

Who is it? he thinks. *The woman in the photo? My wife? Is that my—*

He uses the car to steady himself, digs the toe of his shoe beneath the woman's ribs, lifts, trying to send her over onto her back. The body stops rolling when the spade handle hits the tool bench. It remains on its side, blood dribbling from the smashed face.

"Bloody hell . . ."

It's the woman from the picture. His wife. But not his wife.

Who am I? he thinks. More bits of memory come back to him, float homeless in his mind, alien. *How did I get into this house?*

Inside, the telephone stops ringing.

The automatic garage door clicks and rises, letting bright sunshine in. James lifts a hand to shield his eyes against the sunlight, tries squinting to see who, if anyone, is coming in. A silhouette approaches. As it comes closer, James makes out a man, tall, crisply dressed.

The man stops in front of him, pulls James's arm down from his face.

"No need to hide now, Philip," he says, twisting his lips into what is probably supposed to be a smile.

James is reminded of shark's teeth.

And the voice—the voice is that of the caller, the one who called him "fuckface."

"I'm not Philip," he says, frowning. "My name is James Grundson, and—"

"You're not James anybody," the man with the shark's teeth says. "You're whomever I want you to be, and I want you to be Philip."

James just looks down at the body at his feet, then back up to the man in the sharp suit. "This body," he says, motions toward it. "I don't know who did this, or how I even got into this house."

"None of that matters, Philip. You're feeling better, aren't you?" the man says. "No more of those stomach pains, those nasty cravings, am I right?"

James waits a moment, realizes that the man *is* right. The pains of the past few hours have diminished to the point where they're just a dull ache in his belly, a patch of crusting blood on his head, a miasma of vomit around his nose.

He nods, lost in the man's impossible reasoning.

"Good. That means you almost understand." The man smiles again, pats James on the shoulder, leaves his hand there. It's warm, comforting, like the sun's heat coming through the open garage door. "Your name is Philip Emmelson. You murdered your wife last night in a fit of rage. Plunged a shovel into the back of her head. Her infidelity is what made you so angry, but you feel no remorse for what you've done.

"This," the man says, dropping his hand from James's shoulder, and waving his arm in the corpse's direction, "is what your life has led up to. Everything you did as James Grundson means less than nothing. Any kids you might have, any job, any philosophies or ideals, any portion of the person you think you are, is completely and utterly wiped away, and you are now Philip Emmelson. You will always be Philip Emmelson."

Confused, James bursts into tears. Sobs wrack his frame, and he blubbers words that the man in the crisp suit with the nice, white shark teeth cannot understand.

"Now, now, come on," the man says, "don't be blue. This could have happened to anybody. We're all one person anyway, when you really think about it. All of the same mind, the same passions, loves, hates, indifferences. Nobody really cares about anybody else, because nobody really cares about themselves. It's nothing new. This is old news, Philip, and I'm sorry if you're confused, but I really don't know how to make it any more clear."

James just slumps to the ground, next to the body of somebody else's murdered wife. One of his knees is in her blood.

"I'm sorry it has to be this way, Philip. But forget about being James Grundson. It will only cause you more pain, and I'm sure you weren't enjoying yourself in there, were you?"

No answer.

"Think of it as taking one for the team, okay, Philip?" the man says. "Humanity owes you one." He turns to leave, takes a few steps toward the open garage door, then remembers something, spins on his heel, comes back to where James is crumpled.

"Nearly forgot. Here's your ID." The man produces a passport, birth certificate, and driver's license, throws them into James's lap. He gazes down.

Sunlight shines brightly on James's face, casting shadows beneath his eyes where he sits with his head hung low, feet splayed beneath his body like a discarded marionette.

The man with the shark's teeth kneels down, leans in close to James, whispers in his ear: "I'll make sure the old Philip Emmelson appreciates your sacrifice. I'll tell him you understood that this was necessary, that the guilty are not always held responsible because sometimes . . ."

Something passes quickly across the sun, sending a brief shadow darting through the garage interior.

"Well," the man continues, "sometimes, they find someone to take the fall. Someone like you, Philip. Someone with a big heart and a weak soul."

The man stands up, straightens the lines of his suit.

The sun comes back out in full force, even brighter than before.

A neighbor walks his dog past the front of the house, looks in, sees a man kneeling in a puddle of blood, a woman beside him, a shovel jutting from the back of her head.

The neighbor's mouth forms a round O of surprise. He starts moving again, his footsteps faster now, given purpose.

"Remember, Philip," the man says as he's walking away, "this could have happened to anyone."

As the garage door falls shut, James Grundson tries desperately to remember who he is, where he lives, what sort of life he has, but he can only remember the name Philip Emmelson. The clothes he is wearing expand to fit his shoulders better, come in around the waist to hug him a little closer, the shoes shrinking just the tiniest bit, becoming a perfect fit. He sees the lumpy shape of his dead wife beside him—

—that fucking cheating whore—

—and it starts to feel . . . right.

He sits in the dark, smells the blood, listens to the street noises and the sirens coming closer.

Philip Emmelson falls asleep against the side of another man's car.

And dreams of nothing.

FAIRY FORT

Peadar Ó Guilín

Kevin and I leaned on each other. Neither of us had drunk before, but we'd earned a month's wages and spent the money as wisely as our mothers had feared. "I'd still prefer we fought it out like two men." I said, "Like the King and the Kaiser."

"Sure you would, Paudy!" Kevin's splotchy face spun slowly in my vision. "You're twice the size o' me! This way's fair." And in the whiskey haze, it all made sense. Fear never came into it. The braver of the two would ask Peggy to dance at the end of harvest, the coward would renounce all interest in her.

The moon hung low in the sky, illuminating the mound. Fruit trees grew atop it, but neither man nor bird had touched them. Such mounds cover the Irish countryside. We called them *lios na Sidhe*—Fairy Forts. Even now, my heart beat steadily and unafraid.

"No music," said Kevin and stamped his feet. "Stupid stories! No dancers. It's just old folks' superstitions like the priests say." He turned to go, but I held him fast. My heart quickened *thump, thump, thump.*

"Who has fear on him now?" I asked. My English was poor despite years away from the Gaelic-speaking part of Ireland I called home. "Is it me that has the win?"

"There's nothin' there, Paudy! Use your eyes." But I held him fast.

Although Protestant, and therefore above peasant beliefs, the farmer had built a stout fence around the mound to keep his beasts off. He'd gone to the expense of hammering iron nails closely together 'round the top so that the head of each nail touched its neighbor and formed a closed ring. We looked each other in the eye and it was like being friends again, like we'd never clapped eyes on Peggy Mahon.

The moment ended. Kevin climbed the fence and I matched him step for step feeling the rough grain of the wood, the chill of the iron nails. We landed together on the far side. At once the music began, wild and beautiful, played faster than mortal hands could dream of. I gasped. The hill had changed, become larger and steeper. More trees grew there now. At the top, figures danced, kicking and leaping. Their feet tapped the ground so hard we felt the rhythm *thump, thump, thump* in our own bodies. Kevin gripped my hand. I didn't shake him off for a coward—I wanted to run too, my heart wanted it. I felt it like a sheepdog in my breast, dragging me backward and whining. Then Kevin let me go and began crawling up the slope. If I stayed behind now, I'd have to stay behind at the harvest dance too.

So, I followed, clinging to the cover of bushes. Now I could see the dancers, though not the musicians. Men and women of perfect form, giving every appearance of joy. I could see Kevin's feet tapping and realized my own were doing the same. I'd danced every winter of my life and always loved it.

The *Sidhe* smiled widely and glowed with sweat. Dawn was near. The dance must have gone on all night. Some, like a blond girl in a squirrel-fur kilt, looked exhausted, but never faltered in step or smile. I felt terrible spying on her, but couldn't take my eyes away.

Beautiful, I thought, beautiful. I longed to join her—to forget for a while my life of toil—until one of the dancers switched partners and I saw his empty eyes, large and glassy like a dead bull's. I shivered, and began moving backward down the hill, keeping my eyes on the *Sidhe*.

And then, the blond girl stumbled.

The music halted and dancers froze. Nobody stopped smiling, not even the blond girl. Then all of them ran at her and flung themselves upon her, and clamped their mouths to any part of her they could find.

"No!" I screamed. What possessed me? I ran forward, and Kevin, every bit as drunk and stupid, joined me. I lifted bodies up by their scruffs and flung them away, their smiling faces now bloody. Holes the size of my fist covered the blond girl's body. She had stumps for legs and one of her arms lay chewed to the bone like an apple. Worst of all was the fact that even when the rest of the *Sidhe* had been pulled away, she continued to worry gobbets of flesh from her own shoulder.

"Ná deán sin," I said. "Stop that!"

"Paudy!" Kevin screamed. I turned to see a half dozen *Sidhe* leap upon him. A sharp pain ripped through my calf. What was left of the blond girl was sinking its teeth into me, and others joined her, lots of others, biting hard with their blunt little teeth, each bite burning like the fires of Hell. I flung them off me and started rolling down the hill. Ferns slapped me in the face, furze ripped at my skin and the remains of my clothes. I had to keep rolling at any cost.

I hit the base of a birch and stopped. I looked up, thinking to see my death, but instead I saw the dawn.

I used the trunk of the birch to help me to my feet. The

great hill we'd danced upon had shrunk back to the size of a mound. Little red marks no bigger than the bite you'd get from a horsefly covered my hands. I felt woozy and wondered if the whiskey that had brought me here had planted dreams in my head too.

"Kevin?"

I found him curled into a ball and weeping. Dried blood covered his clothes, but he too seemed unhurt when I pulled him, at last, to his feet.

"They tried to drag me in there," he said, pointing to a rabbit hole. "It was big as a tunnel under the moon."

We helped each other over the fence, and you'd think that would be the end of it, that we'd have learned our lesson.

Around the fire, with old Mahon torturing the fiddle, the younger Mahon talked up a storm. "Why should we do their fightin' for them?" He waved a clay pipe toward the Protestant farm. "The Kaiser's never done us no harm, but them English! We all know what they done for us!"

Murmurs of agreement.

I kept out of the discussion. I lay on my back chewing a stalk. I'd worked two full days with only a night of terror in between them to rest. It was backbreaking work too: cutting rye with a sickle and piling it into stooks to keep it dry. Every muscle ached and I wished I'd more of last night's whiskey for the pain and for the thought that an endless succession of such days stood between me and my grave.

Peggy Mahon bent close to her father with a mug. Blond hair fell over her face and reminded me of the fairy dancer the others had attacked and all but eaten. Her left hand carried tea for her father; her right held the old rosary that never left her sight.

"God protect you, Peggy Mahon," I whispered, "and if He won't, I will!"

I suspected Kevin lay in the darkness nearby plotting his own way into her heart and I wondered if our friendship could ever be mended.

Fresh lines creased Peggy's brow. I dreamed I could smooth them away, that I, Paudy, from the back of beyonds, with no land and broken English, could stand with her before a priest. In the firelight, my mind drifted and I imagined she might kiss me.

Abruptly, Peggy straightened. She strode over to my side and knelt next to me. Before I could splutter, she pressed her lips to mine.

Old Mahon gasped. "Peggy!"

A look of confusion crossed her face, followed swiftly by fright. "Not again!" she whispered and ran from the fire with everybody staring after her. Old Mahon threw me an angry look.

"I didn't do a thing!" I said.

"You'd better not, Paudy Sullivan," his voice rasped like an old millstone, "or I'll have you out of here quicker than scour through a sheep!"

He went into a huddle with his bewildered son and a few of the others. They probably couldn't understand how a religious girl could commit such a sin and so publicly. I decided to sleep away from the camp until they cooled down.

But I needed the cooling more than they! My lips burned and my heart beat even faster than when the *Sidhe* had attacked me. Her lips—the curve of her chin in the firelight tormented me.

A hand grabbed my elbow as I moved away from the fire. I felt a moment of panic.

"It's me, you big lummock!" laughed Kevin. "Did you

think the *Sidhe* had come back for you? They might as well now after what you did with Peggy!"

"You sound happy about it! I think you want old Mahon to send me home." He could still hurt me, my ex-friend.

"You should have kissed her out of sight, when you knew you could. Like me. I kissed her first!"

"What do you mean?" And then I remembered Peggy exclaiming "Not again!"

"Oh, you know my meaning, Paudy!" His eyes glinted in the moonlight. "So easy, it is! I was after takin' a little rest behind the cart and I . . . Ha! I just, I dunno, I just called her to me . . . I touched her chest."

No wonder Peggy had seemed so upset earlier! I flung myself upon him. Poor Peggy! I punched him a few times in the ribs before he wriggled away. I ran after to hit him some more, but stopped when I saw he was crying.

"I know I did wrong," he said. "But what chance has the likes of me with the likes of Peggy Mahon? Beautiful—"

"Kind—" I added.

"With a dowry?" He sat down on an overturned bucket and I moved to stand beside him. "One kiss, in my whole life. It was over in a minute, but . . ."

He'd no need to finish the sentence. Not for me who felt the same.

"When I saw you kiss her too," he continued, "I wanted to kill you. But then I knew you'd never be able to do it again and so—"

"How did you know this, Kevin?" I asked. But when he wouldn't look me in the eye, I realized *he* must have tried again and again to make her come to him after the first time.

I didn't want to hit him anymore, so I left. I tossed for a while. I tried not to imagine Peggy coming to me in the night, and then I begged God's forgiveness, because I couldn't stop doing it. Did the *Sidhe* feel guilt when they took what they needed? God must have heeded my prayers for I fell asleep all alone on the far side of the byre.

Nearby fields held a rival team working just as hard as we. All knew the terrible luck that befell the last team in a district to finish the harvest. So we had to work harder now, faster, backs doubled and in such pain we feared they'd never straighten again. Stroke after stroke of the sickle, three handfuls of grain to the sheaf, ten sheaves to the stook and the sun watching all without mercy.

Peggy came from time to time with a ponger of cold tea. She always seemed to miss me, though I knew where she stood in the field without looking. Kevin went thirsty too. "I can't stand it," he whispered at me, "she won't even look at me."

"With your face so spotted, 'tis no wonder," I said.

"Shut up!" said Kevin. "Shut up!"

"Back to work, you two!" shouted old Mahon from the far side of the field. "Ten minutes more and we're done here."

But it was already too late. Whoops erupted from a neighboring field and laughter. A voice called over the hedgerow: "Mahon, me boyo! Mahon! We're after chasin' her over the hedgerow."—By "her" he meant the bad luck.—"Ye hear me, Mahon? We're after chasin' her over to ye!"

Many of our gang flopped to the ground.

"What do I care," Kevin hissed. "Sure wasn't I born with bad luck already wrapped 'round me neck? I'll tell you this, Paudy Sullivan, I've had enough of it."

"You can do nothing for it," I said.

"No?" said he. He straightened and waved his sickle at

me, a shocking breach of manners that could get you thrown off a team. "I'll have that woman," he said, "and not God nor the saints nor old Mahon himself will stop me!"

The gang acted even colder toward me that evening, especially Peggy, as if it was me that had lost them a year's luck. Maybe old Mahon would give me my marching orders the next day and that would be that. No money for the winter. I was sorry now to have spent the little I'd had on whiskey.

I slept alone again, tortured with the idea that I'd leave Peggy with hatred in her heart. I tossed in my blanket. I wondered what would happen if I explained the whole, mad thing to her. She might forgive me. She might—dared I dream it?—she might confess love for me too! Madness, of course. But her lips had been so soft. Maybe the magic had only freed her to do what was already in her heart.

I decided to risk it.

I left my blanket and moved 'round the byre. The Protestant dogs came sniffing after me, wagging their tails. I'd made friends with them early on and they rewarded me now with licks and silence.

I could see blanket-wrapped bodies in the light of the embers, but I couldn't tell which was Peggy. What if old Mahon woke as I picked my way among them? Or worse, what if Peggy called out in fright?

While I struggled to come up with a plan the dogs began hopping with excitement. Then, I saw it too. A figure was moving away from the camp toward the fields. I knew that shape, that mincing walk.

Kevin!

But what could he be up to? His form crossed the first field heading north. Toward the *lios*.

I hid my blanket and tools beneath bushes at the base

of a wall. Then I followed his purposeful form over dry stone walls for two more fields until he stood at the fence around the *lios*. Now he hesitated. I saw him get to his knees as if to pray, but then he shook his head and stood again. He put something heavy in his pocket and climbed the fence as though it were a mile high and made of sickle blades. I knew how he felt. The terror of the Fairy Fort already gripped me.

I caught him perched at the top, shaking like a leaf. He nearly jumped out of his skin when I gripped his arm.

"This is madness, Kevin," I said.

"Then why did you follow me, Paudy Sullivan?" So bright shone the moon I could see his face as clear as carrots on my spoon.

"We were only in their presence for heartbeats," he said, "and heartbeats is all the power lasted."

"You will not live this time, Kevin," I said.

"And you think you will, Paudy?"

"I didn't come here for that, Kevin, it's wrong, it's—" But he wasn't listening.

"Well, I don't care if they kill me, you hear? Better I never kissed her. But I did kiss her and I won't live without it again." His sweat gleamed in the moonlight. I knew how he felt and tried to lay a comforting hand on his elbow, but he shook me off. "You're worse than I am, Paudy Sullivan. You pretend you have honor and religion, but they're no deeper in you than the scum on boiling porridge. May God strike me dead if I live to see Peggy Mahon in your hands!"

With that, he leapt to the other side of the fence. I knew then, that if I stayed behind, either he would die—and die in sin—or worse: Kevin would be the one to taste Peggy's kisses, and I the one to live without.

My limbs shook as I climbed the fence. As soon as I

set foot on the far side the music began and trees that had been small were mighty oaks.

"God save me and guard me!" I whispered, but I knew that by my own will I'd stepped beyond His reach. I moved up the hill in search of Kevin. The music grew ever wilder and more beautiful. Halfway, I espied leaping shadows that turned my tongue to a dry lump of old oatcake in my mouth. There seemed not enough air in all the world to fill my heaving chest. I wanted to turn back, but I glimpsed Kevin some way ahead, fondling something in his pocket. *A rosary?* I wondered. Much good it could do him in a place like this. I stumbled after him. Soon, I was close enough to see the *Sidhe* at their graceful, grinning dance.

Kevin moved behind a tree and I behind a bush no more than five yards to his left, both of us closer to the dancers than to each other. I couldn't move to him without crossing open space, nor could I call out, though I heard breathing even more ragged than my own, which I thought came from him. I tried to wave to him, but he had eyes only for the dancers.

Kevin pressed his forehead against the trunk of the tree. The ragged breathing grew louder. I heard it even though his lips were pressed together. Could it be coming from someone else?

Then he stepped into the clearing and the music stopped. He took a shiny new horseshoe from his pocket and raised it over his head. The *Sidhe* seemed to freeze.

"Now," said Kevin, voice shaky, "now we'll see how you like my iron, eh?"

They pulled back, grins gone, black eyes fixed on the horseshoe.

"Ye have something I want. Not your gold! Ye can keep that!"

They stepped farther back as he advanced to the center of the clearing at the summit of the hill. Some of them moved to the edges. I heard the ragged breathing again, in the undergrowth. No matter how I looked I couldn't find its source. My eyes turned back to Kevin.

"I'll not burn ye if I get some magic. Ye hear?" Kevin had always been smarter than me, but now he revealed himself to be braver too. Brave enough to win the greatest prize of all.

The *Sidhe* had pulled around in an arc. I feared they would spot me, or hear the terrible breathing nearby. But all continued to stare at Kevin: beautiful women with dainty features, handsome youths, staring, staring, some with mouths agape, some with strands of saliva dribbling down their chins like threads of moondrunk silver. In moments a full circle would form about my friend.

I wanted to run. I *would* run, but first, I'd call out a warning that might give him a chance to flee before the circle closed. The breathing stopped. I opened my mouth to warn my friend.

Instead I screamed. Claws tore into my calf and I fell to my knees, while some creature behind me slobbered and bit. I reached back, almost fainting with the pain, all spines and fire. In the distance, I heard Kevin cursing and shouting. Sounds of frenzy filled the glade.

My hands fixed on a neck and squeezed. I pulled the beast away, feeling a chunk of my flesh tear with it. I swung the thing around to smash it against a nearby trunk and stopped. I recognized her blond hair. The others had eaten parts of her face and one of her breasts. Her body ended at the ribs, the last of which lay exposed and alive with maggots. Her chest heaved for breath. She fixed me with her remaining eye and wheezed: *"Le'd thoil, a thiarna . . ." Please, my lord,* in Gaelic, my language, the language of old people and yokels. It sounded more like the moaning of wind than a human voice.

"What do you want of me?" I asked. Her lips were smeared with my blood.

"Feoil," she replied. *Meat.* I threw her from me and turned to flee. But a dozen of the *Sidhe* had appeared on the hill beneath me. The music began again and they took to grinning as they drove me up to the top. I heard Kevin weeping and hope filled my heart. Together, maybe, we could make a stand.

But I arrived in time only to see him dragged feet first into a burrow little wider than his body. His hand, chewed off at the wrist, remained outside, clutching the horseshoe.

The iron had hurt them: gashed and smoking bodies lay scattered about it. I moved toward the horseshoe, but a princess, lovelier than Peggy Mahon would ever be, blocked my path. Others followed until I stood alone in a circle of grinning *Sidhe* with only the music for comfort.

I could feel blood ooze from the back of my leg and sweat drenched my brow. Some of the *Sidhe* bore injuries worse than mine from Kevin's iron, limp arms and legs where the bones shone through. They all looked hungry.

I grinned at them. What else could I do? Then I laughed and began dancing in time to the music as my mother had taught me. The grins of the *Sidhe* widened. Perhaps this was what they'd always wanted from me. I leapt into the air, arms perfectly by my side. I spun and capered, fighting exhaustion, fighting the pain of every landing on my injured leg. Then they joined in, all of them at once, even the wounded.

Hours seemed to pass. I never felt more alive, more beautiful. I was one of them, truly one of them. At times, my gaze met that of the Fairy princess who promised things Peggy Mahon couldn't name. And I wanted those things. More than anything, more than I wanted a lifetime of toil with every Sunday on my knees.

The moon lowered in the sky. And then, one of the injured ones gasped and collapsed. The others fell on him and began to feed.

I woke on the small mound with blood on my lips and tatters of flesh between my teeth. I swallowed them. I would live now as the Fairies did, free of saints and shame.

The dogs whined and fled when I came to collect my blanket. Only Mahon and Peggy watched me go, he with a frown, she with bowed head and rosary.

"Good riddance!" he shouted after me. "My daughter wants no part o' ye!"

I laughed and skipped down the road. I stopped in the shade of an apple tree where Peggy joined me after an hour, her possessions all packed up in a blanket of her own. Later, tangled in that same blanket, she asked me if I was surprised she'd run away with me.

"Not at all," I said with a yawn, "it's just as I imagined it." Her plain, human face already bored me. Soon, I promised myself, soon I would take her dancing.

THE ABANDONED

Jeffrey Thomas

Maria had been told she was lucky to have acquired work in the city of Tartarus, so soon upon her arrival in the netherworld.

It wasn't much comfort. She could only take the word of her coworkers—her fellow slaves, more precisely—that to be employed here brought a measure of protection from the Demons in place of the punishments inflicted on those beyond the city's borders. It was as reassuring as being told that she should be thankful for having one leg chainsawed off instead of two.

Seeing the Demon city of Tartarus for the first time had been the third greatest shock of her afterlife. The first shock had been that there was an afterlife (she had been one of the only Mexicans she'd ever known not to be devoutly religious) and the second greatest shock had been that the afterlife adjudged for her was as a citizen of Hell.

Mexico City was dwarfed by Tartarus, though to Maria's mind the population of her own former city might have been greater. Perhaps that was only an illusion because of the vast scale of this place, which rendered all (mock) life microscopic, and because of its absence of streets, of commerce. Its very expanse and scope made it seem empty, its fullness made it desolate, and most strangely, its hideousness made it terribly beautiful.

Every structure was a skyscraper, many of them vanishing into the almost solid layer of slowly churning cloud that forever obscured the sky. These skyscrapers were not so much ranked beside each other as *merged* with each other, so that often the only way one might tell them apart (if indeed they were in any sense apart) was to notice how the color of one was shaded slightly darker or lighter than another, or how a building composed of nothing but uncountable, tiny opaque windows faded into a building that appeared to be entirely constructed (within as well as without?) out of gigantic auto parts blended with a madman's plumbing system combined with computer circuit boards . . . some of this machinery glossy smooth, other sections corroded rust red. Though a building might be a ghostly pale hue and another so dark it seemed one existed in day while the other loomed at midnight, there was a bleak sepia tone over the whole of the city that made it weirdly homogenous.

Her own former city had been notorious for its smog, but sectors of this city seemed to loom out of a more subtle mist that blurred its edges, while other areas stood out with a sharpness of line and detail that stabbed the eye. White, luminous fog wound like a living entity between the fissures and irregular gaps in the mountains of concrete and metal, and steam plumed out of apertures, some of these like grates or exhaust ports while others were more like organic orifices. Because worked into the weave of Tartarus was an unmistakable organic element, as if the city wasn't actually built from concrete and metal, plastic and stone, but had been *grown* like one titanic living body.

There was thick tubing that looked both flexible but

vitreous and that snaked down the faces of buildings, that ran in and out of their very bodies, like arteries. There were huge, glassy bulbs or boils or tumors of some kind which were filled with that glowing mist or else with seething black masses like gigantic worms in rows of immense egg sacs. There were portions of the city that looked formed out of translucent bone, out of some calcified matter like a coral reef, out of tons of oxidized fossil. Buildings that seemed made of polished insect chitin, structures that were not linear and hard-edged but fluid and asymmetrical and a chaos of shape and design.

All of these things in unlikely conjunction were Tartarus, unified by its leached brown color however it might shade, compressed so tightly together it was like one colossal building alone, unified by its strange silence despite the ringing and hammering heard here and there as its mechanical flanks pumped and pistoned, unified by its atmosphere of hopelessness and loneliness . . . like an abandoned city haunted only by ghosts. Of which Maria was one.

Maria had been raped again. It was bad enough when a Demon raped her, but much worse when one of her coworkers did. She expected better from them, since they shared her plight. She supposed these men needed to vent their terrible, frustrated rage. Or else they simply felt that this world was a place where evil was expected, being the very substance of the walls, their masters, of their own mock flesh. Still, they expressed their humiliation by humiliating her. Spent their bottled anger by filling her up with it instead.

A Demon had come along the narrow corridor in which they lay, and had kicked the man hard in the ass. The man had scampered to his feet, his slick cock bobbing ridiculously, and scampered off down the passageway to wherever his workstation was. The Demon had then strolled on, not bothering to help Maria up from the floor. As she rearranged her wrenched and ripped clothing, she watched the Demon recede. He hadn't been concerned for her, but only for the work that waited to be done.

The first man who had raped her, on her second day in Tartarus, she had afterward struck across the back of the head with a huge two-handed wrench swung from over her shoulder. He had dropped to her feet with blood already pouring heavily out of his nose and ears. An hour later, the damage almost entirely regenerated, the rapist had sought her out with a lead pipe in his hand for his own club . . . but a Demon had pushed him away and told him to leave her alone. "Thanks," Maria had told the creature.

"Go back to work," it had rasped at her. And several days later, she thought it was this very same Demon who raped her against the wall of a hiss-filled boiler room . . . though it was hard to tell some of them apart, especially the ones like this who were less human in form.

Brushing off her bottom with both hands, Maria resumed her interrupted journey to her current workstation for the beginning of her shift. She picked up her pace, afraid of being late, and thus punished. She had been allowed a period of sleep so as to recuperate from yesterday's seemingly endless shift, and the workers were even given food to eat. These sham bodies they possessed did not really require sleep or sustenance, just as it wasn't true blood that ran in their veins or live sperm that spurted from rapists' pricks. (And nerves did not really scream at the touch of a torturer's brand or blade, however it might seem they did.)

The bodies of the Damned thought they were still

alive, and so they had the urges and instincts of the living.

Tartarus was one of those far-spaced cities of Hell in which its Demonic population was not only trained for their duties . . . but made.

This was Maria's line of work. She was, for all intents and purposes, a manufacturer of the very creatures that had rustled her up for this employment.

Shifts were long. Workers often burned or froze their hands, depending on what sort of Demon—or what stage of that Demon's progression—they were working on. Toward the end of today's shift, a gust of hot steam had scalded Maria's left hand . . . but already, on her way to this floor's showers, the pain and angry redness were fading.

Whenever she was badly burned, by steam or splashed corrosive chemical or by bumping into a red-hot metal surface, Maria was reminded of her father. His right arm had been terribly scarred as a toddler, when he had tipped a pot full of boiling water off the stove top. He had told Maria that his mother was passed out on the sofa at the time. He had told Maria that his mother was a worthless bitch and whore, and a neglectful mother who ultimately left her husband for a man who was younger but just as drunken as herself.

Maria's own mother had met her father while she was living for a time in San Antonio. He was white, she a Mexican. When Maria was eight years old, after an escalating series of terrifying fights, her father left her mother. She had never seen him again, and her mother had moved them back to Mexico to be with family.

Maria had thought that her father loved her; that he would never leave her as his mother had ended up leaving him. Now, she couldn't even remember his face clearly. But she remembered the scars on his arm. They had never faded away, like the burn on her own hand today.

Maria nodded in mute greeting to the three men who stood watch outside the women's shower area. The Demons had not assigned them to this duty; they had volunteered, to protect the women from other men who might enter the showers to attack them. On the rare occasion, though, a Demon or even a pack might enter into the showers, and for them the men lowered their eyes and stepped aside.

Maria stripped and angled her wide pretty face toward the pelting hot streams, turned slowly around, her long hair plastering to her back. Opening her eyes, stepping back a little, she gazed upward as she exposed her underarms to the irregular streams that fell from the machinery high overhead, the fallen water then trickling into a grated floor rough against her bare feet. This large chamber was not intended for this use, but the Demons shrugged it off, didn't bother stopping them. High above, cloudy cocoons in row after row were suspended pendulously like a crop nearly ripe for harvesting. The raining water rinsed these subtly pulsating sacs. Here and there, Maria could see a more pronounced bulge where a limb or wing pressed at the membrane that sheathed its owner.

A reverberating thud made her step entirely out of the torrents for a moment or two to listen. An explosion, perhaps. Another boiler blown? It wasn't too uncommon. A dangerous mistake on the part of a worker (though even if shredded to chum, he would reconstitute) or simply an overtaxed machine. No further detonations followed, and Maria ducked back into the downpour.

After bathing herself, she dipped her shed uniform into a mechanical recess in one wall that had collected a puddle of this falling hot water, so as to clean it as best she could—then she changed into her fresh uniform and headed out of the shower chamber, her hair still dripping wet. At the entrance, one of the guards (his name was Russ, he'd recently told her) smiled at her again and shifted in his hands the heavy mallet he carried as a weapon. "So Maria, how are ya?"

"I'm fine," she told him, smiling a little. She couldn't believe people could still ask such inane questions. Empty civility. Like robot servants after a nuclear war, making tea for mummies long dead in their armchairs. Russ was that robot and that mummy at the same time. She dropped her eyes and hurried past him without trying to look obvious about it. "You?" she called back over her shoulder obligatorily. She saw he was watching her go.

"Okay. Goin' to the mess hall?"

"Yup."

"Maybe I'll see you there in a few."

"Sure."

He was cute enough, she supposed. White. A redhead. And she could not conceive of falling in love with any man here in Hades. As numb as she was, as hollowed out inside, as automaton-like in her work and her daily routines, she was not some robot with a bolted-on grin. Her programming had been shorted out. Civility had been an illusion all along.

Affection was a sham better left to the living.

When Maria turned a corner of the cramped hallway, the rainfall hiss of the showers still in her ears, she looked up to see a Demon plant itself in front of her.

"What is your sin?" it snarled, and backhanded her across the jaw.

The Demons didn't apparently use names to distinguish one infernal race from another, but for their own convenience (since they had to manufacture them), the workers had given them designations, and this species was called a Caliban. It was like a cross between a sumo wrestler and an insect, bulgingly soft in some places and armored in others, the same sepia brown as the exteriors and interiors of Tartarus, except that its eyes glowed a bright white and its primary forearms shaded to almost black at the ends of their scorpionlike pincers. It was one of these appendages that had just sent Maria to the floor.

"What is your sin?" it demanded again, taking another threatening step toward her so that she smelled the choking incense scent burned into its dimpled flesh and glossy chitin. She might have made this creature herself for all she knew.

Her mouth lubricated with blood, which drooled out over the middle of her bisected lower lip, Maria managed to get out, "I have forsaken the Father."

It was true, wasn't it?

On the night of the great and final fight, that frightening last battle like some apocalyptic war, after her father had left, Maria had found a crucifix on the floor. She recognized it as her father's, and realized her mother must have wrenched it off his chest in their shoving and slapping. Without her mother seeing, she swept it up in her fist. And buried it under her pillow that night. But the next day, the first day of her father no longer being in her life, Maria had taken the chain and little cross out into their backyard and buried it there, partly out of angry rejection, partly out of despair.

Was it that some neighbor child or even adult had seen her dig the hole, and had dug up the silver crucifix? Or was it that her vision had been so blurred with tears at the time? Whatever the case, when Maria went to exhume the crucifix out of guilt and longing a week later, it wasn't in the spot she had thought it would be. She tried another spot: and there she came upon a bundle in a green plastic trash bag. Now she remembered what she had buried in this vaguely familiar spot; their cat, which had been hit by a car a year ago. Disinterring this poor corpse was too great a punctuation mark to her pain. She reburied the cat, and didn't try to find her father's necklace again.

She had left it buried. And with it, her faith in family, in solace, maybe even in love. She had continued to attend church with her devout mother. But she had narrowed her eyes in contempt at the larger version of that symbol hanging above the altar. The man with his hands pinned where they could do no one any good.

The Caliban seemed satisfied with her answer. It shambled on down the hallway, and Maria pulled herself to her feet, blood still running off her lip. She had refused to cry, however. She prided herself on holding her tears even when she had no control over the flow of her blood. But the wound would heal, so that more wounds could take its place. Hadn't it been the same, pretty much, when she had still been alive, before she was raped and murdered?

Maria continued on her way. But not to the mess hall. She felt vaguely apologetic as far as Russ was concerned, but she had lost her appetite.

When she reached the enormous chamber in which she had been assigned a place to sleep, Maria realized that the explosion she'd heard earlier had occurred in here.

This chamber was circular and disturbingly organic, its ceiling lost in gloom but apparently taking the form of a dome. Honeycombed into the curved walls were row upon row of elliptical openings like slots in a mausoleum waiting to be filled. Formerly, this had been a tank in which were nurtured a species of Demons since discontinued. They had been one of the more humanlike breeds, and perhaps it was because of their human traits that a number of them had rebelled in the infernal city of Oblivion. Most of these Demons had been killed by now, but there were still those that had escaped the purging.

Her own little cocoon space was in the third tier, and she kept a few belongings inside, which no one had ever deemed worthy of stealing. There, she would rest between shifts, curled like a fetus, reborn—or aborted—every day in an endless cycle.

But today there had been some unknown mishap, and from the room's obscure heights, torrents of a thick, orange-colored gelatinous fluid were raining down to plop and puddle. Fortunately, the floor was subtly concave and the ooze was draining slowly toward a grille in its center. The foul-smelling matter put Maria very much in mind of the gruel they were fed in the mess hall—the only sustenance they were given—though that substance had a chemical-sharp citrus smell and taste, like slurping orange-scented dish detergent.

The irregular deluge went largely ignored by a few weary laborers who had also skipped mess hall and preceded her into the chamber, and who now climbed toward their cramped sarcophagi. Maria stared up into the leaking darkness only a few moments herself before navigating between aggregations of the viscous slime toward her section of the wall. Having arrived at it, she hoisted up one leg to begin the ascent to her own depression.

She hesitated, however, as her eyes were attracted to where some of the rotten-smelling matter had flowed down the wall and accumulated in a particularly large, glistening heap. She saw that there were several bones protruding from it: some ribs, and the batlike struts of a wing. Not the bones of a human; humans reconstituted, their bodies were notional, they could not be killed. Demons, however: they could die. But there was more than the bones. One spot in the mound was subtly but definitely pulsing. Also, Maria could just discern a muted gurgling sound with an unsettling, familiar quality.

Holding her breath against the reek, she crouched by the edge of the pile, and from it drew a loose leg bone. She then used this to probe the slime in the area where it was undulating. There was resistance as she prodded a mass buried within it. And then, a tiny arm thrust up through the jelly, its stubby fingers wriggling.

Maria used the bone to paddle away as much of the slime as she could around the arm. Then, leaning forward carefully, she reached out and took hold of it. It was slippery, and cold, and she was repulsed by the fingers that squirmed against her wrist, but she pulled . . . and in standing, she extracted a body drooling streamers of muck. She held the thing out at arm's length to examine it. Pudgy legs pedaled the air sluggishly, eyes squinted open in its sliding mask of ooze, and its wings moved as if to fan the goo from them. Free of the half-congealed amniotic fluid in which it had once been nurtured, the Demon gurgled more freely, but not loudly enough for anyone else to have noticed as yet.

Though Maria had never seen a mature version, she realized what this creature was. One of those discontinued Demons that had been nurtured in this chamber before it had been emptied and converted into barracks. It was a miracle—or, more accurately, an oversight—that it had survived this long. Overlooked in the cleansing that had eliminated all its siblings. Now, accidentally but belatedly miscarried.

Maria was afraid to bring the infant Demon close to her, but was even more afraid of being seen holding it. She glanced behind her furtively, but determined that her back had as yet shielded her find from anyone who might have looked in her direction. She then did the first thing that came impulsively to mind. Rather than drop the immature creature back into its afterbirth, rather than fetch an adult Demon to tend to this matter, she again hoisted up a leg to begin climbing to her tiny nook. In so doing, she was forced to fold the creature close to her chest.

She was afraid that at any moment, the larval Demon would snap its jaws onto her throat. But instead, it merely mewled faintly, and instinctively clung to her so as not to fall.

Working through her interminable shift, knowing what she had left hidden in her skull socket of a bed chamber, Maria was agitated and distracted and made a number of clumsy mistakes. Her function, of late, was to pour large glass jars full of maggots into molds that crawled past her on a conveyor belt. The squirming, pale brown things were not truly maggots, but close enough for the workers to refer to them as such. A coworker, Patty, told Maria how this particular process reminded her of a carbonated soda plant she'd worked for in life, where bags of hard plastic pellets were melted down so as to be shaped into the two-liter soda bottles they would become. But here, Patty and Maria were molding containers of flesh instead of those of plastic. To be filled with bile, venom, and vitriol instead of corn syrup and caramel color.

Patty would hand Maria a bottle of the maggots, which she would tip into one of the molds (today, they were for Baphomets, a towering Demon with a blackened, goat-like head enshrouded in a caul of cool white flame). Maria would pass the empty jug back to Patty, who would set it aside to be reused later.

At one point Maria fumbled and dropped a bottle, which shattered below the little platform she stood on. Patty jumped back as the pool of writhing, half-alive matter spread at her feet. Fortunately, they were able to sweep it all up and dispose of it before any of the Demon supervisors could see them.

Sometimes, when there were no supervisors in sight, Maria would spit into the open molds as she filled them.

She was relieved when the shift ended at last, but also dreaded returning to her sleep chamber to find her secret discovered . . . or expired. Before she could check on it, however, she first had a stop to make.

Russ the shower guard was entering the mess hall as Maria was just leaving it. He looked like he was coming off his regular duties; his uniform was stiff with caked Demon blood, from recycling old bodies for the recasting of new. When he saw her, he grinned and said, "Hey! There's the pretty senorita. I missed you yesterday."

Maria could not speak. In her mouth she held some of the orange, gel-like gruel she had been served in a bowl by one of the human mess hall workers. She tried to smile at Russ, rubbing her belly and wagging her head as if to indicate she didn't feel well. Concern flashed into his face and he stepped aside to let her pass.

"Are you going to be sick?" When she nodded, he asked, "Can I help you?"

She shook her head, patted him on the arm as she moved forward again (hoping he didn't take the contact as having flirtatious meaning) and left her would-be beau behind.

It was not unrealistic for him to believe she might be ill. In Hell, there were microscopic Demons, or at least infernal creatures, that could infest, infect, cause grief to the Damned. Maria knew this well; from the irregular holes rotted open in the walls on the fifty-third floor of this building, she had been able to look outside at a narrow building that reminded her of a spinal column, in which these viruses were manufactured by other workers like herself.

"Hope you feel better!" he called after her.

When Hell freezes over, she thought.

She had walked only a few steps when she heard Russ cry out in alarm and pain. Turning, she saw that a Caliban had loomed up behind him and seized him in its pincers. One of his wrists, pinned, was half severed and jetting blood. Another pincer had ripped his trousers down, while a third was closed around his genitals as if to masturbate or castrate. The weight of the immense body doubled him over and the creature was no doubt entering him.

"What is your sin?" the Demon wheezed.

Russ and Maria held their eye contact. Russ looked more ashamed than in pain. Maria was ashamed, too, that there was nothing she could do for him. She knew the next time they met he would be physically healed, at least . . . and she knew they would not discuss this.

As she left him behind, she heard the Demon grunt more demandingly, "What is your sin?"

We have forsaken our Father, Maria thought. And He has forsaken His children, the ultimate deadbeat dad.

There were more people in the sleep chamber than there had been yesterday, when she had retired without a trip to the mess hall first. Many of the orifices were already occupied, like eggs filled with termites that would hatch tomorrow to take to their labors. She climbed up the riblike ridges that protruded between two columns of the elliptical hollows, and then ducked into her own in the third tier.

Against the back wall of her sleep space, her spare uniform lay crumpled up. And that crumpled heap was subtly moving, like the heap of gelatin had been yesterday.

Maria pulled aside her clothing to reveal the larval

Demon lying on the glassy hard surface beneath it. Its eyes shifted toward her, held her gaze, blinking. Its fingers plucked and kneaded at the air. Her eyes trailed down to its puny genitalia: it was a boy.

She pinched the infant boy's nostrils shut. The creature's squirming became more pronounced, and she was afraid he would cry out. So far, he hadn't cried or made any loud sounds. In fact, even his soft burbling sounds had decreased over the hours of her rest period, which made Maria both relieved and concerned. Was he making less sounds because he was content, or because he was ailing, growing weak?

The thought of clamping her free hand over his mouth came into her mind. The Damned were immortal, so that they might suffer through eternity. The Demons could perish. The Demons were only machines, so to speak. This diabolic cherub was at her mercy. He was one of the many genera of her tormentors. And her torments might be increased in severity if she was found to have been hiding him. He was the enemy . . .

Last night, she had considered smuggling him out of this room and abandoning him in some little-used corridor, or in the space between two machines, and leaving him to the Fates. But there were no Fates, just Demons, and if they found him they'd kill him to further the factory recall, or genocide, of his species.

So what if they killed him? So what?

But it was *because* they'd want to kill him that she hadn't killed him. Though still a Demon, he was now something kindred to her.

Maria pinched his nose, but didn't cover his mouth. His mouth opened in a disgruntled gasp, and leaning over him, she drooled the orange, citrus-flavored gruel out of her own mouth into his, like a bird feeding her winged but flightless chick.

* * *

One could still dream in Hades. Sometimes, Maria dreamed of Los Dias de Muertos. Markets filled with flaming marigolds and family crypts in pastel shades. Seeing through the eyes of a plastic ghost or ghoul or devil mask. Rows of sugar skulls with sequin eyes. Sometimes, in her dreams, Maria imagined these skulls were the heads of Demons waiting to be attached to their bodies, and come alive. The bread called *pan de muerto.* Edible crucifixes, in a kind of communion . . .

Sometimes, Maria would dream of paging through the blood-soaked tabloid *Alarma!* and seeing photos of her own raped and murdered corpse there for the entertainment of the masses.

Tonight, she dreamed of sneaking out of her mausoleum nook . . . of stealing down the curved wall of the sleep chamber . . . of creeping out into the maze of hallways with a bundle tight against her breasts.

She dreamed of climbing staircase after staircase, or scrambling up ladders, or mounting inclined ramps, until at last she had reached the fifty-third floor of the structure she worked and lived her undead life in. The level—perhaps near the top, perhaps only halfway up—where great, irregular holes had rotted open in the resinlike, semiorganic walls. Holes looking out upon the immensity of the Demon city, Tartarus, where winds whistled or wailed between the tightly packed skyscrapers of bone, winds which set her long black hair flapping as she neared the lip of one such opening.

She uncovered the face of the infant in her arms, and he gazed up at her dumbly. Not crying, not cooing. She had no idea what thoughts, if any, breathed in his head. Would his interrupted progress resume? Would he mature to an adult, or remain at this stage forever? Though he would be helpless out in the world of the underworld, she found the latter possibility agreeable. That he should remain an eternal innocent.

Maria unwrapped the creature's swaddling, and as if he guessed her purpose, his wings began to flex and fan. She held him under his arms, held him up at the level of her face. For a moment, she almost kissed his bare belly, where there was a navel though it had never had a umbilicus fed into it. But she didn't kiss the white flesh, instead turned the infant in her hands to face the city sprawling beyond. She stepped closer to the rim. She held him higher aloft. Her arms slipped out into the biting wind of the air, beyond the lip of the wound. And then, she let him go.

She was afraid he might plummet, but he did not. Instinctually, his wings began to beat so quickly, like those of an insect or hummingbird, that he was buoyed up, and the currents of air howling through the canyons of skyscrapers did much of the work. Up, he rose, and up. Out over the darkness of unseen depths below. Up and into the mist between two particularly gargantuan edifices . . . until he was lost from sight. Until he was free.

In a building so close to hers they were practically conjoined, she saw a figure in one of the windows. A witness to her act. But just as the figure turned away, she recognized who it was and became less afraid. She knew that her father would not betray her this time.

When she awoke and uncovered the Demon larva beside her, she found he had expired while she was asleep, his lids half closed over his already clouded eyes.

Maria did not stir for a long time. She was almost late to work because of it. But at last, she covered his head again under her spare uniform . . . and this she carried with her to work as she often did, so that she might wash it in one of the basinlike recesses in the shower chamber when her shift was over.

She waited until there were no patrolling Demon guards or supervisors in view. She waited even until Patty, her coworker, had briefly left to roll in another cart loaded with bottles of maggots. Then, swiftly, she dragged out her bundle from under the conveyor belt. Unwrapped it . . . took the immobile, rubbery little body in her hands . . . and dropped it into the next open mold. Then, she poured the contents of one jug of maggots over that. She watched the mold be borne away along its track.

Today they were making Calibans. Would the humanlike Demon live on, in some sense, in the body of a new Demon despite its different form? Or had her act been purely one of defiance? Would the Caliban born from this mold be more human, like those rebellious Demons who were being hunted down and cleansed from existence . . . or would this new Caliban one day rape his own mother?

When Patty returned with the cart she became concerned for Maria, touched her arm. She told Maria she had never seen her cry before. But Maria laughed a little, and touched her arm in turn, and they resumed their work.

It was not Russ's turn to guard at the entrance to the women's showers today, but Maria sought him out in the mess hall, and found him, seated herself directly to his left. He turned and looked a little surprised to see her there. Her smile made his rising shame over the other day drop away again.

"Hi," she said to him.

"Hi," he said, sounding a little confused at her open tone. Maria had always been reserved with him, her smiles polite, not showing teeth. Now she smiled more warmly at him.

She stole her hand under the long table they sat at, and rested it upon his own hand.

Russ's uncertain smile grew, as well. But now it was his turn to avert his eyes shyly. He didn't withdraw his hand from hers, however; instead, curled his fingers around it.

They ate like that, side by side. Almost like a husband and wife. Almost like parents at their supper table.

PARTING JANE

Mehitobel Wilson

Now I am nine. I got this notebook and I am tired of cartoons so I wanted to write in it. I will call it the Hospital Book.

Cammy is sick again, so for my birthday I came here and had mashed-up peas and a bad drink. They took out blood and then today they had to give me a lumber puncture. I did not like the way that sounded. Daddy had bought lumber for the deck and I remember splinters. The nurse said, okay, I could get a spinal tap instead. That sounded better.

This is not like when you tap on the glass to get Cammy's bug-eyed goldfish to come over. Not like that. They take something out. It didn't hurt too much but now I feel like someone thumped me on my backbone.

When the doctors came I had made a joke for them. Tap-tap. Who's there, said the brown one in the doctor clothes. Spinal! I said, and the brown doctor made the little green square over his face puff out.

The very black doctor smiled shiny, and I'm not going to tell him any more jokes.

Mom cries when she talks about Cammy. She does not cry when she talks to me. She just seems mad. She was so mad about me saying I didn't like the very black doctor that she could not talk. She made Daddy come in instead.

They always call Cammy "blue-eyes." My eyes are brown. While Daddy was sitting on my bed he was talking quiet and I tried to see which color his eyes were. I never saw, even when he started talking louder. He never pointed them at me so I could see.

He said for me to like the doctors, that they were important, that Cammy is very sick and that if I made things hard for the doctors she might die. He also said that no matter what color doctors are, they are very smart and work hard.

I told him that the very black one had too many sharp parts. Daddy said that needles are important. I know they are! But this doctor brought his sharp things with him everywhere. Daddy said that doctors must always be prepared.

This makes sense.

Now I just stay here at the hospital. Back-and-forth trips got very close together. I went from my little plastic air mattress at home to a littler plastic-crackling bed here, over and over, sleeping one night in my good cuddly jammies and the next in the crispy ones with knots in the back, until they just stopped taking me home.

I haven't written in a super-long time. Candy stripers come around with carts full of books and I pick three each day and read them all. There are better books than when I was in school, big fat books. In school we only had very skinny books with pictures. There are lots of books on the carts here with no pictures at all. I read very fast, the candy stripers say.

There was one on the cart called *Camille* that I stayed away from for a long time, but finally I read it, and it made me start to think of names. I wonder if people become like their names, and if they do, who started it? Somebody must have had that name for the very first time, and somebody must have filled that name up with power, so that when other people get the name, the same things happen to them. Cammy's real name is Camille and she is a lot like the lady in the book. She gets whatever she wants, and coughs up blood, and she lays around sick and everyone loves her for it. Then the Camille in the book dies.

Too bad she didn't have a sister named Jane.

I've started to look forward to when the doctors come. They come to take things, but that's okay. That way I know that Camille is still alive, and that I haven't been forgotten.

This morning I saw Mom walk past my door. She looked away from the glass but I know it was her. She's dyed her hair and the grays are gone, but I still recognized her.

She didn't come back when I called for her.

I only get to write for a couple minutes at a time now. They strap me down to keep me from trying to run away. I can only write when they bring meals.

The candy stripers bring their own books to me, because I've read all the ones on the carts. I can prop a book up between my thigh and the bed rail, and even though my hand is tied, I can turn each page by shaking the book a little. I'm glad I have good eyesight. Dad used to hold books right up to his face to read. I read *Jane Eyre*. I think I'm more like the wife in the attic than like Jane, no matter what her name is. "Jane" must be a name without any power at all.

My hair is very long. I have been thinking of cutting it off. I'd like to do it myself, with something sharp.

I could ask the sharp doctor. He's got plenty of things. Even his eyes are sharp on me in my sleep. I feel them a lot these days. They cut.

He comes behind the plain doctors and looks over their shoulders. He gets eager and his cracked eyes grind the light. When he bounces, happy, and points at the clipboard, the impossibly black mask over his mouth looks terrible and deep. It doesn't shimmer like his sharp things do.

It's better when he wears the mask. I don't like to see him smile.

When I scream at him, the doctors say hush, and bring out their own needles to make me sleep.

Today I read *The Exorcist*. The girl in it got spinal taps too, and had to go to the hospital a lot. Her mom was wild with worry.

I have had this diary for two years. I am in here for Camille, and I haven't even seen her ever since I came here. I wonder if she has seizures, or if she screams?

Thanks to the dreams, I'm supposed to take sleeping pills now. In *The Exorcist,* they give Regan (the girl, she gets possessed, and wow, does she cuss) psychiatrists, and they hypnotize her. They try to talk to her to see what's the matter, and they only give her shots when they need to knock her out, to keep her quiet. They tie her down too, to keep her from hurting anybody, including herself.

Nobody's bothered to talk to me. Just straps and shots and pills, but they mutter about the effect of the pills on my liver, and don't want to get too many drugs in my blood. I know why they worry. It's because they might need to take more from me, and whatever they take needs to be clean.

The sharp one: I saw him.

No anesthesia this time, no drugs—I was wide awake and I saw him. He was alone this time, not looking over anyone's shoulder or glittering through their eyes. This was a week ago, I think. A while ago. The hospital wasn't too happy with the fit I threw and I was sedated for a few days, at least.

After they started letting me be awake again (Camille must be sicker; they must need my parts to be very clean) they let the candy stripers come back. One's here now, reading a magazine about boys. Her name's Rose. I asked if she'd read *Eight Cousins,* and she hadn't. She knows I like books, though, and I think she feels sorry for me, thinks I'm lonely. She said she'd stay with me while I wrote in my journal.

Rose has a runny nose, and I don't want to catch her cold. If I do, they'd all have to wait until I got better again before they could get more from me, and as much as I hate them, I need them around.

Maybe Rose will see the sharp man. Am I the only one he visits? Nobody listens when I ask. I've gotten sly about it, though, more subtle. I don't want them to think I'm hysterical.

When he came, he stood at my door in the dark. The light from the hallway outlined his round head and gleamed on the pitted stethoscope around his neck. He was standing there when I rolled over. I hadn't heard him come.

The only light in my room comes from the call buzzer. That wasn't enough for me to see anything but shadows and shine, but I couldn't use the buzzer, either, because he'd know I was touching it if he couldn't see the orange dot anymore.

But what I did see was bad. He held things in his hands, things so clean and pointed that they caught light out of nowhere. The things ticked together, though I didn't see him moving.

Then I heard a longer sound, something metallic rubbing along the length of something else, and he shifted, and light spangled where his eyes should be. He stepped to the side, away from my doorway, and I couldn't see him anymore, but I could hear him, and I heard every wet, shuffling step as he left. I knew the doctor bags that covered up his shoes were full of blood.

I'd been crying all along without knowing it. When I realized he was gone, I cried harder, and ended up screaming.

Then the nurses came running, and I was glad to see them. I told them, yes, sedate me, but let me take pills. No needles.

Rose says it's time for her to leave now.

The volunteer who gave me *The Exorcist* came back today. His name is Todd. He's half Japanese and pretty cute. Part of me looks forward to seeing him, just so I can look at him and maybe get a good book; the rest of me doesn't want him here, because I'm ugly, and I don't want him to see.

Todd was mad about something. He's sixteen and wants to be a doctor, so he pays attention to the way the hospital works. He eavesdrops and reads people's charts. He wouldn't tell me what was wrong, but he said he'd be back tomorrow just to see me.

I'm glad I didn't cut my hair. Maybe I'll get to see Rose tonight, or one of the nurses might be nice and let me use a little bit of her makeup or something.

* * *

Todd came right before lunch today. He'd brought me a double cheeseburger, onion rings, and a sweet tea from a fast-food place. God, that burger was good. I had grease and ketchup running down my arms right in front of him and I didn't care!

Then he gave me a present, an electronic book thing that I could fill up with all kinds of books and read just by pushing a button. Plus, the screen has light, so I can read at night.

He kissed me on the forehead and that was weird enough, but then he said happy birthday and, well, I'd lost track of things like that, but the chart says that I turned twelve today.

Todd said I'm scheduled for surgery again tomorrow, a pretty big one. I didn't ask, because I don't care, but the way he was talking suggested it was going to be an organ. Liver, maybe? Lungs? Can you take lungs from other people?

His eyes got very shiny, too, but not like the sharp doctor's. Todd's were more wet.

Daddy—my father—came last week after the surgery. I was pretty knocked out so I didn't talk much. Now my father has shaved off his beard, and his hair is cut different. I don't remember when I last saw him.

He and my mother are taking Camille on a trip. A charity is paying for them to go to Hawaii to pet dolphins.

He didn't ask how I was doing. He didn't say happy birthday. To be mean, I said happy birthday to *him* even though that's not until December, and he looked at me like I was crazy and said thank you.

Then I started to cry, and he got very worried, which was good for a minute. He kept patting the mattress—not me, he never touched me—and asking me to please stop crying.

Then he stood up and reached across the bed so he could grab on to both sets of guard rails, and he shook the bed so hard I was afraid that my IV would come out.

He told me not to cry. His teeth were clenched. He looked straight at me, rattled the bed, and said that if I cried I would get dehydrated and then they couldn't use me to make Camille get well.

I wanted to throw up and aim it in his face, but that didn't happen.

He called the nurses and said I needed water and electrolytes and shots. They wouldn't give me pills because they thought I might choke.

When the nurse gave me the shot I saw the jagged doctor standing behind her. Then I went to sleep, where it's safe.

Daddy's eyes, by the way, are brown and red.

This is a hospital. It's full of sick people. I've been here longer than most of the staff has.

A lot of things have happened and I have not written them down, ever. I did not want to remember them.

Now, I think I should tell you, whoever you are, so you can see.

Once upon a time there was a bald blue-eyed baby girl named Camille Fallon Wakefield. Her father, Winston Daniel Wakefield the Third, was happy to see that his daughter had blue eyes. His wife, Gillian Ayers Wakefield, played sonatas and French tapes while Camille was still in her womb.

When Camille Fallon Wakefield was two, she was diagnosed with leukemia.

Gillian Ayers Wakefield went to the hospital to have tests done to see if she would be an okay donor for

Camille. While there, she was surprised to hear that she was pregnant again.

She asked for an abortion. The doctors said, gosh, we understand that you have a lot to handle right now, but here's a thought: this child might be a candidate for a match, too.

So along came Jane No-Middle-Name Wakefield. Jane was judged, through prenatal testing, a match. Hurray for Camille.

Jane, who had brown eyes and blond hair, was prescribed dietary supplements, hormones, and so forth. Jane needed to be strong. Besides, since the doctors kept draining Jane's blood, they thought it might be smart to feed her extra stuff to keep her alive. She needed to be alive.

Jane spent so much time in the hospital as a child that she knew nothing else. When Camille went into remission, Jane went home (a week after Camille did) and slept on an inflatable mattress in the hallway until they could clear a spot for her in the storage room.

Jane—I—was five then, and Camille was seven.

When I was eight, Camille got sick again, and everyone went back to the hospital. When I turned nine, I was given a diary.

So far the doctors have taken:

Blood. (Sometimes little bits, sometimes all of it. Lots of times, at least ten, they have hooked me to a machine that sucked all of my blood out, filtered stem cells from it, then pumped the blood back in.)
Bone marrow.
More blood, more bone marrow, more and more.
Lots of spinal fluid.
A hunk of liver called a lobe (I don't know how many

lobes I have left, but I only had that operation once).

Scleral scrapings for cellular compatibility testing; retinal measurements, and other eyeball stuff in the event that Miss Blue-Eyes needs one (though nobody's going to be happy if she has one brown eye and one blue one).

They took all that. But they also took other stuff, life things. I like reading old books better than watching TV or reading new magazines because I know the worlds in old books don't exist, either. Better to read about places and times that aren't around than see places on TV that will be gone by the time I get to them.

Not that I could walk around any of those places, anyway. I haven't actually been allowed to get up, but I can tell. My legs wouldn't hold me now.

Except for the walking part, I must be the healthiest kid in the world. Otherwise they wouldn't want so much of me.

Sweet how much the other Wakefields love Camille, isn't it?

Not so sweet how much I wish she'd just die so I could get out of here and keep the rest of myself.

Straps are off my arms today because Rose is here. She's boring. I hate her.

Rose is back! I'm sorry I said I hated her. I love Rose! Guess what she told me?

My mother is pregnant again!

I have no idea what day it is. Nobody has come in a week at least. They must be doing tests on my mother to make sure the baby will work out okay.

* * *

I swear Rose said my mother was pregnant. No way I could have dreamed it. No way. I asked the nurse how long until the baby was ready to take my place and the nurse said, what baby? Said I must have been confused, said I was doing just fine. Gave me a sponge bath and put jellied aloe and cold lotion all over the soles of my feet.

Lots of meds, very sorry but they keep me strapped facedown now so my feet stay up and today I saw over my shoulder and the nurse was sliming my toes and then the nurse was suddenly the very black sharp man and when I kicked a little because I was surprised and, okay, very scared even with the meds, he cut me by mistake I think, and there was blood and another nurse came in and at first she yelled and then she said *it's okay Susan* and the sharp man was just the other nurse again.

Why the fuck do they keep me fucking strapped down when I can't even walk anyway? Explain this. Strapped down on my fucking stomach. Hard to write.

Dreamed maybe that Todd came? And he was not in his uniform and he had an earring? He was very mad and tried to take off my straps and he was pulling on me but I don't know if I was awake. Of course, if it was a dream, then I was awake in the dream but not really in real life. Confusing.

These pills are heavy. The IV drip has made my arm swell up and there is one in my neck now which is so gross that sometimes I faint just thinking about it.

Anyway. Todd said that Camille died in August.

Obviously that part was a dream. I don't know what month it is now, anyway.

But then Susan saw him and called security guards,

who came and took Todd. He called them motherfuckers and his nose was bleeding.

Susan never came back. A really ugly nurse came today with one of my normal doctors.

The normal doctor always wants me to call him Dr. Dan but I'm getting tired of kid names. Besides, I don't want to talk to him.

Dr. Dan smiled a lot and his teeth were very wet. Nurse Ugly looked at him like she's in love. Just stared up at him the whole time.

She didn't see his shadow. I did.

His shadow wore a mask of blackness tied beneath his shattered-lantern eyes, and carried scalpels.

Then they put me to sleep. Now my feet are wrapped up and hurt like hell.

Dr. Dan took me out again today. My feet still hurt way too much.

New juice in the drip today, something tingly. Neat. My ears are buzzing. It's kind of fun.

Hey, you know why my feet hurt? Old Dannyboy peeled them like socks. So that's what the shadow's knives are for: they took my sole! Ha.

There's a candy striper now that zips around in an electric wheelchair. Zip up the hall, zip down the hall. The sound cracks me up. *WreeeEEEEEEeeeeer*. Goes so fast past my door that all I see are wheels and stripes and I have no idea if it's a boy or a girl. One of these days whoever it is will get tired of hearing me laugh and stop in to yell at me. I hope so. I'm bored. And tingly!

* * *

A whole new doctor came in today. Dr. Macalester. He was a hippie, I think, if I'm not wrong about what a hippie looks like.

He was goofy. Big happy voice: *Hell*-LOW! *You're a real sport, not scared at all, are you! You beautiful little thing. We're only going to take a lobe today, you'll be fine.*

I said, how many more do I have?

Then we went around in circles for a while until I figured out that he was confused. I told him I'd already had my liver lobe taken. Turns out there's just one they can take.

He said hmm and chewed on his lip somewhere under the beard he had. Then he poked his pager and went away.

Dr. Dan was back and he was more shadow than doctor this time.

Lungs have lobes too.

The wheelchair person is named Phillippa. I can't talk with the tubes still in me, but this turned out to be lucky, because Phillippa went past—*wreeee . . . eee . . . wreewree*—and came into the room. Usually I laugh, she said, and she wondered why I was quiet.

I wrote her some notes and she told me she'd heard that Todd was dead. Said he'd been attacked with scalpels by one of the nurses, who must have gone crazy from all the pressure.

Susan Something, she said.

I wished I'd had some parts left over to give to Todd.

Everything is happening much faster now. I can't close my eyes without hearing the jingle of blades, the ticking of needles. He is here often. Doctors come and go, and every face is just another cut of meat worn by the sharp man. Every voice rings with a steel echo. Every hand, empty or not, leaves a slash.

A corrugated plastic tube fills my throat. It keeps the screams silent. No more need to drug me.

The sharp man is not everywhere, you know. He knows the doctors, maybe, but I never once saw him glitter behind my parents.

There were times when I worried about this diary—what if someone found it, read it—would they think I was insane? Would they take it away from me?

Today I learned not to worry. There are score marks on the pages, a cut through one page here, one that goes nine pages deep there. Pinpricks encircle words. Every instance of *Jane* is laddered with slits and framed with punctures, but is intact.

I think that's his idea of a joke.

Last week the room looked flat when I woke up.

When the nurse came and her face melted to ink and split to brandish the tines of her smile, I saw my reflection in her shattered eyes. One of my own eyes is gone.

I was sleeping today and came awake with a song in my ear. The voice was wet and hollow, meat and metal. It sang, "Oh, no, you can't take that away from me, no, you can't take that away from me."

It was a happy song.

I sang along.

The tube was gone from my throat, but my voice, too, sounded full of clots and echoes.

My hand, I found, was full of steel.

I could not see the sharp man anywhere.

It only took a minute to cut the canvas straps at my wrists. Took longer to cut the one across my chest, but it's done.

My scalpel is very sharp. It gleams. It shows me nothing but shadows and shine when I look for my reflection.

I'm now writing this using my whole arm. For months—more—I've had to write one word at a time with twisted fingers, then pull the page across the mattress half an inch and write the next word.

Soon one of the doctors will come, and I know he'll come alone, wearing his own meat, without the sharp man to look over his shoulder or lurk behind his skin. The sharp man is here with me. I will show the doctor how easy it is for me to write. Now that I'm free I can write HUGE or tiny.

Now I can pull my arm high into the air and stab right through the page to end the sentence.

LITTLE MISS MUFFET IS DEAD, BABY

Michael T. Huyck Jr.
and Michael Oliveri

I'll probably die here in the next couple days, seeing as how I sucked up the last of the free water from the shitter about ten this morning. I used the straw from Wednesday's breakfast and about broke my neck reaching the back of the flush hole. When I tried flushing again to replenish the supply, nothing came out. I'm guessing the town's well is on the blink. Or maybe there's a spider jammed up in the machinery? It'd serve the bastard right.

Wednesday's breakfast . . . my last meal. Heh. What's today?

That was four hours ago by that tail-wagging, eye-swishing Felix the Cat clock on the wall opposite my cell door. The last water, that is. I drank *it* four hours ago.

I'm confused.

How long can a man go without water? Three days? Five?

I thought about jumping to the ground and taking them on. But I ain't that brave and I ain't that thirsty. Yet.

I might get there. Who knows? I have Betty Mae's boot knife, and it's plenty sharp. Sharp enough to cut through those bastards anyway. Unless they got that whatchacallit . . . carapace? That armor insects sport.

Supposed to be tough stuff. Or is that just ants and beetles?

I'm rambling. Sorry, I don't have the time or space, but that's what it's like trapped with a couple of rotting human bodies down the hall and no fucking water. Jesus, I was drinking from the shitter. Who'd have thought it? And I'm still thirsty. Dry.

Dry, dry, *dry*.

I need to stay focused. I need to make sense.

Sheriff Evans picked me up Tuesday night, before those . . . things . . . showed up. I'd been sifting for treasure behind the Farris Superstop and Truck Wash, taking my time in a row of Dumpsters, when I found a small garbage bag of day-old fried chicken. To think, just then I'd thought it my lucky day. Hell, it had white meat! I like white meat because it's not as greasy. Some bastard must've heard me . . . and that bastard called the law.

Evans came creeping around the building in his cruiser, lights off and engine barely a rumble. I didn't hear him, what with the tractor-trailer rigs idling in rows and roaring in and out of the gas pump islands and all. Only saw him when he spotlighted me.

He's the quiet type, talking low and even. Didn't cuff me once. I thought a lot of him at first.

And then—get this—he called me "indigent."

So I said, "No, I'm Welsh."

He didn't laugh.

These one-horse towns still office their sheriffs and deputies in Barney Fife holes—painted brick and mortar buildings with light oak counters and avocado green Naugahyde benches. Evans had his name and rank scroll-cut from a chunk of wood and sitting centered on the front lip of his desk. Two other desks told me that he had help, one with a similar scroll-cut for someone only named "Stanley" and the other with a cross-stitched sign on the wall behind it declaring the area as "Betty Mae's Property." I wondered aloud why it was the real sheriff picking me up at night and not some dick-slappin' deputy. Being the strong, silent type, he didn't answer.

After an hour of bullshit and paperwork, he stored me in cell 1D. It was easy enough to see that I had the whole block to myself, as the doors of the other three cells were swung wide open. He took my shoelaces, then. And my belt. Like I'm planning on spanking myself? But outside that he wasn't too bad.

Because I'm a deep sleeper, I managed to snooze through breakfast delivery. Only when the whimpers started slipping in through the bars did I come to. Well, they were more whines than whimpers, really. Like the pitch of a hungry stray.

To be honest, I didn't give the noise much thought after I saw the tray. I normally dig my meals out of rubbish and refuse, you remember, and Evans didn't let me finish my chicken the night before.

It sat on the floor waiting to be eaten, just inside the bars. There's a gap at the bottom of the door, like they cut the bars too short, and the tray slid in clean beneath it. It couldn't have been there long, 'cause the eggs were hot on the inside and the bacon only broke if you stretched it far enough. I savored that first bit of pork; wiggly bacon is heaven. Just as I wondered if they had any pepper sauce, I heard another whine.

Since they took my shoelaces, I'd already tossed my tennyrunners off into the corner. They didn't match each other anyway. I hadn't thought about it, but my bare feet and creaky joints didn't peep once when I got up to eat. Know why I know? Know why it's as obvious as a turd in a tuna fish sandwich?

Because I looked up, just as I was thinking hot sauce, to find Betty Mae's ample ass throwing me a sideways smile through a mirror. I'm guessing it was Betty Mae, the girl from the desk up front, mostly because I needed a name to put to the smile. That's why. I nearly sucked a mouthful of wiggly bacon into my windpipe.

The cells run four in a row and one deep (considering the size of the town, this had to be a county joint), with barred fronts, swing-out doors, thick and blurry security windows in back, and three walls of cinder block around. On the wall opposite each cell's front hung a shelf, a clock (all four different, and all four stupid cartoon characters) and a big, round, stainless steel mirror angled toward the entrance hall.

Just then, as I breathed bacon and looked into *my* mirror, I saw them in front of cell 1A. The oddly stretched image of Sheriff Evans pumped from inside the cell, his khaki pants down around his knees. Betty Mae stood outside, *her* pants down at *her* knees. And they were slappin' nasties through the goddamn bars!

Hell, everyone has a fantasy. I never figured a cop for wanting to do it from behind bars, though. Or through bars, as it were. Needless to say, I choked silently on the bacon, gave it a few more chews, and continued my breakfast mouselike. Didn't figure it'd hurt me or help me if they knew I knew, you know? And I like entertainment with my meals.

I'm dry and goddamned dry again. It's a good thing I can write and don't have to talk, because I've gone four hours and ten minutes without water now. But that's not long, is it? Not as long as it's gonna be.

I'm getting there.

Evans and Betty Mae abruptly finished their fuck by the end of my second bacon strip, so I'm thinking the sheriff is no woman's dream. Even in the scratchy steel mirror I could see her fingers sinking into the pasty bastard's uniform shirt, and I could see him staring out over her shoulder like he was watching a movie. By the time I bit into the third bacon strip they had their drawers up and zipped. I didn't chance the eggs until they left, but I also didn't move. Instead I inspected each of the cells as best as I could via the mirrors.

They were mostly the same as mine, with a single, recessed light, a single bunk, and open toilet and integrated sink, and one window. Sparse. Or Spartan for you optimists out there. (Shit, I'd kill just for the half empty glass right now.) The other cells were empty. No one here but me and my cooling eggs.

There've been three waves, and I didn't see the first one. I was asleep, see.

After breakfast I left my tray where I found it and hit the bunk for a nap. Just as my eyes were closing I saw Evans stroll up real slow, like each boot weighed a few hundred pounds. He lingered at my door, his moves so deliberate they might've been scripted, and unlocked it. It swung open on its own accord.

"Come out here."

I opened my eyes completely, first checking the floor for my breakfast tray. It was there, so I thought he'd come to pick it up. Might be.

It lay at his toe tips and he never looked down.

Sheriff Evans never took his eyes off mine, not even when he kicked the tray, so it's goddamn unnatural how good an aim the man had with those boots. What was left of the eggs hit me mid-chest and the tray glanced off my left shoulder before coming to rest on my pillow. The milk straw landed under the sink. I didn't find it until later.

I sat up reflexively with the impact, then shook it off and stood.

"Out here," he repeated sternly.

There's a little man that shows up in my head sometimes, a yelling, beating, screaming sort of alarmist fellow. As the years go by I've learned to listen to him more and more.

I shook my head, crossed my arms, and stood fast.

He nodded his head and motioned me forward with a finger.

I shook my head again. He stamped a boot; I shuffled my bare feet.

"Sheeeeeeeeeerrriiiiiiiiiifffffffff?" Betty Mae sang out from somewhere beyond 1A. He sneered, then slammed the door and walked away.

After cleaning up with a wad of toilet paper, I decided to get some exercise. I'm a stickler about that, you know, as my diet's not the best. One has to make concessions if one wants to look forward to decades of Dumpster diving. I started with laps of the cell, because that let me keep my eyes up so I could move quickly to the rear if I had to. Plus, it gave me something to count. Kept my mind busy.

Maybe I made it around one hundred forty times, maybe I didn't. I ain't sure. Close enough to a mile, I think. I was on the backside of that one hundred fortieth lap when Betty Mae waddled down the corridor.

Did I say she had an ample ass? It's true, of course. Looked like two soft watermelons packed in the backside of her Wrangler jeans. She wandered in, flats slapping the floor, half an hour after Evans walked away. Right off I knew she came to draw a line with me, just like the sheriff had.

What was it with these people?

I'd returned the tray to its spot beneath the door, and she bent over to pick it up without a word. Her eyes shot fire and her cheeks were flushed bright red, but she didn't say a thing. I'm thinking Evans told her what I'd seen before she came in, so now she thought of *me* as the guilty one. Hell, I was the only one who *hadn't* chosen to be there.

She wandered off with the tray and without a peep, and for a second I thought I was getting off easy. I'm thinking the tray couldn't have made it any further than her desk, however, as she returned a few seconds later.

She held a clipboard and a pen and starting firing out questions before her feet came to a complete stop. Name, address (yeah, right), and phone number (ha!). Then a bunch of irrelevant shit that left me snickering. And every time I snickered, her face grew two shades darker. She spat questions. She paced.

After I snorted at her description of the difference between a daytime telephone and a nighttime telephone she threw her pen at me. Held it by the tip and flipped it end over end like she was a circus sideshow knife thrower. It went wide and bounced off the wall behind me. I quit laughing, faked a pout, and got up to give her the pen back. That's when she tossed the whole clipboard my way. After palming the pen, I veered toward the board and paper. That's when she pulled her boot knife.

I thought about her pen toss and started walking a little slower, picking up the clipboard and the legal pad that'd dropped off it. Then, slowly, I walked her way. Slowly, I say, but I didn't stop. Not even when her lower lip trembled and her eyes watered. I raised my hands, tilted my head forward, and walked all the way up. The street teaches you these things.

She bolted off, but within thirty seconds she was back with another pen and another clipboard. She ignored my offer to return what she'd tossed at me and leaned back against the opposite wall to finish up the questions. I tossed the paper and pen on the floor and leaned forward against the bars, allowing one to press on each temple. She kept asking, and I answered in a low voice. No more laughing. No more fun. She had a knife now. Betty Mae wasn't all whining and watermelons. It also occurred to me that I might be able to get some of the same action as Evans. My little guy hadn't seen any wet 'n' wild in ages. Hell, it wouldn't even have to be a fantasy this time. I'm a real prisoner and my door's really locked. If that's what gets her off . . .

Right. Talk about your garden-variety fantasy. The chick may dig sex and bars, but bums dressed in stains and scruff probably wouldn't pull her duty. Chances are she's into power, what with her fucking the sheriff and all.

After she quit, I stuck my hands deep in my jean pockets and wandered about in slow circles again. Stared into the shitter and the sink as well. Searched the walls for initials or crude graffiti. Then I gave up and dropped onto the rack for the nap Evans had stolen from me.

It took a gunshot to wake me the second time. Betty Mae screamed right after that, the sound not too far off from her sex noises, but louder. Then a scuffling came into the corridor and I jumped out of bed as the shotgun roared again. Betty Mae's next scream died in a gurgle and a pair of thuds outside my cell.

I ran front and center to check out the mirror, and *that's* when I saw the spider thing.

Now, calling these things spiders isn't quite right. They only have half the legs, and they're not even in the right place. Instead they have one leg centered in each quadrant. Their bodies are teardrop-shaped and skins black and leathery. Their abdomen flesh bears a lustrous shine, but their legs are wrinkled like a weathered biker jacket. Each of their feet ends in four claws, each a good inch in length. They apparently walk and run on the tips of those claws, because the ones I saw never retracted them. At the teardrop's skinny end, presumably the front as they have no eyes to speak of, a single black proboscis thrusts out a foot or so. Calling them spiders is just a matter of convenience. They weren't from *this* earth, I'll tell you that. And I've read enough discarded *National Geographic* magazines to know it, too.

From just the angle of its legs, I guessed the first one I spotted must be on its back. One side was tore up and amber liquid stained the floor. Blood? But it wasn't the spider that'd screamed. It was Betty Mae, and maybe it was Sheriff Evans.

Sheriff Evans. The man with the keys to this damn cell.

I stepped close to the bars and pressed my face close to them to get a better look, but knew before I made it all the way what I'd find. I could *hear* it.

The sheriff lay on his back, head toward me. Another one of those black things, this one still alive, straddled the big man and fed off him. I could tell about the feeding because it was obvious enough that its thin, black tube penetrated his belly below the shiny star on his starred uniform shirt. And the slurping sounds helped, too.

Betty Mae wasn't any better off. She lay in front of the next cell, but I could only see one leg jutting into the corridor and her hand near the wall bordering the two cells. Her boot knife fell just inches from her fingertips. I quickly wedged myself between the bars and the cot and thrust my forearm out to grab the knife. With a good stretch I pinched the sharp end with two fingertips and pulled it back in.

The sheriff's shotgun also lay on the floor, just about centered between us. There wasn't a chance in hell of me reaching it, even if I *was* willing to stick my hand out between the bars again. If there was another one alive out there, it no doubt saw me grab the knife. Which made the knife the only weapon I had. I stuck it in my passenger-side rear pocket, taking some comfort in its solidness.

That's when the window scratching started.

Stupid me, I turned to look. What did I expect to see scratching at the window, hmmmm? King Tut? Marlo Thomas? Hell no. I should have expected what I saw, which was a single black leg with four black claws. It leaned back, out of sight, then practically fell up and against the window's center. *Thunk.* Then it dragged down to the sill—*screech thump. Thunk, screech, thump . . . thunk, screech, thump.* Repeat as necessary.

Part of me backed up reflexively and part of me didn't, because the one in the hall was a helluva lot closer than the one out of doors. I mean, I had a prison cell wall on that side at least. Right?

Turning again, I found the one out in the hall paying all its attention to me now. Having finished up with the good sheriff, it was trying to figure out just how far it could get one of its legs through the bars. That leg stretched mightily in my direction. Mightily. It was straight out, dipping its lightbulb body down up front for more extension. The circular edge of its mouth tube likewise reached toward me, the circular hole in the tip fluttering and slurping—*tasting*—as it dripped the sheriff's blood. No eyes, no ears, no nose. Not even a single fucking antenna. Just the tube mouth flopping.

The thought occurred to me that I could jump on the leg and probably break it. It wasn't very thick, like the narrow end of a baseball bat. But that thought died lonely because my body shivered and refused to play. Instead I dropped onto my ass in the middle of the room.

I forgot about Betty Mae's boot knife.

The handle hurt like hell under my ass, and goddamn if the shock of sitting on it didn't send a few lightning bolts through me. I leapt straight up in the air and howled.

Closed my eyes and hollered up at the ceiling just as loud as I possibly could. When nothing came of it, I opened one eye to find myself staring at a drop ceiling.

Heh-heh. A drop ceiling. A *jail cell* with a *drop ceiling.* What kind of mind-numbing ignorance did the local architect suffer? I traced it with my eyes until it passed out over the bars. Yep, a drop ceiling in the hall outside. If there were beams, you could probably get through the whole place up there. Crawl all around and, just maybe, crawl out to freedom. Spiders willing, of course.

I stared at the spider-thing. Its claws didn't give it much purchase on the concrete floor, so three of the four just paddled away as it tried to force its fat body through the bars. The fourth stretched straight out between the bars, as if it could pull its way in. I offered one of my rare, succinct prayers.

Please, Lord, let it always be that fat. Let all the rest be fat, too.

At least three of the bastards were around me: one dead inside, one alive inside, and one alive outside. Probably more. No reason not to think so.

The thought hurried me.

The toilet served double duty, its cool chrome top offering a step up. I balanced atop the flush valve and reached up, sliding the closest ceiling panel back and away. As luck would have it, a ceiling joist ran straight above me. I checked my balance, then jumped up to grab it. With two small swings, I built up enough momentum to get one leg up and over it. It wasn't easy, and I definitely felt my age, but with pulling and grunting I managed to get on top of the joist and get me a seat.

The prison's architect wasn't as stupid as I first thought, but he wasn't the sharpest tool in the shed, either. There was a way out, just not what I'd imagined.

The bars came up through the false ceiling to enormous bolts pinning it to a slab concrete ceiling. The cinder-block walls continued up on each side and the rear in the same fashion. The only breach in the cell was a broad-mouthed duct leading up to a roof ventilator. It was centered over the joist I perched on, so I was able to scoot down and stick my head in the ventilator's mouth.

The caps of four small rivets pinched the rotating ventilator fan to its square facing. I grasped the joist between my knees, braced myself with my left arm, and reached back into my pocket for the knife.

Thank you, Betty Mae.

I slipped the blade into the tight seam between the fan and the facing. Maybe it was the darkness in there. Or maybe the slick galvanized steel didn't offer much purchase. Either way, the blade slipped up and hit the rotating vanes, shooting out a staccato *RATTATATATAT.* I pulled off quick as I could, but not quick enough. I might as well have blown "Reveille" for the critters. Or maybe "Taps" would be more appropriate.

Shifting the knife to my other hand, I used my fingertips to quietly slow, then stop, the vanes. Then I chanced the lack of bracing and tried to pry the rivets with the knife while holding the fan still with my other hand. I'm amazed at how quickly they gave way.

For a few seconds I pondered the benefits of slowly slipping the ventilator free over letting it drop and just sticking my head right out. Since I'd slipped with the knife, I didn't see much opportunity for surprise, so I slipped it in my pocket again and pushed the ventilator off.

Blue sky greeted me, filling the two-foot-wide mouth left after I beheaded the ventilator. The heat was oppressive, and already the smell of tar and hot stone sank down into my dark perch. But I noted nothing else. No black tubes or scurrying legs. No rushing of taloned feet.

I put my hands together—both palms out—and went out the hole that way. Hands, arms, then shoulders and head together. Still nothing. Precariously I stood on the joist and turned in a full circle. Nothing. Just five other ventilators—three that had to be for the other cells and two, considering the spacing, for the front office area. There was also an access hatch that went back into the jail somewhere past the cells, but it turned out to be locked from the inside. The roof was tar and pebbles. A sun-faded Frisbee, probably once green, lay near the front edge. No spider-things at all.

I hadn't been that happy in months. Hell, years. Too bad it didn't last.

I about strolled straight to the roof's edge before realizing I may not want to be spotted. The little rocks covering the roof hurt my feet and forearms, so I couldn't crawl to the roof's edge, either. Instead I scooted on my butt, letting my jeans take the brunt of the scraping. I made for the front of the building and almost got to the edge when crashing glass and screaming stole the silence.

I think I caught the front end of the business, but my eyes may have been lying to me. It couldn't have been that way. Not in my world.

Near the front edge of the jailhouse, I flopped on my back and rolled to my stomach. So, at the beginning, the girl ran upside-down. As I rolled over, she made it across the street and to the front door of a mid-seventies Cadillac coupe parked at the opposite curb. I'm guessing the door was unlocked.

She slammed the driver's side door to the hinge's limit, tossed herself across a bench seat, and pulled the door in after her with her toes. The spider-things came after her.

Fuck *me* if I can figure these bastards out. They move like bubbles on wet porcelain, rotating left or right while zigzagging in whichever direction might be construed as forward. Each of their four-pointed feet swerved to keep the body moving in one direction or another, with alternating pairs of legs closing together or spreading apart to keep the motion up. It was dizzying.

Four spiders converged on the Cadillac, and the *TIC–TIC–TIC* of their nailed feet against its metal and glass filled the air. She still screamed, although muffled, and I could barely hear her over their arachnid tap-dancing. They stretched their legs up onto the windows, the hood, and the deck lid. A fifth one joined them, rotating clockwise like a cartwheeling jester as it scurried over from Pappy's, the convenience store and gas station on the closest street corner. All five worked the car, beating the glass and poking its steel flanks, but none actually got up *on* the vehicle. Even as they rotated, changing which set of claws explored the car, they always kept two or three of their legs on the asphalt. Like they wouldn't—or couldn't—leave the ground.

I drooped my head further to find three of the things on the sidewalk directly beneath me, each with two legs on the wall and two on the sidewalk. Another, legs tucked beneath it cat-style, paused in the open jailhouse door. As I watched, one of the creatures left the car and spun over to the wall beneath me. It jostled for position and forced the end spider to cartwheel until there was sufficient room for four in a row.

I quit my perch and gave up on stealth as I walked gingerly around the building's roof. Seven of the spiders surrounded the building, with twice that many walking the streets and the alley behind. I heard gunshots and more screams. Maybe half a mile down the main street a huge fire burned, filling the sky with black smoke. The Farris sign rotating nearby told me it was the same truck stop the sheriff picked me up at.

Walking over the beheaded ventilator I'd come through, I dangled my feet down into the shaft and stared off. Not really looking at anything; just listening. From a distant somewhere above me a jet rumbled. A car engine revved. More screams. More gunfire. A door slammed.

Looking down into the dark of the shaft, I considered my options. No ladder on the outside, so the only way down from this roof was to jump. There'd certainly be spiders at the bottom, and they moved fast. I saw that much. Even if I was lucky enough to not break something upon landing, I couldn't get away. Not even as far as the Cadillac and the screaming girl inside.

Yeah, I still heard her.

The ventilators over the jailhouse lobby area could come off. There was one, probably two of the spiders in there, but two enemies sounded a helluva lot better than the apparently infinite number on the street. If I could shut the door to the street in time, that is. Kill the two, get some of the weapons, try and make my way to one of the sheriff's cruisers. Maybe even figure a way to get the girl out of the Cadillac.

Maybe I could get some panic leg off her. End of the world and all that.

If the other ventilators didn't want to come off, I could go back to the cell and try for the cell keys. Assuming the one living spider in the building hadn't left yet, it would eventually. When it got hungry again. Or not. There's no telling how stupid these things might be. It could just wait outside my cell until it starved itself to death.

Eventually the girl in the Caddy stopped screaming. I walked back to that edge of the roof and saw her still inside and still surrounded by spiders. She moved, barely, her mouth open. She'd either gone hoarse or mad, I couldn't be sure. I shook my head and walked back to the roof vent, intending to go back inside.

Instead I just sat there, butt on the rocks and feet in the hole, until the sun went down. I watched the same stars rise that I'd watched a thousand times before. I listened to the sounds of man dying all around me. I couldn't see the spiders, but their nails clacked on the cement, like random drummers tapping on random snares.

I nodded off for a while. The first rays of sunlight poked through the clouds and I went back to check on the girl. At some point the spiders got her. The door was open, and I wondered whether they got lucky or she opened it for them.

On my arrival, two spiders turned to look at me. *Little Miss Muffet's dead, baby,* they seemed to say to me. *You're next.*

I wondered who sat on the tuffet and brought these suckers down on us. And what the fuck is a tuffet, anyway? What does a damn spider care if someone sits on it?

For lack of anything else to do, I dropped back into the cell to rediscover the pen and clipboard Betty Mae "gave" me. Flipping off the spider, I picked up pen and paper and started writing. At the time, I figured writing all this down would keep me sane. Now I'm not so sure. It's starting to get dark again, and I don't even remember when the power went out.

I guess I also wanted someone to know what the sheriff and his fat bitch have condemned me to. Lousy fuckers couldn't even make it ten more feet before croakin'? Then I might even be able to reach the keys and the shotgun. And what kind of sick fuck locks a man up for stealing from a trash bin and then nails his secretary in plain sight? It's a fucking double standard, if you ask me. Good thing the spiders got Evans, because I think he had plans for me. He and Betty Mae. Who the hell would listen to my side of the story, right? I'm just a drifter. So, in a way, the spiders may have done me a favor. How fucked up is that? Still wish they could have croaked the two of them a bit closer to my cell. They're starting to stink something fierce.

The pen was low on ink when I started, and now it's about out. I suppose I could prick my finger with the knife and draw some blood to keep it going.

Come to think of it, I could use the knife to draw a *lot* of blood. Something in the neighborhood of all of it and just finish this whole thing. Just a quick flick and that's it.

Naw. That'd hurt.

My wrist is killing me. There's nothing left to say, so I'm done writing. I guess I'll sit a spell and wait this out. Maybe the hunger'll get me. Or maybe I'll go mad, like Caddy Girl, and jump off the roof. Maybe the spiders will find a way in first.

If you're reading this, I'm guessing you already know.

"THE KING" IN *YELLOW*

Brian Keene

The man stood rotting on the corner. Frayed rags hung on his skeletal frame. Ulcerated sores covered his exposed flesh, weeping blood and pus. He stank. Sweat. Infection. Excrement.

Despair.

Finley considered going the long way around him, but Kathryn waved impatiently from across the street.

He shouldered by; head down, eyes fixed on the pavement. Invisible.

He can't see me if I can't see him.

"Yo 'zup," the rotting man mumbled over the traffic. "Kin you help a brutha' out wit' a quarta'?"

Finley tried ignoring him, then relented. He didn't have the heart to be so cold, although Kathryn's yuppie friends (they were supposed to be *his* friends too, but he never thought of them that way) would have mocked him for it. He raised his head, actually *looking* at the bum, meeting his watery eyes.

They shone.

He glanced across the street. Kathryn was incredulous.

"Sorry, man." Finley held his hands out in a pretense of sympathy. "I'm taking my girl to dinner." Feeling like an idiot, he pointed at Kathryn. "Need to stop at an ATM."

"S'cool," the vagrant smiled. "Ya'll kin hit me on da way back."

"Okay, we'll do that."

He stepped off the curb. The man darted forward, grasping his shoulder. Dirty fingernails clawed at his suit jacket.

"Hey!" Finley protested.

"Have ya'll seen *Yellow*?" the bum croaked.

"No, I don't think so," Finley stammered, clueless.

"Afta' ya eat, take yo' lady t' see it."

Cackling, he shambled off toward the waterfront.

Kathryn shook her head as Finley crossed the street.

"So you met the Human Scab."

"Only in Baltimore," he grinned.

"Fucking wildlife," she spat, taking his arm. "That's why I take my smoke breaks in the parking garage. I don't know what's worse—the seagulls dive-bombing me, or the homeless dive-bombing me."

"The seagulls," Finley replied. "How was your day?"

"Don't try to change the subject, Roger. Christ, you've become so liberal." She paused and let go of his arm, lighting a cigarette. In the early darkness, the flame lit her face, reminding Finley why he'd fallen in love with her. "But since you asked, it sucked. How was yours?"

"All right, I guess. Pet Search's site crashed, so I had to un-fuck that. FedEx dropped off my new backup server. On *Days of Our Lives*, John is still trying to find Stefano and Bo found out about Hope's baby."

"Wish I could work from home. But one of us has to make money."

"Well isn't that why we're going out to dinner? To celebrate your big bonus?"

They crossed Albemarle Street in silence. Ahead, the

bright lights of the Inner Harbor beckoned with its fancy restaurants and posh shops. The National Aquarium overlooked the water like an ancient monolith.

Kathryn's brow furrowed.

"Beautiful night," Finley commented, tugging his collar against the cold air blowing in across the water. "You can almost see the stars."

Kathryn said nothing.

"What's wrong?"

She sighed, her breath forming mist in the air. "I feel—I don't know—old. We used to do fun things all the time. Now it's dinner on the couch and whatever's on satellite. Maybe a game of Scrabble if we're feeling energetic."

Finley stared out across the harbor. "I thought you liked coming home every evening with dinner made, and spending a quiet night around the house."

She took his hand.

"I do, Roger. I'm sorry. It's just—we're both thirty now. When was the last time we did something *really* fun?"

"When we were twenty-one and you puked on me during the Depeche Mode concert?"

Kathryn finally laughed, and they walked on, approaching Victor's.

"So why did your day suck?"

"Oh, the lender won't approve the loan on the Spring Grove project because the inspector found black mold in some of the properties. Of course, Ned told him we were going to rip out the tiles during the remodeling phase, but he—"

Finley tuned her out, still nodding and expressing acknowledgement where applicable. After ten years, he'd gotten good at it. When *was* the last time they'd really done something fun? He tried to remember. Didn't this count? Going out to dinner? Probably not. He tried to pinpoint exactly *when* they had settled into the comfortable zone of domestic familiarity. By mutual agreement, they didn't go to the club anymore. Too many ghetto fabulous suburbanites barely out of college. They didn't go to the movies because they hated the cramped seating and symphony of babies crying and cell phones ringing.

"—so I don't know what I'm going to do," Kathryn finished.

"You'll be fine," Finley nodded, squeezing her hand. "You can handle it."

She smiled, squeezing back.

The line outside Victor's snaked around the restaurant. Finley maneuvered them through it, thankful he'd had the foresight to make reservations.

The maitre d' approached them, waving a manicured hand.

"Hello, Ms. Kathryn," he said, clasping her hand. "I'm delighted you could join us."

"Hello, Franklin." She curtsied, smiling as the older man kissed both her cheeks. "This is my boyfriend, Roger."

"A pleasure to make your acquaintance. I've heard much about you." He winked and Finley grinned, unsure of how to reply.

"Give them a good view," Franklin told the hostess, and turned back to them. "Sheila will seat you. Enjoy your meal."

"I come here a lot for lunch," Kathryn explained as they followed Sheila to their table. "I told Franklin we'd be coming in tonight. He's a nice old guy; a real charmer."

"Yes, he does seem nice," Finley mumbled, distracted. Not for the first time, he found himself surprised by how little he knew about Kathryn's life outside their relationship. He'd never thought to wonder where she spent her lunches.

In many ways, they were different. Strangers making up a whole. She was the consummate twenty-first-century yuppie—a corporate lioness intent upon her career and nothing else. He was the epitome of the Generation X slacker, running a home-based Web-hosting business. They'd been together almost ten years, but at times, it seemed to him as if they were just coasting. The subject of marriage had been broached several times, and usually deflected by both of them. He needed to devote his time to developing his business. She wasn't where she wanted to be in her career.

Despite that, he thought they were happy. So why the disquiet?

Maybe Kathryn was right. Maybe they needed to do something fun, something different.

"—at night, isn't it?"

"I'm sorry," he stammered. "What'd you say, hon?"

"I said the harbor really is beautiful at night." They were seated in front of a large window, looking out toward the Chesapeake Bay. The lights of the city twinkled in the darkness.

"Yeah, it sure is."

"What were you thinking about, Roger?"

"Honestly? That you're right. We should do something *fun*. How about we take a trip down to the ocean this weekend? Check out the wild horses, maybe do a little beachcombing?"

"That sounds great," she sighed. "But I can't this weekend. I've got to come in on Saturday and crunch numbers for the Vermont deal. We close on that next week."

"Well then, how about we do something Sunday? Maybe take a drive up to Pennsylvania and visit some of the flea markets, see the Amish?"

"That's a possibility. Let's play it by ear, okay?"

They studied their menus, basking in the comfortable silence that only longtime partners share.

That was when Roger noticed the woman.

She and her companion sat at the next table. The flickering candlelight cast shadows on her sallow face. She was thin, almost to the point of emaciation, and there were dark circles under her eyes.

Heroin, he wondered, *or maybe anorexia?* She obviously came from money. That much was apparent from her jewelry and shoes. Her companion looked wealthy too. Maybe she was a prostitute? No, they seemed too familiar with each other for that.

What caught Finley's attention next was the blood trickling down her leg. Her conversation was animated, and while she gestured excitedly with one hand, the other was beneath the table, clenching her leg. Fingernails clawed deep into her thigh, hard enough to draw blood. She didn't seem to care. In fact, judging by the look in her eye, she enjoyed the sensation.

Kathryn was absorbed with the menu. He turned back to the couple, and focused on what the woman was saying.

"And then, the King appears. It's *such* a powerful moment, you can't breathe. I've been to Vegas, and I've seen impersonators, but this guy is the real thing!"

Her companion's response was muffled, and Finley strained to hear.

"I'm serious, Gerald! It's like he's channeling Elvis! The King playing the King! The whole cast is like that. There's a woman who looks and sounds just like Janis Joplin playing the Queen. And a very passable John Lennon as Thale. The best though, next to the King of course, is the guy they cast to play the Pallid Mask. I swear to you Gerald, he's Kurt Cobain! It's all so realistically clever! Actors playing rock stars playing roles. A play within a musical within a play."

Her voice dropped to a conspiratorial whisper, and Finley leaned toward them.

"The special effects are amazing. When the Queen has the Pallid Mask tortured, you can actually see little pieces of brain in Cobain's hair. And they have audience participation, too. It's different every night. We each had to reveal a secret that we'd never told anyone. Tonight, I hear they'll be having the audience unmask as well during the masquerade scene!"

He jumped as Kathryn's fingertips brushed his hand.

"Stop eavesdropping," she hissed. "It's not polite."

"Sorry. Have you decided what you're going to have?"

"Mmmm-hmmm," she purred. "I'm going with the crab cakes. How about you?"

"I think I'll have the filet mignon. Rare. And a big baked potato with lots of sour cream and butter."

Her eyes widened. "Why Roger, you haven't had that since your last visit to the doctor. What happened to eating healthy, so you don't end up like your father?"

"The hell with my hereditary heart disease and cholesterol!" He closed the menu with a snap. "You said we need to start having more fun. Red meat and starch is a good start!"

She laughed, and the lights of the bay reflected in her eyes. Underneath the table, she slid her foot against his leg.

"I love you, Kathryn."

"I love you too."

The woman at the other table stood up, knocking her chair backward, and began to scream.

Silence, then hushed murmurs as the woman tottered back and forth on her heels. Her companion scooted his chair back, cleared his throat in embarrassment, and reached for her. She slapped his hand away with a shriek.

"Have you seen the Yellow Sign?" she sang. "Have

you found the Yellow Sign? Have you seen the Yellow Sign?"

She continued the chorus, spinning round and round. Her flailing arms sent a wineglass crashing to the floor. Her date lunged for her. She sidestepped, and in one quick movement, snatched her steak knife from the table and plunged it into his side. He sank to the floor, pulling the tablecloth and their meals down with him.

The other patrons were screaming now. Several dashed for the exit, but no one moved to stop her. Finley felt frozen in place, transfixed by what occurred next.

Still singing, the woman bent over and plucked up her soup spoon from the mess on the floor, then used it to gouge out her eyes. Red and white pulp dribbled down her face.

Voice never wavering, she continued to sing.

Kathryn cringed against Finley. He grabbed her hand, pulling her toward the exit. Franklin the maitre d' and several men from the kitchen rushed toward the woman.

As he hurried Kathryn out the door, he heard the woman cackling.

"I found it! I can see it all! Yhtill, under the stars of Aldebaran and the Hyades! And across the Lake of Hali, on the far shore, lies Carcosa!"

Then they were out the door and into the night.

Kathryn sobbed against him, and Finley shuddered. The image of the woman digging into her eye sockets with the soup spoon would not go away.

After they'd given their statement to the police, they walked back to Kathryn's building.

"How could a person *do* something like that?"

"Drugs maybe." Finley shrugged. "She looked pretty strung out."

"This city gets worse every year."

They arrived at her building and Finley walked around to the side entrance leading into the parking garage. He'd taken the bus, so that they could drive her car back home. Kathryn didn't follow, and he turned to find her stopped under a streetlight.

"What's wrong?"

"I don't think I'm going to be able to sleep tonight."

"Yeah, me either. Let's go home and get you a nice, hot bath. Maybe you'll feel better after that."

"I need a drink."

"We can stop off at the liquor store—"

"No," she cut him off. "I need to be around *people,* Roger. I need to hear music and laughter and forget about that insane bitch."

"You want to hit a club?" He heard the surprised tone in his voice.

"I don't know what I want, but I know that I don't want to go home right now. Let's walk over to Fell's Point and see what we can find."

The buildings in Fell's Point had been old when Edgar Allan Poe was new to the city. By day, it was a tourist trap; six blocks of antique shops and bookstores and curio dealers. Urban chic spawned and bred in its coffee shops and cafés. At night, the college crowd descended upon it, flocking to any of the dozens of nightclubs and bars that dotted the area.

They strolled down Pratt Street, arms linked around each other's waist, and Finley smiled.

A figure lurched out of the shadows.

"Have ya'll seen *Yellow*?"

Finley groaned. He'd forgotten about the homeless man—the Human Scab.

He thrust his hand in his pants pocket and pulled out a rumpled five.

"Here," he said, offering it to the rotting man. "I promised you I'd get you on the way back. Now if you don't mind, my girlfriend and I have had a rough evening."

"Thanks yo. Sorry t' hear 'bout yo' night. I'm tellin' ya, take yer girl ta' see *Yellow*. Dat'll fix ya right up."

With one dirty, ragged finger, he pointed at a poster hanging from a light pole.

"Ya'll have a good 'un."

The bum shuffled off into the darkness, humming a snatch of melody. Finley recognized the tune as "Are You Lonesome Tonight." He shuddered, reminded of the crazy woman at the restaurant, raving about the Elvis impersonator that she'd seen. He tried to remember what it was she had been singing, but all that came to mind was the image of her gored face.

The eight-by-ten poster had been made to look like it was printed on a snake's skin. Printed over the scales, pale lettering read:

Hastur Productions Proudly Presents:

YELLOW
(The Awful Tragedy of Young Castaigne)

Banned in Paris, Munich, London, and Rome,
we are proud to bring this classic 19th century play to
Baltimore, in its only U.S. appearance! Filled with
music, emotion, and dark wonder, YELLOW is an
unforgettable and mystifying tale! Not to be missed!

Starring:
Sid Vicious as Uoht
John Lennon as Thale
Mama Cass as Cassilda
Janis Joplin as the Queen
Karen Carpenter as Camilla

James Marshall Hendrix as Alar
Jim Morrison as Aldones, the Lizard King
Kurt Cobain as the Pallid Mask, or, Phantom of Truth
and
Elvis Presley as the King

Also featuring: Bon Scott, Roy Orbison,
Freddie Mercury, Cliff Burton, and more.

One Week Only! Nightly Performances
Begin Promptly at Midnight

The R.W. Chambers Theatre
Fells Point, Fedogan St. & Bremer Ave.
Baltimore, MD

The breeze coming off the harbor chilled him. This was what the crazy woman had been talking about—actors depicting dead musicians depicting characters in a play. *This* play. The coincidence was unsettling.

"Sounds like fun, doesn't it?" Kathryn asked. "You should have tipped him more money."

"Only in Baltimore can the homeless get jobs as ushers. Come on, let's find a pub."

"No, let's go see this! Look, they've got actors pretending to be dead musicians playing actors. How cool is that?" She giggled, and looked at him pleadingly.

He told her what he'd overheard the woman say.

"Then that's all the more reason," she insisted. "Once people read about the connection in tomorrow's *Sun,* we won't be able to get tickets because of the demand. People love morbid stuff like that."

"Don't you think it's odd that this all happened in the same night? You said you wanted to forget about what happened. Don't you think that attending a play that this same woman went to will just make it that more vivid?"

"Roger, you said that you agreed with me; that we never do anything fun anymore, that we're not spontaneous. Here's our chance! How much more spur-of-the-moment can we get?"

"Kathryn, it's almost eleven thirty! It's late."

"The poster says it doesn't start until midnight."

Finley sighed in reluctance.

"All right, we'll go to the play. You're right, it might be fun." He allowed her to lead him down the street and into Fells Point.

The R.W. Chambers Theatre wasn't just off the beaten path—it was far, far beyond it. They picked their way through a maze of winding, twisting streets and alleyways, each more narrow than the previous. The throng of drunken college kids and office interns vanished, replaced by the occasional rat or pigeon. Kathryn's heels clicked on the cobblestones, each step sounding like a rifle shot.

This is the old part of the city, Finley thought. *The oldest. The dark heart.*

The very atmosphere seemed to echo his discomfort, accentuating it as they went further. There were no streetlights in this section, and no lights shining in the windows of the houses. The buildings crowded together; crumbling statues of crumbling nineteenth-century architecture. The street smelled faintly of garbage and stale urine, and the only sound was that of dripping water, and of something small scuttling in the darkness.

Kathryn gripped his hand tightly, and then—

—they emerged onto the corner, and the lights and noise flooded back again. A crowd milled about in front of the theatre. Finley's apprehension dissipated, and he chided himself for being silly. At the same time, Kathryn's grip loosened.

"Look at this crowd!" Kathryn exclaimed. "It's more popular than we thought."

"Word of mouth must have spread fast."

"Maybe your homeless friend has been pimping it."

Finley grinned. "Maybe."

They took their place at the end of the line, behind a young Goth couple.

The theatre had seen better days. The water-stained brickwork looked tired and faded. Several windows on the second floor had been boarded over, and the others were dark. Some of the lightbulbs in the marquee had burned out, but *Hastur Productions' YELLOW* and the show time and ticket prices were prominently visible. One side of the building was plastered with paper billboards promoting the play. Others advertised bands with names like "Your Kid's on Fire," "Suicide Run," and "I, Chaos."

The line snaked forward, and finally it was their turn. Finley stared at the man behind the glass window of the ticket booth. His skin was pale, almost opaque, and tiny blue veins spiderwebbed his face and hands. Gray lips flopped like two pieces of raw liver as he spoke.

"Enjoy the performance."

Finley nodded. Placing his arm around Kathryn's waist, he guided them into the building.

The usher in the lobby had the same alabaster complexion, and was slightly more laconic than his sullen ticket booth counterpart. Without a word, he took their tickets, handed back the stubs and two programs, then silently parted a pair of black curtains and gestured for them to enter.

The theatre filled quickly. They found a spot midway down the center aisle. The red-velvet-covered chairs squeaked as they sat down.

"I can't get over it," Kathryn whispered. "Look at all these people!"

Finley studied the program booklet. Like the posters, it was designed to appear as if it had been bound in serpent skin. He struggled to read the pale lettering.

> YELLOW was written in the late 19th century by a young playwright named Castaigne. Tragically, Castaigne took his own life immediately upon completing the work. When YELLOW was first published and performed, the city of Paris banned the play, followed by Munich and London, and eventually most of the world's governments and churches.
>
> It was translated in 1930 by the scholar Daniel Mason Winfield-Harms; who, in a strange twist of fate echoing that of the original author, was found dead in Buffalo, New York, after finishing the adaptation.
>
> YELLOW takes place, not on Earth, but on another world, in the city of Yhtill, on the shore of the Lake of Hali, under the stars of Aldebaran and Hyades.

Kathryn stirred next to him. "You know what this reminds me of?"

"What?"

"When I was in high school. At midnight on Saturdays, we'd go to see *The Rocky Horror Picture Show.* It has that feel to it."

"Maybe they'll sing 'The Time Warp.' "

The lights dimmed, plunging them into darkness. The crowd grew silent as a burst of static coughed from the overhead speakers. Then, an eerie, unfamiliar style of music began.

A light appeared at the back of the theatre. The performers entered from the rear, each of them carrying a single candle. The troupe walked slowly down the center aisle, singing as they approached the stage.

"Have you seen the Yellow Sign? Have you found the Yellow Sign?"

As they passed by, Finley forcibly resisted the urge to reach out and touch them. The resemblance to their dead alter egos was uncanny. The actress playing Janis Joplin (playing the Queen) was a *perfect* duplicate, down to the blue-tinged skin that must have adorned her face in death. Following her were Jim Morrison (a bloated Aldones) and John Lennon (a Thale with fresh bloodstains on his clothing). Mama Cass, Jimi Hendrix, Sid Vicious—the procession continued, until two dozen actors had taken the stage.

"Look at that!" Kathryn pointed to the quarter-sized drops of blood left in the Lennon actor's wake. "Gruesome. I can't wait to see what they did with Kurt Cobain. . . ."

Finley shuddered. "Good special effects, that's for sure."

The singing swelled, the upraised voices echoing like thunder.

"Have you seen the Yellow Sign? Have you found the Yellow Sign? Let the red dawn surmise what we shall do, when this blue starlight dies and all is through. Have you seen the Yellow Sign? Have you found the Yellow Sign?"

They repeated the chorus two more times. On the last note, the candles were extinguished and the lights on the stage grew brighter.

The first part of the play concerned the intrigue of the royal court. The aging Queen was pestered and plied by her children: Cassilda, Alar, Camilla, Thale, Uoht, and Aldones, all claimants for the throne to Yhtill. They vied for the crown, so that the dynasty would continue, each one claiming to be the rightful successor. Despite their efforts, the Queen declined to give the crown away.

Then the Cobain character appeared on stage, his face hidden beneath a pallid mask. When he turned his back to the audience, the crowd gasped. Hair and skull were gone, offering a glimpse of gray matter.

Finley had trouble following the plot. Cobain's character, the Phantom of Truth, pronounced doom upon the Queen and her subjects. The threat apparently came from a nonexistent city that would appear on the other side of the lake. Reacting to this news, the Queen ordered him tortured.

Though Kathryn seemed enraptured, Finley grew restless as it continued. He found it incoherent to the point of absurdity. One moment, a character professed love for another. The next, they discussed a race of people who lacked anuses, and could consume only milk, evacuating their waste through vomiting.

The characters rambled on, and Finley slipped into a half-conscious state—his mind adrift on other matters, but the actor's lines droned in the back of his head.

"There are so many things which are impossible to explain! Why should certain chords of music make me think of the brown and golden tints of autumn foliage?"

"Let the red dawn surmise . . ."

"Aldebaran and the Hyades have aligned, my Queen!"

"What we shall do . . ."

"Sleep now, the blessed sleep, and be not troubled by these ill omens."

"When this blue starlight dies . . ."

"The City of Carcosa has appeared on the other side of Lake Hali!"

"And all is through . . ."

He wasn't sure how long he stayed like that; head

drooping and eyes half shut. Kathryn's light laughter and the chuckles coming from the rest of the audience startled him awake again.

He checked his watch; then glanced around at the other patrons. Immediately, his attention focused on a couple behind them. The woman's head was in her lover's lap, bobbing up and down in the darkness.

Before he could tell Kathryn, he noticed another display; this one in their own row. A man at the end was lovingly biting another man's ear, hard enough to draw blood. His partner licked his lips in ecstasy.

"Kathryn—" he whispered.

She shushed him and focused on the play, her face rapt with attention. Her cheeks were flushed, and Finley noticed that her nipples stood out hard against her blouse. Without a word, her hand fell into his lap and began to stroke him through his pants. Despite the bizarre mood permeating the theatre, he felt himself harden.

Just then, there was a commotion at the back of the theatre, as another actor entered. The crowd turned as the actors pointed with mock cries of shock and dismay.

He wore a gilded robe with scarlet fringes, and a clasp of black onyx, on which was inlaid a curious symbol of gold. Though his face was hidden beneath a pallid mask identical to the one Cobain was wearing, there was no mistaking the trademark swagger. He swept down the aisle, pausing as the crowd burst into spontaneous applause.

"Thank you. Thank you very much."

He bowed to the audience, and then took the stage in three quick strides.

"Behold, the Yellow Sign upon his breast!" cried the Queen. *"It is the King of Carcosa, and he seeks the Phantom of Truth!"*

Hendrix, Lennon, and Vicious entered the audience, each with a burlap bag slung over his shoulder.

"Masks!" they called. *"Everyone receive your masks! No pushing. There's plenty for everyone!"*

Finley pushed Kathryn's hand away in alarm. They were passing out *knives*—real knives rather than stage props. The lights glinted off the serrated blades.

"Kathryn, we—"

His statement was cut short as her mouth covered his. Greedily, she sucked at his tongue, her body suddenly filling his lap. The scene replayed itself throughout the theatre. Men and women, men and men, women and women. Couples, threesomes, and more. Clothes were discarded, and naked, glistening bodies entwined around each other in the seats and on the floor. All the while, the dead rock stars waded through the crowd, dispensing knives.

"Kathryn, stop it!" He pushed her away. "Something is really fucked up here."

"Have you found it, Roger? Have you seen the Yellow Sign?"

"What?"

She slapped him. Hard. Then, grinning, she slapped him again.

"Now, you slap me," she urged. "Come on, Roger. You said you wanted to do something different. Make me wet. Hit me!"

"No!"

"Coward! Pussy! You limp dick motherfucker! Do it, or I'll find someone else here who will!"

"What the hell is wrong with you?"

It's like she's hypnotized or something! All of them are! What the hell happened while I was asleep?

On stage, what appeared to be a masked ball scene was underway.

"You have questioned him to no avail!" Elvis's voice rang out through the hall, echoing over the mingled cries of pain and ecstasy. He was addressing the actors, but at the same time, the audience as well. *"Time to unmask. All must show their true faces! All! Except for myself. For indeed, I wear no mask at all!"*

As one, the crowd picked up their knives and began to flay the skin from their faces. Some laughed as they did it. Others helped the person sitting next to them.

He turned, just as Kathryn slid the blade through one cheek. A loose flap of skin hung down past her chin.

"Kathryn, don't!"

He grabbed for the knife and she jerked it away. Before he could move, she slashed at his hands. Blood welled in his palm as he dodged another slice. Then, finally, he slapped her, leaving a bloody handprint on her cheek.

"That's it, baby!" she shrieked. "Let me finish taking my mask off, and then I'll help you with yours."

"All unmask!" Elvis boomed again, and Finley turned to the stage, unable to look away. The King removed the Pallid Mask concealing his face, and what he revealed wasn't Elvis. It wasn't even human. Beneath the mask was a head like that of a puffy grave worm. It lolled obscenely, surveying the crowd, then gave a strange, warbling cry.

Kathryn's skin landed on the floor with a wet sound.

The thing on stage turned toward Finley, and then he saw.

He saw it. He found it.

Roger Finley screamed.

"Excuse me?" The bum shuffled forward.

"Just ignore him, Marianne. If we give him money, he'll hound us the whole way to the harbor."

"Don't be ridiculous, Thomas," the woman scolded her husband. "The poor fellow looks half starved."

The bum shuffled eagerly from foot to foot while she reached within her purse and pulled out a five-dollar bill. She placed it in his outstretched hand.

"Here you go. Please see to it that you get a hot meal, now. No alcohol."

"Thank you. Much obliged. Since you folks were so kind, let me help you out."

"We don't need any help, thank you very much." The husband stiffened, wary of the homeless man's advances.

"Just wanted to give you a tip. If you like the theatre, you should take your wife to see *Yellow*."

He pointed at a nearby poster.

The couple thanked him and walked away, but not before stopping to read the poster for themselves.

Roger Finley pocketed the five dollars, and watched them disappear into Fell's Point, in search of the Yellow Sign.

He wondered if they would find it, and if so, what they would see.

THESE STRANGE LAYS

Tom Piccirilli

Holder's father had been in the ground for almost four months and he figured it was about time to see the grave, say whatever he had left to say.

Woodland Cemetery sat out on Route 9, bordered by a high school soccer field on the south and deep woods behind Fall Gardens, a psychiatric hospital, to the north. Holder sped down the back roads as the afternoon sun settled in the horizon, with that vicious autumn glare cutting down like a cleaver. He'd never been inside the Woodland acreage before and was surprised at how large and well-kept it was. He parked in an empty lot, puzzled that the place didn't have more visitors, considering all the dead.

It was a good thing the old man was under six feet of dirt. The well-trimmed lawns, carefully pruned hedges, neat rows of graves, and methodically placed trees would've driven the old man berserk. He would've torn up the place in his four-by-four on general principle.

Dad had some issues but he liked to laugh, especially when cops or security guards were chasing him. Holder could see it now—the truck tires spitting grass and topsoil, looping around the place in wide circles and crashing through the freshly planted shrubs, with the wild drunken guffaws booming over the fields.

A shard of sorrow worked loose in his chest and Holder chewed back a groan and let it slowly shift to a sigh. It took him almost fifteen minutes of hunting along aisles before he found the right grave. Somebody had left a Bible, a pint of whiskey, and a slice of cheesecake half buried in the loose dirt. It gave him pause, thinking about which of his old man's girlfriends might do something like that.

None of them had names in his mind, just vague descriptions as they flounced around his father in the bars. Chubby chick with the rose tattoo on her neck whining about a dental hygiene night class professor. Way too young Latina mama with the horse teeth pawing bucks for baby food. Black leather micro-skirted, mother-daughter tag team bottled blonds hunting eight-balls at four a.m. Holder wondered which might be the Bible-toting, cheesecake type.

He had the same name as his father and seeing it carved into stone made Holder grimace. On occasion you came face to face with your fate all on your own, and sometimes they sort of threw it up at you. He thought about what he wanted to tell his dad now—how much he missed the man already, and how he wanted to hear that robust laughter again—imagining him down there with a grin, his eyes only slightly hooded, peering into the dark.

Everybody dealt with the devil in his own way—you cut and ran or maybe you had the guts and faced up. You dodged the pea soup and sat in the first pew, ogling Christ on his cross and standing in line to dig up some kind of confession. You beat your lust out of yourself and tried not to buy too much filth on the Internet. Or, if you were like Dad, you slid a half-pint of shine Nick's way and offered a cigar. Then you pinned his hot, pointy ears back to his head, took a gander around your particular corner of hell, and decided what the fuck to do first.

A sound tugged Holder's attention aside.

His father's voice was so loud in his mind that it took a moment to realize someone else was singing, high and resonant, almost like a hymn. He wagged his chin hoping to dislodge his thoughts. That song had an edge to it, drifting through the trees and up the cemetery's promontory. He turned and scanned the area.

He half expected to see the chubby chick with the rose tattoo on her neck come stumbling along. She had enough meat in the keester to suggest she enjoyed a cheesecake or two now and then.

Flitting through the thickets bordering Woodland was a girl, sort of prancing in the steady breeze, doing the kind of Irish jig you did when you were too drunk to realize you weren't doing an Irish jig at all. He tilted his head and watched her rushing across the graves the way you weren't supposed to do, stepping on all the heads, where the earth was always a little soft. It took him back some and made him curious. She glanced up the hill and saw Holder there and made a sudden looping arc toward him, capering without a care.

She waved to him and he raised his hand in return, thinking, All right, we're about to get into something here.

A few things ran through his mind at once, including the possibility that this might be one of his father's other kids that were undoubtedly running around out in the world. Tadpoles that had turned into people, looking for what? Money? Vengeance? It made Holder a touch wary, imagining her coming up, grabbing him by the collar, slapping him around some and then throwing herself down in the dirt, wailing. You had to be ready for just about anything.

When she got up to him she said, "I'm Megan."

A melancholy but compassionate face, with crow's-feet at the corners of her mouth from smiling too harshly, for too many hours at a clip. He kind of liked the wrinkles there because she was young, midtwenties maybe, and it gave her a little extra touch of the exotic, as if she'd seen more than she should've and had a hard time handling it. Jesus, maybe she *was* his sister.

She wore inmate togs. Light gray jammies and her feet were bare and stained green and he got to thinking how he'd like to wash them for her, the water warm and plenty of bubbles around on her slick skin. Tussled blond bangs framed her heart-shaped face, and she clawed her hair off her forehead, pursing lavish bee-stung lips. She breathed deeply, on the verge of yawning, like she'd just gotten out of bed.

Some girls had the kind of look you wanted without having to do a damn thing for it. Nature set it up inside your head and you couldn't fight it no matter how you tried. Holder felt his throat closing up, his breath growing rapid.

"Hello, Megan," he said, and his voice was thicker than it should've been.

He took a step forward and saw that her eyes were hazel with bits of gold in them, and now she gave a grin that made him step back again. He had no idea exactly how he should handle the devil. Do you offer up your throat or do you back off slowly, try to get to the car without making much of a fuss? She looked behind her at the hospital buildings maybe a half mile away, then checked in the other direction toward the high school. And then she angled herself to stare beyond the fields at the rest of town, where flawed denizens returned home now after work to ooze into couches while the television ranted and laughed hollowly.

Holder decided to hold his ground. He could always dash for cover later, crawl on his belly through the woods to get away if he had to. Maybe he had more brothers and sisters shambling toward him at this minute, babies creeping along the tree line. Megan pirouetted past and sat on the soil, digging her heels in deep, wedged against the stone.

"Lady, that's my father's grave."

"Do you think he'd mind? I mean, really?"

Holder tried to imagine it. A lovely young woman's ass perched over his dad's dead face. This was the sort of thing his old man would've gotten a serious kick out of, always telling Holder to get out and enjoy life, have some fun, get laid more, do something a bit crazy.

She went for the bottle of whiskey and he said, "Don't."

"He isn't going to drink it, is he?"

"It's for him anyway. Leave it."

"Okay. Can I play with the Bible?"

"No."

"Did you hate him?"

"No, I loved him more than anything."

It seemed to surprise her, like he had all the wrong answers. "Really? Why?"

"He made life interesting and he laughed a lot."

"Oh."

There it was, another tiny temptation that worked through his veins, the right neurochemicals slithering around inside his mammal brain. It slipped in like a blade under the heart. Holder liked the way she made the sound. Damn near an *oooh* but not quite. He didn't want to think about what kind of a home life she came from where loving your own dad was so alien an idea.

Leaves spun past in the growing wind. Her hands moved as if making charms, dirty feet leaving marks against his name on the stone. You could read symbols into so much around you that if you didn't let it all go at once you'd spend the rest of your life chasing after it, studying false signs. He had a tendency toward that sort of shit.

Her frown softened and eventually faded until she let loose with a soft giggle. "Spank me."

The words slid into him. He realized they were both stuck in other roles right now and didn't know what to do about it. He wondered which bastard he was supposed to be in her head. Prom date gone awry? Greasy-pawed Uncle Freddie? Or could you actually find a part of yourself adrift in somebody else?

"Sure," he told her.

He was his own father, who used to enjoy situations like this, and she was the naughty child she'd once been, going all out to get under the skin, and both of them were this close to letting loose with screams for the hell of it. You cut loose once in a while and bled the steam off, if you could.

Megan didn't help him and that was all right. He wanted to touch her but didn't want to be touched, really, and the thought bothered him. Funny the things that could trip you up. He couldn't have *that* dirt on him so he pulled her up by the wrists and drew her against the stone. Some of your craziness was okay depending on its position. She slipped out of her pajama pants, arching herself over the gravestone. Dad had to be scratching at the coffin lid by now. She pulled her blouse open and Holder moved to her, her nipples in his hands as he finally leaned in to taste her tongue and kiss those pouting, pulpy lips.

No more than five seconds went by before she broke his grip. The animal in him started crawling out of the hole, the rage stirring. Megan twisted around and bent way over, resting her arms atop the tombstone, showing off her ass. This is some freaky shit, he thought, but not much different than some of the other situations he'd been in. His first screw had been with a black prostitute named Rosy weighing in at 270 that his father had brought home for him when he was thirteen. You got used to strange lays after that.

"Come on, slap my ass."

"Sure," he said.

"Let him watch. Let Daddy watch."

It irritated him, hearing that. Holder began spanking her with his right hand while running his left underneath her neck, squeezing lightly. He worked his way down to toy with her clit, still swatting her pretty roughly.

She turned and gave him the slow once over, sort of disappointed. "Harder, really punish it."

"Okay." He let loose and gave her a few open-handed whacks that echoed like gun shots across the cemetery. Her ass grew instantly red. He thought about the Pope in Vatican City suddenly flinching so severely that his big funny hat flipped onto the floor.

Some people would've thought it a little weird to be doing this but he knew his dad would've enjoyed the scene, had probably done plenty similar in his life, though maybe not on his old man's grave. It gave Holder an extra incentive and he planted his heels, throwing all his weight into it as he swatted her. When did this turn to abuse and violation? When did it close in on murder? She was grinning now, clenching her teeth and letting out a low moan broken by bitter snorts. The nasty crimson of her ass grew deeper and deeper. Here he was thinking of bubble baths and now this. It made him scowl and he started to feel a little out of it, thinking, Am I supposed to dig this? Where's the payback? I don't want my heinie hurt. He stopped in mid-whap and she quivered while he licked her neck. Better, much better, none of this hostility. You let that out on the rude, ugly pricks of the world, not on the young beautiful girls.

You could kill your demons with kindness. She bucked and heaved backward as he pressed his groin up behind her, dry humping her as he strained against his shorts. Rosy had liked it this way, urging him on going, "That's it, honey, that's the stuff. Uh huh." This might actually get good. Megan reached behind and undid his jeans, unzipped and yanked him out in one fluid motion, slipping it in without ever glancing over her shoulder to look at him. She was close already and when he thrust into her she was so wet that drops splashed into his pubic hair.

Dad's roaring laughter filled Holder's head. Rosy's laughter too. And Matilda's and Jade's and Patricia's and others he remembered but whose names had disappeared. His father had been very generous there for a while. A couple of them had been murdered the next year during the summer of the Icepick, when a killer had worked the streets taking the ladies out. It had been an ugly time. Bartenders had started getting the stink eye, cops coming around to all the pubs and back rooms, rousting anybody who came within a hundred yards of an ice pick. Holder would stand around while the police tried to shake something loose, describing the way the ladies were found. Sixty-four puncture wounds. Ninety-seven. Twenty-five in each eye. Holder threw up a lot that summer.

He held on to her hips and screwed her from behind even more forcefully, not caring where he was any longer as his nuts tightened and her hair whipped back into his face. She had good control and nabbed him with her muscles, snickering while he moaned. He caught a whiff of some sort of extra-strength shampoo, no fruit or tropical oils, just straight detergent. He wondered what went on up in that hospital to beautiful crazed women like this who danced on top of the dead.

The stone tipped an inch as she cried, "That's it, that's it, for Daddy, as hard as you can," chanting it, in rhythm with his lunges. He nearly quit then, that Daddy shit was getting on his nerves, but he let the tension go, rising up the back of his neck until it drifted free. He wanted to kiss her but couldn't figure a way to turn her around to face him without losing contact. It worried him, the idea that she might just run off if he didn't keep his hands on her like this, so he kept hold of her.

A strong scent of sweat wafted in the air and made him a little heady. She thrust backward, fiery hand prints atop alabaster flesh. You could see Nick everywhere if you wanted to. He snorted into her neck and she whispered, "You can bite me if you want." He did but not very hard, just enough to gather some of her flesh between his teeth as he locked up.

He slumped and laid his cheek on the spot between her shoulder blades, panting. When his eyes focused he checked her skin for teeth marks. He found a couple of spots that looked like small puncture scars and his back teeth ground together.

Is that what happened to the Icepick killer? Did he crack wide open in his real life and they tossed him in the Falls for a nervous breakdown? Did he stalk around pressing the pick to the backs of little girls, hard enough to bring up a drop of blood or two but not so deep that he'd draw attention to himself again?

Couldn't you get through an hour of life without having to wonder about some crazy bastard lining up new victims? There were other evils to worry about, but sometimes it just didn't feel like it.

"I needed that," she told him.

"Me too," he huffed.

With a rough touch Megan pushed him off. She waited as he pulled his pants back up. She patted his groin like a new pet and then drew her own bottoms on. It worried him some, that pat.

"Let's go," she said, smiling with a real understanding. This girl knew more about Holder than she should have and it scared him.

"Where?"

"Home, of course," she said, and he understood exactly what she meant.

"Oh, Christ."

But he could almost feel his father urging him on in this game, telling him to play it out.

He headed for his car but she walked the other way, down the hill, so he followed. They traipsed into the woods like Hansel and Gretel and came to the fifteen-foot chain-link fence separating the cemetery from the hospital. He kept glancing at the buildings as they jutted and spiked the sky. She knew the way easily enough and the matted carpet of sticks and craggy rock didn't appear to bother her as she walked on. He'd driven by Fall Gardens a thousand times before, staring up at the indistinct faces peering down from their screened windows and seeing so many other versions of himself. The people he'd barely avoided becoming.

They broke from the underbrush at a spot where the fence had been carefully cut through, at the beginning of the long manicured lawns. It had once been poorly restored and then the wire clipped again. Cutbacks, everything was cutbacks, the state didn't want to pay to replace the entire chain-linking.

She led him on without a care, nobody else around, until they got to the main admissions building. It looked like a converted Victorian, quaint and homespun as a Rockwell painting. He didn't know what to expect but it wasn't the openness and freedom he found. Goddamn, it was a lot nicer than his own apartment complex. You could get jealous of damn near anything. He thought there'd be nurses, security guards or lemon-faced doctors around, somebody in charge handing out medication or pushing the group therapy folks around like in *Cuckoo's Nest.*

But there were just a few other patients playing Ping-Pong, reading in lounge chairs in the brightly lit corners. It looked like a resort and he felt another twinge of resentment.

Megan ushered him to an office with the words FREDERICK HENDERSON ADMINISTRATOR on a beveled glass door. She didn't knock, walked right in, and tugged him by the sleeve to follow. There was a nurse seated at the secretary's station but Megan walked past and entered the inner office.

Frederick Henderson was a fat guy, gray hair at the temples, big thick jowls hanging. He probably pushed 350 and his clothes were way too tight, like he refused to believe he was that overweight and decided it wouldn't be true so long as he never went up in waist size. Rosy had done the same thing but at least she'd worn skirts with elastic. Holder had read that tight clothing could cause all sorts of troubles, from poor circulation to internal organ damage. Freddy didn't have to worry about it anymore. He was dead and had been for hours. Holder touched the man and found the corpse already in rigor. Near as he could figure it was heart attack.

Freddy's cologne wasn't holding up well in light of his recent turn of events. The room was filled with the same smell Holder had come upon four months ago when discovering his father behind a local bodega, half buried in the trash, smiling with his eyes open.

You could do your best to keep yourself on the narrow

but once you fell off, you never quite stopped falling, you never got to the bottom. Holder sighed deeply. He didn't turn around because he was sure he'd catch the ghost of his old man standing around back there, doubled over and red-faced, hand over his mouth to hold back the snickering.

Freddy's ring of keys lay beside him. Holder scooped them up and shoved them in his back pocket, hoping the doors weren't being locked behind him, one after the other, as he'd walked down the halls. Who would he have to fight to get back out again? Which of the patients would bet their broken cigarettes on him?

The nurse entered, wearing a stethoscope, her uniform unbuttoned too far, opened down to the waist. Loops of long black curls coiled across her shoulders. She had huge, looming brown eyes and a mouth a little too large for her elfin face. But odd enough to be appealing.

She had the kind of smile you wanted to mash out of existence with your lips. It was that indecent. He wanted to cry out for Rosy and have her come save him—Oh, Rosy! You could trust Rosy, but this . . . you just couldn't be certain what kind of perdition this was going to lead you into. The nurse shrugged and the uniform started to slip from her shoulders. A small growl worked around the room and Holder hoped to Christ it wasn't him doing it.

The stethoscope lay between two small upthrust breasts topped with pink aureole she'd actually rouged with lipstick. Holder hadn't seen that for a while and the sight hit him in the right place.

"Let me guess," he said, "you're the doctor in charge now."

"Of course."

"Uh-huh. You folks have quite the run of the place, huh?"

"It's no different than anywhere."

He thought about that and decided it was true. Even behind bars and in cages you got away with murder. If you got out and wandered around, who would know so long as you came back again?

"On your knees," she said.

"Boy, do you got the wrong person." He grabbed for the administrator's phone but saw it had been yanked from the plug hard enough to tear loose the wiring. Holder sighed again. He tried the one at the nurse's station and it was the same. He turned to ask Megan where another might be. Before he could swing completely around he felt an incredible black pain in the back of his head and went down.

A sheen of burning yellow blazed across his eyes, flickering white lights dappling the edges of his vision. He heard something shatter and hoped it wasn't his skull. He tried to stand and his knees gave out but he didn't hit the floor this time.

Their hands were on him, tugging and tossing him onto his back across the nurse's desk. They got his pants down and Megan let loose with that giggle again. It was really starting to piss him off.

Holder struggled to hike himself up but the nurse had some meat and power behind her and kept shoving at his shoulders, pinning him down. He swung a fist, or tried to, but his hands were bound together with something. Freddy's necktie. Ain't this some shit.

Shards of glass covered the desk. Must've been a paperweight. Who the hell actually had enough free papers around that he needed a big globe of glass to hold them down? He was suddenly filled with an intense dislike for Freddy.

He wanted to fight but it was too late, they'd yanked his pants off and gotten him up and were already toying with him. Megan licked and let him hook along her top teeth. It was a pleasant feeling until the nurse wrapped her hand around Holder and stroked way too hard, like pulling a fire alarm. Oh, Rosy, help me! He'd already climaxed a half hour earlier and was still sensitive. It hurt like a bastard at first. He clenched his teeth and groaned, and Megan took over and slowed the pace, much more gentle.

Holder let out a moan of relief. He almost said thank you. She kneeled on the floor while the nurse crouched over him, lying across his waist, using her tongue to probe. Now this was therapy. No wonder no one ever got any better. She started moving her mouth in circles, too quickly, everything too rough. Freddy never had a chance, the poor fat bastard.

Megan moved around savagely, teasing, the kind of shit that made men burn down whorehouses. He couldn't stand it any longer and shoved. They both used their tongues covering every inch of him, working up his thighs now, across his belly.

The nurse finally mounted him, easing herself open with one hand while guiding him in with the other. He noticed a few spots on her chest that could've also been puncture scars. Was he imagining things again? Did the Icepick wander the halls just sticking the pick at everybody he came across? Did all the patients wear his hideous work in their flesh?

Black hatred filled him and a part of him wanted to give in to the fury, release it, go hog wild, but he didn't have his old man's delight. One man's pleasure could leave blood on the walls. He twisted his hands in a way that tightened Freddy's tie around his wrists. Some of the insane knew nothing of insanity, and the rest of us do.

He wanted to ask his father, Did you ever make it with two deranged inmates at the same time with a murdered porker lying twelve feet away in another room, with a killer possibly loose in the halls, stabbing folks in the night? He had to wager against it. A trace of pride filled him. It was a fair bet but still not a guarantee. Dad definitely had stories left to tell at the end that never got said.

Nick was nearby. The nurse kept their movements slow, rocking lightly as he pushed harder. She was wonderfully tight and gasped aloud as he found the rhythm and started enjoying how her chest bounced each time he moved. He tried to focus on the marks but sweat stung his eyes. Megan had herself poised over them, just observing now, elbows on the desk, her chin in her hands. He'd seen a porno like this once, some boring piece of French crap. A sudden bout of insecurity gave him a few doubts, but he slogged on, and soon the nurse began trembling. She kept her gaze locked on Holder as she swayed above his body.

No wonder Freddy's clogged arteries had given out. He'd eaten baby back ribs for lunch and his tie smelled of grease and barbecue sauce. The nurse dropped, clung to him and drew her nails across his chest in the same spot until thin lines of blood oozed free. She let out a harsh *Ngg* noise that actually made him feel pretty good, despite the strange lay. She kept her eyes on him and so did Megan, both of them staring, deranged. Almost enough to put him off his game, but not quite.

The nurse shuddered so hard that her knees cracked. Did the Icepick make her feel that good when he was stabbing her, cutting her up? Megan leaned over him and said, "Do it again for us, let me see you do it again." Under normal circumstances it was the right kind of talk that would've set him on fire, but now it just brought him back to where he really was, staring down at his bound hands and seeing dead pigs in his mind.

Holder almost lost it for a second but the nurse wouldn't let him fade out. She slapped herself down hard on his groin and kept up with those *ngg* sounds, her face darkening as she flushed.

He stiffened and bucked, trying to ride the wave—that tickle doing good things to him in the right place. When she was satisfied that she'd finished him off completely, the nurse slowly moved away.

"You are two very fucked up chicks, you know that?" he asked.

"Yeah," she said, "we do. But we don't mind. Do you?"

There was no point in trying to figure any of it out. He held his wrists out and Megan carefully unknotted the necktie.

Holder wandered around the place until he finally found a phone and called the police. He left then and made his way back across the lawns and the woods to his father's grave.

It was evening but the bright moon squatted three-quarters full.

Dad down there smirking, pleased with his boy.

The old man would've told him to have fun, and Holder looked forward to visiting again in a few nights. He still had Freddy's keys. He'd make copies and leave the originals somewhere on the property, near the front doors. Cutbacks, everything was cutbacks, and the state wouldn't want to pay to change all the locks. He'd find the Icepick killer if he was hiding in the hospital. Holder would walk the halls and hunt his prey, whether it was actually there or not. Sometimes you couldn't go wrong, and sometimes you could.

You must. You had to be ready for just about anything.

He needed to have one last drink with his old man. Holder uncapped the whiskey, took a long pull, and poured the rest into the dirt. It vanished immediately and he took the empty bottle with him as he staggered into the darkness, grinning so wide that his teeth lit the way.

LA MER DES RÊVES

Caitlín R. Kiernan

"Aye, there's the very reef what scuttled the *Asrai* back in eighty-nine," the fisherman says. "There's her bowsprit, poking up above the waves," and Emmie opens her eyes to see. Salt spray like icebitter needles against her face, the clammy, armored thing still wrapped up tight in her arms, and she blinks as the room undissolves, congeals around her. Four stark walls the color of nothing healthy and the door to the hall—long hall of closed and threatful doors and a stairway crouched at one end. The flat she shares with Caroline, their mattresses and brown paper grocery bags of filthy clothes, the candle stubs and windows all painted black so the winterpale Boston sun can't get in.

If it were only disappointment, falling from the old man's weathered sailorvoice to this ugliness and the dank, infection-sour smells that seem to seep from the plaster walls—if it were *only* that, she might feel no more or less cheated than any other junky dragged back into the waking, conscious world. She might sit and stare vacantly at the door, shivering beneath her orange blanket, burntorange wool with leaping white rabbits, and no emotion but the sicksweat fear that Caroline may not come back this time, the anger that she hasn't come back already and in a little while Emmie will start to hurt.

But it isn't only that.

"Mr. Gearty?" she whispers, her breath a handful of fog in the freezing air and she pulls the blanket up around her ears. "Mr. Gearty, I think I've slipped away again."

The January-raw wind like hungry dogs slinking around the brick and mortar corners of the building and she closes her eyes.

"I didn't mean to, I swear to god almighty I didn't mean to go," straining to sound as sincere as she can remember how to sound, and then she can hear the waves somewhere behind the wind and not so very far away after all. Thinnest drift-net membrane cast for her, flung across the wide gulf between Here and There and all she has to do is listen, just shut up and pay attention to the rise and fall, rise and fall, rise and fall of the stormweary sea so the mackerel-tangled weave can snag her.

"You gotta keep an eye on that undertow, missy," the fisherman says. "Gets its hooks into you, it'll carry you all the way down to hell and Davy Jones."

And the little boat bobs and rolls on the water like a toy while the old man fusses with the sail, tattered lateen canvas and his hands cracked and bleeding from the ropes. Her and the huge seahorse huddled together in the bow and Mr. Gearty in his yellow southwester cap, Mr. Gearty like an ad for frozen fish sticks.

"The *Asrai* was just rounding the Cobb there," he shouts, shouts to be heard, and points a crooked finger towards the horizon, pointing straight into the silverblack heart of the storm, and Emmie squints but all she sees is the restless blur of rain and sea and sky.

"Lost her foresail and got turned round with the wind on her port side," and then the sea lifts the little boat high on the crest of a wave and the old man curses to himself, wrestles with the backstay as they ride swiftly down into the next trough.

The seahorse struggles in her arms, rolls its dark and cowsad eyes and Emmie wishes she could think of anything at all to say so it wouldn't be so afraid; one word of comfort, and "That's what done her in," the old man says. "Got dragged up on the rocks and had her belly ripped out."

The seahorse makes a sound like a small child whistling and curls its long tail around Emmie's bare ankle.

"Shhh," she whispers, her chapped lips pressed against the slippery place an ear should be, if fish had ears. "We're almost there. It's almost over now," but the seahorse doesn't hear her, or it doesn't understand, or it simply doesn't believe a word she's saying.

The wind rustling through canvas like the flutter of terrible wings, like the dark birds hanging low above the place where the sea batters itself against the shore, and Mr. Gearty chews at his pipe and shakes his head.

"She knows we're coming," he says.

"Maybe they haven't seen us yet," Emmie replies, even though she knows better. Knows that the terns and gulls and snake-necked cormorants, the kestrels and clockwork ravens are all the Duchess's willing, eager eyes.

"Eh? What's that?" and he spares her a quick, disapproving glance.

"We might be lucky," Emmie whispers and the seahorse whistles again. "We might."

"If we drown 'fore she finds us, aye, that we might, missy. I wager the Lady's at the headlands by now. She'll have the black gulpers and the bristlemouths—"

A crackling roar from the sky, then, so she can't hear the rest and the next wave tips the skiff perilously to starboard, tosses it and the greedy sea is sloshing in; all the fisherman's junk in the bottom washing around and rattling about, an oar and an empty lobster pot, his tackle box and the pear-shaped Spanish mandolin.

"Easy!" he shouts. "Easy there now! Ye watch yourself back there!"

But Emmie slips anyway and the seahorse lands on top of her, pricklesharp spines to jab and slice her flesh, to tear the clinging fabric of her soggy dress, and both of them floundering helpless for a long, long second or two while her mouth and nose fill up with brine and her eyes are burning from the salt. She coughs, spits out a mouthful of ocean, and the boat rolls violently to port before Mr. Gearty finds a patch of calmer water, a fleeting pocket of saner wind.

And the old woman opens her eyes in the hospital-white room and listens to the mechanical sounds of the machines that keep her alive, that breathe for her and piss for her and strain the poisons from her blood. Woman as old and brittle as the last day of November. Tears streaming from her ambercloudy eyes and her mouth too dry to speak, her tongue an Arabian desert, but the dream so much more real than these antiseptic walls, the fluorescent ceiling, and *Find me quick,* she thinks. *Find me quick, Mr. Gearty.*

And the Duchess, then, the ebony-and-crimson-scaled Lady of Abyssal Plains, the Dowager Oneirodes muttering across the worlds, words to burst like fat and greasy bubbles inside Emmie's head—*Stay awake, old woman. Stay awake or we'll make a basket from your ribs. We'll plant coral and anemones in your shriveled skull.*

We'll leave you here.

And the pretty, young woman in her white nurse's uniform and squeaky nurse shoes bending over Emmie, woman with round sand-dollar eyes and hair the green-brown of a kelp forest. Her suctioncup fingertips at Emmie's thin wrist and something scribbled on a clipboard; she smiles a lipless barracuda smile and "Are we feeling better this morning, Miss Carmichael?" she asks. "Are we having bad dreams again?"

"There!" Mr. Gearty shouts, the storm snatching at his voice and Emmie sees it; past the tall and jagged stacks like Neptune's rotting teeth, the towering sea arch where shale and sandstone have been carved away by a hundred thousand merciless years of wind and rain, frost and waves. The high rock span and the current driving them towards it, as if it knows, as if that one thing in all the wide and godforsaken sea has taken their side. The birds wheel above the little boat, screeching their shrill warnings and alarms for the Lady's blackguard and the old man curses at them and gives the backstay more slack.

You don't have to die with him, the Duchess whispers, her voice laced between the freezing drops of rain. *We can forgive everything. We can send you home.*

"Hurry, Mr. Gearty," she says and the seahorse shudders in her arms. "She's found me. She's found us all."

He coughs, wipes water from his eyes, and nods to show that yes, he's heard her; the lunatic sea beneath them heaves and roils like the draining edge of a flat planet, last cataract before the endless plunge through stars and the gaseous skeletons of stars. Final nightmare that would be kinder than whatever's waiting for them and Emmie hugs the seahorse and whispers a half-remembered prayer.

A hundred ships gone down in this narrow cove, a hundred barques and brigs and sleekhulled schooners, brigantines and whaling boats, so what's this tiny bucket of kindling and pitch against those odds? What's one old fisherman against the lost souls of captains and admirals and pirate kings?

Open your eyes, my dear. We'll look the other way.

And the ocean parts for them, then, splits itself wide like Moses raising his arms and God on his side; Mr. Gearty turns and shouts something that Emmie can't understand as the boat tilts forward and slips suddenly down the steep and frothing face of the water, racing itself down towards the bottom of the sea.

Emmie makes a grab for the tiller—desperate, clumsy lunge and losing her grip on the seahorse anyway, the terrified, whistling animal sliding helpless from her arms and she only succeeds in knocking a pencil off the edge of her desk. It clatters to the floor and rolls a few feet, just out of reach, and she looks up to see if Dr. Farish has noticed.

"So, it then becomes a question of precisely what the image of the siren, the nymph, and the mermaid meant to all these *fin de siècle* painters," he says. "And to poets like Silvestre and Swinburne, as well."

Emmie leaves the fallen pencil where it is and stares out the third-floor classroom window at Washington Square instead, the Manhattan late afternoon sun turning the weathered, white marble of the Arch the softest shades of gold. Trying to remember something that seemed so important only a moment ago, something forgotten but its aftertaste lingering on the tip of her tongue, and "Duplicity and seduction," Dr. Farish says, "and the essentially cold-blooded, predatory nature of women, unrealized by the naive fisherboys."

A small bird at the window then, a wren or a sparrow, and Emmie wouldn't know the difference, ornithology never one of her strong points, and it hops about on the sill and pecks once or twice at the smudgy glass.

See, child? You can have this life, if you want it. You can have any life you ask for. Any life at all.

A moment's panic for such a strange thought, strange

and ravenous voice speaking without words from somewhere behind her eyes or the bird is talking and she opens her mouth to scream and vomits salt water. Hot bile and a cold bellyful of the Atlantic gushing past her lips, her throat on fire, and then she lies down on her side in the stinking mud and seafloor slime and waits for the roaring, whirling walls of the maelstrom to collapse. Waits for the bewitched water to fall in a final, crushing curtain and then she can finally be dead and no one can ever say she didn't try.

She can see the shattered keel of the little boat half buried in the mud, the graygreen slurry of silt and living ooze, dying fish and the wriggling bodies of spider crabs and trilobites, squid and moray eels all snarled in the stranded, sargassum tangle. And the fisherman, too, on his knees and one of the anchor's iron flukes driven through his chest, his head flung back as if one last view of forfeited heaven might redeem them all. Dark blood trickles from his mouth and into his beard, and his eyes are wide and empty as the sky far, far above them. But there's no sign of the seahorse anywhere, her charge shepherded halfway around the globe, so maybe it escaped, she thinks. Maybe they haven't failed, after all, and even now the Duchess is fleeing back into the depths, dragging her demons and blackguard with her.

No worse than any other lie that Emmie's told herself and she doesn't shut her eyes or look away as the Lady rises from behind the ruined skiff, spreads her stickling angelfins and lifts the severed head of the seahorse in one webbed and phosphorescent hand.

"We would have kept our promises to you, dear," she says, her voice the sound of continents tearing themselves apart to drift and air bubbling from the lungs of drowning men. "A billion worlds, a hundred billion lives merely for the asking. We didn't want to see you come to this."

Mr. Gearty makes a rheumy, strangling noise that might have been words or only his last, hemorrhaging breath, raises his left hand and Emmie sees the big boning knife clutched in his fist a second before the Duchess reaches down and tears the old fisherman in half. She steps over the body, bluepink intestine loops and wet, white bone, and kneels in the mud beside Emmie.

"Did you think we were lying to you, child?" the witch asks her, something like regret pooled in her sharkflat eyes, and "No," Emmie says. "No, Lady. But I had to be sure. I had to make the right choice. And I had to find my own way."

And, in the end, the trick so much easier than she ever would have dared imagine. The gauzy smell of thunder and pain like chitinous fingers pinching at her heart, pinching at her soul; the Duchess's long jaws swing open, slackjawed understanding come too late and it's over before she can scream, before she even begins to believe what's happening, and Emmie stands with the seahorse's severed head, staring down at herself writhing broken in the mud.

"You can have this life," she says, "if you want it," and the Duchess looks back up at her from Emmie's own discarded eyes. Blue eyes filled to overflowing with simple, mortal horror as the whirlpool spins around once more, one last, clockwise revolution as the magic frays and the sea finds gravity again and crashes down upon them.

AN OUNCE OF PREVENTION IS WORTH A POUND OF FLESH

Brian Hodge

Dear Wendy,

You've probably never received a letter like this before, and I know for sure I've never written one like it. For that matter, I can't remember when I actually sent you a letter on honest-to-god paper, instead of just picking up the phone or sending an e-mail. Probably when we were kids and M&D would send us to different camps and we'd mail our pitiful notes back and forth about how miserable we were, or how we'd fallen in love with this or that counselor from the boys' side.

And you probably can't help noticing: There are two letters here, actually.

Do me a favor. Don't open the second one unless you have to. Just leave it alone, sealed in its own fat envelope, and put it away someplace where it won't tempt you . . . a file cabinet drawer you hardly ever open, or better yet, your safety deposit box.

Yes, I hear you . . . how are you supposed to know if and when you should open it? Trust me . . . *you'll know*. And I'm not unaware of how cruel this must seem. All I can ask is that you fixate on that word a couple of sentences back: *trust*. Ever since we were little, we've kept each other's secrets when it mattered. That's all I'm asking, Wendy. Keep my secret. But this time I'm asking you to keep it from yourself, too . . . at least until you hear something about me that makes it seem like opening the second envelope is without doubt the thing to do.

With a little luck (or maybe a lot, I don't know), it'll never come to that. And then, someday in the distant future when we're both old and our bodies are puckered with scars from all the nips and tucks we've gotten to assuage our vanity, we can sit down where nobody can see us slip on our old-lady glasses (yours will be the pair with the rhinestones) and tear open the envelope and *then* I'll share my last secret with you . . . and maybe by then it'll just seem like a bad dream.

So put it away. Right now, before you weaken.

I trust you.

And love you,
Corri

Okay Wendy, now you've done it . . .

You've either betrayed my confidence to an extent you never have before (but I forgive you for it, because I know the position I put you in), or the worst has happened in one form or another and I'm no longer able to speak for myself. At least not in the way you deserve to hear things from me, with all the details intact.

That's what this mystery letter is all about: telling you my side of things, before you hear too much from anyone else that might poison you against me. I realize that puts you in the position of trying to salvage what everyone else in the family might think of me, but then, you're good at that. You were always the diplomat. Unless I've forgotten something, in all our petty arguments, you only called me an evil bitch once, and that was over a guy whose name neither of us has probably spoken in years. It's important to me that you don't end up thinking that the label actually applies.

It's important to me that *I* don't end up thinking the label actually applies.

Please just keep this one thing in mind: *I'm still me.*

As I write this, it's been about ten months since I signed the lease on the condo where I live now. I sent you a few pictures then, so you know what the buildings look like, these faux-Tudor facades. There's around a dozen of them in a ring, along the outer edge of a circular drive. The inside of the drive is like a little island, and more or less communal property . . . plenty of trees, and they use sprinklers to keep it green over the worst of the summer. That's where the pool is, too, and it stayed busy this summer, with the schoolkids on break and anyone else with enough leisure hours to lie around doing nothing.

But now the pool's just an empty blue pit. They drained it weeks ago and covered it to keep out the falling leaves. So most people no longer have any reason to come over to this middle area . . . myself excepted, of course.

In front of the pool is what they call the clubhouse, even though it's devoid of life most of the time, and there's no club to belong to. Upstairs is almost entirely one huge room with a fireplace as big as a BBQ cooker and lots of comfy plump chairs. You can reserve the place if you want to, for parties or meetings or whatever . . . but I never have any reason to go there.

I only ever go downstairs. That's where the weight room is, and as dingy and sometimes dank as it is, it was probably the clubhouse basement that sold me on living here.

Here's why: On my own, I probably would never have

made the association between exercise equipment and medieval torture instruments, until one time in a so-called health club this guy on an adjacent weight machine did it for me. And of course he did it with a leer. Picture some knotty-looking guy with a god-awful tan and too much body hair and this mustache so butch it's kitsch. I took one peek at him and all I could think was that he looked like a porn star from the seventies, and probably had the mentality of one, too.

That whole singles-bar-on-steroids atmosphere, where to stay fit you're also forced to put up with unwanted invitations for coffee or lunch or microbrews . . . that's the sort of thing I became adamant about avoiding. So when I found this place, with the clubhouse, it was just a match. Go down there late enough in the evening and you're almost guaranteed to have the place to yourself. Judging by how infrequently I find changes in the way I racked the weights during my last workout, I've always gotten the impression that hardly anyone bothers to use the place at *any* time of day.

And before you object that something could happen down there that's bad enough I'd be better off taking my chances with the seventies-era porn star, I never head over without my pepper spray.

OK. Enough background. Now we're getting into it.

A few nights ago, Thursday, I walked over to find a sign on the door:

Closed 'til further notice. Problem with sewage back-up.
DISEASE RISK—DO NOT ENTER!

It was a quickie job, hand-lettered in black Magic Marker, with strips of electrical tape crossed over the face of the deadbolt lock. It had to be Enrique's doing. There's no reason I've ever had for mentioning him before, but

Enrique handles maintenance for the complex, along with a couple part-timers. According to neighbors who've lived here long enough to remember the prior guys who held the position, Enrique puts them all to shame. I imagine they're right. He really does seem like a dependable guy, conscientious. And I've noticed this fall that he wields a mean leaf-blower.

So, with my key in hand, I stood there at the clubhouse door and weighed the alternatives:

A. Obey. Turn around and go straight back to my condo. Shower, bed. Miss the night's workout and wake up with limbs feeling as though the muscles have turned to custard. One night's broken habit becomes two, then three, and by the end of the week I can't imagine lifting another weight in my life. In a few more months I'm miles down the road to developing the world's saggiest ass.

B. Bend the rules a bit to thwart the terrible consequences of A.

You know me well enough to realize there was no debate. At least I was careful about peeling the tape off the lock so it would fit back into place. I figured I'd open the door long enough to give it a sniff. If it didn't stink, there probably wasn't much of a problem and Enrique was just being Enrique, cautious to a fault.

I didn't smell a thing. So I slipped in, smoothed the tape back over the keyhole, and locked up behind myself.

What you have to understand now is that the basement is divided up a lot more than the upper floor. At the bottom of the stairs, the weight room is to your left. I tried the air again, but it smelled the same as always . . . this chilly scent of iron plates and a residue of old sweat. Enclosed the way it usually is, with the ceiling-level windows shut, you'd think if there really was sewage on the loose, you'd be smelling it by now.

I put my towel and water bottle on the main weight bench and decided to make one last check before starting my workout. Like I said, when you come to the bottom of the stairs, the weight room is to your left, but if you go right, you're in this narrow corridor with a few storage closets, plus the bathrooms and a pair of showers. Which weren't spotless, but there were definitely no signs of muck backing up from below.

So by now I was starting to wonder if the stuff on the door wasn't someone's idea of a prank, and a lazy one at that.

At the very end of the hallway, that's where Maintenance works out of. Unless someone's in there, even during the day, the door's always locked, because they keep a lot of tools in there . . . although it's not really very secure. I guess so they can take what's essentially a workshop and make it seem more like an office, it's the only door downstairs with glass set into the top half. If you wanted to steal the tools, all you'd have to do would be smash the window, reach down past the blinds, and let yourself in. Seems awfully trusting to me, but they aren't my tools.

I was about to turn around and get on with my workout when I noticed a light at the edges of the drawn blinds, about what you'd see if someone had left on a desk lamp. It didn't necessarily mean anyone was there . . . except then I heard a thin scrape of metal from behind the door, and then this gruff voice, but murmuring, so I couldn't make out all the words. But I heard this much:

". . . worse trouble . . ."

Of course I took it personally—that there really was something to this infection risk after all and I was busted. So I called out Enrique's name.

I'd never known him to be here so late. He doesn't live

on-site, either, but then again, maybe he wouldn't want to. He'd probably never get more than an hour's peace during his off-hours, like a doctor at a party: *Hey, as long as we're talking, would you mind taking a look at this rash?*

Nobody said anything, so I tried again. Even if the sign really was legit and now I was where I wasn't supposed to be, I doubted that Enrique would be angry. I suppose he has to get angry *some*time, but I've never seen it, even when there's a good reason. Back in the summer, I saw one of his part-timers run over a garden hose with a mower, with predictable results. Enrique didn't get angry—he just scowled a moment, then laughed it off and gathered up the pieces like dead snakes. I remember thinking at the time that he'd probably make a good father, with that kind of patience.

I told you that because I need you to know up front that he's not some kind of hothead. This is something I had to remind myself of at first.

I heard that metallic scrape again, and what sounded like the shuffle of footsteps, only clumsy, and finally I got an answer from the other side of the door:

"Hey! Can you get me out of here?"

Not Enrique. *Definitely* not Enrique. In fact, it wasn't a voice I recognized at all.

It didn't make sense to me, so I said something silly, like, "Why—is the door stuck?" But even if it was, I was thinking, What's this guy's problem, anyway? He's the one in there surrounded by all the tools.

He only shouted at me: "Hurry, would you? Jesus!"

I tried the door, but it was locked. So I went to one knee and put my eye to the glass, to look through a little gap in the blinds. And I was right, it was just a little desk lamp burning in there, so it was dim enough, and the peephole small enough, that it took awhile for me to make out what I was looking at across the room.

The guy inside couldn't go anyplace because he was sitting on the floor with his hands overhead, chained to a vise. Remember Daddy's workshop when we were kids, and the vise he had bolted to his workbench? This one is twice that size. You could use it for a boat anchor. I once saw them use it to hold a huge mower blade while they sharpened it with a hand-held grinder.

You'd probably react about the same way I did . . . totally clueless and no idea what to do about it. Should I get a loose free weight and break the glass? Go straight home and call the police? But then, too, a part of me was thinking, Well, if he's chained up in there, it's possible there's actually a good reason for it. He looked young, but I couldn't tell for sure. So I asked who he was.

"Does that fucking matter right now?" he yelled. He said he could see my outline against the blinds, staring in at him, so I had to know his situation.

Except I *didn't,* really. I didn't know his situation at all, only what I was seeing at that moment. I asked who left him like that. I didn't even realize that Enrique was there by now, behind me, at the opposite end of the hall. Not until he spoke up to say that *he'd* done it.

"I've got pepper spray with me," I told him. Showed him, too, although I couldn't believe how calm my voice was.

"OK," he said. "You can leave right now if you want, and do whatever you think you should do. But before you decide, I'd really rather talk to you a few minutes. You can hold the spray on me the whole time, and I promise not to come any closer than you want me to."

That was when the guy in the workshop started shouting for me to use the spray on him *right now.*

But there was something about Enrique's eyes, and the

look on his face. It wasn't like I'd caught him in the middle of plotting something terrible or some kinky game he was playing. He looked ashamed. And sick. Not physically ill, but like something had made him sick to his heart, and that if I was intent on turning him in, he wouldn't do anything to stop me.

He pointed toward the weight room, so we'd have more privacy . . . but I didn't like the idea, still didn't totally trust him, I suppose. I mean, if we got in there, we could stand on opposite sides of the room, but he could throw free weights at me from farther away than the pepper spray shoots.

So we decided on the stairs, me at the top landing, him at the bottom. That was good. If he rushed me, I could blind him, then kick him back down. But by the time we got there, I was pretty sure it would never come to that. He was having me tell him where to stand the whole time, like all he wanted was for me not to panic.

First, I had to know who he had in the workshop. Enrique said his name was Kevin Stapleton. From one of the other buildings, only on the opposite side of the complex from mine, so there was no reason he'd be familiar to me.

Next, how old? 16 or 17, Enrique thought.

And finally, *why*? For as long as I live, I'll never forget the look on his face when he answered. Because even then I could tell he wasn't totally convinced, but the fear that he might be right was eating him alive.

"I think he's one of those kids that's about to blow," Enrique said, "and wipe out as many people at his school as he can."

It just hung in the air like that, because I didn't know what to say next. There was a time, not even all that long ago, when if you'd said that about a boy of 16 or 17, everyone would react as if *you* were the crazy one. Well, not anymore. We know damn well they go off and do that sometimes, a few of them, and they always come from towns and suburbs just like this one.

Tell me I'm wrong.

Now maybe you know how I felt sitting at the top of the stairs looking down at Enrique.

"Corri," he said then . . . which caught me by surprise, him calling me by name. I wasn't sure he even *knew* my name. It's one of those situations where you see someone three or four times a week, and you wave or say hi because it's a familiar face, but there was no reason he had to put a name with mine. I can't have introduced myself more than once, when I first moved in. He must have one hundred names around here to know and all *we* have to remember is Enrique. It just impressed me, that he must've made a point of remembering who people are.

Anyway.

What he said: "Corri . . . I've got a little sister that goes to the same school."

Which explained his apprehension, if not the rest of the situation. I mean, God knows our family has its own baggage there, too, right—high school cruelty. And all these years later, we're still living with the repercussions.

I asked, "How do you know this about him?"

Turns out it was because of the ants.

This past summer, a few of the buildings developed a problem with little teeny red ants. A bunch came in from somewhere and decided to colonize. It's not a ground floor thing, either. I'm on the third floor and still see them come out of the woodwork along my kitchen counter. Because it's a problem that affects whole buildings, and not just individual units, it's Maintenance's responsibility. So the guys have been making the rounds once a month with this contraption, sort of like a hot-glue gun only bigger, and they use it to leave dabs of poison around. The ants eat it and carry it back to the colony, and *everybody* gets sick . . . genocidal I'm sure, from the ants' perspective, but come on . . . N.I.M.S.B.

Not in *My* Sugar Bowl.

If you're not going to be around on poison-bait day, they want you to make arrangements so they can get in anyway . . . leave a key, with them or a neighbor. That's what tripped Kevin up. His parents split years ago, and it's just been him and his mom. And she'd been gone all week—a business trip or a convention, something like that.

You're probably thinking the same thing I did at first: If she's gone but her son is still around, why does she need to leave a key with Maintenance? To answer that, all you have to do is think back to how reliable you and I must've been the first year or two after we started driving.

So it was late afternoon when Enrique made it into the Stapleton place, and had to use the key to let himself in. The fact that so many people have no problem with him coming into their places when they're not home shows you the kind of trust everyone has in him. Which must be why he seemed embarrassed when he told me about looking over the papers that were lying out in plain view on the kitchen snack bar . . . like unless he's totally blind, he's committing a violation of privacy.

But he showed them to me then, and I can see why they caught his eye.

You know how something looks when it's been handwritten, but appears to have been done by someone at different times and in two completely different moods? Almost like it's been done by two different people? That's what these were like. Parts of them were really precise, *painfully* precise . . . straight diagram lines, lettering so neat it could've been done by a monk in an abbey. You could picture someone hunched over the paper trying to be soooo careful.

But the other parts? It was the kind of thing that's frightening to look at, even before you know what it is, because of the state of mind it reflects . . . a place of such uncontrollable rage: swirls of black and red ink, slashes back and forth so hard they'd nearly worn through to the other side of the paper. Words, too, so jagged they were barely legible: DAY OF JUDGMENT, he had that one a couple of times. LET GOD SORT EM OUT, that one once, except then he'd crossed out GOD and replaced it with THE DEVIL. In one place, BITTER NECTAR, which didn't seem nearly as obvious. Lots of FUCKs, of course, with a different object every time . . . sometimes a first name, once a big angry EVERYBODY.

But I mentioned diagrams, right?

Enrique thought it was his school, and I had to agree. Hallways, classrooms . . . nothing was labeled as such, although some seemed to be marked with abbreviations, others with numbers, like a sequence of events. Some were marked with symbols, too. A few resembled bombs; others were bullets, from one to five in a row, like a rating system. They couldn't have looked any more perfect and lined up if they were printed in a magazine. That was the most disturbing aspect about this whole thing: the layout done so painstakingly, then the rest layered on top of it, like an explosion.

So Enrique had me now. It didn't take much persuading for me to see the same potential bloodbath that he did.

And you're wondering how Kevin ended up in the workshop like that, right?

Even though Enrique still had a few more places to do, after he left the Stapleton place, he came straight back to the clubhouse. You don't just discover something like this and then go on about your work. Except when he got back there, that's when he found Kevin in the weight room, pumping iron like there's no day-after-tomorrow.

Of course I didn't see it happen, but it's not hard to picture the scene: They look at each other, and Enrique's surprised in a way he ordinarily never would be, so Kevin cues right into that. He sees the poison-bait gun and *knows* where Enrique's just come from. And Enrique knows he knows. All this going on between them without either one saying a word.

Enrique didn't remember what he said, finally, just that he pulled the papers out of his back pocket and Kevin went ballistic. Whoever started it, the fight couldn't have lasted long. Enrique may not be very tall, but he's sturdy and wiry at the same time, like that guy you dated awhile in college, the one on the wrestling team.

Whether or not it was right or wrong, while Kevin was basically out of it, that's when Enrique chained him to the vise.

I know what you're probably thinking now, because they're the same reactions and questions that came to me there on the stairs:

(1) Why didn't you just call the police?
(2) That was nearly four hours ago. What have you been doing all this time?
(3) How does Kevin explain what you found?
(4) What are you planning on doing with him?
(5) Don't you realize that the longer you let this go on, the worse it's going to be for you?

And Enrique seemed contrite enough. He realized he'd panicked, and things got out of hand before either of them could stop it. Yet despite everything, even if what Enrique was doing was wrong, maybe it would've been a worse wrong to just let it go.

So I'll answer those questions more or less the way Enrique put it to me, and hope you'll understand why I started seeing things . . . not *his* way, that's not it, more that I wanted to mediate this situation to the best possible conclusion for everyone concerned. I was frightened for both of them, but in Enrique's case, I *knew* he was a good man; where Kevin was concerned, I didn't know a thing about him.

Anyway, your answers:

(1) and (4) Enrique didn't call the police because technically he was the criminal at this point. He may have been motivated by good intentions, but it was still kidnapping. It wasn't that he'd ruled out the police, just that he hoped he might have something more concrete to give them when they showed up, so what he'd done might seem more reasonable.

(2) After he put Kevin in the workshop, Enrique was still shook up, and it took him a while to come up with a plausible reason to keep other people out of the building, in case someone came over. (Obviously, for me, it still wasn't good enough.) After that, he went back to the Stapleton place and starting looking for anything he could find to build a case against Kevin. Except, under the circumstances, Enrique felt that he wasn't being very methodical and all he was doing was going in circles. That's where he was when he eventually looked out the window and saw the lights in the clubhouse basement, after I'd turned them on in the weight room.

(3) Kevin's explanation for what he'd left out on the counter was that they were rough layouts for levels in a video game he was designing.

(5) Enrique understood he was in deep and digging himself in deeper. That's why he was so desperate

to find something at Kevin's place. And why I was inclined to let him have a little more time to do it.

OK, it was more than that. Not just let Enrique have more time . . . but help him.

"I don't know anything about computers, Corri. I never had any reason to," he told me. "But Kevin's got one over there in his room, and what if it's all on there? These kids that snap, you always hear about these journals they keep and nobody finds them 'til it's too late."

Here's what I told him: "I'll do this, but only under one condition. I'm not going to invade this boy's home and possibly his most personal thoughts until I meet him." Which Enrique understood. "And if I don't find anything that points in the direction you think is there, you're going to have to call this off and face the consequences. This can't continue."

So he gave me the key to the workshop.

I'm still not sure what I was expecting. After these kids explode, you see their pictures in the papers, or on the news, and there's always a disconnect with how young they look and the adult hatefulness of what they've done. Kevin was working at a disadvantage, though. He looked nothing like a yearbook photo. He'd gotten sweaty hours earlier, and never cleaned up. He had a bruise on his jaw and dried blood on his lip. Worst of all, he'd had four hours to sit there fuming with his wrists chained to a vise.

I swear to you, he wasn't very big but he didn't look young. Or frightened. He looked like he was ready to kill someone. I tried to put this evaluation behind me and remember *why* he might've looked this way. Now, there *did* seem to be a peculiar little vibe when I first walked in, something I couldn't quite put my finger on . . . but it was only later that I realized it was more than just the situation and not my imagination.

"Oh, let me guess," was the first thing out of his mouth. "You come down here and already you're taking his side."

"I'm not on anybody's side," I told him.

He sneered, but not like he was copping an attitude. You can sneer like that out of hopelessness, too. He said, "Oh yeah? Then tell me this: Between me and Enrique, who would you rather testify against in court?"

God, Wendy, he knew. He knew I wanted him to be the guilty one so I wouldn't have to implicate Enrique for making a stupid mistake.

There was an oil stain on the floor a few feet from where Kevin was sitting. He stared at it, like it gave him a focal point and an excuse not to look anywhere near my direction. Just like Sherman when we were growing up, the way Daddy used to tell him that he probably knew what the tops of his shoes looked like better than he knew any of our faces.

"That's OK," he said, finally. "I wouldn't believe me either. It's just funny, is all. Usually, a video game's got to *exist* before it gets you into deep shit . . . and it's always with people who don't understand that somebody my age can actually make the distinction between reality and animation."

I asked him, "If that's all those plans were, you don't think it was an overreaction to attack Enrique when you saw he had them?"

Kevin said it happened the other way around.

When he looked up, he remarked on my workout clothes, why I'd come down here in the first place. So we talked about weightlifting awhile. As it turned out, we both bench the same, which is why I could come over and usually find things the way I'd left them . . . although it obviously bothered Kevin to realize he wasn't doing any better than someone twice his age and female.

Then he recovered. You know the way boys are: "I didn't even think someone as old as you would want to go near weights."

Why, you little shit, I thought. *You just about lost me with that one.*

But then I looked at his arms and chest, lost inside the T-shirt he was wearing, and knew why he was coming over . . . that something at school was making him desperate to bulk up but it wasn't working for him because nobody had ever taught him that you don't quit as soon as you get tired, that you have to keep going a little longer after it starts to hurt.

So I explained it: keep lifting through the pain, that sort of thing.

"I know that," he snapped at me. "You think I don't know that?"

Which is about when he started staring at the oil stain again.

I tell you that so you'll know how difficult it was for me to go into his home. There's something so crushing when you see the fragility of all that bravado. Especially since he wasn't complaining about being chained to a vise nearly as much as you'd think he would.

Maybe he *wanted* somebody to stop him, I thought. Maybe he wouldn't admit to anything, or *couldn't,* until it was forced out in the open.

So I took the next key from Enrique.

Breaking and entering, that's a new one.

And I told you earlier, but maybe it's time to remind you: *I'm still me.*

With his mother gone, he was living about the way you'd expect. So did we, remember, when M&D would go on vacation after we were old enough to leave alone . . . at least before the thing with Sherman. So, all that mess and clutter, I tried not to see it as one more symptom of a disintegrating mind, just the habits of a kid with no supervision and a one hundred percent pizza diet.

Enrique had spent most of the time over here looking for weapons, obviously without finding anything, so I didn't bother with that. Even if Kevin did have them, he could've been storing them elsewhere . . . or with some-*one* else, if he wasn't planning on acting alone.

I went straight for his PC, instead. That's all I'd agreed to, right? While it was booting, I sat at Kevin's desk, surrounded by his walls, trying to soak in anything that would give me a clue as to his mind-set . . . the pictures, posters . . . that odd teenage boy blend of tough-guy stuff and vulnerability . . . pop star bimbos and actresses he knows he'll never have, and bands that look brutally angry even in still-life, and a few steroidal wrestlers, maybe for gym inspiration.

But all this did was remind me how much of our lives at that age consist of total fantasy. It was no gauge of anything, just the same stuff I'm sure you could find on millions of students' walls or inside their lockers.

So it hurt. One way or another, I was going to have to rat out somebody—either a screwed-up kid or the overprotective big brother of one of his classmates.

His PC: I started with his e-mail archive, because it's more centralized, and also on the theory that if he was planning something with a partner, he wouldn't have deleted all their communication. Nothing, though . . . so I moved on to the much bigger task of the rest of his hard drive.

After an hour and a lot of keyword searches, the only thing that seemed like a possibility was a folder whose entire contents were password-protected. The folder itself was labeled "Fryday"—judge for yourself whether or not the misspelling was intentional. But considering all this was happening on a Thursday night, it seemed important to get to the bottom of it.

If Enrique was expecting an expert at cracking encryption, he'd overestimated me. I do midlevel investment banking, for god's sake. All I could try was guesswork, stuff off the posters, but that didn't go anywhere. Then I thought back to the diagrams he'd shown me, and tried a few of the slogans from it.

You know what finally let me in? "FUCK EVERYBODY."

It was all there, Wendy.

Written plans, some of which corresponded with the timeline on the diagrams. A hit list. Bomb-making instructions he'd downloaded. Rants. Poetry. A journal going back more than a year. It was the mother lode and it broke my heart, and I imagine what allowed me to feel that way . . . for Kevin, and not so much for the names on the list . . . is because he hadn't actually *done* anything yet.

Here's a line that stood out to me:

> *I can't remember a time when humiliation wasn't a spectator sport.*

And how about this one:

> *I keep praying I have one more growth spurt in me, but I don't know why, cause I should know by now that even if there is a god, he's on their side and not mine. I don't have to be a giant, trade being one kind of freak for another, I'd just like to stand tall enough so I could walk by and the assholes of the world would have to think twice about fucking with me.*

That's the one that really got me. Sound familiar? It's not word for word, and maybe you never heard it, but I remember something very close to this coming out of Sherman back then, in a rare moment of honesty instead of trying to squash it all down and put the best possible face on his pain.

So I read as much as I could stand—more of which I'll get into later—then shut down the PC and turned out the lights.

As you can imagine, Enrique was extremely anxious by this time. Back at the clubhouse, I found him in the upstairs area, sitting in front of the fireplace, although it was cold and dead. He didn't have to say anything . . . all the questions were in his eyes.

"From what I could see, everything looked like they really were designs for a video game."

It was out of my mouth before I even knew I was going to say it.

"A pretty tasteless video game, maybe," I added, "but that's no crime."

I was hearing myself say these things and wondering where they were coming from. My voice and someone else's words.

Poor Enrique, though . . . one look at him and you knew he was on the verge of getting sick. I took the workshop key again, then had him give me one last key: for the lock he'd used on the chains. I patted him on the arm and told him to wait there, let me see what I could do to smooth things over.

And Kevin . . . I don't know if he suspected where I'd been all this time or not. I'm sure he had to. He wasn't stupid. Even if he still played innocent at first.

"Let me spell it out for you," I said. "F–R–Y–D–A–Y."

He still wasn't giving in without a fight. Said so what if I'd run across the recipe folder for his home ec class.

I unfolded one of the papers I'd just run off on his printer and started reading his own words to him: "'All these motherfuckers can die, die, die. Give me matches and gasoline, stakes and ropes and kindling, and I'll give you a barbecue of legend. I'll grind the ashes of their bones into a powder and fertilize a field of thorns, and then I'll drive their children through it naked and raw with my whip at their bleeding backs.'"

Now he didn't have much to say.

So I said, "Some barbecue recipe."

Now, finally, he admitted that what Enrique had found was no video game. It was exactly what it looked like. Except he didn't really mean it, he said . . . he was just blowing off steam, putting everything down to get it out of his system.

But it was getting easier and easier to see through the lies. As long as he'd had that room for doubt, he could maintain a plausible level of denial, but now that it was gone, he was crumbling along with it. He started to cry then, and the most awful thing about watching this was that he couldn't even wipe his own nose, he had to turn his head and smear it across the sleeve of his T-shirt.

I couldn't *not* unchain him.

"You just don't know what it's like," he kept telling me.

You can probably guess what I had to do next.

I told him about Sherman.

I think it was the only thing I could've said at this point that would give me any credibility with him. And it did seem to make a difference, even if it happened nearly fifteen years ago. Having a brother who went to school one morning on his own two legs, and after the end of the day never walked again . . . Kevin could relate to this, no matter how long ago it happened.

"A thing like that, and they got away with it?" The way he was asking, it was like this confirmed every fear he had about the world.

All I could tell him was what we'd been told until we were sick of hearing it: that what happened was an accident, it was just a friendly game of football, that Sherman shouldn't have been playing with bigger, older guys that way.

And then the other half, what we knew but couldn't prove: how they'd hit him from three directions at once when he didn't even have the ball; that maybe they hadn't meant to go as far as breaking his spine, but they'd definitely meant to hurt him.

Kevin sat there awhile, taking it all in, then asked, "What did you do?"

"What do you think we did?" I said. "We lived with it."

"Those guys who did that to him . . . didn't you want to waste them?"

Now how was I supposed to answer that one honestly and still avert a potential tragedy?

I need to tell you something else now. At first it may not seem connected, and maybe it really isn't . . . but I've come to the conclusion that it is.

I've been into the general idea of fitness all of my adult life, but there came a marked turning point seven months ago when it seemed to take me over to a much greater extent. I know exactly when and why this was, because it didn't happen in a vacuum.

Two things, back to back:

The first was when Lynette divorced Sherman, and what that did to him. If he wasn't my brother, maybe I could've understood her perspective a little better, but Jesus Christ, she didn't know what she was getting into when she married him? He wasn't *standing* there waiting for her while her father walked her down the aisle, he was *sitting in his wheelchair*. Then one day she wakes up and realizes she's got a gimp for a husband? I'm sorry if it sounds harsh, but I despised her for it.

The second thing came on the heels of this. The mail brought another annual alumni newsletter from my high school class. You probably get them too. I don't even want the things, and have never once sent in an updated address, but no matter where I move, they always find me. If we'd gone to a public school, we probably wouldn't have to contend with these intrusive little flashbacks, but because we went private, I suppose we're obligated to feel we're part of some grand legacy.

I'll usually flip through the newsletters in case a name jumps out that can still make me smile, but this time . . . I suppose it was bound to happen, that it shouldn't have come as a surprise, but it was just the timing, you know? On that page three feature "What Are They Up To Now?" there he was: Matt Standerfer. It was a family photo, Matt with an anemic-looking wife and two little kids who appeared to have a good start on growing up to look just as listless as their mother. As for Matt himself, he didn't look all that different, mostly a little heavier, although I spent a minute wondering what about him was different that wasn't so physically obvious. Then it came to me: He looked like he'd worked hard to lose that "entitled-to-everything asshole" air that I remember about him. He looked like it was important to be everybody's friend now. I can't explain how I knew, but even before I could force myself to read the write-up, I thought, "Oh my god, it looks just like a campaign photo."

That's right. State Senator Standerfer, that was the latest plan. And why wouldn't it work out for him? Everything else has.

Except I could *not* shake the feeling that everything he has, this little empire of business and family and now so-called public service that he's constructed, at least what wasn't handed to him on a platter . . . it was all built directly on Sherman's broken back. That never being held accountable for instigating that incident was the single greatest lesson in Matt's life about how the world would work for him and people like him.

Having my nose rubbed in this within days of hearing the news that Sherm's wife was abandoning him . . . that's when I started working out so obsessively.

I can't overstate how therapeutic it was for me, because I thought I'd gotten beyond the anger, yet here I was, totally unprepared for the way it flared up again. It was so utterly consuming, Wendy, and forced me to confront what a deep, black well of hatred I still had inside for Matt Standerfer and Anthony Chapelle and Doug Van Der Graff. Because not only had they never been held accountable for targeting our brother the way they did . . . to my recollection, not one of them even said he was sorry.

This was almost fifteen years ago, but it was still eating away at me the way it did when I walked into his hospital room and saw him lying there after the first surgery. No matter where life leads us, there are times when it feels like we've hardly managed to take a single step.

But I had the weights and the privacy, and the desire to make at least *something* constructive come out of all this negativity, so that's where I channeled it. I'd work out until it burned, until I could hardly move my arms and legs, and it wasn't even like I was doing it out of vanity anymore, the way I first got into it. It wasn't about looking better, or even feeling better in the normal sense. The closest thing I can compare it to would be an exorcism. I'd work and work until I was drenched and it felt to me that somewhere in all the burning and pain and exhaustion, one more little piece of the fury I'd never turned loose of was squeezed out and I could finally leave it behind.

So. Now you know my mind-set of a few months back.

And how does this possibly relate to the events of the other night?

I'll let Kevin take over for a minute, word for word, with some entries I found in his journal, from about six months ago:

> *I don't know her name, but O.M.F.G. is she hot. She's older, and normally that'd be telling me to step off right there, but it's like in this case it doesn't even matter. She's got this killer hardbody and in my head I'll stand her next to girls at school, especially the ones with the shorty tops hoisted up to show off the belly button rings pierced into their doughy guts, and I'll just be thinking, You pathetic twinks, you can't EVEN compare, so why don't you just stop embarrassing yourselves.*
>
> *It's staying light out later now as spring goes on, and that's just KILLING me cuz it's not dark anymore when she gets over to the weight room!!! As long as it was night out, I could sit close enough to those ground windows that look down into the basement and she'd never know I was there. So I've decided I hate the sun now cuz of what it took away from me, and I'm just living for the fall and longer nights again.*

Now this one, from a few days later:

> *Yeah, I'm a world class perv, what of it?*
>
> *At first I thought it was gonna be just some conso-*

lation prize, like, well, I can't watch her work out, so I'll take what I can get. All I have to do is watch out my window and see when she leaves the clubhouse and I can be over there a minute or two after she's gone. Mom's still an idiot, actually thinks I'm going out for a walk to clear my head and get some air.

I guess THAT much is the truth. If I get over fast enough it's like she's still there, in the air. I can smell her and if you think about it, that's almost as good as touching her would be, cuz what's a smell but molecules, right? So I'm breathing her down inside me.

Some nights it's obvious she's had a superintensive workout, cuz her sweat will be all over the vinyl on the weight bench, and

Jesus, I'm such a pussy!!! Can't even come out and type it when nobody else will be reading it.

The first time it happened I wasn't even thinking. I just did it. Or let it happen. Like, oh look. A few minutes ago that was inside her skin. Now here it is. And now it's inside mine.

You wouldn't think it would burn as much on my tongue as it does. Not that I mind. It's a good kind of burn, actually. Like a good hard workout must feel.

Over the next several entries he goes on with various fantasies, which I see no reason to repeat, or things in his daily life that have no relevance at all. After a couple of weeks, Kevin gets the idea that he should take up lifting too, because if he goes through the exact same motions that I do (and apparently he watched me long enough to get my routines down), immediately after I've done them, and in the same place . . . then in his way of thinking, it's a way of getting closer to me.

Or as he put it: *First I get inside her space, then I get inside her skin.*

But eventually a strange thing happens. After a few

weeks of hitting the weights, he seems to all but forget about me. Ordinarily I'd think that was the healthiest possible outcome, that even though the way he first got drawn into lifting was a little kinky, in an adolescent way, now he was beginning to see results and it was setting off a positive chain reaction: that he was developing some self-esteem and confidence, that he could turn his attention to girls his own age instead of playing it safe with this voyeuristic infatuation with someone twice his age who wasn't even aware of him yet.

Except I don't think that's precisely what was happening.

From early August:

> *I must suck at this, cuz I'm not really getting much better at it I don't think, but by now it's like that's the last thing that matters. The cool thing is all the shit that starts to go through my head while I'm doing it. I don't even have to try, I just show up and it starts to flow. Like I'm this omnipotent FORCE OF NATURE and can do whatever I want to right all the wrongs and there's not a fucking thing anybody can do to stop me cuz there just isn't.*
>
> *Tonight it was Barry Swain.*
>
> *First I cut off both his hands, so he can never use them to shove me down ever again. But before he can bleed too much I use a blowtorch to cauterize the stumps. And all that heat, you know, it makes him thirsty. So I give him some water. All he wants, gallons of it, he's one grateful chugging motherfucker. Then I take a pair of vise-grips and clamp off his prick so he'll never piss again. Then I just let the pressure build, a couple hours, until he's screaming even worse than when I hacked off his hands. And just when he says he can't stand it anymore?*
>
> *That's when I turn the rats loose on him.*

So they're eating him alive, right, except he doesn't know how to feel, cuz on the one (amputated) hand it's the worst pain he's ever felt in his worthless life, but on the other, he's praying for the rats to hurry up and burrow through his gut to relieve the pressure.

Jesus, that had me going all night.

That's bad enough on its own. But there's one thing that makes it worse:

It went through my head first. Almost fifteen years ago.

I know the prevailing feeling is that girls just don't have things like that going through their minds, but I can assure you, with no small amount of shame, that they do. It was one of a few revenge fantasies that I entertained a few weeks after they put Sherman in the hospital, and it was becoming hard to ignore the fact that our family was never going to see justice done.

You were always more of an optimist than I was, and I suppose that, being the middle child, I had that classic way of hiding in plain sight, where I took these ghastly scenarios and turned them over and over in my mind, the same way you might take a mound of clay and keep making new forms from it. It helped get me through that time . . . not just Sherman's pain, but all the stress that M&D were under while trying to keep it secret from us.

In time, I let it go. Or thought I had, until seven months ago.

Then I tried to work it out of my system for good. And was pretty sure I had. I just didn't realize it was possible to leave it where someone else could find it.

So. One more partial entry from Kevin, from late August:

Another school year, Day 2. I thought it might be different now, but I guess that was just the stupidity talking.

I'm there and I'm not. Meaning my malformed body is there in the hallways and in the seats, but my brain's a million miles away.

Actually, the solution is simple.

I don't know why I never thought of it before.

I'm responsible, Wendy. By some mechanism I don't understand, could never have anticipated, I am at fault. I could probably put it all down to coincidence, if not for that one thing: his coming up with such a vicious, specific fantasy that follows mine as closely as a script.

However it happened, I can only believe that what I left behind most nights in that weight room infected him.

One woman's therapy is another boy's bitter nectar.

So now maybe you can understand why I lied to Enrique. I knew what I thought I *should* do, but when pushed up against it, in that moment I couldn't go through with turning Kevin over to the police . . . not when he was in a situation that I suspected I'd helped put into motion.

But then, the longer I talked with him in the workshop, and the more the past and present swirled around me, the more I realized that, no, I hadn't been the one to put it into motion after all. That was someone else's doing, when Kevin was still a toddler with no idea of the kind of cruelty that passes for amusement.

When we finally came up from below (it was close to midnight by this time), I took him to see Enrique. The poor guy had been waiting it out the whole time by the fireplace.

I told him, "Everything's okay. Nobody's spending the

rest of the night in a cell, not over an honest misunderstanding."

They shook hands and each mumbled an apology, but neither one of them wanted to look the other in the eye. A couple minutes later, after Kevin had gone home, Enrique couldn't thank me enough, and asked how I'd done it.

"He just needed someone to listen to him awhile," I said. "After that, everything else just fell into place."

Now the hardest part.

I wish I could say I had a clear recollection of everything that transpired in the workshop toward the end of the night. Except I don't.

So much of the earlier hours are stamped so indelibly in my memory that it was easy to recount them almost word-for-word. But then I get to a certain point and there's a blackout zone, sort of like when you're driving and your radio reception will fuzz out, then come back in clear again a mile later.

As we left the workshop, here is what I'm absolutely certain of:

I know that although Kevin had two handguns and some pipebombs stashed at his father's house, he'd gotten past the intent to use them the next day. And he didn't. I'd tried to get him to take a long look at the consequences, and imagine as vividly as he could how he would feel twelve hours later, if he was even still alive. How he would feel if he accidentally gunned down just one person who wasn't on his list, that he didn't feel deserved it. Maybe this helped. Or maybe it didn't much matter what we talked about, so long as someone was listening.

And I know I tried to leave him feeling that he could talk to me in the future if he needed to vent or something. By this time I was obviously aware that I'd had a hold on him, if not so much now then at least not long before, so I wanted to exploit that. Not in a manipulative way, just . . . well, you know. For the greater good.

I know these things for a fact. It's just that there's this deeply shadowed stretch that I didn't even think much about at the time . . . fifteen minutes, half an hour, I'm not sure. I mean, this was a heavy discussion at the end of a heavy night for all concerned, and we were worn out. All our defenses, they were just gone, eroded. Toward the end, Kevin broke down into tears again, and of course this time I did too.

And then . . . ?

Next thing I knew, we were walking up the stairs to square things with Enrique.

As I said, I really didn't give it much thought the rest of that night or the next day or even the next. Not until I got a call from Alexis Warwick asking if I'd heard about Matt Standerfer. Maybe you've heard about him by now too . . . or maybe not, since you were three years ahead of us and it probably wouldn't ripple through your class the way it would ours.

At this point, they don't know who killed him and neither do I, although the obvious theory is that it's tied to next month's election, somebody who didn't want to wait for the ballot box to sort it out. Maybe it is. I *pray* that it is. Then again, maybe the timing is just coincidental.

At this point, all I know is that for the past several hours, Kevin is nowhere to be found. And maybe that's the coincidence.

But if you're reading this . . . unless you went ahead and have read it before you had enough reason, even though I asked you not to . . . then I suppose that means the finger of blame has been pointed at me.

So I have to go back to the other night, and what I can't even remember: Did I say something I shouldn't have . . . exploit Kevin's attitude toward me in the wrong way? Did he volunteer? Were we just so worn down and exhausted by our emotions that in the end we were conquered by the hatred that I'd found so hard to overcome . . . and now it's out there on its own, free to do what it's always wanted?

And what do I do, Wendy? Knowing what I *don't*, should I try to contact Doug Van Der Graff and Anthony Chapelle, and warn them about what *might* happen . . . or just let things take their own course for now?

I imagine the fact that I've spent hours and hours preparing this, to tell you my side of things, before even asking myself that question, gives an indication as to its answer.

Because I keep thinking that if it really *wasn't* Kevin, then I'll have betrayed him in a far worse way than if I'd turned him in the other night.

I don't know what you must think of me by now.

I'm still me, though. *I'm still me.*

Even if tonight I have no idea what that means.

Ever your sister,
Corri

RELEASING THE SHADOWS

Paul Melniczek

The trees slumbering along Chestnut Street looked weary.

Bark was peeling from the gray and brown trunks like pieces of dead skin, clumps lying on the crooked sidewalks, vein-cracks streaking through the faded cement. Rectangular patches of grass formed crude sections between property lines, an attempt by construction designers to add a sense of order and control. But now the aging neighborhood appeared as little more than a forgotten relic of suburban sprawl gone lazy and decayed, the residents moving on, and the few that still remained growing old along with the stone and wood.

Jordan walked beneath the skeletal branches, listening to the dried leaves skipping and tumbling in a November dance. They scraped along the street as a mischievous wind awakened to tease them once more. It snaked upward, catching and spinning a weather vane on the top of Mo's Corner Grocery, the bleached-white sign dangling loosely on a pair of twisted, rusty chains.

The store was closed, empty and silent.

Jordan paused before the brick and stone building, remembering the penny candy and round bubble gum, sweet sticks of every possible flavor, enough to satisfy a young boy's sugar-coated fantasy. Standing there now, he hoped for a special tingling, a warm sensation in his chest reminding him of the joyful days of his childhood, but instead there was only a cold void, barren and vacant.

The neighborhood had changed so much . . . Had it been only ten years ago? It seemed like a lifetime. Jordan's expectations had been high, looking for a pleasant rush of fond memories spilling across his inner vision. The memories came, but he found them clouded and confused.

He felt a chill as the wind prodded at him, squirming between the collar of his tight jacket and placing cool, invisible fingers around his neck.

Gazing at the steps of the store, he could almost hear the laughter of his friends, the joking and playful shoving as they ripped apart candy wrappers and stuffed them into trouser pockets. The brags and dares, the plans and games. They'd never left trash on the ground out of respect to Mr. Mollins, the store owner. The man had been at least seventy back then, with grizzled white hair, thin eyebrows and soda bottle glasses. A kind man, it was not unusual for him to hand out special little gifts to his favorite customers, the neighborhood children. Sugar straws and string licorice. The cherry ones had been out of this world.

The store looked like it had been unoccupied for a while, and Jordan sadly wondered if the man were still alive. He told himself he didn't really want to know the answer, and he trudged onward along the sidewalk.

This part of town was quieter, the homes sparser. Two blocks behind him sat three-story Victorian monoliths, once the regal dwellings of proud community members, local politicians and industrialists. Old money. But their individual fortunes had long ago trickled away, their owners abandoning them, selling the structures to out-of-town investors looking for fixed income and cheap property. They'd been converted into apartments, rented primarily to local college students who attended the town's modest university—the only graduate institute within half a county. And most activity gravitated toward the school and its greener district in the town's business section. Not toward Jordan's old stomping grounds.

He passed along a rotting fence which had once bordered Josh Miller's place and Gladys Hyken's small but cozy rancher. Friendly neighbors, Jordan recalled. He pictured the man's face—an earthy smile, with a quick joke always buried somewhere in the deep pockets of his work trousers. And Gladys, with the apple and lemon pies sitting on the shelf of her kitchen window, which was open wide on warm autumn days, the aroma of cinnamon and spice drifting across the backyards for what seemed like miles to the nose of a hungry youth.

He looked further, spotting the home of his childhood. Jordan had contacted the current owners out of curiosity, finding them rude and uninterested in his wistful musings. They'd been too busy to answer Jordan's questions, as he wondered how the place was holding up these days. Disappointed, he decided not to intrude. People had their reasons for privacy, he supposed, and he was old enough to realize he couldn't return to his youth. He sighed, pausing before the redbrick Colonial.

Like the other homes, it seemed to have lost its dignity somehow. The house appeared gloomy and shrunken, lost to the gentle memories held within its durable stone heart. Jordan felt depressed, feeling no flicker of the quiet happiness that he'd anticipated. It was a powerful moment, as polarizing emotions rippled through his chest, leaving him with that cold, empty sensation again.

Jordan walked past it, wishing things could be different. But part of him wasn't really surprised by the melancholy air surrounding the street. He wanted to believe otherwise, telling himself that the neighborhood would find itself once more, perhaps within the fresh faces of children new to the area, their young parents eager to renew the suburban promise offered beneath the tall streetlights and watchful hedgerows.

But he'd been dreadfully wrong. His thoughts turned a shade darker. He shuddered, telling himself it wasn't because of *that* particular reason, the one lurking deep within his mind.

Jordan shrugged aside the unspoken idea, and turned down a grassy walkway separating his old home and another. Bushes loomed to either side, unclipped and dirty. Cobwebs flapped lazily inside the strangled overgrowth, and he remembered the frightened look on Jimmy Miller's face as the boy had reached into the shrubs looking for a lost baseball. Some of the wood spiders living there had been nearly as big as his own hand.

He continued on, slowing as he reached the main alley. It had been a popular haven for him and his friends, secure from the prying eyes of parents, home to a slew of natural hiding places and with enough open space for a world of adolescent adventures. Garages sat on both sides, the white paint chipped and faded. The windows were broken in many spots, jagged edges filling the gaps, and Jordan felt a new surge of frustration, finding his favorite haunt in the same disrepair as the rest of the street. The whole area was like an abandoned pet, unwanted and uncared for. The pit of his stomach was queasy, an uncomfortable feeling tingling deep within his bowels and plucking much deeper at his conscience.

He felt sorry for the neighborhood and its forgotten residents. Sorry for the shadow-memories that still lingered, once pleasant but now only a twilight dream-fragment buried within the whimsical hopes of a returning optimist. And he was especially sorry for himself, thinking it would be any different.

Jordan felt keen with remorse. As if he'd lost a friend.

And in reality, he had.

Not wanting to face that terrible moment of his past he'd tried to believe otherwise. But now, standing again in the backyards of his youth, he could no longer deny the truth. It had happened here.

Right here.

His gaze swept the forlorn alley, and the place had not changed much over the years. The area was located in the heart of the little town, but somehow it had always managed to be something of a frontier to him and his friends. Cars never used it, as it became a dead end further ahead. Shaded by trees and hedges, naturally dark. The bushes seemed to have grown even taller and thicker, neglected over time by the careless owners. Oak trees towered overhead, the tiny nuts scattered along the ground, fodder for the numerous gray squirrels which made their homes beneath the gnarled branches.

Yes, it had been right here that Tommy Wilks had disappeared that fateful November evening.

Jordan's eyes turned inward as he replayed the events. He, Jimmy Miller, Tommy, and Brett Hunkil had been playing kick the can, one of their favorite pastimes. They would meet after supper for a late afternoon frolic, pushing back the pencils and schoolbooks until later, running outside, galloping and laughing until they could no longer see, and their parents would shout for them to return home for the night. How Jordan had loved those magical evenings.

And then, on *that* unforgettable, terrible evening, Tommy had vanished.

Right during the middle of the game, with the boys all in hiding, and with Tommy guarding the rusted can with reckless pride, like a miniature knight from King Arthur's court. The others had schemed, whispered, giggled beneath the split poplar tree, and waited patiently for their chance.

Tommy had been *it,* and they were determined to get him.

Brett played scout, snooping low to the ground, crawling snakelike on his belly to spy on the other boy. He'd come back partly confused, partly excited. There had been no sign of Tommy. They'd exchanged smirks, wrinkling their noses, snickering, and crept back toward the danger area, where Tommy just *might* be hiding, waiting to spring upon them with the youthful vengeance only a young boy could muster.

And they had never seen Tommy again.

Gone.

Without any indication of where or why. They yelled for him up and down the alley, ran across the yards, went to his house, the store, even the school. At that point his parents became extremely worried, and called the police. By nightfall, the entire town had been put on alert. Search parties scoured every block and alley as word went out.

His own parents had offered hopeful words—that Tommy would be found and was playing a joke on everyone, or perhaps had hurt himself and needed help.

Jordan had wept bitterly, staying up all night, hugging his pillow, staring out the window. It had been a clear night, the moon leering in at him from the sky. His mother came into his bedroom, comforted him, but the pain wouldn't go away.

And much later, although he could never be completely certain even until this very day, a high, thin voice came echoing through his own backyard, spilling through the window that Jordan kept open, only just a crack, to permit the cool air. The words, utterly strange and haunting.

Olly olly oxen free!

Jordan felt chills race his spine in recollection. Had it been Tommy, giving him a signal? He'd stumbled over to the window, staring outside with frightened eyes. The landscape was painted a ghostly white from the moonbeams, the night silent. But nothing more . . .

Just as alarming had been his conversation with Tommy earlier that evening. He remembered the words his friend had spoken with him before supper, as they sat together lazily beneath the poplar tree, discussing plans for the coming night.

Tommy's eyes had been dreamy.

"I wish I could stay here forever, you know, and never have to grow up. Why do we have to grow old? And Jordan, sometimes I think there are other boys in our alley, playing along with us. Like they're waiting for something . . ."

His voice had trailed off, and Jordan had felt troubled by his friend's words.

The next morning, the police made a terrible discovery. About half a mile from their block was an old quarry, now filled in by a deep, cold lake. A red shirt was found at the highest point above the canyon, near the edge. They had identified it as one of Tommy's. The authorities were convinced that Tommy had met with disaster. He'd fallen into the lake, they concluded, although his body was never found even after the dark waters had been dragged for days.

But Jordan wasn't convinced.

He believed that Tommy had actually jumped in on purpose, killing himself. Changed the course of his future so that he would never have to worry about growing up.

He'd left his friends during his favorite game, and hurried off to meet his fate.

And that was why the street and its people had died.

Looking for other answers, Jordan now realized the truth. Perhaps he'd always known, but didn't want to admit it to himself. He stared at the alley, tears trickling down his cheek.

Tommy. Too afraid to grow up.

Jordan felt incredibly weary. He pulled his jacket tighter against the coolness, stamping his feet.

He stopped abruptly, feeling icy hands grip his throat at the sight of a rusted can beneath the poplar tree, noticing it for the first time. A twist of cruel fate, chiding him with a bitter reminder? Jordan slowly walked forward, pausing before he reached it. The wind awakened, stirring the branches over his head, disturbing the leaves. Twilight was swiftly approaching.

He suddenly sprang forward, kicking the dented can high in the air, sending it several yards ahead and directly into the poplar tree. It dropped, falling dead on the ground. He closed his eyes. Jordan sobbed, knowing that his past was as elusive as the stars in the sky. His throat dry, he considered his own life and expectations, his future.

All his failures . . .

The lack of a consistent career. A poor, misunderstood relationship with his parents. The absence of any female companionship.

Not surprisingly, he realized that everything revolved around that fateful evening when Tommy had disappeared. When life couldn't have been any better, when the troubles of the world meant nothing to a group of innocent young boys, and when their neighborhood was a gentle, loving entity, looking out for those nestling within its collective breast.

With all these things carefully in place, Tommy had run away from his own future, finding a permanent and terrible solution that guaranteed his youth would continue forever. The boy wouldn't be growing old.

Staring at the rusted can, Jordan wondered how cold the water of the quarry was in November.

And beneath the poplar tree, the shadows moved on their own.

WHOEVER SITS BY THE SHORE

Brian A. Hopkins

(For Marie-Simmone Lizotte, the real little girl in the story, with grateful acknowledgment and appreciation to Pierre Béland, from whom I first heard her story.)

August 14, 1978, from the Lighthouse at Pointe-au-Père, Quebec

My name is François Laurent. I am a lighthouse keeper. I am a very old man now, seventy-five years old today, on this day that I write to ask that the weir at Rivière-Ouelle not be reconstructed as proposed.

I know the weir. I was born and raised, you see, in Rivière-Ouelle, and watched my father set those weirs which were so productive from 1915 to 1918. My grandfather and his father before him worked the weirs, taught perhaps by the very first to set such traps, the Indians who once numbered in the tens of thousands before they were confined to the Kahnawake Reserve. Stadacona and Hochelaga were the names of their villages when Jacques Cartier found the natives in the fifteen hundreds. He dubbed them *les sauvages,* but when he lost twenty-five men to scurvy in 1536, it was a Huron chief who taught Cartier to grind and boil the bark of the common arborvitae. This tea worked so well that Cartier took arborvitae saplings back with him and planted them in the royal garden at Fontainbleau, where they thrive to this day. This is history. The St. Lawrence is rich in history. History and tradition. These are things I understand, things that make us Quebeckers who and what we are. They are our heritage. And the weir is a part of all that.

You ask then, why I oppose reconstruction of the weir at Rivière-Ouelle, why I ask you to spare the lives of a few whales whose presence only hurts Quebec's fishermen? I am asking for my sister, Lizette, who cannot ask, but would if she were still with us.

I will try to explain.

All my life I have lived by the sea—or, if you will, the St. Lawrence River. But you and I know that the St. Lawrence is as much an extension of the sea as it is a river. It flows downstream only half the time, its current reversing every six hours with the tides. Twice a day, millions of gallons of brown river water are flushed downstream, exposing the skeletal splines of the Saguenay fjord on one bank and clam worms wriggling in the red mud on the Rivière-du-Loup side. Sailboats anchored at high tide in the marina at Rivière-du-Loup will be left sitting in the mud six hours later. Until the green sea waters flood the shore again, bringing in seaweed, marine fish, seals and whales, sea level (or *river* level, if you prefer) is as much as eighteen feet below normal. Gazing up- or downstream from my lighthouse, I see nothing but water as far as the horizon. This is true from the mouth of the Saguenay to the Gaspé Peninsula. There are white caps and surf, and if there was white sand instead of the red muck and biting worms, Quebec might draw a beach trade. Large enough to carry her own weather, weather that culminates in vicious storms that often rage across the Great Lakes, the St. Lawrence has taken many a ship and more than her share of seamen. That is why those of us who live by the St. Lawrence River, also call her the sea.

The Canadian poet Louis Dudek said, "The sea belongs to whoever sits by the shore." I have sat on these shores all my life, watched the ebb and flow of tide and life and time. If you will just bear with me, I will explain what I believe Dudek meant by that enigmatic statement. The sea, you see, belongs to me. And it belongs to Lizette.

When the merchant Jacques Dumond Lévesque came to speak with Papa, I was twelve years old. Lizette was six. It was 1915. There was a great war being fought across the Atlantic. Just that year, the first Canadian troops had engaged the enemy, digging themselves into the soggy trenches near Vimy Ridge in France. It was one of the first times Canadians had taken a part in world affairs, for once setting aside our time-honored policy of avoiding *l'affaires des Anglais.*

I saw the war as a magical thing, a place to go and prove you were no longer a boy. I deeply regretted the fact that the recruiters saw through my lies. A tall boy of fifteen, like my brother André, stood a good chance of fooling them, but not a small lad of twelve. What I didn't know was that most of those Canadians, many of them boys no older than André, were digging their graves in France.

The war had created a new economy. There was a demand for all manner of goods, including whale products. Hunting the big whales was still a tortuous endeavor in those years prior to the invention of the harpoon gun. The smaller whales were far easier to come by and much easier to kill. Beluga leather is smoother and softer than cowhide, with virtually no grain—a fine Moroccan leather, I've heard it called. More importantly, the oil from the beluga's melon was selling for a dollar an ounce in New York City.

When Lévesque told Papa how much he would pay for the oil and that each whale might yield at least a barrel's worth, Papa simply nodded and said, *"C'est beau. Oui, c'est très, très beau."*

We cut the trees that autumn: more than seven thousand twenty-foot maple and birch saplings. We removed all but a crown of young branches and sharpened the base, creating something that looked like a plumed dart. Working through four low tides, we took those darts out on the flats and drove them into the mud of the river bottom. It wasn't hard to find where to place them; the flat was stippled with the rotting shafts of poles left by our forefathers. Since 1705, this had been the traditional site for the weir, there by the mouth of the Rivière-Ouelle.

Along a straight line starting just below the high-tide mark, we placed poles at three-foot intervals, forming the "wall." The wall ends in an oval pen called the "yard," which is more than a mile long by three quarters of a mile wide. The poles around it are set close together. There is only one entrance to the yard, facing the upstream side of the wall. The "door" is about a quarter mile wide; its upstream frame, aptly called the "hook," curves sharply inward like a gigantic fish hook. Pursuing fish on the tide, the belugas enter the mouth of the Rivière-Ouelle. When the tide reverses, the water is murky with sediment, and the belugas cannot see the poles. Instinct tells them to swim toward the open sea, but they are hampered by the wall, which to their acoustics must seem impenetrable. They follow the hook and ultimately wind up trapped in the yard.

When the tide retreats, the whales are left stranded in the mud, flukes slapping feebly, sides heaving, whistling that eerie cry from their blowholes, the sound that earned them the nickname "canaries." Some of the larger belugas weighed over a ton. Some of the younger ones weren't much bigger than dolphins. All that were caught in the weir were harvested.

I remember that first morning. More than a hundred beached whales struggled within the long curve of the weir, their bodies glistening milky white in the sun. I waded out with Papa and the other men of Rivière-Ouelle, the mud sucking at my boots, the cold water lapping around my calves and finding its way down into my woolen stockings. The dawn had a crisp taste, a frozen pinch about the ears, and a sharp needling of the nose. The water was the color of bricks where it lapped against the sides of the white whales.

"This is how it is done," said Papa, showing me the broad-bladed, rusty claymore he carried. "You must strike them just behind the blowhole."

Done right, the claymore shatters the whale's skull, cleaves its brain, and kills it instantly. But I rarely saw it done right. In fact, even that first morning, the whale thrashed and screamed as Papa repeatedly struck it with the claymore. Blood sprayed across the whale's broad white back, splattered Papa's earnest face, speckled my shirt, deepened the murky hue of the water until it rippled like a cloudy burgundy wine. The whale's deep black eyes rolled in agony. Its flesh parted in a vee under the multiple blows of the claymore, widening like the trunk of a tree beneath an axe. Chunks of meat splashed into the St. Lawrence and stuck to Papa's waders. The air became heavy with the heat of whale blood. I watched with a detached combination of revulsion and fascination as bone was revealed in the pink crevasse of the whale. Watched it shatter. Watched the whale eventually fall silent with a last great shuddering of air and a pink bubbling from its blowhole. Its cries ceased, but there were similar whistles coming from all around me as the men of Rivière-Ouelle set about the harvesting.

I had seen my father butcher hogs. Had watched him hang and strip the entrails, hide, and flesh from deer. Seen squirrels and pheasant and other assorted game reduced to dinner. This was no different.

But then I saw my sister Lizette on the shore, her hands over her mouth, her eyes wide with terror, the wash of red foam on the beach nearly touching her shoes. The old Mohawk we all knew as Beagle (after a dog he had once owned) was standing behind her, one hand on her shoulder. The old Indian's face was set like stone; there was absolutely no emotion written in the many deep lines carved around his eyes and mouth, as if he'd been clumsily hewn from a redwood post. But Lizette . . . her face was twisted with revulsion and fear. She, too, had watched more than her share of butchery in her short life. This should have been no different for her. And yet . . .

The whales—sometimes dead, sometimes still struggling—were slit along the spine and belly from fluke to melon. Hooks were sunk into the heavy skin and then mules were used to strip it and the underlying layer of blubber from the carcass. Papa showed me how to use a knife between the white hide and the dark mass of muscle beneath so that it pulled loose easier, showed me how to cut around the pectoral fins as the skin ripped away. The heavy mat of hide and blubber was dragged to a shed and rolled onto a trestle where the blubber was scraped away, run through a grinder, and then tossed into a boiler. Scarcely any heat was required to render the oil, for the beluga's blubber was so soft that it would liquefy if left lying in the sun.

The hides were folded and buried to cure. When retrieved after a few days, they steamed in the cool morning air and stank like a possum I'd once seen my dog gnaw on for four days. Any remaining flesh and blubber was scraped away with a spade; then the hides were covered with salt, folded, and stacked in barrels. Barrels of oil and hides were then taken upriver to Lévesque in Quebec City.

The meat and muscle were stripped from the whale carcasses, ground and cooked as feed for our hogs. The bones and organs and head were left rotting on the beach, their unbelievable stench permeating the entire village. Beluga oil slicked the tidal wrack, gluing sand and pebbles into a shimmering beach mosaic lapped by the crimson waves. It looked like a scene out of some horrific nightmare, but unlike any nightmare I'd ever had, this was in color: the bloated blue organs, the line of congealing blood marking the waves' reach onto the beach, the glistening bone, the shimmering oil, and the roiling black clouds of flies.

That night, after the slaughter at the weir, we celebrated, a *fête champêtre* like none I had ever seen in Rivière-Ouelle. The music was loud and the liquor flowed freely. But the women would not dance with the men because they stank so bad, because their hands were still slick with beluga oil, because the laces of their boots were still clotted with blood. I found my father in a dark corner, sullen and brooding, his gnarled hands clamped around a bottle, the glass hazy with his oily fingerprints. "Your sister," he said, "she will not speak to me."

"She'll get over it," I told him. "She's just a stupid girl."

"She listens too much to that old Mohawk. He fills her head with nonsense. Perhaps I should have a word with him."

"Beagle's harmless, Papa."

"Perhaps," he said. Then he reached out and stroked the threadbare lapel of my jacket and let his fingers trail down over the too-tight shoulder to the sleeve that ended midway between my wrist and elbow. "With the money from the whales, we will buy you a new coat, eh, François?"

"Thank you, Papa."

He grunted and took a long pull from his bottle, then looked strangely at the wives and single women on the far side of the room. I wasn't old enough to recognize the look then, but something of his longing and pain must have struck a chord in me, because it's forever this look that I remember, and it's the look I most often recognize when I confront myself in the mirror. Papa had been alone since my mother died just shortly after Lizette was born. He never took another wife. In his eyes that night, I saw how incredibly lonely he was.

Finally, he pushed me away. "You go, François. Play. There has been too much work this day, eh?"

So I went looking for Lizette to ask her to go easy on the old man.

"Beagle says the beluga whale is a spirit guide," said Lizette.

"A what?"

"They take the souls of warriors to the next life. Beagle says so. Beagle says we shouldn't kill them."

I laughed at her. "Beagle's people have been hunting the whales since the dawn of time, Lizette." It was true. When Cartier reached the upper estuary of the St. Lawrence in 1535, he found the waters teeming with "a species of fish which none of us had ever seen before . . . the body and head as white as snow." The Indians called them *Adhothuys* and told him that they were very good to eat.

But Lizette wouldn't listen. She dreamed, she said, of our brother André caught in the weir, of his struggles, of the blood and the pain, and his body rotting on the beach.

"The whales will bring him home," she said, which made no sense, even when played against the Mohawk's mysticism, because it wasn't home where the whales took spirits, but to some other realm, some ancient Mohican version of Heaven. Lizette refused to listen to me with all the stubbornness a six-year-old can bring to bear. When I called her a baby, it just made things worse.

She refused to have anything to do with Papa because he stank of the slaughter. This broke his heart because, while he had always treated his sons with a certain male standoffishness, Lizette was his baby, his sole source of comfort since the death of our mother. Gone were the nightly hugs and kisses, gone the long evenings reading to her in the rocker by the fire, gone the hand-holding and hair-brushing and giggles. Lizette avoided me as well, but I was a boy of twelve with all of Canada's natural splendor as my backyard; what did I need from a girl of six? But I saw how it hurt Papa.

Lizette wouldn't touch anything bought with the money that came from Lévesque, not the new shoes Papa bought her, nor the pretty blue dress. She wouldn't eat anything cooked in beluga oil. Wouldn't eat pork because the whale meat was fed to the hogs. Wouldn't eat fish because local fishermen said it was a good thing that the whales were being culled because they ate too many fish. She grew thin and pale. Her hair, once so lovely and golden in the sun, hung lifeless around her shoulders. The rotting stench that pervaded Rivière-Ouelle seemed to suck the glimmer of life from her eyes.

"Papa," I said one afternoon over the boilers, "we have to do something about Lizette."

"I have tried, François. But she does not listen. What can I do?" He fed the last of a bucket of blubber into the cauldron and shrugged before going to the grinder for more. "Besides, soon the season for whales will be over. Things will return to normal. You will see."

For a time, he was right. September storms swept the rotting carcasses of the belugas back out to sea and wiped the beach clean. The wind stripped away most of the odor from Rivière-Ouelle. Unless you went looking for it, went prowling around the shacks on the beach where the rendering gear was carefully stowed away for next season or stood in the tack room and smelled the waders and boots and hooks and claymores stored there, you wouldn't know the village had been the site of such mass slaughter. Lizette, though still weak and thin and adhering to her principles of touching nothing related to the harvesting of the whales, became more like her old playful self. She became Papa's shadow again. But her dreams continued. Worsened, in fact. Letters from André did little to assure her that he was fine. She would wake screaming in the night saying that she could feel him drowning.

Fighting after the Battle of Flanders consisted of trench warfare. The Allies were on the offensive with attempts to force a breakthrough at Neuve Chapelle and Arras. The Germans unsuccessfully attacked Ypres, using clouds of chlorine gas, the first time in history that gas was used in this manner on a large scale. A French assault between Reims and the Argonne Forest took the Germans' first line of trenches, but was stopped at the second. Canadian troops took Vimy Ridge in the Battle of Arras, but their victory was a hollow one as Gen. Edmund Allenby's British army was unable to effect a breakthrough. The war stymied, bogged down in mud and blood and endless agony. Our boys began returning home, some crippled—emotionally or physically or both—some in pine boxes. We waited for word from André, whose letters had ceased several months before.

And we waited on the next whaling season, eager for Lévesque's money.

But something came home with those young Canadian soldiers. As we set the poles for the weir and sharpened our claymores, a respiratory ailment snuck on quiet and deadly feet through Quebec's little villages. Soldiers who had come home broken soon turned up dead. Family members began to show symptoms.

On the day we received the government's letter about André, Lizette came down with a temperature of 104°. *We regret to inform you that André Laurent gave his life in France.* Weeping, Papa packed a poultice of cooked onions around Lizette's neck. *Though we can never adequately express our condolences or thank your family for the sacrifice that you have made . . .* I was forced to stay away from her for fear that I would catch what she had. *. . . please know that your son died that others might live and that still others might know the freedom so highly prized in our own country.* I could not comfort my sister, nor share with her my own grief for a brother who would never return.

It wasn't until 1941 that it was discovered that influenza could be controlled by a vaccine containing the virus. Father's poultices and hot ciders and homemade remedies were no match for the most destructive epidemic of modern times. The Spanish flu had already swept across Europe and was now being introduced to North America by soldiers returning from the war. It's estimated to have caused more than twenty million deaths, most due to complications of bacterial pneumonia.

Lizette kept saying that she felt like she was drowning.

I would sneak in to see her at night, unable to sleep in spite of my exertions at the weir. She kept asking about André, wanting to know if he was home yet. When I tried to explain to her that André was dead, she would just look away and whisper that he was coming home soon.

"It's my fault," she said one early morning. "I didn't save them."

I tried to shush her, but she just repeated her confession. "Didn't save who?" I finally asked.

"The whales." She began to sob softly, struggling to breathe against the phlegm in her throat.

I wiped her nose, dried her eyes. "Hush, Lizette. They're just fish."

"No, François. They're spirit guides. It's my fault. André can't come home because of me."

"Lizette, André is—"

"You have to take me to them, François. Take me to the whales."

I shook my head. "You are too sick. You have to stay in bed." I tucked her poultice tighter around her neck. Pulled the covers up under her chin. Wiped the sweat from her brow with a cool rag. She was burning up.

"François," she said, "if you ever loved me, you will take me to the belugas."

"I'll go get Papa."

"No! Papa will make me stay in bed and you'll be in trouble for being here. Take me to the whales, François." She placed her burning hand on mine. "It's my dying wish. And it's the only way we'll ever see André again."

What was I to do? I bundled her up and cradled her in my arms. I was strong from dragging beluga hides and lifting buckets of blubber, but she weighed next to nothing, so tiny and wasted in my arms. Her face burned my shoulder as I took her out into the first faint grey of dawn. The stars were retreating, but there was a brilliant moon hanging over the St. Lawrence, its beams all wrapped up in the rippling water and the last wisps of a fog. There were whales in the weir, just as there had been the last three mornings in a row, but the tide had not retreated enough yet to completely strand them. They shifted restlessly, back and forth like pacing dogs, blowing great plumes of mist, exhausted from a night of searching the weir for an opening.

"Do you see them?" asked Lizette.

"I see the whales," I replied, the cold water now lapping at my bare feet.

"No. Not the whales. Do you see the soldiers?"

"Lizette, I don't . . ." But I did. There. In the fog. The indistinct shape of men moving among the whales, pairing up with them. The men of Rivière-Ouelle had come early to the river, I thought, but no one had awoken me. I waited for the brutal chop of a claymore against flesh, a distinctive sound that carried far across the water, but it didn't come. The shapes stood in the gloom and the mist and the cloud-shadowed moonlight, waiting with the whales.

"Take me to them."

"I need to take you back to bed, Lizette."

"Just take me to see them. One last time, François. Please."

So I waded out until the waves were slapping against my waist. Any further and Lizette would get wet.

"He's coming," she said.

And I saw him. God help me, I saw him. And it came to me at that moment that home might have a broader and far grander meaning than our little village, that his journey might only be starting here.

The mortar that had ended his life had laid open the entire left side of his chest. Ribs lay exposed like bleached driftwood in a mottled gray bed of deflated lung and tattered infantry green. His heart, also exposed, had ceased to beat, yet he stood before us, one hand clutching his abdomen, the other trailing into the water to rest on the broad back of a beluga whale. His eyes were lackluster, lifeless, but still they sought out my own.

Lizette reached out her hand to him. "André," she whispered weakly.

"We can't get out," he said, black blood running down his chin as he spoke.

"You have to help them," Lizette told me.

So I carried her to the beach and set her against an overturned dinghy. Then I waded out among them, my heart hammering so loud that I couldn't have heard the most impressive nor'easterly had it come raging down from the Gaspé Peninsula. They stood in their uniforms, the moon-drenched water lapping at their gaping wounds and the stumps of their missing limbs, toying with the shredded remains of their trench coats. They stood with the beluga whales . . . with the spirit guides.

I swam out to the wall of the weir and began pulling up saplings. The wood had swelled in the water, wedging them tight in the ancient holes in the river bottom. To remove them, I had to go underwater, brace both feet against the bottom, wrap both hands around the pole, and pull with all my might. Ironically, had I not worked so hard at the harvest the last two seasons, I would not have been strong enough to do it.

When I had a half dozen or so removed, I called to my dead brother. He came and the others followed, leaving sluggish wakes in the St. Lawrence, wakes that I could not determine were really from their passage or just from the whales. The others passed through the gap in the weir, vanishing into the shifting river fog, but my brother stopped and waited.

"André," I called to him, tears streaming down my face, "I cannot believe—"

But he held up a hand to silence me and turned toward the shore, waiting.

There was one more whale.

And one more spirit.

"No . . ."

"We will see you again, François," my brother said softly. And: "Stay away from the war. There is no glory to be had in the killing fields. You'll find your own worth here." And he pointed toward my heart.

Lizette stopped at his side. She reached out as if to touch me, but withdrew her hand at the last instant, as if she feared what might happen or how I might react. I felt the chill of her hand's passage, felt it all the way to the core of my being.

"Thank you, François."

"Father will be lost without you, Lizette."

"Please take care of him for me."

"I'll try."

"And stop them from killing of the whales."

"I don't think they will listen, Lizette. I don't think they will believe this."

"You must make them believe."

And then she, André, and the two beluga whales accompanying them slipped from the weir, escaped the trap that was this life, and vanished into the mist. "He's coming home," she had said.

I waded back to shore, where I found Beagle cradling Lizette's lifeless body. We slipped back into the house and tucked her into bed. She looked at peace. The glisten of fever sweat and the hacking cough were gone. Her bed no longer radiated that intense heat and that smell of sickness. Her eyes, though open and lifeless, were clear and blue.

Father found her the next morning as the men of Rivière-Ouelle were discovering that their catch had escaped in the night. We buried her beside Mama and André, in the little cemetery on the hill overlooking the river, the same cemetery where I would eventually bury Papa.

When they tried to blame Beagle for pulling up the saplings, I confessed and did my best to explain why I had done it. They didn't believe me. The saplings were replaced three times, but each time I swam out in the night and removed them, taking down more of them each time. Though he didn't believe my story of the ghosts and the belugas, Papa defended my actions to the rest of the village. Because of our loss, not just André but Lizette as well, the villagers thought us both mad and took pity on us. The fourth time that I went out to remove the saplings, Papa went with me. The villagers had hidden in the shoals in their dinghies and came out to drag us back to shore, but that night no belugas entered the weir. Nor the next night or the next. And then miraculously, the season was over. The belugas had moved on. And the following year, Lévesque did not come to renew his offer. Rivière-Ouelle turned to other trades as she celebrated the end of the war and a bittersweet victory. Freedom had been secured, but at such a tremendous cost.

I grew into a man, buried my father (who was never the same after Lizette's death), and sought my own solitudes. For years I wandered northern Canada where, as poet F. R. Scott put it, the land is:

Inarticulate, arctic,
Not written on by history, empty as paper,
It leans away from the world with songs in its lakes
Older than love, and lost in the miles.

I was escaping civilization, fleeing man with his penchant for violence against himself and the species with which he shares the planet. And I was escaping the ghosts.

You see . . . once you've seen them, you *always* see them. There is no escaping their injuries, their lost gazes, their tragic voices. But in the far north, there are places where no man has walked, where no ghosts have fallen, where a man can truly find solitude. Places where I could sit and ponder what I could have done differently to save Lizette, where I could wonder where she'd gone and when I'd see her again . . . when I'd go home.

When I eventually returned to civilization, more animal than human by that time, I took this job as the lighthouse keeper at Pointe-au-Père, where the massive lens of the lighthouse keeps the spirits at bay and I cannot see the destruction taking place all around me as we sacrifice our world for Lévesque's jaded coin.

I sit in my lighthouse and hide from the ghosts of men and belugas, staring down the St. Lawrence to the fjord lurking in the fog at Rivière-du-Loup, where the water is some 400 feet deep. Ancient sea water resides permanently in such troughs, reminders of a sea some 20,000 years gone, reminders of a Quebec covered in glaciers. Whales and seals fed at the exposed continental shelf of the Atlantic. Finback, humpback, bowhead, narwhal, and harbor porpoises plied these waters, along with the harp, bearded, and hooded seals . . . and, of course, the gentle beluga.

Today, Canadians make more money in a single year hauling tourists out to see the beluga whale than was ever made killing them for oil. But the belugas' numbers are dwindling. They've been compromised by lead and mercury, DDT, dieldrin, mirex, and other insecticides, polychlorobiphenyls, and the most carcinogenic molecule known to man, benzo pyrene.

I sit by the shore and the sea belongs to me, but the sea is dying, as am I. Will there be a guide for my spirit when my time comes? Or will I wander this world alone, as I have done most of my life, for all that remains of eternity?

I want so much to see my family again. But to do that, I must beg you to protect this fragile world of ours, to accept your own ownership and place on the seashore.

AN ENDING

Steve Rasnic Tem

There is nothing more he can say. Perhaps he's told too much already. His daughter used to complain he had an answer for everything, and now he knows she felt bad about saying that for some time, and now he answers to no one, no matter how much they ask. But there is nothing more he can say about that.

Now that he cannot speak, his thoughts are loose in time. *No matter how much she asks,* he thinks, as if she could ask, as if she were not gone. Just like him, unable to bear witness to the world. Just like him. So does this mean he, too, is dead?

Of course not. Of course not. Not so long as the neurons fire, illuminating the brain, filling the sky with light. Broadcasting the voices.

The songs they sing are measured in broken air and shattered bone. The power of them lies in the stray wind in the high mountains felt and heard by no one. When they cry the earth cries, and the earth cries often. The darkness that is their subject knows no bounds real or imaginary, rubbing at us all.

But she was correct just the same. Once upon a time he did think he had the answers for everything. Now he understands how little he knew. But he cannot tell her.

And if he could speak, what might he say? What would he talk to her about? What message would he bring to the dead to show he understood even a bit of their plight?

He might say no. He might say yes. He might yadda yadda yadda.

He might say there is a new flower growing in the window box. A yellow tulip, his wife's favorite. He might tell his wife he still loves her. He might tell her that he loved her and he loves her and he always will. What better thing might a person say?

The strangest thing about his immobility, he thinks, is how much he moves inside it. His chest rises and falls, ever so slightly, not much more palpable than his thoughts, but still discernable. Sweat traces his face like the fingertips of blind angels. Fluids and gasses move deep inside him, down in the hidden chambers of the self.

And his eyes move, even though he is rarely aware of it. He sees, but what he sees could be the dream he's having, he has no way of telling. He has no way of telling anyone. His eyes might even be cameras, replacements for the eyes he used to have. Click and click again. Can they do such things? They can do so many things he does not understand. He does not understand.

And the world moves, changes and spins because of something he has done. He is done. The world changes colors and brings forth strange and wonderful creatures who dance and lick and scream, and he knows he is the cause, but he does not know how.

In the other bed his wife stares at him. She may have died but he cannot be sure. Sometimes he thinks a look can last longer than a life. She has stared at him so intently for a very long time. She does not miss a thing. He understands that for a very long time she stared at him with a love beyond anything he had ever experienced before, beyond anything he might imagine, but he suspects the intention of that gray-eyed gaze has changed over the time of their imprisonment to become of another kind of focus and intensity, but he was never quite sure what words might best describe this new state. In his more fanciful speculations, in fact, he imagined that his wife invented a brand new emotion: one that goes beyond love, one that factors the despair of knowing, the knowledge that comes from living with death so close at hand.

He prefers to look not into those hazy gray eyes but at her hairline, at that place where the hair parts above the middle of her forehead, where the combined scents of shampoo and brain heat so often gather, where she smells clean and vital, where her smell is like a taste of the entire of her, where he would live forever if he could.

The phone rings again, a physical tearing of the sour air in the bedroom. His daughter's answering machine picks it up. A loud click followed by another loud click, as if something is snapping. As if the bones of this sorry animal, this answering animal, are breaking, and soon it will answer no more, its sad carcass draped over the nightstand.

Once upon a time it did answer, and so efficiently recorded the details of their daughter's death, which he would not believe at first, because she only went out for some milk, she promised them both (although neither of them could answer) that she'd be right back, and who could die in such a way, on such a small errand?

The voice on the machine had been so crisp, so professionally sympathetic as it delivered the terrible news, who could not believe it?

Now the male voice on the machine asks, *"Are you there? Pick up. Pick up. Are you there?"* with an urgency that surprises him. Some boyfriend he does not know about? Was that where she was really going when she left here? Did she tell him about her parents, so that maybe he'll think to call the police and send them to her house?

There's always a chance. He used to tell her, from the time she was a little girl, there's always a chance, sweetheart.

"Are you there?" Even if he could answer, he does not know what he could say.

His daughter left on her little errand eight days ago. He knows because of the calendar on the wall just above his daughter's desk. He can barely see it, tucked around the corner there, but it is still clear enough. Kittens above the black, dated squares. He cursed her sweet name for her arrogance, so convinced with her nursing degree that she could take care of them both. No nursing home, no nursing home, Dad. Damn her carelessness. And her driving has always lacked caution, no matter how much he tries to teach her. She thought she knew. She thought she knew. Her father's daughter, she took after him.

No one knows he is here. And no one knows her mother is here. Now the eighth day is passing, slipping like ooze from broken hydraulics, dripping off the edge of the table and out of sight.

And damn her for being dead. She's broken his heart. And now nothing can be right. There is nothing he can say. Even when there is so much to say.

His wife's arm hangs limp off the side of the bed. She's been strapped down, but in that last seizure the cloth tears, the arm flopping free, then limp. He'd wanted to be closer then, but all that moved was his desperate tears.

Eight days and some strong smells have faded, some gradually making their presence known. The smell the body makes as fluids give way. The smell of the orange on the sunny table. The stench as the body dies incrementally. The reek of time, wasted and misused, the days thrown away. The foulness of regret, accumulated until the very end.

His wife was always fussy about matters of toiletry. She had no more odor than a glossy magazine ad. She cared for no variety of incense or perfume, and found even cooking odors somehow rude. He never understood how she managed to be so odor free. She could not be said even to smell *fresh*. She was cured. She was sealed. She was statuary. Her nose was an anchor for her eyes and nothing more.

Illness, as he would have told her had she just asked, brings indignity. He was the first to fall, robbed of speech and mobility by a blood clot, and he greatly admired the way she put aside her prejudices in order to take care of him. Even changing him when the aide was off duty. She didn't complain, not even involuntarily. She simply did what needed to be done for someone she loved. Could he have done the same for her? He wasn't so sure. At least not with such care, such equanimity.

She'd been bent over him, rearranging his pillow, making it so that it fit perfectly beneath his ears, and he was feeling absurdly grateful, because a crease in the case had been torturing him for hours. When he detected an ever so faint aroma of urine, and he stared at her in surprise as her expression changed, as if some startling idea suddenly entered her consciousness, and almost immediately he knew it was a stroke—she'd been assaulted by the fairies, and she fell away from him and he couldn't even shout his outrage at the terrible thing. The anger leaked out of him a bit at a time over the following hours, weeks, and months.

What is left of the woman he loved in the nearby bed he cannot know. There is so much he cannot know.

*   *   *

He does not know when the ringing in his ears first began. It seems a recent event but he cannot be sure. He suspects it's the song the brain sings when it dies but of course there is no way for him to know if this is true. Sometimes it is loud and sometimes it is quite soft. Sometimes it is all he can do not to weep when he hears it.

One of the things his wife and he enjoyed most was listening to music together. Now those days are gone, he thinks, or are they? Perhaps even now they are listening to the same tune.

Suddenly there is quiet as if a door has been closed. This is the way. This is the way. When the view becomes unbearable, then shut the door.

He closes his eyes against her death and a loud voice grows, singing from somewhere far below him. It is his own voice he hears, even though his lips do not move.

He has heard, of course, that as the brain dies neurons fire indiscriminately, and what the mind perceives in such circumstances is not to be trusted, is fanciful in its last, desperate attempts to complete a train of notions, and all that is witnessed under these conditions is a product of an electrified imagination.

So what, he thinks. When you are reduced to brain, and the various senses which are accessories to brain, what more could there be, and certainly, what could be more important than that first trip into insubstantiality where only the imagination can report back, strapped to a shuddering, unhesitant engine of unreason?

So he isn't alarmed to see the great goat stroll through the door, like some new owner surveying the premises purchased for a hard price. The goat gazes at him only briefly, a polite but dismissive look at an eager would-be lover found wanting.

Instead the goat lingers at his wife's side and he is suddenly overcome not only by a bare, numbing grief for her but also by the very reek of her, suddenly more powerful than ever before, like a focused sample of every undrained outhouse and waste pool, every foul abattoir avoided by so-called decent, civilized people. He is terrified, tries to turn away and when he knows the attempt useless, closes his eyes tight as his love for her.

But the goat's huge laughter tears his eyelids open and he has to look at the thing, prancing and dancing over his wife's disastrous bed, now her grave. The goat rises on its hind legs and pounds the ceiling with its split hooves, shaking down plaster and lathe, wiring and insulation batts, jangling pipes and a steady and gorgeous fall of fine white powder, continuing long after the goat has settled back onto its haunches, long snout pushed heavenward, eyes closed in pleasure over the bath it is receiving.

He surprises himself thinking how oddly beautiful it all seems, the abstract patterns of debris framing the now snow-white animal fur, the blissful yard-long smile spread around the goat's huge head.

Then quickly the goat mounts his dead wife's bed, licks the disaster of her with its long red tongue, and lowers itself, and lowers itself, until it can begin its thrusts effectively, a great back and forth of ripping and damage as it enters his wife's sad remnants of flesh, forcing a terrible gasping of air out of her mouth in a hideous parody of orgasm.

After the great goat has done whatever it can, it rises and walks off the bed, dragging remnants of the woman he loved most of his life still stuck to fur, to belly, to genitalia, most of it disintegrating as the goat strides to the door and out, her skin and hair shattering against the floor like bits of frozen twig and leaf.

* * *

A darkness begins to seep from scattered corners of the bedroom. It breaks into wings and the things that wear wings, insects and disasters spat out and eager to escape. Their flight soon fills the room, until he can see nothing else. When their edges fly too close he can feel his skin tearing, but not enough, sweet lord, to bring him release.

In the middle of the world a huge wind begins to turn. In the distance his life shimmers like a beautiful, barely noticed thing, and as he watches the dark shapes rush to surround it: the almost loves and the never agains, their narrow heads brightly plumed with the naive prayers of children.

So he has his release, his ending, his final day. And he's ashamed to say he's grateful not to have suffered what his wife had to suffer. He's grateful to have had some peace at the end, deserved or not it matters little. He's grateful.

What more is there to say at the end, even when he can say nothing? He said all he knew to say a long time ago. Some things can only be said in the language of angels.

Dad? Dad, are you awake? Did you sleep well? Time to get up now. Time for dinner.

He is awake, his eyes wide open, but only now beginning to see. He is so absurdly grateful he begins to weep. No ending here after all. He wasn't ready, he wasn't ready. And somehow the angels knew.

So kind of his daughter to wake him. She's always been a good daughter, a wonderful daughter in fact, and he is grateful. So many fathers have not been as fortunate. So many fathers have children who leave them, children who stay away even when they are home, children who pretend they have no fathers or mothers, children who have this other life, waiting for their fathers to die.

Dinner, Daddy. Don't let it get cold.

He gazes around the bedroom and again it amazes him how clean she keeps it, how everything seems in its perfect place, how it had no perfect place until she put it there. The bed he lay on so carefully made, barely disturbed even as he eases from between its crisp white sheets. His wife's bed, equally well made, and laden with roses to honor her memory. When did she die? He's not quite sure, because her passing was so peaceful—their daughter has taken such good care of them both he knows she passed with a minimum of fuss and pain.

He had so many fears about this time—how foolish it had been to worry and obsess about what must come to us all. How much better to ease into it without struggle, to see it as simply another stage, no better or worse than any other, just another adventure at the end of your days.

Daddy, please. I don't want you to starve.

She's just being silly now, because he could use a few missed meals, a man of his size with a history of little self-control. Eating always made him feel better, so why not do what made you feel better? Store enough up to last you through the lean times, was the way his father had always put it. The world had a way of eating at you, so what better way to survive than to have more of you against the world's angry appetite.

"Smells good, sweetheart. Smells wonderful!" He almost laughs, because he's so surprised to hear the sound of his own voice. It seems forever since he's heard the sound of his own voice. But of course it was only this morning, or perhaps last night, certainly no further away than yesterday afternoon. He and his daughter speak every day, after all: long, serious talks about politics and morals and her many dreams. She's always had so much ambition. She takes after him. She takes after him. Even to the point of sounding like him: his voice, her voice, indistinguishable.

He's just had so many bad dreams of late in which he wasn't able to speak to her, he wasn't allowed to speak to her, and he'd been so hungry for conversation. He is so hungry.

Dad, I'm not telling you again! Dinner!

He's always been late for dinner. He'll get so busy sometimes, there is always so much to do, and a person of ambition can go on and on without replenishment sometimes, building on what he has already done, using the same words, the same thoughts again and again, reusing the dreams he's dreamed a thousand times before.

That line of thinking is making him vaguely uncomfortable. Better to get on to dinner, otherwise he might hurt her feelings. Nothing wrong here. Nothing is wrong.

She's kept the kitchen as spotless as the rest of the house. Gleaming countertops, crystalline glass, shiny silver of the utensils. The finest linen. But where's the food? He doesn't see any food.

Not that he needs to eat, however hungry he may feel. He's gotten so fat of late, he could lie in bed a year or more and live off all that he contains.

Better not to think of that. Better to keep a positive attitude. He has so many bad dreams. He has so many awful things in his head.

"Sweetheart," he says. "Sweetheart. I don't see the food."

Look down, Daddy, she says from the other side of the wall.

He looks down at his plate but there is nothing. There is nothing to eat. "There's nothing here, sweetheart."

Don't be so helpless, Daddy. Make yourself a meal. Make yourself a meal.

He can feel the sheets gathered around his head. He

can hear his wife's body torn asunder and carried out of the world. He can smell the reek and decay of everything he has ever loved. He tries to cover his ears against the screams of this world but he cannot move. He cannot move.

Make yourself a meal, her voice says with finality.

He gazes down at his ponderous belly and fumbles at all the utensils suddenly spilling off the edge of the table: all the sharp edges, all the knives of the world.

The telephone rings. The answering machine picks it up. "Are you there?" the male voice asks. "Pick up. Pick up."

"I'm not here!" he says. "I'm not here!"

Make yourself a meal, she says, and grabbing the sharpest knife, he does.

About the Editor

John Pelan is the editor of several anthologies, including the Bram Stoker Award–winning *The Darker Side*. With Edward Lee, he is coauthor of *Goon*, *Shifters*, *Splatterspunk*, *Family Tradition*, and several short stories. His novella, *The Colour out of Darkness*, is available from Cemetery Dance Productions. John's solo stories have appeared in numerous anthologies (including this one), and a major collection is forthcoming in 2005. As a researcher and historian of the horror genre, John has edited over two dozen single-author collections and novels of classic weird fiction and SF and is currently working on assembling collections by Fritz Leiber, Charles Birkin, and Daniel F. Galouye for publication by Darkside Press and Midnight House. John lives with his wife, Kathy, and their six cats in Seattle, where they have just celebrated their twentieth wedding anniversary. Visit his site at www.darksidepress.com and buy lots of stuff.